DATE DUE

blue night

A NOVEL

blue night

Cindy McCormick Martinusen

TYNDALE HOUSE PUBLISHERS, INC. | WHEATON, ILLINOIS

Designed by Julie Chen

Edited by Lorie Popp and Ramona Cramer Tucker

Published in association with the literary agency of Janet Kobobel Grant, Books & Such, 4788 Carissa Ave., Santa Rosa, CA 95405.

Scripture quotations are taken from the *Holy Bible,* New International Version®. NIV®. Copyright © 1973, 1978, 1984 by International Bible Society. Used by permission of Zondervan Publishing House. All rights reserved.

Scripture quotations are taken from the *Holy Bible,* New Living Translation, copyright © 1996. Used by permission of Tyndale House Publishers, Inc., Wheaton, Illinois 60189. All rights reserved.

This novel is a work of fiction. Names, characters, places, and incidents are either the product of the author's imagination or are used fictitiously. Any resemblance to actual events, locales, organizations, or persons, living or dead, is entirely coincidental and beyond the intent of either the author or publisher.

ISBN 0-7394-2629-x

Printed in the United States of America

To David
This would not be, without you.

In memory of Brady Shawn Harman (3/30/97 to 7/4/97)
Despite the short time we spend in this world,
we can change lives in profound ways.
You have, and we miss you.

I will repay you for the years the locusts have eaten—
. . . and you will praise the name of the Lord your God,
who has worked wonders for you.

JOEL 2:25-26, NIV

Austria
November 28, 1944

Lukas Johansen didn't deserve her. He knew this. Yet he must ask anyway.

She'd say yes. He knew that, too, though he feared she shouldn't.

His breath was a long stream of white as he leaned against the cold bark of the black oak. He glanced behind him and then relaxed, allowing his mind to anticipate her arrival. It was a wonder they could grow love in the desperate world surrounding them.

His eyes strained against the glare, searching for movement where the rough trail disappeared over the hillside. Susanne's sun-white hair would appear first; then her soft gait would bring her head in and out of view until he'd see her forehead and face. Finally all of her would be framed against the horizon. She'd be smiling as she wound around rocks and mud in her hurried pace to meet him. Her easy grin and quick laughter were addictive. Lukas couldn't get enough of the life that poured from her.

He stared toward the hillside where deep blue mountains rose sharply above the trail. Below, thin plumes of smoke rose from chalets dotting the valley floor. Late-afternoon light was falling slowly to evening; then it would move swiftly into night. Lukas' impatience grew. As soon as Susanne reached him, he would ask.

The words were not practiced. Lukas had no clue what he'd say. No getting on one knee—he wanted to look her straight in the face. He'd probably find himself trying to talk her out of saying yes. "You should not marry me. I do not deserve what you give. If you knew who I was, you would hate me. My past could destroy our future."

He worried he'd be too convincing.

Yet the guilt always remained behind him like a hound after its prey. Justice meant he should suffer—all the days of his life. The frayed patches of his present work could never fully cover his past sins. But Lukas would ask her. And Susanne would say yes. They might both regret it.

Where was she? He pulled out his watch and checked the time again. Perhaps she didn't get his letter after all. She could be home wondering why he hadn't written as promised. It had been several days since he'd seen her—too many days for him. He wished she didn't have to take the morning train away from him at the beginning of every week. He knew good work required sacrifice these days, if work could even be found. But the first three days of every week were empty without her. He knew it bothered her, too. But she said they had to be thankful she didn't have to work away from the village every day like others did. Susanne could always find something good in the world. Soon he would take her away from this place of insanity. *Soon*, he would promise her.

Lukas glanced over his shoulder again. His hidden life compelled frequent looks behind. No place possessed complete safety. Not a large oak in the crook of two hillsides. Not even the mountain peaks above. Security was found in the moment past. If you were alive tomorrow, then today had been safe. He longed for that to end.

He reached for his gold pocket watch but then couldn't wait any longer. His feet moved faster into a jog and then a run on the soggy ground of the alpine trail. A sudden urgency pushed him. He stopped only before the last rise to her house. He bent down, trying to calm his breath and burning lungs. At last he took a long, deep breath and moved ahead.

His eyes swept the yard and then the house. She wasn't hanging white sheets on the line or tending geraniums in the window boxes. The front door was ajar. There was no lazy smoke from the chimney. His step quickened. The cows in the field behind the cottage stretched their necks between the wooden poles and moaned. Lukas stopped at the open gateway. Boot prints—of more than one person—smeared mud across the stone walkway. Lukas pivoted, awaiting the trap. Then he saw them: red dots and splotches bright against a lasting pile of snow by the porch. Turning quickly, his eyes caught more splotches and smears along the porch, doorjamb, wooden siding, and posts as he rushed inside.

Dishes lay broken on the kitchen floor; specks of red splattered the table. The pine cupboard's contents had been yanked out and shattered across the counters, sink, and floor. It appeared as if a starving beast had ripped the room apart except for a distinct heel print near a pool of blood beneath a wooden chair.

Lukas stared at the dark red pool that streamed along the ridges of the pine floor planking. He'd seen such pools before—always beneath chairs or tables or walls where someone had been held and hurt for a long while.

"Susanne!" His voice echoed up, frantic, against the beamed ceiling.

Through each silent room, he searched upstairs and down. The door to Susanne's grandmother's room was the only one closed. He pushed it open—afraid of what he'd find, yet urgent to know. No one was there. He turned to leave and heard a noise like the whimper of a small animal. Lukas followed the sound behind the door toward a darkened corner. Susanne's grandmother was on the floor, her back to the corner like a punished child. The woman was hunched over, her skirt bunched around her knees. She clutched something against her chest.

"Frau Olsen?"

The whimper became a sob as his footsteps creaked against the wood floor. She gazed up at him, tears streaming from her red-rimmed eyes. Terror cried from her worn eyes even while her mouth continued its sob.

He knelt in front of her and noticed what she held against her chest—Susanne's childhood rag doll in the gingham dress.

"Where is she? Where is Susanne?" Lukas asked softly.

He touched her bowed shoulder. She wrenched away, letting out a wail that echoed through the house. Lukas left her there, even more desperate to find Susanne. Had she been taken? There must still be hope. He stood in the kitchen, telling himself to think, and think wisely. He could save her if he kept his head. She might be at the police station in town being interrogated. If they knew who he was, they'd want him instead. But how could he barter with them and exchange himself for her freedom?

His eyes roamed the room and his mind sought the first step. Then he realized there was a trail to follow. A blood trail. It led outside. He ran out the door, along the porch, and down the steps to where the snow displayed blood in crystals of red light. At the corner of the house he slipped and fell on a patch of ice. He rose slowly, the roof dripping water from long icicles next to him. His feet walked almost woodenly over the slush.

She was facedown, her arms straight at her sides. The beautiful sun-white hair had come undone. It lay twisted in the snow and around her back.

"God, please, no," he could only whisper. Carefully he turned her over and cradled her head in his lap. He tried to wipe the blood from her face but smeared it across her cheek.

Lukas looked wildly around for someone who could help. It couldn't be too late. How could he love her and yet not have known what was happening to her? Why hadn't he come sooner?

He held and rocked her back and forth, hoping somehow that God would change his mind. Waiting in numbed silence, he gazed above the mountain peaks. But a prayer would not come to his lips. Still he hoped for a miracle. That God would realize he'd made a mistake. That today was not the day of death for Susanne Olsen. That God would say to her as she stood in front of him, "You are too early." Then he'd turn to the Death Angel. "Return her. The world yet needs her."

The cows stared from the corral. One bawled mournfully. A breath of wind swept through the trees. From the house he heard the old woman's continual wail. Stillness closed around him, suffocating him.

And night pressed in. As it slowly consumed the light, Lukas studied her face. He'd hoped to see the peaceful gaze of an angel, not the look of death he beheld.

"I came to ask you to marry me. I want to be with you always." Her expression remained unmoved, a resolute statue, not Susanne at all. "You cannot leave me yet. What will I do now?"

There was no answer.

Lukas knew that at last justice had reached him. But Susanne had paid the price.

⋯⇒◎⇐⋯

VENICE, ITALY
Spring, Three Years Ago

Kate Porter walked along the edge of a wide canal. Water lapped gently against its side. In her life a place like this was a postcard-sized thought or a setting in a romantic movie. But the world had suddenly grown smaller. Today she stopped and stood before tall, flat-fronted buildings and awakening shops.

Her husband awaited her return to their hotel room, not far down a winding alleyway. They had stepped inside the postcard. They were vacationing before Jack's conference within the frames of a movie scene. A passport and a United Airlines ticket, and Kate had awakened to stroll along the streets of Venice to buy espresso and brioche from an Italian café.

Venice. A city built upon water with the width and breadth of lives and dreams divided by vaporettos, gondolas, and cool breezes. Little wonder that artists and writers had been drawn to this city for centuries. Kate had never thought she'd see it for herself. After all, her spot on earth was a simple home in a simple American town. The history, culture, and ambience of this place reached beyond that. It was overwhelming, but she also loved it and wanted to see everything this world could offer.

Kate walked slowly to memorize each step along the Riva del Vin toward the towering Rialto Bridge. The bridge appeared above a low mist, an ancient arch spanning the waters. Its curved rail, trimmed in stone balustrades, carried the echo of centuries-old footsteps. Once the only means of crossing the widest canal in Venice, the Rialto now provided a center-stage view of the Grand Canal, where morning travelers already passed through the dark waters in black gondolas and touring boats.

She couldn't wait to share all this with Jack. It would be the best business/pleasure trip of their lives. A part of her wished they had brought their daughter. How Abbie would love this place. When Kate passed a row of wooden posts, rising like sentries from the canal water's edge, she decided the three of them must come back sometime soon.

It was good for her to be alone this morning, to brave the foreign soil she once thought she'd fear. That was the real reason she'd left the hotel in search of food. And she'd passed her own test. The girl who had never felt the need to leave the United States was now conquering a Venetian walkway.

But the unexplored would have to wait just a little longer. The pastry warmed through the bag she carried and the espresso cooled with every step.

Jack had better be awake.

"I'll be back in just a little while," she whispered to the city, pausing at the entrance to their hotel. Leaving the morning breezes for the stale indoors, Kate made a mental schedule of the day ahead as she climbed the stairs. They had several days before Jack's archaeological conference began. The wafts of pastry made her stomach yearn for the Italian treat.

The door was locked. When Kate tapped with her elbow, a flick of paint cascaded to the ground. Only in Italy would they pay such a price for a "quaint" hotel room with faded walls and worn carpets. Jack must be asleep or in the shower. Kate balanced breakfast and extracted her room key from her pocket.

"You should be proud of me," she said, pushing the door open.

The shower water was running.

Setting the pastry and espresso on the tiny table, Kate dug into her carry-on bag for her travel guide. They must try gelato after lunch and Italian espresso after visiting the Basilica di San Marco. She bit off a piece of pastry as she paged through the guidebook.

If Jack would just get out of the shower.

Perhaps she should pull one of their evil cold-water tricks. Kate sneaked toward the bathroom, but the door's creak ruined any chance of surprise. Then she noticed the shower curtain. It was scrunched open against the wall, and a puddle had pooled on the floor from the spray.

No one was there.

She turned off the faucet.

"Jack?" She peeked behind the door, already knowing he couldn't fit there. "Okay, where are you? You know I hate these kinds of surprises."

Her gaze moved around the bathroom, then back into their room. The wardrobe doors were open. Jack's suitcase was still zipped shut. She had opened their dual shaving and cosmetic case.

Perhaps he'd gone to find her. But his clothes were on the floor.

The bed was a mess of sheets and covers. The pillow she'd used was flat and off center. But Jack's pillow looked as if it had been fluffed and adjusted just right.

And there was something on the pillow.

Shaking off the beads of water from the shower, Kate walked toward the bed as if in slow motion. On the pillow was a piece of broken blue ceramic.

She had never seen it before.

But it was here. And Jack was gone.

part *one*

Hours continuing long, sore and heavy-hearted,

Hours of dusk, when I withdrew to a lonesome and
unfrequented spot, seating myself,
leaning my face in my hands;

Hours sleepless, deep in the night, when I go forth,
speeding swiftly the country roads, or through the city
streets, or pacing miles and miles, stifling plaintive cries;

Hours discouraged, distracted—for the one
I cannot content myself without.

Hours when I am forgotten (O weeks and months are
passing, but I believe I am never to forget!) . . .

—WALT WHITMAN, *Leaves of Grass*

CHAPTER ONE

CORVALIS, OREGON
Present Day

K ate Porter could feel a distant urging. It
nagged at her like a light tap on the shoulder or a drip of water
from a faucet she couldn't see. She cast it aside as always and
let her thoughts drift with the slow creak of the porch swing
and the flow of dark clouds rolling across the moonlight. Such
nights had the power to quiet the distant highway or even the
wind in the trees. Once they would have bred dreams and
plans for tomorrow. It was no longer so.

Yet even this dreamy night could not calm the uneasiness
that moved in her—like the first hint that a season was changing. She tucked the flannel blanket around her crossed legs
and leaned her head against the chain of the swing.

Tonight felt different somehow. Kate wondered about it,
listened to the night sounds. Life had continued on one
consistent plane for so long. A gentle night like this had not
been allowed. Instead it prodded her to search harder, try
more, scour her thoughts again and again for an answer. That
day in Venice had changed who Kate had always been. Like

clay spun in the hands of a potter, she had been shaped, molded; then suddenly something had gone wrong. The wheel continued to spin with her there, awkward and misshapen, abandoned on the wheel.

Kate had become accustomed to it.

Yet the distant tapping seemed to say she'd forgotten something that morning three years earlier, something that was essential for her now.

Remember. Remember.

She tried. What was it? What else had she lost that day, besides everything? Kate kept circling that nagging something, but she always ran without finding the answer.

When the French door scraped open behind her, Kate realized she'd been ignoring her daughter's call—without really knowing it.

"There you are, Mom. Look what I found." Her daughter's bare feet padded across the wood-planked deck.

"What is it?" Kate asked, her eyes blinded by the light from the windows. She tried not to feel annoyed at the interruption as she adjusted a pillow in the empty place beside her.

"Daddy wore this shirt on our daddy/daughter night." Abbie spread a beige shirt over Kate's lap. "See my milk shake's still on his sleeve."

"Yes, I see. And I remember." Kate wondered why her daughter had been in the walk-in closet looking at her daddy's clothing. It was becoming a regular habit.

Abbie hopped up beside her. Her thin legs dangled, but not straight out like when she was smaller, when the bend of her knee didn't reach the edge of the swing. Abbie had always gone to bed easier if she spent a short time on the swing with Kate or Jack or all three of them together. It had been a long time, longer than Kate realized, since they'd been on the swing together.

Abbie pulled the shirt around her shoulders and rested her head against her mother. They rocked back and forth with the distant sound of cars and crickets and bullfrogs. Kate glanced at her daughter engulfed in Jack's shirt. How that represented their life. Jack so clearly with them, in everything they did. Yet now he was only an empty shirt with no arms inside to give them strength or warmth. Kate slid her own arm over the shirt and around Abbie's shoulder.

"Mom, will he ever come back?" Abbie met her mother's gaze. She wanted the truth. It was the same question Kate asked every day.

Kate placed her feet down to stop their rocking. She touched the tip of Abbie's chin and wished she could take back the last three years—for both their sakes. The old life of family time, dance recitals, and church involvement had been shattered into police interviews, unsuccessful searches, and a mixture of hope and loss. Now confusion, fear, and nightmares were as normal as car payments, shopping, and the growing pile of unopened gifts to Daddy. That Jack Porter had vanished without a trace was a fact. But how? Why? Would he return?

"I don't know. If he was coming . . ." Kate paused, not sure she wanted to admit this even to herself. "If Daddy was coming back, I think he would have been here by now."

Abbie nestled her head against Kate again and gathered Jack's shirt more tightly against her thin frame. "God can bring him back."

Kate pushed her feet from the deck into a soft swing. How could she argue with the faith of a child?

"Mommy?" Abbie hadn't called her Mommy in years.

"What, my girl?"

"The sky looks blue."

"Yes, it's a blue night. You don't see them often. The moon behind the clouds and I don't know what else, perhaps the season. It makes the night blue."

"I like it."

"I do too."

"It's God's way of telling us Daddy is okay, and he's coming back."

Kate wanted to give her a long explanation why that wasn't true. Why tomorrow's dawn would start a new day for both of them, another new day without Jack. She only held Abbie tighter. Sometimes a child's faith was really a futile wish. Perhaps that was what faith had always been.

—◦═◉═◦—

For two and a half years, Abbie had slept in Kate's room. It was mutual need. For six months now her daughter had decided to sleep in her own bed. Kate missed her presence and would welcome her back, but it must be a good sign for Abbie to not fear sleeping alone. If only Kate could reach that place.

Kate stood in Abbie's doorway. The antique bedroom set would need restoring soon, she thought, chiding herself for paying too much for it. Kate knew better with owning her own antique shop. But when the set had come onto the auction block, she couldn't resist. The carved walnut headboard with a tiny light built into the center matched the dresser and bedside table. It was perfect in here.

"Tell me again about the day Daddy disappeared." Abbie tugged the purple, flowered bedspread up over her head and held the lace edge with her fingers.

When Kate didn't move or answer, she peeked out from under the covers. "Mom? Are you going to tuck me in?" She pulled the covers over her head again.

"You wouldn't let me forget," Kate said with a smile. While lifting Abbie's arms, Kate pulled the covers neatly over her daughter's lap. The blankets tucked perfectly beneath her.

"Well?" Abbie asked.

"Well, what?"

"Tell me again."

"I've told you too many times. And we were supposed to start *The Voyage of the 'Dawn Treader'* tonight. In this book, we'll see what it's like at the end of their world."

"You and Daddy were in Italy," Abbie said with a determined look. Kate couldn't distract her daughter so easily anymore. "You went to get pastries in the morning and you came back and he was gone. All that was left was a little broken piece of blue tile or something. And we've never found him."

Kate brushed Abbie's bangs back and kissed her forehead. She wished a seven-year-old—*her* seven-year-old—didn't know such a story. But there was no protection from the truth.

"Let's start a new story." Kate meant the C. S. Lewis book on Abbie's nightstand, but then she realized: *they* needed a new story for their lives. It seemed they awoke each day to the same page and repeated it again and again. Time was passing, but they were stuck trying to change the past or at least mend it. If they didn't move on, was there any chance for a future?

"Okay. I wonder how they will get into Narnia this time," Abbie said. Her eyes were already blinking heavily.

Kate noticed it was an hour past her bedtime. "Let's start tomorrow. I had no idea it was so late. We spent too much time on the porch swing."

Abbie gave a long groan. "Well, then, will you sleep in my bed tonight, Mommy?"

Abbie's eyes pleaded and another "Mommy" worked a knot inside Kate's middle. "It's too small for both of us. You could sleep with me."

"No, I should stay here."

"I'll snuggle till you fall asleep."

"Good." Abbie moved over and opened the covers.

It took another fifteen minutes for Abbie to stop smiling and asking little questions and finally allow her body to drift into slumber. She turned and curled with her back toward Kate. It was the same sleeping process since she was a toddler. Her eyes would start to droop, she'd give one last attempt to stay awake, then she'd turn to face the wall and sleep would come.

As Kate watched the back of her daughter's cotton night-gown move in slumbered breath, her own thoughts rummaged back through Abbie's questions. Kate still couldn't shake the feeling that she'd forgotten something. That day in Italy was a wrinkled page of paper she'd clutched so long her fingers had worn through it. It still amazed her how entire lives were destroyed by a single rift in time. She'd sought every detail or any phrase spoken strangely. But had she missed something?

Few mornings could compare with that morning. Certainly, the first dawn of their honeymoon when they kept calling each other "husband" and "wife"—just to hear the sound of it. Or the hours after Abbie's birth when Jack held their infant daughter to the window and introduced her to the world. But their morning in Venice would have been listed soon after those other memories.

The city of dreamers, painters, and lovers had been a long way from Oregon rain, new buildings, and short history. . . .

Kate awoke gently as if she'd simply taken a breath of fresh air. Light through thin curtains warmed the room, reflected light that had first danced from ancient walls and frescoes and then discovered the play of their room. They were on a quiet street with only the footsteps of morning travelers and an occasional slap of an oar in the canal nearby. The walls were soft yellow, and terra-cotta pots of red geraniums were arranged on the floor and table. Bright paintings of Tuscany's vineyards and coastlines brought the feel of Italy indoors.

Jack faced away from her, his breathing heavy and deep. Blankets and sheets were twisted and pulled over them in odd directions like legs and arms entwined together.

Kate tugged on the blankets and slid herself against the length of Jack's warm body. His breathing moved against her chest.

"Jack."

He didn't move.

"Remember where we are?" She rose up, propping one elbow on the bed, and stroked his earlobe.

He grumbled; she smiled.

"Jack, we're in Venice."

He rolled toward her, stretching and rubbing his eyes. He always awoke like this, though Kate hadn't taken the time to watch in quite a while. Back home, mornings were alarm clocks, coffee, day planners, and lists. But this is what they'd have. It started now.

"We don't have to hurry this morning," she whispered. Although his eyes remained closed, she could see half his smile.

"But you want me to wake up now."

"We don't have to go anywhere."

"But you want us to go everywhere, right?"

"Yes," Kate said, kicking the covers away and getting out of bed. She couldn't wait to see what last night's darkness had hidden from view. She pushed aside the curtains and fully opened the creaking windows. Several stories down, a storekeeper arranged a display. Ripples of light reflected from the canal waters. What kind of world waited beyond their window?

Kate turned and could feel Jack watching her. Did he think she was beautiful standing in front of the window, light haloed around her dark hair? The look on his face said he did.

She moved slowly toward him, then hopped on the bed, bouncing up and down while he tried to grab her. "Get up, get up! We have to see Piazza San Marco, Museo Correr,

Basilica di San Marco—do you like my Italian accent? I don't care how expensive it is to ride that gondola; we're doing it. Magnifico!" She jumped, acting like she would land on him as their laughter mixed together.

"Your guidebook is going to disappear." His threat dissipated into a gasp as she landed on his chest. "Jet lag. Doesn't that count for anything?"

"I think it's more than that," she said, kissing his chin.

"Another night like last night and we may only see these four walls."

She jabbed her fingers below his ribs. "I'll tickle you awake."

"Okay, okay!" He grabbed her hands. "Should we call home and check on Abbie?"

"Don't try to distract me. Anyway, it's midnight at home."

"No wonder I'm so tired."

Kate studied his smile, which was more of a half grin, and tried to memorize the moment. They'd talk about this morning when they were an old couple walking in their garden. She'd remember his face, slightly tanned after his last dig; his sleepy gray-green eyes and dark messed-up hair; the small scar beneath his left eye. His hand behind his head as he watched her watch him. She'd never forget this.

"The day has begun," she whispered.

"It's midnight, remember?" He tried a fake yawn.

Kate got off the bed and opened her suitcase. "Okay, I'll go to the bakery, get some Italian pastries and an American paper, if it can be found, while you hop in the shower."

"You shower first; you're the slow one." He sat up, twisting his fists into his eyes.

"I'm hungry now. Can't you smell fresh-baked pastries through the window? Besides, I'll be showered and dressed by the time you've read your paper. Unless you can skip one or two sections this morning."

Kate rummaged through her suitcase and dressed quickly. She brushed her teeth in the bathroom, then put on some lipstick and tucked her hair into a clip. "Full European makeover when I get back. You won't recognize me."

"That doesn't sound good," he said, smiling. "I kind of like you the way you are."

"Be back soon. The bakery is only two or three doors down." She leaned close to kiss his forehead, nose, lips, and chin.

Jack grabbed her arms and pulled her toward him. "Look at you in bed again," he said. "We're in Italy! We have a million things to do and see. Unless you'd rather have break- fast in bed." He grinned wickedly.

"Go take your shower and be awake when I get back." She grabbed her jacket and their room key and opened the door.

"Be careful," he said as he sat up. "And could you get me some coffee? I think I'll need it."

Kate would hear those words again and again. Simple morn- ing words and requests. They were the last she'd hear Jack say.

The wind chime outside Abbie's window softly woke Kate from her thoughts. The night-light cast a soft halo around the room and on the top of Abbie's light brown hair. And suddenly, there it was. Like a gentle whisper in her ear, she knew it. Kate sat up and stared at her daughter. What—or rather whom—Kate had forgotten was right beside her. Kate had been physically present every day. But while Abbie was growing up, Kate had focused her energy on finding their old life.

I didn't forget Abbie, she told herself. But tonight she seemed able to look at the last three years more clearly. On the outside, she'd performed her motherly duties—bedtime stories and kisses—but Abbie had not been fooled. She had clung to her mother at first, trying to draw her back. But the years had brought Kate further away, and Abbie had become accustomed to it. They'd given their full effort in trying to find Jack, and in doing so, Kate had become a part-time spectator in Abbie's life—not the mother she'd once been and always hoped to be.

That morning in Venice, Jack had asked if they should call Abbie. How she wished they had, even if it had been midnight. Perhaps it would have stopped what happened. Jack had thought of Abbie at first dawn. The days since that morning had slowly torn Kate from keeping her daughter at the dawn of her thoughts. Finding Jack—whether he was dead or alive—had been her goal. Yet suddenly she knew what he would want—for her to be there for Abbie first.

Kate tucked the covers once again around her little girl. Sliding Jack's shirt from under Abbie's pillow, she held the fabric against her face, hoping to find some scent of his after-shave. There was none. Too many years had passed.

"Abbie, I promise to be a better mother," Kate said tenderly to her sleeping child. "We're going to get through this and put it behind us."

The book on the nightstand caught her eye. The time had come for a new story. They'd waited for Jack long enough.

But had she missed anything else?

CHAPTER TWO

The vow was breaking.

Lukas Johansen didn't know if he was ready.

After nearly six decades, they would not only speak but also meet once again.

Long ago, five men had vowed their loyalty: Karl as their leader, Jantes who would die too young, Oskar the intellect, Edmund with his serious loyalty, and Lukas himself. They had fought side by side, watched one die in their arms, and discovered together that victory would not bring the peace they'd hoped for. The war ended. And these men who'd survived as one were forced into another vow—to never meet again.

If ever they crossed paths, passed on the street, attended the same gallery opening or political event, there was to be no acknowledgment that they'd ever known one another. Not one of them could attend Edmund's funeral, which dropped their original group of five—then four when Jantes died—down to three. They might know what was happening in the others' lives, but only through individual investigating. Spouses knew little. Children even less. So why meet now? Why threaten the secrecy and break the silence?

Lukas felt the descent of the plane in the dizzying drop of altitude he always disliked.

"We'll be arriving at Phoenix International Airport at our scheduled time in about fifteen minutes." Lukas ignored the rest of the pilot's words as he clicked his seat belt in place. He glanced out the small window and blinked his eyes wearily to the inaudible sound resonating in his ears. It was the sound of waiting.

Waiting was a noise that drew a person into reminiscent places, away from where he stood in a line or stared at a telephone willing it to ring, or as he checked his watch for the tenth time. Dread, anticipation, anxiety, expectation—all fell under the wing of waiting. Lukas didn't hear it with his ears but with every part of his being. Waiting was like a rodent, or a hundred rodents, with sharp, tiny teeth that gnawed from the inside out.

On the Lufthansa 747 bound for Phoenix, Arizona, United States of America, staring from his first-class window seat, Lukas realized he had been waiting. He'd waited for this day for over fifty-five years, hoping he'd escape into the grave instead. A reunion brought people together who sought to see one another, though there was no reason Lukas should not desire to see these men. He'd say he loved them if asked, though he wasn't sure he actually did. These men had been his world when the rest of the world had been destroyed. He'd survived on them as much as he survived on food and water. But without word or contact in so many decades, now they were strangers with ties closer than brothers. They were also the past he wished left behind. What images and emotions would arise when their eyes met once again? Would they even know each other now? More than their faces had changed from youth to old age. The days when five men fought one enemy now seemed like a movie he'd once seen, even played a part in.

Minutes and seconds fell away as the plane touched ground, wheels bouncing and screeching. He watched the pavement and ground whirl past; then they slowed the way he always imagined the last seconds of life would be like. Time would slow, slow until one second was an hour and then eternity loomed ahead.

Lukas would have to go through customs first. An ache always formed in his stomach whenever he crossed a border or passed through customs. His ulcer, he'd told himself, until he realized it always happened at borders. He knew there was nothing to fear. But that nothing tensed through him, though in his life he had walked through customs over a hundred times. He wore a tailored suit and carried expensive luggage. There was nothing suspicious in his manner. He was respected, a retired diplomat no less.

The plane maneuvered toward the gate. Beyond the tarmac, the gates, and customs agents, two men waited. Maybe they sat side by side, stood at the window watching the plane taxi in, or bought coffee from the airport McDonald's. Surely neither had digressed to wimpy Starbucks. Men like them drank coffee dark and strong and would not be seen at a trendy coffee-house. Things changed, but not some things or some people. At least, that was his hope—or perhaps his fear.

Lukas remembered their vow made long ago, in another dimension: "I promise to keep this pledge. We each vow loyalty to one another. I become a brother to these men."

Five men had repeated those words that now sounded so idealistic and unnatural in the world he lived. Lukas had first met the entire group in the hidden room beneath Karl's home on the night of their pledge. They didn't trust Lukas at first; he was the newcomer to the group. But they trusted their leader, Karl. And Lukas would prove whom he served again and again. At that time, it was the only way to survive. And with the memory of those men came other memories—memories he wished to leave buried.

Susanne. Her name was right on his lips. He had not spoken her name in decades except for once, when one of his ex-wives said he called to her in his sleep.

"Who is Susanne?" came the morning scrutiny. Thinking back, he recalled that it was Bernadette who had asked, since Vera would not have cared. But Bernadette would take it as an insult to her own beauty that he could possibly call for another. Lukas could never explain who Susanne was, despite the argument it caused.

"Susanne was brave and valiant," Karl, her brother, had recalled on the night the five men gathered. "She believed in an Austria free from Fascism and Nazi terror. We will continue the work she believed in. And we will avenge her death."

Karl's past words rang oddly in his ears as the pilot thanked the passengers in both English and German for choosing his airline. Loyalty and brotherhood didn't fit the time and place now. Lukas Johansen was a powerful man. His grandchildren watched MTV and surfed the Internet for Hollywood movie stars. Words like *loyalty* and *brotherhood* were either as old-fashioned as phonographs and switchboard operators, or they alluded to some secret cult or neo-Nazi clan. The average man wasn't called to such words anymore—at least not in today's world.

Time changed the world.

Lukas already longed for this meeting to end. It would be only two days, he told himself. He should be able to endure that and would insist on sleeping in a hotel. Yet memories he thought exorcised now arose like ghosts haunting his mind. Perhaps they would tell new stories? Or simply laugh at the antics of comrades now gone? He hoped, how he hoped, that they wouldn't talk about the losses and those things that caused them to depart from each other's lives. He hoped this was simply his old friends' desire to meet war buddies before age took them all.

Yet something inside told him otherwise. There had to be a greater reason behind this reunion.

Did he have the strength to face it?

⚬⚬⚬

Lukas felt inward relief as the customs agent stamped his book and nodded him forward. In all the times he'd passed through a crossing, he'd never shown what he felt inside, even long ago when he'd had real reason to fear the sight of a uniformed guard at a national border.

A large family flowed around him, hurrying to the baggage claim. He'd brought only a carry-on, so he followed the exits to the departure area. His walk was always slow now, but today even more hesitant. He began to scan the groups of people.

Then he saw them.

Karl Olsen and Dr. Oskar Gogl waited against a wall. They stood next to each other without smiling. A surge of emotion built within Lukas' chest, surprising him by his lack of control. The years had worn against their bodies, though Karl remained a tower of a man with wide shoulders and a belly that had grown with time. Oskar stood straight, his inquisitive eyes reminding Lukas of a harmless schoolboy you'd ask to help with your homework. Their age surprised him, but he'd know those faces anywhere.

Lukas suddenly wished for the hugs and tears he'd criticized earlier. He walked toward them in a steady pace, pulling his suitcase behind. They walked toward him—Oskar's smile growing wide and Karl giving a nod of great approval. Lukas felt a tinge in his sinuses up to his eyes that he feared he could not control. Everything he'd achieved—the power and success—these men were the reason. Yet he'd forgotten his roots. Each of them had vowed to forget. They were brothers, long lost and nearly forsaken.

"Lukas," Karl said, his voice catching.

Lukas stopped in front of them, completing the triangle. Never had he realized how much he missed them until their flesh joined in vibrant handshakes. The stir and noise of the airport with its sounds of many air conditioners and muffled movement and voices faded around them. They would soon laugh and reminisce and tell about life so many years ago. Yet those stories wouldn't sound true even to the teller's ear, for time seemed to have slipped those years into a dream. All that was real were the years of war together and the moments ahead.

Suddenly Lukas knew that some vows were *meant* to be broken.

CHAPTER THREE

Clouds of gray and white danced and whirled like a portrait van Gogh would have painted. A few raindrops, tapping against her window, were like fingers drawing her attention.

"Showers likely today in Corvalis with a high of seventy-one degrees," the weatherman had forecast that morning.

Kate paused from her work and gazed out the window. Her backyard flowers called to her to come and play. Her geraniums had done well through the winter, and green shoots poked from the rich soil where she'd planted bulbs last autumn. The dark sky above promised a drink to the bordered plants and lawn.

Rain was healing to Kate, and Oregon provided much therapy. Yet the same rain detracted her from the task at hand. Instead of doing paperwork or profit-loss charts, she yearned to be in her workshop, where the steady rhythm of the rain would beat on the tin roof. She'd gladly trade in her paperwork for the smell of wood stain and the feel of sanding an antique bureau and offering it a second chance. But there was a business side to owning Restorations, and that was her downfall. If she merely had to varnish and paint, take the old and restore, add new pegs, or strengthen a brace, Kate would be wealthy.

She forced her focus back to the pile of papers that had grown beyond ignoring in the past weeks. Discipline was needed even on a cloudy day, even with raindrops pleading— at least until Abbie's return from school. Kate put a stack of receipts in an envelope and noticed one of the files in her in-box.

It was Jack's file. Once Jack was the man she'd stood beside on a cloudy day at the beach and promised her life to. Now Jack Kenton Porter was a manila folder of information. Or, rather, many folders. She'd kept a section for each year within the cabinet beside her. Jack had his own cabinet. Inside those files were missing persons' information, other disappearances in Europe, Italy, and Venice itself. She had photographs available to send to police stations and phone numbers of people she'd called and called, who now only took messages through their secretaries. The first-year section was crammed with papers and folders organized and labeled. She had packets of information from Amnesty International, Missing Persons Bureau, and on and on.

The next year's section was a little sparser, the following even more. The current year was one folder thick and kept in her in-box. She'd noted the retirement of a local FBI agent she once called regularly, a new missing-persons Web site she'd yet to contact, and other odds and ends. Kate had begun clipping articles on tragic and mysterious occurrences. They bore no relation to Jack—an article about organized crime in Eastern Europe, a bite-sized sidebar on violence statistics in American small towns, a newspaper reporting the trial of a Chilean leader for human rights violations.

Perhaps she put such items within Jack's file to add something to the emptiness. They were the only things she could add to her life with Jack. The rest of their marriage was frozen in a moment of time while the world kept moving.

Quickly, before she lost her courage, Kate opened a cabinet and put the current world of Jack Kenton Porter inside. She closed the cabinet hard enough to rock it slightly. The files were reminiscent of her last few years. At first so full of activity. Friends and family calling, helping, supporting. Other people were against her and wrote letters of accusation: "We know you did something to him."

She'd been determined and full of faith and hope, sure that truth would prevail. Now few people besides her closest friends and family called. She'd wished for in-laws to share the struggle—people who'd known Jack since birth and loved him as much as she did. But both his parents had passed away—his father when Jack was young and his mother the first year they were married. Jack's brother worked on a fishing boat in Alaska and rarely visited.

Life had moved on, and they didn't know what to say. Kate reminded some people of their own fears about the unfairness of life. God didn't keep anyone from the scars of living, no matter how involved in church you were. If it happened to the Porter family, it could happen to anyone. Their name had gone from one of the upstanding, Christian families to a tragic and unthinkable mystery. What do you say to that?

Kate could still see suspicion in some eyes. "What *did* happen to Jack Porter?" She heard their silent questions when they kept their children from staying the night or were always "just so busy" to follow through on setting an actual date to get together.

Something *had* happened to Jack.

The people who knew Kate best assumed he was a low-life creep who abandoned her or perhaps had somehow fallen into one of those Venetian canals that ran murky water through the city. A body could stay under forever or wash right out to sea.

Then there were those who knew Jack better. Jack could make a friend anywhere. These people knew he was strong. Jack couldn't slip and die in some canal when he'd done dozens of dives and underwater explorations. And he wouldn't abandon his family. So they questioned Kate's motives.

Family and neighbors who weren't "religious," as they called Jack and Kate, held mixed opinions. Everyone had an idea behind her back. One cousin was sure Jack had been taken by aliens. An outspoken neighbor once announced too loudly in the grocery store about those "hypocrites in the church who have worse problems than normal people." Everyone had a theory, but the answer would probably never be known.

A long raindrop ran in a stream down her window.

It was time to move on.

The decision itself was difficult enough, but to actually put it into action seemed nearly impossible. Kate was stuck in quicksand. Even though she now reached for a branch to escape, it didn't mean she'd make it out alive. How did she say good-bye to someone who wasn't there? A grave or a jar of ashes would have provided a focal point—something to grasp or shed tears upon. And what if—what if she'd missed something?

Kate rested her head in her hands, her elbows on the stacks of papers covering her desk. There was also a pressing fear she'd ignored for three years. Without her husband, without the world they'd built together, without the search and the dedication to prove her innocence to every doubtful person—without all that, who was she? When all alone, with everything stripped away, who was she?

Be strong. Don't search too deep. Take one day at a time.

Remember you have a daughter who needs you back. Get your work done.

Kate returned to the file of invoices. This was part of her renewed focus on Abbie. She must consider their financial future, when instead she only wished to drift away. There were no insurance settlements or social security to help those with a missing husband. But Restorations was doing well, considering its rough start and the competition of online auctions. With the small shop as her sole income, Kate had barely kept them afloat for several years. Garage sales, budget shopping, and a loan from her family helped. Kate had refused to sell the house—what if Jack called or came home one day? How would he find them? Now the shop was on its feet after gaining a good name and regular customers, and their debts were getting paid off. They were going to be all right. Kate needed to work at organization and the taxes she was behind on. Someday there'd be insurance money when enough years passed for the courts to pronounce Jack dead. It would provide Abbie with a college fund, a first car, a nice wedding.

But what of her own future? That appeared cloudy. The fog would someday lift from her life. Perhaps she should make a few small goals, something just for her that didn't ride on answers to the questions of the past.

Her wall clock down the hall sounded the half hour. Kate straightened and realized she was actually looking toward the future. Wasn't that progress? Survival had been the game for so long. Now the years ahead were opening before her eyes.

She studied the drops of water gathered on the hydrangea blossoms outside the window. There might yet be someone inside her. She needed time to get to know herself again. Time to feel really alive, to be able to give Abbie spontaneous and unmasked love like she used to. They should do something together, something fun and carefree. Perhaps a short trip, such as to an indoor swimming pool. Their family had always loved the water. Jack and Kate had taught Abbie to swim as a very young child; it had been one of their favorite pastimes. Boating or snorkeling, anything water related. Kate hadn't done those in so long. She tried to recall the last time. It had been before Jack disappeared—that she knew. It was before her love of water had turned to fear. All because of the words of an Italian *poliziotto* three years ago. "Your husband is floating in that water, isn't he?" The image of Jack under some canal had never left her, even as time passed.

She remembered the officer spoke terrible English, and she could barely understand him. Kate tried but continually had to ask him to repeat his words. Finally, they waited for an interpreter. All the while Kate fought panic and the shock that Jack could not be found. She was alone in a foreign country with its unknown procedures and was suddenly the object of suspicion. She was sweating and shaking at the same time.

"You must know something," the *poliziotto* said. His eyes bore through her in a way that made her wonder if she actually could be somehow involved. Was she going insane? Did she know something more? But she didn't; there was nothing. Jack was simply gone when she returned.

"Was your relationship volatile?"

"Whose idea was it to come to Venice?"

"Where did the grant funding for the conference come from?"

"Do you have the information for this archaeological conference?"

"We will contact the conference director to confirm your story."

"What happened last night?"

"Did you go to a restaurant?"

"Was there an argument?"

"Did you make love?"

"Tell us again what happened. Start at the beginning."

She had answered again and again, feeling dirty and fearful and frantic. The translator grew tired. Officers came and went, continuing to ask her questions. Some had been kind, the one brutally suspicious. She continued to answer. No, they weren't politically involved. She was a mom and owned a small antique shop. He was an archaeologist and taught at the local university. No arguments. Yes, a late dinner at a café. Yes, they had made love. No, no argument.

They checked every source.

The conference was real, the grant legitimate.

They had a daughter at home.

In October, they would be married nine years.

"Something is not right with this story. A man cannot just disappear," the officer had insisted.

"I know that!" Kate had cried, tears spilling down her cheeks. "He was there. I went out for just a few minutes, and all his things are still in the room. Where could he have gone?"

Kate had called her family and could barely speak when she heard her father's voice. He called the American consulate. Hours of terror, hours more with Jack still gone. What if she'd known then that three years later she'd have no more information? It would have driven her mad.

The rain was still falling in long streams against the window. The papers continued to wait and wouldn't organize themselves. Kate turned away from the window, away from yesterday, and propelled herself into today.

Yet sometimes, though she'd feel guilty afterward, she wished it had been her who was lost beneath the murky water's edge.

⋆⇒◉⇐⋆

Karl drove a gray Buick with leather seats and an air conditioner that already fought the Arizona spring heat wave. Lukas was surprised to see where his old friend had made permanent residence. Karl, the man of the mountains, full of might and vengeance, now lived with sidewalks and coordinating land-scapes surrounding every home and business. Perhaps there was safety in anonymity. Or perhaps he had gotten a good bargain for the place.

"Welcome to American suburbia," Karl said as he pulled into the driveway of a midsize, gray-and-white home—a cookie-cutter replica of the ones around it. There were scrubs and sage in the hills above them and droopy, transplanted poplars in the middle of every lawn. Karl had loved trees.

"How do you like it here?" Oskar asked Lukas' unspoken question.

"I have learned to golf." The garage door rumbled upward and then closed behind them as they drove inside.

"I have an air-conditioned work area," Karl said, as if to convince them. Lukas spotted the wooden bench set up with table saw and a neat row of tools pegged to the wall. He thought of his own estate with wooded acres and manicured grounds. He had a woodshop the size of Karl's house, though he rarely took time to work in it. Was this Karl's only option?

Karl's wife, Marta, was waiting with old Austrian hospitality. Platters of cheese, fruit, and bread waited beneath plastic wrap for their arrival. Lukas had always liked Marta and her spunky personality. She was small in stature but had never been afraid to take on anyone. She was an old woman now, moving in careful strides but smiling as broadly as ever. She snapped the kitchen cloth at Karl when he popped a slice of boiled egg into his mouth. Lukas was assured she had lost none of the attitude he'd admired.

They ate and laughed while reminiscing. "Remember when" was the most-used phrase, though they avoided what all of them remembered most—death, struggle, sorrow. They recalled mistakes in the field and drinking until nearly blind and almost being caught by Gestapo agents because of their stupidity. They chided Karl for forgetting some of the native German they all spoke while within the walls of Karl and Marta's home. Lukas felt at home with them again, even in such a foreign place. It had grown dark outside, and remnants of food and coffee surrounded them despite Marta's continued straightening up.

Then, right in the middle of their laughter, Lukas was reminded. There was something more to this gathering. More than a reunion of brothers. He didn't know why he suddenly knew it. The more they talked and laughed, the more Lukas grew uncomfortable. Something wasn't right.

Lukas caught Marta staring at him too long. "You know, don't you?" she asked.

Abruptly, the room went silent.

"What?" Oskar asked, chewing a bite of bread.

Lukas could not escape the hold of Marta's gaze. She nodded gently and smiled. "You are wondering why we asked you to come. You know this is not just a reunion of old friends."

"We contemplate this for many months. Why should I resurrect what is dead a long time?" Karl rested a hand over Marta's. "It was Marta's idea actually."

"We did agree to never meet again," Lukas said. "There had to be a reason for this. Are you in trouble, Karl?"

"Could you slow down for a moment," Oskar said. He pushed up his glasses and looked around the room.

"We all are in a precarious position. Only Marta and I have been the ones to know it," Karl stated flatly.

"Explain," Lukas said.

"We should have met sooner. I cannot describe what it means to see you both. Too many years have passed, and we were brothers."

"But it was necessary for us to survive," Lukas said.

"*Ja,* but do you know that even the Waffen SS and all German divisions have reunions? How can they and we cannot?" Karl said.

"Because they are no longer suspects of crimes—at least not many of them. We could be put on trial, even now," Lukas stated. "You could be deported, Karl."

"This is true. The guilty often flourish the most, but innocents such as ourselves could be accused." Karl shook his head.

Lukas shifted uncomfortably. He had done much worse than Karl even knew. Yet he was the one who'd found success, power, and sizable wealth, while Karl lived in middle-class America. Karl would say that he'd paid for his sins, but Lukas knew that some things could never be righted.

"We cannot undo these years we've lost together, though Karl and I believe we would have done it all differently," Marta said. "But there is something we can do for those years past."

"Something we can do now? What could this be?" Oskar asked, leaning forward.

"I do not know how you will take this news. Marta and I came to the United States and settled in Arizona twenty-eight years ago. We wanted to blend in with the world and hide from the past. But we were unsuccessful. Either I awoke from a nightmare at least once a week, or she did—and this is absolutely nothing compared to what our Jewish friends endured in the camps. Perhaps God hounded us so we would hide no longer. Ten years ago we began to make a search."

Karl paused and eyed each one of them. "During the war, the five of us were given one final mission. Our goal was to find SS officer Wolfram Meizer. Wolfram Meizer was involved in Nazi death squads that murdered thousands of people in the Baltic states. We also knew his reputation as one of the more vicious guards in several camps. As you know, our orders were to find this man and discover exactly what kind of armament was being produced in personal knowledge of Wolfram. Because we were en route to your escape from the Occupied areas, Oskar never knew the reason you were brought in, Lukas."

"I mind my own business. Did then, and I still do." Oskar sipped his coffee. "But what does this have to do with our reunion?"

"Wolfram Meizer killed my sister, Susanne. Neither of you knew that she was working as Meizer's housekeeper several days a week. That led to her death by his hand. I do not need to repeat our old mission or the failure in losing Susanne and Jantes. We almost had Wolfram. We should have investigated his death further. At the time, we believed the records and testimonies."

"What are you saying?" A coldness Lukas recognized from long ago seized him, spreading through him as if his blood were freezing within his veins.

"We now believe Wolfram Meizer survived the war."

Something deep and sharp sliced through Lukas. All he was and had become began to crumble into tiny shards. The idea that Wolfram Meizer could be alive during all these years insulted his very existence. His entire life's work seemed null and void with the thought that his greatest enemy had been free to live and grow old as he had.

"What are we going to do?" Oskar asked.

"We will find him," Lukas said.

"We believe we have." Karl folded his hands as if to pray. "And here lies the danger. We may know his location. But he may also know ours."

CHAPTER FOUR

Kate knelt to inspect the underside of a dusty table-and-chair set. Pairs of feet walked past as she examined it for damage or cracks in the wood. The auction was getting crowded already. She got up and sat in one of the chairs and wrote the table number in her notebook, running her hand along the carved edging. It appeared in disrepair and would be missed by many buyers, but she was familiar with this builder whose business was destroyed by the Civil War. Kate had been looking for a Charles Buchanen table for a long time. She tried to think how she could keep the oak claw-foot table for herself instead of reselling it at her shop. First she'd have to win the bid.

"I made it!" Kate turned to see her friend Connie O'Brien balancing two capped Styrofoam cups in her hands. "Only an hour late," she said wryly, as her purse strap slid off her shoulder.

"Would you like some help?" Kate asked. She took one of the cups of coffee.

Connie plopped into the chair across from Kate with a sigh. "Can we stay here for four or five hours so I can unwind and not hear the ringing of children's voices in my ears?"

"That chair will probably get a higher bid with you in it. With a little help, this set could be beautiful once again."

"I think mucho help would be required to make *me* feel beautiful again," said the harried-looking, slightly overweight mom.

"Wasn't it you who was sure you could balance book-keeping with day care? My home is my sanctuary—yours is the local zoo."

"Was that me? I absolutely don't recall. My mind was snatched by two-year-old T-Rex Randy, who thinks it's his job to bite every dino-child on the playground. Look at my wounds." Connie pushed up her sweatshirt sleeve and pointed, but Kate couldn't see anything except her friend's soft, freckled arm.

"I think we should find a better place to sit," Kate said, motioning toward the auction manager. He'd glanced their way twice.

They moved through the warehouse labyrinth of antique furniture to a snack bar that served only donuts and coffee.

"So how did you escape?" Kate asked as they sat across from one another.

"We only had three kids today since the flu bug landed. My aide is watching them while I take an hour to myself." Connie took a long sip from her cup. "This caffeine fix should help me function as an adult again."

"That would take more than a coffee." Kate smiled.

"Okay, okay. So tell me, *Kathryn*," she said, emphasizing the word like an antiquated Englishwoman would, "how *are* you?"

Kate smiled, recalling their long-standing joke. Connie had once started counting how many people asked Kate, "How are you?" during a single church service. She broke them into categories of whether the *how* or the *are* or the *you* was accentuated. The winner was the "how *are* you?" Connie wanted to enter Kate into the *Guinness Book of World Records* for the most-asked phrase, sure that her friend would win. Kate had often dreaded the pastor's closing prayer, knowing she'd soon be assaulted with the question. Worse, still, was when people stopped asking and returned to the usual "how are you?" After three years, she was just anybody else with another tragedy behind her. So it was nice to hear Connie ask, however jovially she put it.

"I am *just* fine. How *are* you?"

"Settling nicely into this chair, thank you for asking." Connie took another sip of coffee and sized Kate up with her gaze. "Is everything all right? You look exactly how I feel—tired."

"Thanks. Perhaps you need to cut back a little."

"I think you're changing the subject. What's up?"

Kate continued to drink her coffee. She wasn't sure she was ready to face this. Today was about escaping from the world of decisions that plagued her; it was her chance to search the auction for pieces to bid on. Her shop was small, but furniture moved quickly. Her customers especially liked that she always had something new and interesting.

Yet, Kate mused, Connie was never easily daunted. Perhaps if she verbalized her thoughts to another, it would make them real. "Okay," she finally admitted. "Abbie and I need to move ahead with our lives. But I'm not sure how to do that."

Connie's eyebrows rose. She quickly wiped cinnamon-specked whipped cream from her upper lip. "This is something. Waiter, bring us some champagne! Let's sound the church bells!"

"All right, Connie. Don't hesitate to embarrass us."

"When have I ever been afraid to embarrass you? But wait; hold on. These words of yours sound somewhat familiar. Oh yes, they're the very words I've been repeating to you for the last six months. Imagine that!"

"If I didn't love you so much, you would really get on my nerves."

"I know. I'm irresistible." Connie puckered her lips and blew a kiss. Her expression softened. "I can be too pushy. And I was a bit obvious when I went through that phase of giving you those self-help books."

"Ah yes. *Who Moved My Cheese?* and *Severing Your Spirit Hang-Ups* weren't high points in your support."

"I already apologized a million times. But some of the inspirational quotes I e-mailed were good, right?"

Kate nodded with little commitment. Quotes and books and advice from Connie and other friends had been water through her fingers. The gestures were appreciated, but the words did little.

"This hasn't been easy for me either. You don't know how hard it is to see your best friend go through a catastrophe. I want to fix everything for you."

"Some things aren't supposed to be fixed," Kate said and smiled.

"They have to be healed," they said together, repeating one of their pastor's favorite lines, the cause of much laughter between them—however true the words.

"I'm proud of you, Kate. Deciding to move on with your life. But what does this mean exactly?"

"I told you; I'm still trying to figure out that part."

They both sat in silence for a moment.

Then Connie shook her finger as an idea formed. "This is *The Empire Strikes Back.*"

Kate rested her chin in both hands, watching her friend with amusement. Life often mirrored a scene from a movie in Connie's world.

"Remember the part when Han, Luke, and Princess Leia

escaped down a wall panel and fell into that trash compactor room? There's all that garbage and dirty water and an underwater snake that I think Han shoots after it almost eats Luke. Oh, Chewie was there too, 'cause I remember his fur getting wet, and I thought he probably smelled like a wet dog. I hate that smell."

"Are you coming to some point? And by the way, that scene was in *Star Wars,* not *The Empire Strikes Back.*"

"Are you sure?"

"Remember Princess Leia had her hair like two cinnamon rolls on the sides of her head? She only wore her hair that way in *Star Wars.* Anyway, your point?"

"Well, the walls started closing in and they couldn't do anything to get them to stop. Luke was on his walkie-talkie thing trying to get R2-D2 to reprogram them. It gave me the creeps imagining all of them smashed together like when I use my trash compactor and even a green-bean can squishes flat. Can't you just see them all smashed together—Chewie with his wet hair—"

"Connie, return to Earth, please."

"Okay, okay. At last, you realize you need to get out of the garbage heap. And I know you didn't want to get in the garbage cylinder of the Death Star. I know you needed to search the garbage to see if Jack was there, but he's not. He's not. And now the walls are closing around you, and you can't find out how to get out. So you need some help from the outside." Connie smiled as if all should be clear to Kate.

Kate stared at her friend for a long time. "If we hadn't been friends for so long, Connie—"

"Don't you get it? You need a friend to help you get out. So I'm helping you get out."

"How are you doing that?"

"I'm ordering you to get away with Abbie. You need to help her realize that you are both moving on. Take something symbolic to mark the end of that old life and the beginning of the new—I don't know what, but something. I wish those Italian police would have given you that piece of ceramic you found on the pillow."

Kate had wished that too. It was the lone item that could remind her that the nightmare was real. But it was across the sea, locked away as evidence.

"You could have thrown the ceramic into the ocean!" Connie demonstrated for her. "I'm very serious about this. You need something to let Jack go. He's gone, and you need to say good-bye."

Kate recalled similar thoughts she'd had, both about the good-bye and something special for her and Abbie.

"Then you can move on with your life."

"You've never said it out loud before," Kate said in a low voice. "That Jack was really gone."

"I know. I wanted you to say it first. But I wouldn't have pushed you. Even if I did drop some hints the wrong way, I wouldn't have pushed for you to make this decision if I thought there was any chance of Jack coming back. I knew Jack. I loved him too. But I especially know how much he loved you. The two of you were what fairy tales are made of. If Jack were alive, he would have come back by now. If Jack is alive, it destroys everything I believe about love. Kate, Jack is gone."

Kate nodded slowly. Finally she could hear these words and believe them. Finally she knew that Jack was gone forever.

✦══◯══✦

Perhaps they'd always known it. Somewhere inside, when the doubts arose, they had stuffed them away. When they'd been finally free of the weight of a nation and a war that destroyed great cities and many lives, it had been too heavy to pick up again. When a fight has lasted long and leaves the body and spirit downtrodden, when victory is announced, the enemy defeated—quiet doubts can be ignored.

Wolfram's death had been too easy. They'd found Jantes. Jantes, the one who tried to make Lukas laugh because the others believed it impossible. He'd finally succeeded by telling a story so ridiculous that the owls in the trees must have chuckled. Then, the next morning, Jantes had moved ahead to scout the area. Wolfram had been waiting and had assured a slow death for the young man whose only dream was to farm his father's land again. Lukas had found him first. He had held Jantes in his arms and looked into eyes glazed with pain. Jantes' tongue had been cut from his mouth and his stomach sliced with agonizing mortal wounds.

Jantes died in that muddy ditch with Oskar, Karl, Lukas, and Edmund surrounding him in a circle, his blood covering each of them. After that, the remaining four pursued Wolfram with a vengeance despite their actual orders. One thought consumed them—*find Wolfram*. It was pure revenge that drove them. And then they had reached the camp. . . .

They had been silent for several moments now as Karl retrieved documents from his office. The refrigerator hummed from the other room. Marta rose and moved to the kitchen, returning with the percolator to once again fill cups littered around the room. Karl returned, carrying a large cardboard box he set on the floor. Lukas caught Oskar's odd, puzzled expression. It had been a long time since Lukas had seen that look. Oskar had always adopted odd facial movements in difficult situations, as if he didn't know what was happening. But the truth was, Oskar was the most intelligent of them all.

"So, tell me. Was Wolfram helped? Or did he convince the Americans he'd make a good spy against the Russians? Or the other way around?" Oskar's voice actually trembled as he spoke.

"How can you be certain?" Lukas asked. He buttoned his sweater up the front, still feeling cold inside.

"I didn't want to believe it either." Karl leaned against the couch and crossed his arms. "This man killed my sister and Jantes. But let us look at the evidence. None of us actually saw his body. We didn't push to do so, because of what we saw in the camp."

They were silent once again.

The camp had been the final blow. Each remembered and could still feel the skeleton fingers clinging to their wool pants; they saw hollow-eyed skulls who smiled and cheered as they walked among the living dead. The stench of death had permeated their clothing, even their own skin. It caused them to retch and brought madness to their minds. Different from the grief of losing Susanne and Jantes was seeing what mankind could do to mankind. Lukas had known already.

"I want to know—how can you be certain?" Lukas asked again. He wanted to banish the thoughts of yesterday. All this was getting too close and he feared what the memories would do to him. Wolfram's body was supposed to be long decayed. The American soldiers swore they'd seen his shredded body after the camp inmates reached him.

"Look at the photographs," Karl said. He passed several enlarged black-and-whites toward Lukas. Oskar moved to sit beside him. The first photo was old and the man in it was walking away from the camera. Lukas didn't want to believe it. Not until the third photo did he and Oskar feel convinced.

"These were all taken in Argentina in 1956," Karl continued.

"How did you get them?" Oskar asked.

"I have made connections with a group of Nazi hunters."

"Ah, really?" Oskar said, adopting that puzzled look again. "How did this begin?"

"It began with our contacts during the war. I have kept in

touch with the others from the Austrian Resistance. And my role in the underground gave me connections with the Allied army, especially the American army. Those contacts have remained, but of course, I pulled back considerably when the crimes began involving the blue tile pieces. We believed then that it was essential to be clear of any suspicions that would link us to those murders. Now I see that this was Wolfram's doing.

"Marta began to read more about the Blue Tile Crimes. She studied the locations—"

"Stop," Oskar interrupted. "I have not been kept aware of these things you call Blue Tile Crimes. I knew of one murder when you contacted each of us to no longer keep our group together, but I did not know of more."

"I have a file," Karl said. He found a manila folder and dropped it on the coffee table. "We have at least six murders, several of them high-ranking officials. But let us cover that information soon. Oskar, you look through the file and it will connect with what has led us to this gathering. But to return to Wolfram, it was in the records of war crimes trials where Marta found the first testimony about Wolfram. The officer on trial told of an event that took place several days after Wolfram was supposed to have been killed. We first believed it a mistake."

Lukas glanced at Marta and wondered if she'd read the testimonies from his trial also. It had been long ago, and only a few people, including Karl, knew about his time in prison. Had Karl told her? Lukas had had a different name then and had spent those years trying to pay back his old sins. It wasn't so easy.

"I wasn't ready to hear it, and I became quite angry about her prodding. But when Edmund died in the late eighties, I realized that my life would not last forever. Could I go to the grave with such a truth? So we began to dig. Most of my loyal contacts were retired and had time to help. No one knew of our group's connection with the blue tiles, and because we vowed to stay apart, we ensured no one would find out. The Nazi hunters already had Wolfram on their list. That's when we obtained these photographs. But I wanted to tell you something else. Since working on this, I wrote to Edmund's widow, asking if she had found a piece of broken blue tile. She told me that she had seen it years earlier, but that she didn't find it in Edmund's things."

"Are you saying you believe Wolfram was involved in Edmund's death and that he took the blue tile from him?" Lukas asked.

"It is only a suspicion."

"You have known these things and you have not contacted us?" Lukas asked.

"There was little reason in the beginning," Karl said. He lit a wooden pipe that had rested beside his chair. "Lukas, you were still very much a political figure at the time. The last thing you needed was old comrades returning, especially with the problems we faced after the war. Oskar had buried himself in research and lectures. And we didn't know where Wolfram was at the time. It seemed frivolous to contact you with nothing. But let us start with some background."

"Karl has been learning the computer. He made this summary of Wolfram." Marta gave them each a folder with information inside. They had prepared for this reunion well.

Lukas read over the first page, though he knew all the information already. A young Wolfram Meizer had joined the Nazi Party in 1931 while living in Munich, Germany. During the war, he became an SS Death's Head member and later a guard at several death camps, including Dachau and Mauthausen. At the close of the war, he worked at Ebensee in Upper Austria— a subcamp of Mauthausen. The words spoke of knowledge gained firsthand.

"We have a report from one of the survivors who witnessed Wolfram in action," Marta said. Then she read aloud: "'Wolfram Meizer was one of the cruelest officers. He would kill for any purpose. If he was in a good mood, he would kill. If angered, he would kill. Drunk, celebrating, or sick—it did not matter. I was working in the field when Meizer walked by. He tripped over a rock and hurt his ankle. He was furious and pulled out his gun, though none of us looked at him or said a word. He shouted for someone to come to him. None of us moved. He pointed to the young man beside me. The boy begged and cried, but Meizer shot him in the face. He did this to three other men and then left the field. This was one of many instances.'

"A report from another SS member. This took place in what was formerly Yugoslavia. 'We lined them up; they were all women. Meizer shot them in the neck one at a time. I believe there were at least fifty.'"

"And there was also Jantes and Susanne," Oskar said softly.

"What has Wolfram been doing since the war?" Lukas asked.

"He escaped Europe, probably using a false Italian passport. He went to Paraguay and Argentina, where he owned various businesses and two houses, one by the ocean and one in the mountains. In the late 1960s, he even lived in the United States for several years before returning to South America. It was only in the mid-1990s that he disappeared. At first, we feared he had died. But now we believe we have located him once again, using a name—perhaps even several—different from the one he used after the war back in Europe."

"You *feared* he had died?" Oskar took a sip of cold coffee.

"Yes," Karl said firmly. "We want him alive. We want him to pay in this world for what he has done. Marta believes he will get justice in the next life, and I hope that also. God's justice should be even worse since the cries of the innocent are in his ears even more than ours. But I still want justice."

"Why would he change his name now?" Lukas asked as he sifted through the papers in the folder. His thumbing stopped at the copies of the photographs. In one, Wolfram stared from the page straight into his eyes.

"Because he has an important reason for returning."

"Which is what?"

"That is something we do not know. There are several possibilities and locations. I believe he is after something that was left behind."

"As in something the Nazis left behind? Another Nazi treasure hunt, I suppose." Oskar chuckled as he said it. "And what exactly will we do once we find him? What is this justice you speak of? Remember, we are all old men. Our days of revenge are over. Perhaps I am speaking for myself here, but if you have not seen a mirror lately, well, friends, you are old men now."

Karl laughed. "Unfortunately, I do not need a mirror. But there is something we can do. We'll expose him. There are still dedicated war-crimes investigators, also the media if need be. I hope he will stand trial and have prying reporters hound his last days. He has known too many years of freedom."

Oskar scratched his chin, thinking. "You know he will get lawyers to say he is unfit for trial. The other recent trials have gone that way often enough."

Lukas listened to the dialogue around him and read over the papers. He stopped when he found a photograph of a young woman that seemed to have been printed from the Internet. "Who is this?" he asked, holding up the copy.

"Ah yes, this is a delicate matter." Karl glanced at Marta and then back at them. "I need to tell you about a woman who lives here in the States. She may be a link to Wolfram."

Lukas looked at the photograph again.

"Her name is Kate Porter."

CHAPTER FIVE

H e never slept well in someone else's home.
A hotel worked because no one's life was there. But to sleep in
the house where a family or individual lived meant breathing
their air and memories. Lukas should have gone to his hotel as
planned. Oskar, snoring from the couch, was evidently not
bothered by his displacement. Everyone except Lukas had
voted for their staying the night, since the evening had worn
into the late hours.

Perhaps he felt so troubled because of the months he'd spent
hiding in the homes of strangers—strangers entrusted with his
life. He never wanted that dependence again. Or perhaps it
was the flood of this information—something he didn't want
to face so late in life. Wolfram Meizer alive. Memories and
questions about Susanne. An American woman with a missing
husband who somehow tied into their lives, though he
believed there was more to that than Karl had yet revealed.

Lukas turned in the bed and straightened the covers. He
heard muted conversation and a stifled laugh in the room

beyond the wall. Karl and Marta were awake also. They were probably discussing their reactions to seeing wartime friends turned old. Did Marta laugh at how Oskar's nose now looked like a bumpy gourd and that Lukas' own forehead now revealed a gathering of age spots?

He turned onto his back and stared at the ceiling. There was much to process and more to come. They'd finally given up for the night. It was like a maze trying to follow Meizer's path and figure out what he was now seeking.

Another muffled laugh worked through the wall. Suddenly he wondered what it would be like to love and be loved like Marta and Karl loved each other. Did Oskar feel that strongly about his wife also? Lukas' thoughts went to Susanne. But this brought back the questions that haunted him. Had she really loved him as he had loved her, or had she been gaining his trust to discover the truth of his loyalties, whether for the Allies or the Nazis? He'd never known of her involvement in the Resistance until after her death. Did that change what they'd shared?

Lukas' thoughts should focus on the present. His fear that the past would flood over him if he came to Phoenix had come to pass. He considered getting up again. He could look through Karl's information and gain more information on this woman Kate Porter and Wolfram's investments and . . . he should think about those things. But sleep at last began to fall over him, bringing images of Jantes in the mud, the breathing corpses of the camp, and as always, Susanne.

⋆⇒◇⇐⋆

Kate woke early but waited to get out of bed. Not for the same reasons that had kept her there in days past, when it had taken tremendous strength to move back the down comforter, when her feet had felt tender and unprepared for walking and her energy had seeped into the padding of the Sleeper Queen mattress.

With the light growing through the windows, Kate savored this new feeling.

Connie had told her, "Wake up to a new day. You are putting the past behind and moving forward. Tomorrow is that first day." Then Connie had described a movie, which Kate hadn't listened to; she was too busy telling herself to do it. To make tomorrow new.

And it was.

Unlike other mornings that seemed to be a continuation of pain that ached from morning through night into the next dawn, this dawn brought a great sigh of hope. She was caught up on bills, her house was mostly clean, and she and Abbie were going on a road trip—a trip to tell Jack good-bye.

Kate kicked back the vanilla-colored comforter, got up, and hurried to make coffee and waffles. A new day it was. She couldn't wait to tell Abbie about their four-day minivacation a week away. Perhaps she'd let Abbie choose their destination. And sometime between breakfast and next Friday, Kate would help her daughter see the essential need to tuck Daddy away in their hearts and move on. Together they would find the strength to do what only three years' absence made possible. The time had come.

"I want to visit the aunties," Abbie said later between syrup-soaked bites of waffle.

Kate's fork slipped from her fingers and clattered against the plate. Her weathered spinster aunts, wonderful as they were, weren't her idea of time away.

"You said we can't go more than five hours away," Abbie begged. "That means we can't go to Europe to find Daddy or to Grandpa and Grandma's for a visit. I choose Auntie Hannah and Auntie Geraldine, especially since Grandma says that the

aunties are going to die someday and I add a lot of sunshine to
their lives."

Kate hadn't yet picked up her fork. Her child with heart-
shaped face and clear blue eyes appeared innocent of the world
around her. Then she unloaded casual statements across
waffles that spoke what her thoughts really held. Kate closed
the open map of the great Northwest she'd placed on the table.
When Abbie smiled at her sweetly, Kate wondered what this
seven-year-old knew about manipulation.

Once she'd caught Abbie reading one of the "change your
life" books Connie had dropped off. Kate had looked at the
book, a guide to management, and had tried to decipher the
message Connie was sending within the pages of *Who Moved
My Cheese?*

"Rick's boss passed these out to all the employees at Soft-
ware Visions," Connie had said. "It's more for businesspeople
but it also addresses a lot of life issues."

Kate had skimmed the book and laughed again and again.
What kind of management book was written using mice as the
example characters? The short chapters covered the choices of
mice as they sought their cheese. Either they adapted to the
changes of their cheese being moved, or they eventually
croaked. The story was supposed to help employees better
adapt to change ("they keep moving the cheese") and to be
proactive in their work by anticipating change ("get ready for
the cheese to move").

"My cheese didn't just move; it disappeared," Kate had told
Connie the next time they met. "And my cheese is not coming
back. What does a little mouse do?" She was half amused and
half annoyed by Connie's gift.

"But Jack wasn't your cheese; your *life* is your cheese." It
was as if Connie had prepared for this discussion. "Or your
cheese is more accurately your future and your present situation."

CINDY McCORMICK MARTINUSEN

Kate wasn't ready to hear it. Perhaps she was the mouse in the book who was shriveled in the corner, weak from lack of cheese. Kate turned to joking about whether her life was Gouda or more likely Swiss, with holes pressed through it. Connie had sighed and joined in the debate over cheese varieties, adding in movies that included famous "cheese" scenes.

When Kate found Abbie reading *Who Moved My Cheese?* she worried. It was bad enough that her daughter had had few friends in the years since Jack's disappearance. Abbie didn't fit in with little-girl ways and had little patience for what she called "the silly and mean behavior" of many of the girls in her class. Now she was reading a management book for entertainment.

Abbie continued to eat her waffles. Perhaps, Kate thought, her child knew exactly how to get her cheese no matter where it moved.

"Okay, my daughter." Kate paused, wondering what to address first. She went for the reference to Jack. "You want to go to Europe to find your daddy? Is that what you're trying to say?"

Abbie's expression shifted from cherub to surprise. She hesitated, then asked, "Can we?"

"Come here and sit on my lap."

Abbie slowly put down her fork and came to her.

Kate twisted a strand of Abbie's honey-colored hair. She could see highlights of auburn as her fingers pulled through. Was this the moment to make Abbie understand that her daddy was either dead or certainly not coming back? Kate wanted to keep the momentum of her new day, but Abbie's yearnings were too raw to ignore.

"I know you aren't quite ready to say good-bye to Daddy. I don't want to either. If a million prayers would bring him home, he'd be here. The police in Italy, even the FBI and many other people, have tried and tried." Kate touched her daughter's chin. "But you have to understand."

"I don't want to talk about this," Abbie said, jumping from her lap. "Do we get to go see the aunties or not? Can I start packing my stuff?"

Kate's hesitancy produced a long "pleeease" from her daughter, and then Abbie disappeared down the hall at Kate's slight nod. Kate was failing as a mother, right before her eyes. She didn't know what else to do. Abbie could close up her feelings like a door slammed and locked, with a smile covering the pain. Kate often had to search for some hint in Abbie's words or actions to find out how her daughter really felt—and Kate had done little of that in the last few years. Jack had been better at drawing Abbie out. When another child had hurt Abbie's feelings in preschool, Kate knew nothing about it when she picked her daughter up. That evening Abbie broke down on Jack's shoulder and immediately told him the story.

Kate sat in the quiet of the breakfast nook and wondered what to do. "The aunties?" she said aloud. Of all the places to choose. The purpose she'd assigned this trip had just shifted from a farewell to more of a challenge. Kate wished to leave now while her resolve was still strong. But Abbie's school and the antique shop pulled her to that curse of adulthood— responsibility. It turned even worse when she called Aunt Gerdie with the news of their visit. Gerdie suggested that Kate pick them up and then drive all of them to California to see Kate's parents. Abbie was on the other line, cheering for the plan.

"Aunt Gerdie, I only have four days," Kate put in, trying to bring some reason to the situation.

"Where's your sense of adventure?" Aunt Gerdie responded jovially. "And did you realize that's Mother's Day weekend? Your mom would be thrilled, and all of us women, mothers or not, can be together. This is perfect."

"Yeah, perfect, huh, Mom?"

"Perfect," Kate muttered.

"It's an hour and a half to our house and seven hours more to your parents'—not bad for a young woman like you. I once drove for three days straight to see my best friend before she left for the mission field—"

"Okay, we'll do it," Kate said in surrender. The entire plan was hatched by Aunt Gerdie. Kate felt as if a hurricane had come and destroyed her vacation in one swift blow.

The trip was complicated, exactly what she'd hoped to escape. Days later complications increased. Mason called.

Lukas let the warmth of the shower pour over him as the bathroom filled with steam. Once, travel never phased him—now, every muscle complained. The beds in even the best hotels didn't compare to his at home. Chairs were uncomfortable, and several days of leaning over papers at Karl's house had taken its toll on his neck and shoulders. How had he ever slept beneath trees and stars on cold, rocky ground?

For two days, they'd discussed and reminisced. Lukas insisted he sleep at the local Sheraton the second night. Only in America would a hotel offer a shopping and entertainment center with a 166-foot water slide. Children and adults in bathing suits roamed the halls. Brochures boasted of the amenities he didn't require.

Lukas needed to return home. An important election was approaching, and though it hardly affected him since his retirement, there was always the media in need of opinions and party responses. His retirement had not taken away his influence in the government.

And now he needed to be strong for another reason. The discovery that Wolfram was alive would give him something to work toward. There would be little peace now that he knew the man was in Europe—exactly how close to home, Lukas would find out.

The message light was flashing on the hotel phone when Lukas left the bathroom. He still needed to pack and his flight was only three hours away. It was probably Oskar or Karl calling for a final good-bye. He checked the time and realized that Oskar would already be at the airport.

It amazed him that the days had passed so quickly. He would be glad to leave this arid land. Glad to get back to his mountains. The three men and Marta would meet next month at his home in Austria after each of them worked in his or her assigned area. It would be good to welcome them back. Neither Karl nor Marta had been home in nearly thirty years.

And so much had happened during that time. Lukas examined his sagging chest above the paunch of his stomach. Once he'd been lean and fit. Would this body be strong enough to carry out what lay ahead? Not that he needed physical strength. Using the good sense of three men and a woman, they had laid the plans, keeping in mind their limitations. This would not be like the old days of sneaking through the woods, killing sentries in the dark, infiltrating enemy zones—this would be a battle of will and mind. It would mean finding the enemy first and destroying him in ways he would not expect.

Lukas was an old man and not in body alone. He suddenly wondered if it would be worth it. Would he feel any satisfaction bringing down an old enemy—even one he'd hated for so long? If not for the protection of his life and his friends', he would actually consider leaving revenge in God's hands. He'd thought Wolfram was dead once before; it had been little comfort. Why would it be different a second time?

He picked up the phone and pushed the message button while sucking in his stomach and pushing back his shoulders.

"Lukas." Karl's voice on the recording held a steady urgency. "Return this call. I need your help."

Karl knew Lukas' flight schedule. He wouldn't call unless essential. Lukas picked up the phone with a great sense of foreboding.

The line was busy.

CHAPTER SIX

There are mysterious connections between people. Something unexplainable that draws two people together like an instinct uncontrolled. The connection doesn't consist of love or simple attraction, though it could grow into friendship, passion, and later love. Kate would sometimes analyze it: Where did it come from? Was it always mutual? What was its purpose?

Her thoughts wandered the old path of these questions when she felt that connection stir at the sound of Mason's voice on the phone. She was comfortable with the feeling, like a fluffy afghan tucked up to her chin on a chilly day.

"What are you doing right now?" he asked without saying hello.

She smiled and sat in her overstuffed chair by the French doors. Abbie was outside, playing school with Whiskers, the calico cat.

"I'm making plans for a four-day escape from my house and shop."

"How did you work that one?"

"Trudy wanted extra hours, so I'm giving them to her."

"Isn't your daughter in school? You aren't teaching her to play hooky this early in her education, are you?"

"Teacher training Friday and Monday. Worked perfectly, didn't it?"

"I could get envious. Where are you going?"

"To pick up the aunts and drive to my parents.'"

"Let me renege on the jealousy statement. I thought you said something about an escape?"

"I'd had something else in mind, but Abbie made the choice with some help from Aunt Gerdie."

"That explains it. What did *you* have in mind?"

"The open road perhaps. What I really miss is the water— scuba diving or snorkeling, even swimming would do. I've been thinking of water quite a bit lately."

"Not exactly what I had in mind."

"What did you have in mind?"

"Dinner, the two of us."

Kate didn't speak for a moment. Mason always invited both her and Abbie whenever they did something. "Is everything all right?"

"I'm not the best swimmer. And I'd like to talk to you, alone."

And there it was. Kate didn't know what gave it away—the fluctuation in his voice or something more instinctive. She'd wondered with a mixture of dread and anticipation when or if this day would come. She'd always felt a strong drawing toward Mason. It was an attraction that made her want to be near him, to hear his voice and laugh with him. She felt guilty about it often enough, while also wondering if he felt the same. Kate had been alone for a long time. Sometimes her skin yearned to be touched, while her mind turned fearful at the actual thought. She missed being loved and loving someone in return. But the decision to put Jack behind her needed to be with pure motives, not with any thoughts concerning Mason.

Kate and Jack had known Mason for years. Jack and Mason played golf from time to time. They were in the same men's group at church. Mason's insurance company was doing well and kept him busy, so they would invite him to dinner regularly. They'd double-dated when Mason had a girlfriend. When Jack disappeared, Mason was one of the few friends who didn't abandon her. Instead, he checked on her and Abbie, cleaned the gutters in the spring, and did odd jobs around the house. He'd take them out for pizza or Italian. But this was different.

"So, when?" she asked almost fearfully.

"As soon as possible."

◆▸══◉═══◂◆

Lukas sat on the sofa, his hands folded, elbows resting on his knees. Blue and red flashes from the police lights out the window washed across his face. He lifted his head as if it weighed a hundred pounds to look again through the open door where men in uniforms took notes and photographs with their eyes turned downward. He could see the bottom of two gray-stockinged feet oddly twisted and uneven.

After Karl's urgent message, Lukas had called back.

It had taken three tries before he heard Karl's voice. "You have a plane to catch, but I need you to stop by. It is hard to explain." Karl talked like someone afraid of being overheard.

"I will come over."

"Marta is gone this morning with the car. She was dropping off Oskar at the airport. You must take a taxi."

"I will be there in less than an hour."

"Be careful."

These last words told him a lot now. Karl had known danger was near. Lukas had changed his departure and kept

his room at the Sheraton for another night. When he arrived at
Karl's, it was like replaying an old memory. The door was ajar,
though he saw no blood at first.

Karl's desk chair was overturned. Lukas saw legs turned
awkwardly and then the large frame of his friend on the floor.
A small pool of blood soaked into papers that had fallen beside
him. The wound looked minor, possibly caused from his fall
to the floor. There were no other injuries he could see. Karl's
eyes were closed, but there was no pulse.

Lukas hurried to the kitchen for the telephone, a towel, or
something, anything. Karl could still be alive. He cursed his
legs that wouldn't move fast enough, as if quicksand pulled at
his every movement. He was searching the counter for the
phone when he heard a car pull into the driveway. He hurried
to the door; Marta met him there. She froze with a bag of
groceries in her arm. She didn't seem surprised to see Lukas
but instantly knew something was wrong. He tried to stop her,
but she pushed by, dropping the groceries in the entry. They
were still there. Eggs splattered across the welcome mat.

And on the desk above Karl's body, Lukas had found a fragment of blue ceramic. A blue tile. It was in his pocket now.

The coroner arrived and took Karl away. The police began
to leave. After Karl's body was taken, Marta was led away
toward her room. A sob cut through the low voices still there
as if electricity flashed through the house. Then Marta
screamed for Karl. Lukas remembered a scream like that from
long ago. It sounded almost familiar, since he'd heard it often
in his sleep. Lukas' first instinct, crazy at it was, was to find
Karl. His wife needed him. After all they'd endured together,
this was how their marriage ended. They'd made their home in
a subdivision where kids rode by and teenagers cruised too
fast. There were fast-food restaurants and video stores a mile
away. An old man could not be killed in such a place.

"Lukas!" Marta's plea was heard from the master bedroom.

He hurried down the hall and found her standing beside the bed. An elderly woman was trying to sit her down. Marta's face looked panicked, but she steadied when she saw him. "Everybody out." Marta's voice was strong, though tears flowed freely down her face. "I must speak to Lukas."

The elderly woman hurried from the room. A policewoman hesitated, then left also. Marta closed the door and leaned against it, as if thinking. Lukas waited.

She paced across the room and stopped in front of him. "He is gone, Lukas. My Karl is gone."

A sudden sob dissolved her against his chest, her arms around his middle. She hit her fist against his back once and regained her composure slowly. He patted her back awkwardly until she looked up at him. He could see that she might dissolve again at any moment.

"I must be strong, be strong," she said and set her jaw. "I know who you were."

Lukas felt his eyebrows drop slightly. She nodded as if he'd spoken.

"I've known since the war. Your real name is Bruno Weiler. Once you were a Nazi, an SS even. You worked at a concentration camp. You were our enemy before you were our friend. But something made you betray the Nazis—I never knew what. I didn't trust you, but I trusted Karl. And you proved whom you served."

She paced the room and wiped her face.

"After the war, those years you disappeared, you were in prison for crimes you did as Bruno Weiler. Karl and I were the only ones who knew; Oskar and Edmund thought you were lost in the aftermath of war. You could have called on many people to save you. Karl told me some of the people you helped while betraying the Nazis. They were powerful families who could have helped. But you faced those ghosts. And when you were free, Lukas Johansen was alive, that other man gone forever."

His expression didn't change, but inside he was surprised, even fearful. He also wondered if he would ever be free from those ghosts.

"Wolfram, he did not know you as Lukas Johansen. Karl and I know the families you helped during the war. You saved them from certain deportation to the camps. And they helped you after your time in prison. We heard how you fought going into politics because of your past. But your past was too far buried—that was made certain. Until now. Wolfram knew you during the war before you betrayed him. Perhaps you even believed that Susanne was killed because Wolfram knew you were with us. He didn't. Wolfram didn't know you were part of our group. You were brought to our house to help us find Wolfram. You were told that our place was just another safe house. Karl was instructed to be certain of your loyalties before you joined our group."

"Was Karl instructed to ascertain my loyalty, or was Susanne?"

"No. Never. She loved you, Lukas. That was not part of it. I promise you; she loved you. But listen to me. These are things in the past. It is today that you must be wary of. You see, Wolfram might have known about your time in prison, but then Bruno disappeared after several years. No one except a very few have known that Lukas Johansen was ever Bruno Weiler. But now you've come to our house. We did not know he was so close. Otherwise, we would not have brought you here. And we know—" she gestured toward the living room, and tears rolled again even as she clenched her jaw—"this was Wolfram."

"Yes." Lukas took the piece of blue tile from his pocket and handed it to her.

She held it in her open palm. "Do you understand? You and

Oskar are not safe. Especially you. Wolfram knew that Bruno Weiler betrayed him. If he could locate Karl, then he will know that former Austrian minister Lukas Johansen was visiting here. He will know that Lukas Johansen is his betrayer, Bruno Weiler."

It shocked Lukas to realize that the identity he had maintained for nearly sixty years was now compromised. His two ex-wives had not known, nor any of his children—only once did he speak of his past to another. He must not think of this now. Karl was dead, and Marta needed him.

"I am safe for this moment. Wolfram will not move yet. In fact, I am certain this could not be his direct work. Remember, he is an old man also. Perhaps he will wait for me to come to him." Lukas actually had no idea what Wolfram thought or what he would do. But the words seemed to comfort Marta. The reality that Wolfram could have come here and done this without help was impossible. "I will stay with you."

Tears raced over the lines in her cheeks in a continuous stream. "How will I live without him?"

"Let us get through today. We will think of tomorrow when it comes."

The Phoenix Coroner's Office would most likely give a natural cause of death, he assumed. The gash in Karl's head was a result of a fall from a heart attack. Lukas wouldn't object. They need not know what he knew. This was his fight now.

Lukas suddenly felt he'd lived a hundred lives. He was tired of living and getting over tragedies. Old people were supposed to get rest, retirement, peace. He had none of that. And now he must watch his back again. For decades no one but a handful of people knew who he really was. Now Karl was dead. What kind of world stole the life of a man such as this? Lukas knew he shouldn't ask himself, for as soon as he thought it, a hundred faces of good men and women returned—faces of death. How weary he was of hatred and grief and especially of the memories. If he wasn't careful it would all wrap around him and drag him straight into oblivion. But Lukas knew no other path.

CHAPTER SEVEN

The memorial service was held two days after Karl's death. Few people attended. Karl and Marta had no children. They had only a small group of friends in the community, because the past left many fears about growing new friendships. Lukas knew from experience. The service was graveside, short and simple. Then it was over. His friend was beneath the ground.

Though she claimed to be fine, he knew Marta needed him. She cried at night, then upheld her usual strength to any neighbors or acquaintances who stopped by during the day. Oskar stayed at the house with them, taking the first flight back to Arizona from Maine after Lukas had phoned him with the news. But Oskar could not stay long since his wife had just received the news that she had early stages of cancer. Whenever Marta left the room, they discussed what really happened and what to do. Lukas knew he wouldn't have Oskar's help in the months ahead.

The morning after the funeral Marta joined him and Oskar

for coffee. Her eyes were red, but she was dressed, with makeup on and hair in its usual pulled-up style. Lukas and Oskar were discussing the blue tile when she entered the room.

"What do we do now?" she asked.

"We would like access to Karl's office," Oskar said thoughtfully.

"Yes, of course. I'll open the safe also."

Lukas watched her walk with great effort, as if her legs now carried the weight of a thousand years. He admired Karl's widow. He envied what they'd shared—everything. Lukas' ex-wives had known only sketches he revealed during a nightmare or in a moment when he forgot himself. Once while sitting with his second wife as they watched their girls play soccer, he had remarked on his love of playing soccer in his tiny yard in Hallstatt and how the ball always ended up in the lake. Vera had looked at him strangely and said, "I thought you were born in Vienna." But Vera didn't probe because she didn't want to know. Her world was peaceful, and that's what mattered.

Perhaps it would have been different if he'd shared with someone what he'd endured and what he'd done. The one time he *had* told his story—to a young woman not long ago—he'd felt freer somehow. She'd told him about the forgiveness only God could grant. But still he couldn't seem to find it.

Lukas followed Oskar into the office. Marta had opened a cabinet door, revealing a built-in safe. She turned the lock this way and that until they heard the soft click.

"Here's the file on Meizer," Oskar said. He flipped through the papers as Lukas searched the small safe.

"This looks like all the information Karl already shared with us. But it will help."

"What is this?" Lukas asked as he looked at a small cardboard box with address and paid postage but no recipient name.

"Should we open it?"

Marta didn't hesitate. "No, we must mail it. I forgot Karl told me. I asked him why he has this package with paid-for postage. He said it wasn't time yet, but that it must be mailed."

"Should we first look inside?" Oskar asked.

"We mail it, just as it is," Marta spoke firmly. "Karl said this, 'If something happens, mail the package.'"

"You do not know what is inside?" Lukas asked, turning the box over.

"I trust Karl with that."

"Then we'll mail it," Oskar said. He was spreading other papers around the desk, though Lukas could see they were all the same documents they'd explored the first day of their reunion.

"I will make some sandwiches," Marta said in a tired voice. She shuffled away with her shoulders slightly hunched. Lukas wondered if she'd survive this.

They sat around the kitchen table and ate in silence. Marta moved quietly around them, cleaning the counters. After brushing the crumbs from his whiskers, Oskar moved to the couch for his usual afternoon nap.

Perhaps they were all too old for the task before them. If a day searching files and planning the next move was this difficult, how would they ever find Wolfram Meizer's location? Karl's absence was felt in everything. He'd been their leader—now it was up to Lukas to take his place. He knew his position but did not desire it. Too many thoughts moved through Lukas' mind, keeping him from rest. He needed to think—think and breathe fresh air, even if it was Arizona air.

Marta stopped him at the door. "Would you mail this down by the park, a few blocks away?"

"You are sure?"

"I promised I would."

Lukas considered opening it as he left the walkway of Karl's house. It could be important, provide better answers. Without a name on the front, would the package arrive at its destination? The inner wrapping was too tight for him to know what it contained. He could open it and repackage it without Oskar or Marta knowing. Lukas played the thoughts in his head until he stopped in front of the blue mailbox. In the end, he dropped it in after repeating the address over in his mind several times. He hoped they wouldn't regret it.

The subdivision had a small park for neighborhood children. As Lukas walked the two blocks, beads of sweat soaked into his collar though the day had turned unseasonably cool for an Arizona May. He found a bench that faced yellow plastic slides and chain-link swings. A group of young children climbed and shouted while their mothers chatted on the other side of the playground. One mother would get up to break up a squabble or help a child get the gravel from his shoes. Strollers and snacks in Tupperware containers, boxed drinks and sticky faces, birds chirping, and the sun warming the wool hat he'd brought from his closet at home.

What a bizarre and obscure line between this, an average American day, and where he'd been earlier—within the intrigue and spy stories that were as real as these sunscreen-lathered children before him. How did the two worlds coexist without either ever knowing of the other? Chubby smiles and carefree days just blocks from secret packages and a dead comrade. Lukas felt jerked both ways.

He walked by the blue mailbox on his way back and already regretted the mailing. It bothered him that he still clung to such old futility as fulfilling a dead man's request. Nothing would have been harmed if they'd checked the package. Nothing at all. He took a receipt from his wallet and a pen from his pocket to jot down the address before he forgot it. His memory wasn't what it used to be. The more he thought about it, the more Lukas realized how essential it was for him to find where the package was going.

-+≡◎⊂≡+-

Welcome
Restorations—Old & New

Kate turned the sign so it could be read from outside the window. Painted by an artist friend, it was the subject of new customer comments.

"What a lovely sign," the older patrons would say.

Restorations—she was embarking on a restoration of her own. Now that she and Abbie were getting away, it was difficult waiting for the day to arrive.

Kate peered through the front window, surrounded with vines and mini white lights, for any smudges she needed to clean, then walked through room settings of antiques—living room, kitchen, dining room, and bedrooms. She dusted and straightened as she moved to the back section of antique books. It was a peaceful Monday morning with the light rain pattering overhead. A gas fireplace hummed from her living room section, warming the narrow shop that really did feel more like a cozy house than a store. Some of her regulars came and enjoyed sitting in the library area and sipping the variety of teas Kate made available. She was still considering an espresso machine because of all the requests she had received.

Restorations had been her line of survival in more ways than one. Many mornings the shop forced Kate from bed when all she wanted was to hide forever beneath the covers. But she knew that if the shop failed, she would be forced to sell the house, perhaps move, further disrupting both Abbie's and her life.

The shop also gave Kate a place to explore her creativity and provided a short escape from Jack—Jack's search, Jack's disappearance, and memories of Jack. But sometimes she felt she'd leave it all behind for something else, something she'd yet to know or find. It was only an inkling she had from time to time—an inkling she'd pack inside under the heading "Stop looking for greener grass when you have a struggling lawn that needs you."

Now with a short trip ahead, Kate longed even more for the time away. Just a few more days, she told herself throughout the day when her mind kept drifting away from work. She quoted the wrong date on a late-1700s rocking chair and the customer corrected her, frowning as if Kate knew nothing about antiques. Later, Trudy, her only employee, discovered the teapot had been filled with a mixture of Orange Spice and Mint Green teas. Kate had wondered why no one had drunk any.

"You're nervous about tonight," Trudy said with a smirk on her face.

"Why would I be nervous?" Kate wondered how Trudy had heard about her dinner plans with Mason.

"Jane told our Bible study so we could pray for you."

Kate stared at Trudy for a moment. Because of Connie's weekly family night, Kate had gone to her next choice for a baby-sitter—Jane. Jane was Ms. Professional Christian. She traveled often and spoke at retreats. Kate liked the woman and, though Jane was always a flurry of productive activity, she had cared enough to check on Kate and Abbie when few still did. For Christmas the year before, she'd given Kate a coupon book for five nights of baby-sitting. Whenever they saw each other at church—which wasn't often because of Jane's involvement, the large congregation, and Kate's inability to get there on time since Jack had disappeared—Jane would remind her that she still had those baby-sitting coupons to redeem.

So Kate had called and Jane was thrilled, even though she had to switch some things around to be able to do it. "It's all right though—ministry is ministry." Kate didn't know what she thought about a night baby-sitting Abbie being considered "ministry." Sometimes Kate saw glimpses of her own future in

Jane's schedule-dominated life, if her own had not been interrupted. And that scared her to death.

Trudy was explaining how the women's group thought it
was a good sign that Kate was dating again. "It has been such
a long time."

Kate didn't want to be the subject of Bible study gossip and
thought she should explain that dinner with Mason was far
from hitting the dating scene.

The phone interrupted.

"Mrs. Porter, this is Mrs. McDonald at Corvalis Elementary.
Abbie's teacher brought her to the office a few minutes ago.
She doesn't seem to be feeling very well today."

"I'll come pick her up. Is she all right?"

"Well, Mrs. Konner is here and . . . why don't I let you talk
to her?"

"All right."

"Hi, Kate. I'm not sure what is wrong, but Abbie just hasn't
seemed herself all day. At recess I had her stay behind so I
could talk to her and she started crying. When I asked what
was wrong, she wouldn't tell me, so I thought you might pick
her up or come talk to her."

"I'm coming right now."

Abbie looked small and fragile sitting on the couch in the
office area. Her head was bent, and she watched the tips of her
brown shoes bobbing up and down. She spotted Kate and
quickly covered a fake-sounding cough with her fist. "Hi,
Mom," she said with another forced cough. "I don't feel good."

Kate crouched in front of her, looking intently into her face.
"Let's take you home, all right?"

Abbie nodded and Kate noticed tiny tears in the corners of
her eyes. She put an arm around her daughter and told the
office secretary they were going home. They were silent as
they walked outside; Abbie leaned close against her as if to
hide her face from the students they passed.

"Abbie?" Kate began when they were both belted inside the car and she had put the key in the ignition.

Abbie turned toward the outside window. "Mom, I just don't want to talk about it. Is that okay?"

Kate thought for a few moments. "I can't help if you don't talk to me."

"Remember those times when you said you didn't want to talk? You were crying and I asked you why, but you couldn't say why. Now I know what you mean. You just can't talk about it yet." A tear careened down her cheek and she wiped it away quickly. "Maybe it's just my time of the month."

Kate had to stifle a laugh. Abbie was still looking out the window in deep contemplation. Obviously she was repeating a Connie line, not even knowing what it meant. Connie often used the phrase in her descriptions of woes, "and it isn't even my time of the month," or "of course, it would have to be my time of the month so I completely broke down crying."

Kate placed her hand over Abbie's for a slight squeeze and then turned the key in the ignition. At home, Kate made hot cocoa and they rocked together in the porch swing. While Abbie was cheerful again, she didn't approach the subject of her tears. Kate tried different tactics, but Abbie was good at moving around them.

Later Kate walked by Abbie's bedroom, where the door was open only a crack. She was carrying a laundry basket and had come in search of stray socks or clothing when she heard Abbie playing.

"And that's why I must leave forever," Abbie said in a deep voice.

"Daddy, please don't go. I missed you. I want you back." The voice was of a little girl.

"I came home and no one missed me," the deep voice said.

"I did, Daddy. I promise. Take me with you."

Kate knocked lightly on the door as she pushed it open.

Abbie's expression held the word *guilty*. "Hi, Mom," she said quickly, lining up the stuffed animals she was playing with.

"We need to talk."

Abbie shook her head.

"I'm not leaving until you talk to me." Kate sat on the bed next to her.

"I like things the way they were. Now you want to know everything about me."

Kate was taken aback. "I only want us to be close. I want to be a good mom. I want you to tell me what's bothering you." She reached to pull Abbie toward her, but her daughter scooted away. For all Kate's reassuring thoughts over the years that Abbie was coming through the loss of Jack fairly unscathed, it hurt to realize that she hadn't really peered beneath Abbie's smile to what her daughter really felt and thought.

"When will Miss Jane be here?"

"I'm going to call her because I don't need her to come tonight."

"Why? Because of me? Mom, Miss Jane promised to teach me how to cook ginger cookies, and Grandma wants me to make some for Christmas this year. If Miss Jane doesn't come, how will I learn?"

"When did you talk to Grandma?"

"At e-mail lab today. Please, Mom."

"You e-mail Grandma?" Her daughter had a whole life she didn't even know about.

"And Grandpa and Reece. Sometimes Aunt Gerdie, too, when she has time to visit her friends and use their computers. So can Miss Jane still come over?"

Kate nodded, though she didn't want to go. Abbie had moved into her "everything's great" attitude, and Kate suddenly knew that this was the biggest disguise of all. The only way to reach

Abbie was if her daughter learned to trust her enough to share her struggles. It wasn't going to happen overnight.

Abbie continued to weigh on her mind as she stood in front of her closet later and realized she hadn't gone shopping like she'd hoped before this dinner with Mason. Once inside the walk-in closet with its racks of pants, shirts, coats, and the smell of cedar and musty shoes, Kate wished she could slide into a warm corner and hide from the outside paths awaiting her decisions.

Her fingers trailed the fabrics of her clothes that had changed little in the last few years and then moved toward Jack's section. She'd promised herself a dozen times that she'd box his things away. She felt the cottons and acrylic mixes and denim from Jack's Dockers for the university, his khakis for fieldwork, jeans for home and play—they all hung waiting to be picked from their hangers and worn again. With the touch of each fabric came the return of a related memory. The black tie and jacket was their last Christmas party together. Work boots with mud cemented to the edges was a dig she'd worked at with Jack. The gray shirt was a night to a suspenseful movie—her makeup had smeared on the collar where she'd buried her face. The days of their marriage were lined up here in neat rows. She had often tried to reach into the past and live them again. But they were past, she reminded herself now.

Kate returned to her clothing and chose the only outfit she still liked—a black skirt and burgundy blouse. The rest of her hanging clothes were church outfits or scarves, shirts, and pants for the antique shop—all of which she was completely bored with.

Jane arrived at Kate's door that evening with one arm covered in clothing. Jane was in her early fifties, but she always had more energy than anyone Kate knew. "When you said that you didn't get to go shopping, I decided to bring a few of my things in case you felt like something new. Oh, but you already look nice."

Kate followed Jane's quick steps down the hall to her bedroom and surveyed the outfits. On their hangers they looked like professional women who'd gone limp after a long week on Wall Street. The feeling that tonight was a big mistake kept getting stronger.

"Mason is such a great guy. We've tried to find him someone for years. The church's most eligible bachelor, that's for sure. We should have made you an appointment at the salon— manicure, massage, facial, highlighting."

"You're making way too much of this."

"Oh no. This is an important step for you, Kate. I know we didn't meet until after what happened, to your husband, I mean. But it's been horrible for you—we all know that. We can't even imagine it. Tonight is your night."

Kate wished she felt as excited. It interested her that Jane kept sliding into forms of *we* as if the Bible study group or the pastoral staff were such a part of Jane that she had become pluralized instead of a single individual.

"Mom? You're going on a date? With Mason?" Abbie stood in the doorway and stared at the carnage of clothing as if she'd interrupted great plans of betrayal mapped around the room.

"Yes," Jane said with a wide grin. "Do you want to help make Mommy pretty?"

Abbie turned quickly and hurried from the room. Kate found her beneath a sheet she'd earlier spread from Abbie's bed to her dresser to kitchen chairs forming her newest fort. She was curled in the farthest corner with her head on a small lacy pillow. Kate sat on the floor and put the sheet over her head so she was inside the fort too.

"I think I have the flu." Abbie sank her face into the pillow with a groan.

"You were all right a minute ago."

"But now I feel sick. Maybe I have hyper-thernia."

"Hypothermia?"

"Yeah, that."

"You only get hypothermia from being in the cold too long." Kate reached across stuffed animals and books to touch Abbie's arm softly. "Why don't you come out of here?"

Abbie slowly sat up but didn't crawl from beneath the fort. She picked up her sticker collection book and thumbed through it without looking at Kate. "Why didn't you tell me where you were going?"

"It's only dinner with Mason."

"You didn't tell me."

"I should have. We haven't been talking as well as I'd like so it was easier for me not to tell you. And I was worried about what you would think. I'm sorry, Abbie. I think it would be best after today to just cancel."

"Are you in love with him?"

"No!" she said too quickly. "Not at all. I like Mason, and he's been a really good friend. He's been your friend, too, like a real uncle."

"Why didn't he ask me this time?"

"I'm not sure, but he said he wanted to talk to me tonight."

Abbie finally looked at Kate, searching for any additional answers. "Okay, then. You should go."

"I don't feel like it now."

"No, you should go. And I need to learn to make those special cookies with Miss Jane."

"You'll have a good time with her?" Kate made a face that looked like Jane's pert expression.

Abbie giggled. "Yeah, she's pretty nice."

"I rented *Anne of Green Gables* for you."

"Really?" Abbie crawled past her. She hurried into the other room in search of the movie. Kate stayed on the floor and gazed around the disastrous room.

Jane peered into the room and then came in. "She'll be fine."

Kate sighed and nodded. Jane put out a hand to pull her up.

"She has school tomorrow, so bedtime is 8:30." They walked toward the living room. "If she gets her reading homework done, you can let her stay up till 8:45."

"I did finish my reading," Abbie said from the couch.

"Abbie, no inventions without Miss Jane's approval—like when you made the whipped-cream-and-chocolate-syrup sandwiches when Connie watched you."

Abbie frowned. "Okay, but we are making the cookies, aren't we?"

"Definitely," said Jane and winked at Abbie. "We'll have fun without disasters."

"I left the restaurant phone and my cell number on the fridge." Kate leaned over the back of the couch and gave Abbie a kiss on the cheek. "I love you."

"You promise you won't fall in love?" Abbie's eyes scrutinized her. "What would happen to Daddy?"

Kate glanced at Jane, who winced with a this-is-out-of-my-league expression. "We'll talk in the morning, Abbie."

"Kate," Jane said, stopping her in the entry, "you look very pretty." Kate glanced at her reflection in a mirror by the front door and found that she, too, was pleased with her appearance. "I hope you enjoy your evening."

Kate left the house quickly before she changed her mind. As she drove toward the restaurant with the sun fading in the western sky, Kate had a strong sense that she was betraying both Abbie and Jack.

CHAPTER EIGHT

A couple walked ahead of her through the restaurant doors. The man held the door for Kate but then was drawn close to the woman again, like two magnets pulled together. Kate couldn't help but glance at them a few times, though they were oblivious to her presence. It only increased her loneliness.

She turned to search for Mason Phillips. She was late, and she'd seen his car already in the parking lot. Through the open patio door, she could see him. Their eyes caught, and she waved at his smile. Kate wound through the candlelit tables, low voices, and chink of silverware and glasses, her eyes on Mason's the entire time. He watched her with an admiring smile, more admiring than she remembered. Kate found him more attractive than she ever had and knew he thought her beautiful at that moment.

But instead of enjoying the gaze that drew them toward one another, she was jolted back to that morning in Venice when she'd wondered if Jack thought her beautiful. She could see his face vividly in that moment. With effort, she blinked away his image, but Mason's expression showed that he'd noticed the intrusion of something between them.

"Hi," she said timidly.

He stood, and his presence had a powerful effect. "Hello," he said and pulled her chair from the table.

Kate felt awkward as he scooted her in. The evening was warm, and the sky had cleared as the last remnants of evening hung on the horizon. The trees had opened their green wings and white, potted impatiens dressed the open patio.

"Remember this table?" Mason asked, sitting across from her. His dark eyes prodded her to remember. He was handsome with his warm smile and neat, dark hair that receded slightly at his temples.

"We came here for my birthday with Abbie a few years ago. I'd forgotten that. We sat here?"

"Yes. Your thirty-second birthday. Connie was sick and your friend Jane was out of town. You didn't want to do anything, but I made you."

"You have a better memory than I do."

"Are you ready for your trip?"

"Yes. It should give me time to really think about things."

"Time to think? What is churning inside that head of yours now?"

Kate realized she'd just opened the door to a serious conversation, one she wasn't sure she wanted to share with him. She paused for a moment, gazing over the wrought-iron fence toward the shadows of flowers and scrubs.

"It's been a hard three years," she said.

"Yes." He reached and took her hand. His touch stirred something she'd nearly forgotten. Kate looked at his smooth jaw and then at his mouth. She hadn't been touched in a very long time.

"I'm trying to be patient," he said without moving his eyes from her face.

"Trying?"

"For a very long time."

"You've never said so before."

"Didn't you know?"

Kate realized she had. There was mutual attraction between them; yes, she had known that. But that he actually wanted to move past friendship? She imagined she had known even while she ignored the idea. Now it was out in the open between them, and he was awaiting her response.

He sensed her hesitation and turned her hand over. "What do you feel?"

"Mason, I'm not really sure."

"Do you feel anything?"

"Yes," she whispered.

He smiled and looked at their hands. Kate liked his smile; she always had—the way it gave his face more character and life. His touch sent slow tingles up her arm and brought thoughts she didn't know how to cope with. She'd shut down these feelings for so long, and it terrified her to have them awakening again.

"If I only knew what happened to Jack . . ."

His fingers paused their journey over hers. The waiter stopped by and took their drink orders.

When he departed, Mason spoke. "Jack is always with us."

"Yes." She pulled away and stared into the candlelight between them. "I always thought that true love would endure anything, and if two people pledged their lives and hearts, something almost magical took place. Surely I should have some kind of feeling that should tell me what happened to him, whether he's alive or dead. Though I just can't imagine him alive any longer. But there's nothing solid that I can say I know for certain. No answer from God or any intuition. Nothing."

Mason watched her as she spoke. He always listened, but tonight he didn't appear as interested. There was impatience in his face. "Then what do you believe happened? And can we ever get past it?"

Kate twisted the linen napkin in her hand without looking at him. "A few weeks ago I watched a television special called *Disappeared*. The woman they interviewed believed her husband had been murdered." She glanced at him and noticed his interest. "The man's office was ransacked and they found traces of his blood in the room—but no body. For eight years she assumed the worst, until he was arrested in a different state for faking his death and stealing a new wife's money. The women were crying in the interview. Both said they had no idea their husband could do such a thing. As I watched, I wondered if I could be interviewed for that show. I can't believe Jack would do that to me or to Abbie. But those families would have said the same. It scared me. I mean, who can you trust if not someone like Jack?"

Kate didn't mean the words to hit a target.

"I guess it would be hard for you to trust again," he said, though she knew what he was really asking.

"I don't know if I can." She realized the truth as she spoke the words. Mason was a good man, but Jack had been too. A battle raged within her. One part wanted Mason to love her, wanted him deeply, with cheesy soap-opera music in the background. Then the image of a trial appeared in her thoughts, with judge and jury pronouncing her guilty, guilty, guilty. Another voice told her how ordinary it all felt. She'd thought she'd wanted the ordinary again. Dinners with her husband as they leaned over flickering candlelight, family charades and laughter, man-sized socks in the laundry always turned inside out, church on Sundays and Wednesday nights—she had wanted the life she'd had with Jack.

Mason seemed to be offering her an ordinary life again. Yet the pages couldn't be turned back and Jack be replaced by someone new.

Kate shook her head to clear away the thoughts.

"I'll wait for you, Kate. If you aren't ready, I'll wait till you are. I'll wait forever."

"Forever is much longer than you think."

He seemed to search every one of those words. "All right then, I can't say forever. But I have endurance—I've breezed through three years. But I need to ask you to be willing to try also. Could you at least try to let me get close? We will move slowly, a bit at a time. If you need space, we'll back up. And we'll see what happens. Kate, can you give me that much?"

She nodded but felt a growing sickness in her stomach. She'd assured Abbie she wouldn't walk near this path with Mason. She'd told herself the same.

Kate had occasions of great strength. She could make a decision and move toward it fiercely. Mountains would begin to move. But it was the passage of time that gave her trouble. Her resolves weakened; obstacles made her question the path. But none of that strength was with her now. She'd made promises to Abbie and to herself. Now she was making another one to Mason. They were promises that contradicted each other and would surely bring sorrow to someone.

⋅→▬◦◌▬←⋅

Kate didn't want to go in. Jane would be waiting and wanting a report. But Jane was asleep on the couch with her briefcase open on the floor beside her. Papers were in her hands and on the floor. Kate touched her shoulder.

Jane groaned as she sat up. "How was it?" She yawned and

straightened her blouse, then pressed her hands around her short hair to straighten any wayward strands.

"Good," Kate said.

"Mason is a great guy."

"Yes, he is." Kate felt suddenly tired. "Thanks for staying with Abbie. Was she all right?"

"Sure. We made whipped cream–cookie sandwiches after our cooking lesson. She was a happy camper."

Kate smiled. "She gets her way with another baby-sitter. Would you like to stay over?"

"What time is it?"

"Ten-thirty."

"That's it? I can't believe I fell asleep." Jane closed her leather briefcase and blew a sleepy kiss good-bye. "I'll call for more details later. Oh, you have several phone messages I left on the counter."

Kate closed the door behind Jane and leaned against it. The house was quiet and lit only by the living-room lamp. Kate saw the list of messages on the table but didn't reach for it. Instead she shuffled through the mail and carried a few bills that still read "Mr. & Mrs. Jack Porter" to the couch. She could tell that Abbie had already gone through it. Abbie loved to get the mail. Kate had ordered several magazines for her so she could find something with her name on it. The highlight was always a package from Uncle Chris. Her single uncle liked to treat Abbie to anything from a boxing mummy to a cuddly teddy bear.

Kate opened the bills and set them beside her. Loneliness swept into the room like a fog. One of the hardest parts of losing Jack was the loneliness she'd never considered before. After being with someone every day and every night and then losing them, the silence became an enemy and an accuser.

Jack, why can't you tell me what happened? God, why can't I have peace?

Kate noticed a paper partway under the couch. She pulled it out and looked at Jane's typed letter to all the Sunday school teachers about a meeting they were required to attend. Kate read the letter again and again. It was her old life on that sheet. She'd written such letters to the women's group or to the parents of her Sunday school class.

Were her faith and religion as basic as that? They had been more like her career or hobby than the foundation of her life. Kate knew she'd been sincere in her beliefs, but now that she examined her old life from a distance, those beliefs had turned cold as she immersed herself in work. Did she truly love God as she professed? Kate didn't know anymore.

Weariness overtook her. She stretched out on the couch, turned on the TV, and flipped through the channels of infomercials and low-budget movies. Hours later she awoke, stiff and uncomfortable, to a group of exercisers bouncing across the television screen. The clock read 3:30 A.M. She turned off the TV and trudged down the hall, Abbie's night-light leading the way to her bedroom. She shed her nylons and tossed them to the overstuffed chair, where a gathering of discarded clothing already rested. Taking a step toward her bed, she raised her blouse to pull it off when something caught her eye in the dim light.

Something small rested on her pillow, right in the center. She could see its darkness against the cream-colored pillow-case. Kate picked up the small object and, though it had been years, she was shocked at the recognition of it in her hand. It was cool to her touch but felt red-hot, as if she couldn't let go but wanted desperately to be rid of it.

Her other hand reached for the lamp to be sure. And there she stared at the piece of broken blue ceramic that returned her to that room in Venice. Blinding fear coursed through her.

Abbie!

She raced down the hall in fear with the broken ceramic in

her hand. Why hadn't she checked on Abbie when she'd come home? With one hesitant pause, she flipped the switch. Her daughter was there, lying on her back. Her closed lids flinched in the blinding light, but she stayed asleep. She was there.

Kate turned off the light and knelt by Abbie's bedside. Then the house closed around her. The darkness and any creak seemed to possess another presence. Someone had put the broken ceramic on her pillow. Someone had been in her house. Had it been while she slept on the couch? And what if that person was still here?

CHAPTER NINE

The television screen cast white flashes on the walls—the only light in the hotel room. Abbie's head rested against the pillow, facing the TV. She was asleep at last. Kate flipped on a lamp and found the remote to turn off the cartoon. She glanced again at the locked door. After numerous shakings, Abbie had awakened and found it exciting that they were going to a hotel in their own city in the middle of the night, and that they were acting mysterious in the process. Kate tried to make it seem fun, like a surprise party for two.

They were safe here, Kate hoped. Her nerves felt jittery, as if she'd drunk too much caffeine. Now that she was locked within The Corvalis Inn and wasn't required to portray the fun-mommy role, the questions assaulted her. How did the ceramic piece get in the house? What did it mean? When had it been placed there? Kate thought of calling Jane to find out what she knew. Perhaps she'd call her parents, though she tossed that idea, knowing the futile worry it would cause them. She should call the police or the FBI, but every time she picked up the phone she stopped herself.

Kate had habitually called an officer friend in the months after her return from Venice. Until one visit to the station. Adam had been both her and Jack's friend—someone she could count on, someone with connections, even if all the assurance she received was "I'll keep searching." Six months after Jack's disappearance, Adam sat down with her. She thought it odd he'd asked her to come to the station, odder still when he brought her into one of the interrogation rooms—for privacy, he said. But once there, she knew something was wrong. He wasn't acting like himself. Adam went over the months and phone calls and all that he'd done. He asked her why *she* thought there were no leads, none of any kind.

"Jack's photograph and information has been sent around the world. We've had experts in international kidnapping and ransoms, political killings, missing persons, but there's nothing—no ransom note, no terrorist group claiming responsibility, no contact with his relatives or old friends, no sighting of him with another woman, no body washed on shore or found by fishermen. These are the facts, Kate. You have to tell me if there's something we don't know."

Kate was transported to her last experience in an interrogation room. Then she knew: Adam suspected *her*. After months of no information, even Adam was suspicious. He kept her there for several hours, finally admitting that sometimes people tried to cover their guilt by seeming to be overly concerned. He'd let her go, saying that he believed her—though she knew he wasn't fully convinced. From then on, she questioned herself constantly and feared every inquiry and move, asking herself if it made her appear guilty. Added to her already anxious feelings was now the fear of how others saw her. Excessive concern might be construed as guilt. Too little concern could be interpreted the same way. If she did everything or nothing at all—someone would suspect her motives.

Kate picked up the phone, glanced at the curtains covering every inch of the window and at the dead bolt over the doorknob. She couldn't stay here forever. She dialed Connie's number.

"If this is another telemarketer, get your time zones right," Connie grumbled after several rings.

"It's Kate." She heard a rustling on the phone as if Connie quickly sat up.

"What's wrong?" Sleep had raced from Connie's voice and was now replaced by calm fear.

"It's a long story, but I'm at a hotel in town. I could use you right now."

"Kate, what happened? You have to tell me something."

"I found a piece of broken ceramic—exactly like the one in Venice. It was in my house, on my pillow."

"How did it get there? Dumb question, I know. Where are you?"

"Corvalis Inn. Room 253."

"I'm on my way."

Kate slouched into a chair beside a small table. She took the broken triangular shape from her pocket. It looked exactly like the one she'd found in Italy and clutched until the Venetian police had taken it away and locked it away in their evidence room. Any analyses had turned up nothing. Only its presence on the pillow was suspicious.

The room was silent and warm, contradicting the unrest she felt inside. Within fifteen minutes Connie knocked on the door. Kate peeked at the distorted head through the peephole. She opened the door to her friend with disheveled hair and mismatched clothes—flannel sweats and her husband's T-shirt.

Connie hugged Kate immediately and held her for a long moment. Then she pulled away and peered inside the room. "Let me see it."

Kate pointed to the coffee table and bolted the door behind them.

"So this is it? Is it the exact same one?" Connie held the ceramic to the lamp as Kate walked past the bed to sit in the chair.

"I don't know. I didn't have the first one for very long. But it looks like it."

"Maybe it was stolen from the police in Italy, or maybe that jerk officer was really in on this and now he's after you, or maybe this is some kind of a test to see how you react to prove your innocence."

"Connie, this is real." Kate had the feeling her friend was reverting into some fantasy world. Connie's expression cleared and they both glanced at Abbie, who now slept on her side.

"I'm sorry. You must have been terrified."

Kate didn't respond.

"And you didn't call the police?"

"No."

"But this is big. This is important."

"I know it is. And I know I should call. Every time I pick up the phone, I ask myself what it would look like from their end. I mean, who found the piece of ceramic? I did. Is there anyone else who could have put it there? No. Two people were in the house all night. How could someone break in, and why would they? I've touched it so my fingerprints will be all over it. Will there be any others—besides yours? Good chance not. I could see it as an evening news story. Think about it—the disappearance of Jack Porter is still a mystery. Who's suspect number one?"

"You're right." Connie set down the ceramic and began pacing the room.

"I am?" Kate had been prepared for Connie to disagree.

"We need to pray." Connie's face was serious. Kate's mouth dropped. She had expected other suggestions to come from her friend first. That Connie immediately suggested prayer meant she understood the mess Kate was in.

"Well, pray then."

"Mom?" Abbie was sitting up in bed. "Hi, Miss Connie."

Connie waved at her, but she was back to pacing, and the movement of her lips showed that she was already praying.

"Honey, try to go back to sleep, okay?"

"I'm thirsty." Her eyes closed even though she was sitting up.

Kate found a plastic-covered cup in the bathroom, struggled with the wrap, then filled the cup with water. Abbie had fallen back against the pillow but reached for the cup.

"Sit up or it will spill all over you." She helped Abbie take a few sips, then gently laid her back against the pillow.

Connie had stopped pacing. "I'm sorry about all this," she said, her eyes red and hazy. "I pushed you to put Jack behind you. And when you try to, all this happens."

"It's not your fault."

"What is God doing? I could sure use some help here."

"Maybe God doesn't want me to live a normal life. I wish I could understand him even slightly."

Connie didn't respond. They'd discussed long ago how Kate hated to hear the pat Christian responses she'd received when Jack first disappeared: "God works all things for good. The Lord has a plan." Even if the words were true, people used them as a way to shirk off her pain and excuse themselves from any real help or involvement. How could they vaguely understand what it was like to lose half of yourself and not know where it was?

"We'll do it different this time," Connie said firmly.

"What?"

"We need to be stronger, more persistent."

Kate stretched out on the bed beside Abbie and closed her

eyes. The world was suddenly moving too fast, and she had no strength left.

"I saw this show once . . ." Connie paused as Kate shook her head. "No, this was a true report about a woman searching for her missing daughter. She knew her husband had taken her to his homeland in Bolivia, or was it Quebec, or maybe Saudi Arabia? I don't know. . . . But this woman began doing her own searches and hired an international private investigator. Eventually, she got her daughter back—even though she did have to kidnap her illegally."

"Are you saying you think Jack is alive?" Kate stared at Connie.

"I've lost all opinion now. Do *you* think he is?"

Kate leaned on one elbow. She saw a soft glow around the edges of the thick curtains. Dawn was coming. The idea of Jack's being alive—breathing, sleeping, eating, dreaming—even more terrible. "I almost hope not. If Jack is alive, he was not the man I thought I knew."

"But someone put that thing on your pillow. Someone of flesh and blood did that. I think it's time, so let's start making a game plan. Maybe we should get—"

Abbie stirred. "Mom?"

"It's still too early to wake up, Abbie. Try to sleep longer. We'll be quieter."

"For some reason, God's not finished with this in your life yet." Connie sat at the table and held the ceramic fragment again.

"Mom?"

"Connie and I are talking."

"But, Mom . . ."

"I'll turn on cartoons or something. I'll take you to the pool in a little while."

"But, Mom, I have to tell you something."

"What is it?" Kate's patience was weakening.

"I put the tile on your pillow."

Kate stiffened. Her neck turned slowly as if on a creaky hinge. Abbie stared back with a worried, am-I-in-trouble look.

"*You* put it on my pillow?" Kate's face paled. She sat up on the bed. Her stomach churned, and a million thoughts coursed through her. Had Abbie been in danger? Had someone given it to her daughter while she was out enjoying the night with Mason? "This is very important," she said, trying to keep her voice calm. "Where did you find it? And why did you put it on my pillow?"

"Well, I put it there 'cause I remember that's where you found the other one. I was going to tell you, but I fell asleep before you got home. Miss Jane had to make some important phone calls before we could watch the first part of *Anne of Green Gables,* so I went and got the mail. There was a small box, and I thought it was from Uncle Chris—no one's name was on the front part. So I opened it. It scared me to see what was inside, and I didn't know what to do. I thought Miss Jane might get mad at me for opening the mail so I just hid it in my room."

"And when did you put it on my pillow?"

"After Miss Jane put me to bed. I tried to sleep but couldn't. I thought you'd be mad, and I didn't want Miss Jane to be mad at me too. So I went in your room and put in on your pillow so you'd see it. I tried to stay awake, but before I knew it, I was waking up and you were taking me to the hotel. I forgot all about it." Tears rolled down Abbie's cheeks.

"It's okay, Abbie. This isn't your fault," Kate whispered, touching a tear before it streamed off her chin. "Miss Jane never knew about the box?"

"No."

"And it came in the mail?"

"Yes, it was there with just the bills. I didn't have any mail, but I was so excited—"

"Where is the box now?"

"I threw it in the trash, way down at the bottom when I thought I'd get in trouble."

"We need that package." Kate stood. Connie was already handing Kate her purse and keys. "Abbie, you aren't in trouble. This is not your fault at all. I just hope Jane didn't take out the trash."

"Should we all come with you?"

"No, this will be better. Now that I won't envision some prowler creeping through the house, I'll be fine."

Connie's eyes assured Kate she'd make sure Abbie was okay.

"What movie is this from? And does it have a happy ending?" Kate asked Connie as she put on her coat.

"I wish I knew." Connie sat on the bed. "Where are your shoes?"

"I left so quickly I didn't get them."

"How did you check into the hotel—oh, I'll just sit here and imagine it."

"I'm glad you find it amusing."

She opened the door and Abbie ran to hug her legs. Tears burst from Abbie's eyes. Kate bent low and embraced her tightly. Her hair smelled of dried whipped cream and watermelon shampoo.

"It's okay, Abbie girl. You did nothing wrong. No one is upset with you."

"O-okay," she managed between sniffles.

Kate leaned back and looked deep into Abbie's glittering eyes. "You are a very special girl, do you know that?"

Abbie nodded and smiled slightly.

"I promise I'll see you soon."

As Kate closed the door, she remembered saying similar words to Jack when she'd left their hotel in Venice. It always came back to that day.

CHAPTER TEN

Her house appeared unusually shadowed as
Kate pulled into the driveway. Perhaps because she never saw
the outside this early in the morning, with the sun just emerg-
ing from behind the eastern mountains. On the way over,
she'd wondered at every corner if someone would grab her.

The hall was still lit. Kate had flipped on the light in her
hurried and terrified escape with Abbie. Now it seemed loudly
silent as she walked through the entryway.

The overflowing trash can was sticky with the whipped
cream can and chocolate-coated paper plates she pushed aside
in her search. A butter wrapper glued itself to her hand, and
the burgundy edge of her sleeve landed in something brown
and gooey.

Then she saw the box. Kate extracted it from the rest of the
garbage and set it on the counter. There was nothing distinc-
tive on the outside; it was simply an average postal box. Kate
wiped it clean with paper towels, closed the flaps, and
searched inside the trash until she found all the pieces of the

label. There was Poly-Fil inside the box and a Ziploc bag. There was no return address, like Abbie had said, but even more strange was that though her address was printed neatly in blue ink, her name was not on it. The postage label was smeared from the trash contents, but it looked like it was postmarked a few days before. Kate made out a few letters until she had the origin—Phoenix, Arizona.

Phoenix meant nothing to her. Kate had never been there, and she didn't know anyone from there. She had a cousin in Kingman, Arizona, but that had nothing to do with this.

She turned more lights on and carried the box to the couch. Her thoughts went through every possibility as to why the ceramic had been sent, by whom, and what Arizona had to do with it. The time had come to call the police—Adam, probably. She had spoken to him only a few times since that day in the police interrogation room. Kate dreaded the thought of going back there and putting herself in the center of suspicion. She remembered what Connie had said about international private investigators. Perhaps that should be her first move instead.

Connie brought Abbie home a few hours later. They'd picked up fresh bagels, and Kate pretended everything was great for Abbie's sake. They were supposed to leave in two days for their four days away. Abbie told Connie about Grandpa's horses and how Grandma was teaching her how to play card games. Connie said she'd stay the day and had already told her husband and called a substitute to come to her house for day care. Kate was on the couch, having stowed the box and tile in her closet. Abbie and Connie were in the kitchen, their voices distant, as if they were swallowed by a thick fog.

"Let's leave your mom alone for a little bit," she heard Connie say. "Kate, you didn't sleep last night. We'll make plans in a few hours, but rest awhile so you can think clearly."

Kate's thoughts protested, but her body didn't. She went to

her room and stared for a moment at her pillow with the slight indention where the tile had been. She could feel the old, consuming weariness moving over her. She fought it, but she'd forgotten how strong its hold was. She'd struggled with it for so long, some days succumbing and awakening to a lost day. It was a depression or sorrow, or perhaps fear so strong that it made her want to drift away, to go insane and feel nothing. Maybe insanity was really the greatest escape of all—not a fearsome affliction but a respite from a world of pain.

Kate was determined to fight it. She'd sleep and be strong again. For the past three years it had been Abbie and the antique shop that had kept her from falling too deeply—this time it was for herself also. Kate would face this and find the answers—at least enough answers to move on.

Hours later she awoke. It had been good sleep. She was on Jack's side of the bed with her pillow nestled against her. The phone rang, but she didn't reach for it.

A few minutes later Connie tapped on the door and peeked in. "Are you all right?" She looked worried but put on a smile. "Perhaps we should call the doc for some Prozac injections?"

"Why not an IV?"

"This woman has already called twice." She opened the door wider and pointed to the cordless phone she had pressed to her chest. "She's an older lady, I can tell, doesn't quite get the message that you shouldn't be disturbed. Says it's very impor-tant. I can get rid of her again."

"I'll talk. I feel better, much better. Thanks, Connie." Kate sat up and reached for the phone. Connie closed the door as she left.

"Mrs. Porter?" The slight vibration in the woman's voice indicated her age.

"Yes?"

"Very good. I have tried to reach you. I tried calling last night also."

Kate sat up straighter, trying to recognize the voice with its strong accent. "Who is this?"

"Please, if you will listen. You will receive some mail soon. There will be no return address or sender's name. But—"

"I received it last night. Who is this?"

"It arrived already? That was very fast indeed. Did you open it?"

"Yes." Kate was standing now. "But who . . ."

"Then it is very important that we meet and discuss what was inside. I do not want to discuss it on the telephone."

"Who *is* this?" Kate demanded.

"A friend. I am someone who cares."

"Why can't you tell me who you are? Why did you send it to me?"

"If we could talk in person it would be much better than over a phone."

"You know where I live?" Kate queried, instantly wary.

"I have the address, yes. We are currently in Portland."

"We?"

"Please, Mrs. Porter. I know my telephone call and the package must make you very afraid. But we can meet in a public place that you choose. We want to help you."

Kate was suspicious, afraid, curious, and she wanted to know something—anything—after having nothing for so long. She felt herself fading into the person she'd been in the first years of Jack's disappearance—weak and frightened. She had to find a way out.

"I'll meet you."

"Very good. It is important that you trust me and not tell others. There is nothing to fear. I have some information you will want."

Kate turned toward her door as it creaked open. Connie peered inside. "I'll come to Portland. Tomorrow. Give me your number, and I will call on my way."

"Yes. That will work."

Kate pulled out drawers in her bedside table until she had a scrap of paper. She found a green crayon to write the number of the Portland Sheraton.

Connie was standing in the doorway. "I'm going with you," she said after Kate hung up the phone.

"Where is Abbie?" Kate asked. "Did she hear any of this?"

"She's teaching Whiskers the waltz. Who was that?"

"I don't know. Someone who sent the ceramic piece or at least knows who did. The woman says they have my address, name, and phone number—which is not a great feeling."

"You're meeting them tomorrow?"

"Yes."

"Let's call the police." Connie's face looked sorrowful as she said it. She understood what it would mean for Kate.

"This won't be dangerous. I get to choose the place we'll meet."

"I'll wait in the car then."

"Abbie needs to go to school and have someone pick her up. She already missed today."

"What if they're terrorists or want some money? I'm calling Mason to go with you."

"No. It wouldn't be a good idea. Mason can't be involved in this."

"Whatever you say, Agent Scully."

"Who?" Kate had to laugh, knowing it would be some bizarre Connie-thing.

"You know, *The X-Files*."

"Has anyone ever told you that you watch way too much TV?"

"I might have heard that before."

Connie sat on the bed. Kate plopped down beside her. They stared at one another.

"I don't know how to survive this again," Kate whispered. "Everyone says, 'Oh, you will, you will. We'll help you. You're going to make it—just have faith and God will see you through.' They say it must be a comfort to have Abbie with you. Just yesterday I thought I *was* going to make this."

Connie touched her hand. "I don't know how or if you'll survive this. But I'm with you all the way. I can promise you that."

"Only a true friend would be so honest." Kate closed her eyes. Then a thought struck her. Had the box contained only the tile? Abbie always ripped open Uncle Chris' packages to see what they contained before she read the card he sent.

"Where are you going?" Connie asked as Kate suddenly hopped up.

"Agent Kate has an idea."

Connie followed her to the trash can. Abbie was still outside with Whiskers so Kate carefully sifted through the contents again. Down near the bottom, she found an envelope that had escaped her earlier search. Her name was on the front.

"Amazing," Connie said in a hushed voice. "Open it."

> Dear Mrs. Porter,
>
> I try again and again to write this letter to you. I am sorry about what happened to your husband. In some ways, I feel responsible. My hope was to meet with you and tell you everything I know. However, the arrival of this package means this is not possible. You will be contacted soon by others who will know how to help. I have entrusted my blue tile as proof of my sincerity. Please guard it well until you meet the others.
>
> Be careful and keep this confidential. It is of the utmost importance.
>
> Sincerely,
> Karl Olsen

"Kate, there's your proof."

Kate nodded and read it again. "Yes. Finally, something real."

CHAPTER ELEVEN

Lukas sat on the small couch by the window. He flipped through the *London Telegraph* with swift movements, annoyed that this was the only international press he'd found downstairs.

"What is wrong?" Marta asked. She sat on the couch at the other side of the suite. The phone was beside her.

"Why did you say we have information for her?"

"I didn't think she would come without a reason. And we do have information for her, the poor woman."

"You should have let me call."

"You would have scared her straight to the police, if she has not already been there."

Lukas slapped the paper down in annoyance. He was irritated at Marta and upset because of it. She was Karl's widow— the once beautiful young woman who had endured terrorizing events and yet survived to be kind and concerned for others. It drove him crazy. Her worry for Kate Porter had cost them information they needed. She had not confirmed what was actually inside the package, though both of them felt fairly certain. If Marta had let him open the box before mailing it, they would not be in this position at all.

Lukas realized his irritation ran deep. It went back to his arrival in America. He should be home or at least on a plane right now. He'd be in the middle of a midmorning snack or already watching the first movie of the international flight. Thoughts would be turned toward home and his daughters and grandchildren. He'd be dreading the thought of returning to the business and politics of government. Was the euro holding against other world currencies? What scandal was about to rock which official? Would the election preparations swing the current polls? Questions that had once been essential and urgent and pressing.

Yet since the graveside ceremony of his longtime friend and the deep night tears shed by Marta, Lukas thought a government agenda sounded like the squabbles of schoolchildren. That knowledge bothered him. He should want to close his days with banal worries and political issues. He'd yet to truly commit to this search for Wolfram, even though the unanswered questions had pushed him to come to Portland and pursue the lead of Kate Porter. But he still fought it, wanting to slide into the oblivion he'd had before this reunion. What was wrong with him? Had he lost his will to fight for the life of a friend?

"I tried to say as little as possible. What if the phone is being listened to?" she reasoned.

That's when he realized that Marta knew he was grouchy because of her, or partly because of her. She'd thought over her words before speaking. It was wise of her to consider phone tapping, but he doubted such lengths had been taken. Yet what did he know?

"Are we going to eat out or get room service?" Marta asked.

"I have never been to this city. Perhaps we should eat in the hotel restaurant."

"You are a creature of habit, aren't you?"

"What do you mean?"

"You like your paper, your coffee, your safe hotel."

"I am an old man. I need my few comforts."

Her laugh sounded good. It was the first time since Karl had died that Lukas had heard anything of the usual Marta in her voice. His annoyance cleared, and her laugh made him smile.

CHAPTER TWELVE

The Cup O' Day Café was in downtown Portland. A group of regulars already sat at outdoor tables. From hidden speakers funky music played. It sounded composed in a tropical third-world country, with lots of bongos and ukuleles. The café smelled of rich espresso and spicy herbs that antagonized Lukas' nose. He detested trendy coffeehouses. West Coast America believed themselves the inventors of a new fad, while the Viennese had been gathering young and old to their coffeehouses for centuries.

"She was smart to pick a place like this," Marta said as they found a table.

"The coffee is probably terrible, and we will need to go to the counter for our order. No service in America." Lukas cursed in German, drawing a long look from Marta. No, he had not forgotten their decision to speak English while here. "Some words must be spoken in your own language."

Marta clucked softly but grinned. Her expression soothed his anxieties in a way that surprised him. A waiter stopped by for their order, and Lukas checked his watch. They were still early.

"She will come," Marta said.

He didn't doubt it, only dreaded it. He wanted to make this quick—get the tile fragment and any information on her husband's disappearance and then leave before this woman learned too much about them. Lukas now longed for home with a depth he'd only known as a young boy when his mother was very ill and he'd had to stay with his aunt for a month. These American smells and feelings were all wrong. He needed home.

Then he saw her through the large windows. She was younger than he'd imagined—closer to one of his daughter's age. Kate Porter walked inside, pausing at the door. She held her brown purse in her hand like a shield and glanced around the shop. She wore a skirt and blouse—at least she wasn't as casually dressed as most Americans.

Their eyes met. Lukas could see relief in her face. What had she expected?

They shook hands and introduced themselves. Marta had convinced him to give accurate details. Marta had convinced him of a lot of things.

"Did you bring the package?" Lukas asked before they had returned to their seats.

"No."

"We would like the item returned." He knew his voice sounded harsh, but he wanted to get the tile and end this connection. Marta should have told her to bring it. He again wondered why Karl had brought this woman into their lives. He must have known this meeting would have to take place.

"I didn't plan to give it to you." She seemed shaken by his abruptness, and Lukas was glad of it. She must not think they were an elderly couple for her to pat and cajole like children.

"It was a mistake that you received it."

"Did Karl mail it?"

Marta glanced at him.

"I did," Lukas said. There was no need explaining every-thing to this woman. Something about her rubbed him wrong. She sat there trying to figure him out and gain answers he would not give. "What do you know about Karl?"

"Were you involved in my husband's disappearance?"

Lukas could see this would go even worse than he'd expected. "No, I was not."

"Do you know what happened to him?"

"We know he disappeared three years ago. Perhaps you could give us those details."

"You must know something more, or why would you send me the package? And where is Karl if he didn't send the pack-age?"

"Excuse me," Marta said. "We must slow down and talk first. Gain some trust all around. Mrs. Porter, would you like to order something?"

Her eyes flicked briefly to Marta, then back to Lukas. She was afraid of him, but not as much as he wanted. This would not be as easy as he had hoped.

⋅➤═◐═◑═◀⋅

Kate hadn't anticipated such an elderly couple. Except for their heavy European accents, they appeared to be any old couple walking in any Portland park on a Sunday afternoon. He would be a cantankerous, old man, and she the kind, grandmotherly type. What Kate had expected, she wasn't sure. Perhaps people who leaned more toward spy-movie charac-ters—the chain-smoking woman and the dark, probing eyes of the intelligence director, though she felt that this man noted her every word. Yet looks could be deceiving, and she found it true once they started talking. The couple wasn't even a

couple. The woman lived in Arizona—the man didn't say.
There seemed as much espionage possible between these two
as between the couple on *All in the Family*.

"Lukas has three daughters, but I have no children. Do you
have children?"

Lukas did not speak, as the woman did all the pleasantries.
He kept glancing around with a look of distaste, especially
when the beat of bongos increased into a rich South American
song. Kate knew he wanted to get to the reason for this meeting as much as she did. For a moment, she had the sense that
this was all a joke. Could she really be sitting with two people
who were her first link to Jack? Perhaps they knew nothing.
But finally she had proof in front of her eyes that all of this had
happened, that she hadn't lost her mind—and Jack in the
process. The events were real. Jack's disappearance was real. In
some ways, Kate wished she had followed one of Connie's
fantastic plans to wear a hidden microphone, have the police
drag these people in, or videotape the meeting from a hidden
location. But it was Karl Olsen's letter that changed her mind.
He trusted her with the tile, so she would trust him, wherever
he was.

"I have a daughter," Kate said. "She's seven years old. But
could we talk about the piece of ceramic now?"

"Ceramic?" the woman asked, glancing at Lukas as if she
couldn't understand. Kate couldn't remember her name. She
had wanted to write them down, ask for the spelling, and then
try to find out who they really were. Perhaps that was some of
Connie's influence.

"The object in the package. Did you know what was
inside?"

"It is not ceramic," Lukas said. "It is an antique tile."

"Like the tiles in flooring?"

"Decorative tiles are used differently," Lukas grumbled, as if
any kind of explanation annoyed him. "They can be found all

over the world in palaces, churches, mosques—some are very old; others are found in the average kitchen."

"I am familiar with decorative tiles. Where did this one come from?" Kate put her elbows on the table and leaned closer. She had many questions to ask, and the letter was tucked in her purse. The most important questions she'd ask soon; first she'd gain the woman's trust, maybe even the man's by some miracle, and then seek the truth.

Marta glanced at Lukas as if to question how much she should say. Kate wondered about their relationship, how long they'd known one another, what brought them here.

"During World War II, that tile was broken into five pieces," Marta said. "One piece was given to each of five men who were part of the Resistance in—"

"Marta," Lukas said. He didn't have to say more, because it was clear that Marta didn't like the reprimand. She acted as if she hadn't understood his silent message.

"One of the fragments is in a police locker in Italy, and I have another," Kate said. "Where are the other three pieces? And how do you know all of this?"

"You are wrong," Lukas said. "The tile you found in Venice was not an original piece, but only a copy."

"How did you know I found the ceramic—the tile—in Venice?" She suddenly wondered how much they knew about her. "And it wasn't an original?"

"No, it was not." Marta said. "One of the original tiles was stolen in 1945 by a German named Wolfram Meizer. The tile you found matched the shape of the piece that used to belong to Jantes—a friend of ours."

"But how do you know what my tile was shaped like?"

"Marta's husband, Karl, gathered the information about the tile you found in Italy. He had a photograph of it." Lukas and Marta glanced at one another.

"Where is he?"

There was a pause and Marta spoke. "Karl died recently."

Kate and Marta stared at one another for a moment before Kate turned away. Now she better understood Karl's letter. "Do you mind telling me what happened?"

"We believe he was killed, or he died in the process of . . . his heart was not so strong."

"I'm sorry." Kate said the words, then stopped. She didn't want to say that because she had disliked it when people said those two words to her. What did they have to be sorry for? Now she'd spoken the dreaded words.

"Your husband included a letter with the blue tile." Kate opened her purse and set the letter in front of Marta.

Evidently surprised, Marta appeared to fight to contain her emotions. She picked it up. Lukas leaned over and read it to himself.

"How is my husband connected?" Kate asked after several minutes of listening to bongos change into a CD of Mediterranean guitar.

"That is what we are not certain of," Marta said. "Karl knew more, but he did not tell me."

"Why did you send the tile?" She spoke to Lukas. "It seems obvious that you don't want me involved in this."

"That is the way of Lukas," Marta said. "It is a complicated story as to why Lukas mailed the box. He didn't know the contents at the time."

"How are you involved in this blue tile—" The waiter arrived with coffee and pastries for the couple. Kate noticed Lukas peer skeptically into his cup. She ordered a vanilla mocha and caught his frown. The woman said this was Lukas' way, but she felt dissected beneath his gaze.

"These five men who each received a piece of the tile—" Kate leaned back in her chair and watched Lukas—"were you one of the members of the blue tile group?"

He glanced at her with a hint of surprise; then anger over-shadowed his face.

"I want the tile," he said, as if releasing each word as calmly as possible. "It was a mistake for Karl to involve you."

"How can you say that?" Marta said before Kate could respond. "Karl had a reason for this. He said in the letter he felt somewhat responsible for her husband's disappearance. There is more than you know, Lukas. Do not speak of him that way again."

Her words quenched Lukas' anger like a flood of water over fire.

"Kate—" Marta put her hand over Kate's. It shook, but Kate couldn't tell if it was because of emotion or age. "We hope to have some answers about your husband as we do our own investigating."

"Are you working with some kind of police or investigators?"

"We do not work with those agencies," Lukas said solemnly.

"I want to be involved." She said the words quickly, tossing herself in without gauging the warning signs. Kate thought she perceived a slight smile from the woman.

Lukas Johansen's reaction was quite the opposite. "That is out of the question."

"Why?"

"This is about something that happened long ago. These are things you can't even understand."

"Make me understand."

"How can you comprehend something beyond your life and years? This began even before the war. What do you even know about our war? Let me speculate. You took a semester at university? Or you read a novel? You went to the movies and watched *Schindler's List* with popcorn and Coca-Cola?"

Kate didn't answer.

"Lukas," the older woman chastised.

"This is about me. And my husband. Tell me what happened to him, and I will go away," Kate insisted.

Lukas folded his arms across his chest. "I do not know."

"We might know something," Marta said. They both turned to her quickly—Kate in hope and Lukas with an unspoken warning. Marta ignored him and leaned toward Kate. "This is about my husband also. The man responsible for my husband's death is probably the same one for your husband. We do not have evidence yet—we pursue that cause. Yet before you commit to this, you must know what it will cost you."

"I don't know if I can go on with my life without knowing."

Lukas was shaking his head. "To become involved could risk your life. Did you not say that you have a daughter? And probably a comfortable life here in America? Are you willing to risk what you have for the knowledge of what happened? I suggest you think about that. Marta's husband, my comrade, is in the grave because of our search for answers. It is too high a price to pay for answers, even for revenge. This is what you must decide."

Lukas pushed his chair back loudly and left them at the table. Kate watched him glance around the room and storm toward the bathroom. The room was suddenly too noisy, Marta's eyes too inquisitive.

Kate lost her courage again. "I need a little time."

"That is expected."

The two women's eyes met, and they seemed to understand one another.

"Do you think my husband could be alive?" Kate asked.

Marta gently churned her hands and stared at the table. "Wolfram has left a trail of deaths where he has been. I tell you that because I would not want to hope my husband was alive when he was not. But I cannot say for certain. If you are a praying woman, I would pray. This could be the most important decision for you. We will be returning to Europe—Italy and Austria."

"I cannot go to Europe. I have a child, a business."

"I want you to know what could be necessary. Nothing is impossible, but if I had been granted a child, I would be as hesitant—you are a good mother. Take some time. We would ask for the tile if you choose not to help."

"Give me a week?" Kate couldn't believe she was even considering it.

"Of course."

Kate hardly breathed until she was a block away from the old couple inside Cup O' Day. For a moment she leaned against a building to catch her breath. Marta had given her a number to call. She wanted an answer within a week, whether Kate would join in the search or release the tile fragment.

Kate had a decision to make—the most important one of her life.

CHAPTER THIRTEEN

The taxi pushed through traffic and onto the highway. The rain clouds of the Northwest had pattered toward the east, leaving the sky a brilliant blue. Lukas wanted to find fault in the region, but arrow-topped pines bent over lush meadows tugged at his favor. He wondered why Karl and Marta had not chosen an area that resembled their homeland more closely than did the arid desert of Arizona. Perhaps they thought they'd forget for a while. Strange how he had stayed and learned to live with the past behind him, for the most part, while the Olsens had escaped the land but the ghosts of yesterday drew them back. Karl Olsen was dead because of it.

Lukas stared at the whirl of trees and hillsides along I-205 as they sped toward the Portland Airport Sheraton. Marta was silent beside him.

The taxi driver tapped the steering wheel to the beat of a song that he played too loudly for Lukas' taste. A dispatch came through his radio, and he turned it down, though his left hand never missed a beat. Marta stared out her window. The yellow cab swept past a puttering Volkswagen painted to look like a strawberry, and Lukas noticed that RVs seemed to rumble off and on exits in every direction. RVs with white-haired drivers were everywhere in America.

"The West," he spat.

Marta turned toward him. "You are a bitter old man." It was the first time she'd spoken since they'd left the coffeehouse.

"We can speak at the hotel."

"Why? Do you fear you will hurt my feelings?"

"Perhaps." He kept his eyes out the window and glanced from time to time to check the meter on the front dash. "And other reasons."

"I am not weak, and you are not my master, Lukas Johansen." He realized she was furious at him, especially when she switched to German. "I will not have you speak for me or tell me what to say or not say."

He, too, switched to German, even though the driver glanced at them a few times. "You are angry because of the meeting? I should be the one angry."

"And you are."

He turned away to see the crooked peak of Mt. Hood rising in solitude into the sky. That was another strange thing about the mountains of this region. The tallest peaks rose alone from valleys or lower ridges, unlike the massive chains of peaks and ridges at home.

"You are angry, and I am angry," she said. "If I had less respect for you and myself, I would have told you . . . well, my mother's instruction is still in this old woman. But you will not silence me again."

Lukas stared at her profile since she wasn't looking his way. He could only shake his head.

"Kate Porter will choose whether to work with us or give up the tile."

"That was not offered," he said too loudly. The cabbie's eyes appeared in the mirror again. "I walked away for a moment, and she believes she has this choice."

"We are old, Lukas. Do you know that?"

"I know that very well. But this woman cannot help with that."

"We are old and she is already involved. You are recognizable throughout Europe."

"And an American will not stir up notice?"

"Wolfram did something to her husband—most likely his body will never be found. I would want to know. And Karl wanted her involved. He knew we needed her. He also felt responsible—I want to know why."

"So he did keep some secrets."

"We shared our lives. He would have shared this with me at the right time. I was not threatened by things that would worry me. Eventually Karl always told me. Eventually he would have."

"What do you think this is about?" He lowered his voice. "We can't form some secret group like the old days. Those days are gone. But suppose we did—we would never bring in an American mother who knows absolutely nothing about this. It is insanity."

"I decided to offer Kate Porter the chance to help. I would want the same offer. Now, Lukas, I grant you the same choice. Do you want to help me find Wolfram Meizer?"

"What are you talking about? This is up to me."

"No. Karl and I have been searching for more than a decade. This man took my husband. He most likely took this woman's husband also. Perhaps the two of us will work together. I know that you have not committed in your heart. You feel it is your duty because I am Karl's widow and because of old vows and Susanne's death. But we are too old for that. We must seek Wolfram Meizer because we want justice, not revenge. We must commit all of our energy, perhaps the last energy we will give to something in this life. Just as I spoke to Kate Porter, I speak to you. Be certain for yourself and not anyone else."

Marta spoke without looking at his face. Her eyes now turned to probe him, as if she could understand thoughts even he wasn't familiar with.

"You have not been near me in all these years, Marta. Yet you believe to know me so well?"

"I know you. I know both the good and the bad," she insisted.

He shook his head. "You don't."

"I know why you don't like her."

"Who? Kate Porter? I have feelings neither for nor against."

"That is not true." She spoke with confidence, and he hated that this time she was right. He didn't like Kate Porter, though he couldn't say why.

"We can trust her," Marta said, then paused as if considering her words. "She reminds you of Susanne."

Instant anger welled inside him. Marta's eyes were compassionate, but his face burned as if slapped. "How could you speak such words? That woman is nothing like Susanne."

"They do not look alike, and she is older than Susanne was when she died."

"When she was murdered," he corrected.

"Yes. But I find a spirit and a kind of . . . is it innocence to the world? Not innocence, for this woman has endured pain. But she is brave without knowing it."

"You should have written great works of fiction, Marta."

"I knew Susanne. She was my sister-in-law and the only true friend I ever had. I know some qualities of Susanne when I see them. Think about it and you shall see also."

Lukas had begun to pull at a small tear in the vinyl seat when he noticed it and stopped. It bothered him that Susanne was no longer a clear image in his mind. He knew he had loved her laugh and her soft hands with their slight lines of dirt under her nails from the work she did on her grand-mother's farm. He could still make out the pieces of her that he loved, but lately her entire image had eluded him.

Marta's hand on his surprised him, and she softly squeezed. It had been a long time since someone had touched him so gently.

"She was true and honest and good. And she loved you, Lukas. You have wondered that, haven't you? Karl did not believe me, but I knew you were troubled when you learned Susanne was part of the Resistance. She wanted to tell you but thought you would not trust her love. I wanted to tell you, but everything happened so fast in the end." She sighed and moved closer. "She did not want to love you at the beginning because of your past. In the end she loved you despite your past."

Great emotion flooded through Lukas. He turned back toward the window and pressed hard to keep everything locked inside. The taxi had exited the freeway and was cruis-ing toward the airport hotel. He felt as if a valve had been opened and unwanted feelings surged through him. His chin twisted and his muscles tensed. For over fifty-five years he had wondered. Now in a taxi in America with some strange funk music playing and Marta beside him, he had learned the truth.

"Lukas?" Her voice was quiet. "Are you all right?"

He cleared his throat. "Justice instead of revenge. I will have to get used to such an idea."

-◦▬◦◖▬◦-

The tile had been in her car, tucked in the glove compartment in a Ziploc bag filled with cotton.

Holding it in her hand now, Kate propped it against the driver's side window. No light showed through. She examined its ridged pattern of cobalt and wondered about its origin. It wasn't the blue and white of Dutch delftware, but the ridged pattern reminded her of something European. Lukas and Marta wanted this back if she decided not to be involved in their search—their search for some enemy from WWII. It all seemed preposterous as she sat in the driveway with her engine running.

Abbie was at Connie's, where Kate should have picked her up, but she wanted to see her little house first. She sat for a while and gazed at familiarity—the brick walkway and flower beds under the cottage-style windows. She always intended to cut the grass that grew inside the long crack in the driveway, but whenever she approached it, she'd notice how the grass clung desperately to its source of soil, surrounded by cold cement. And she'd leave it there. Sometimes in the summer she even sprayed water its way.

Now as she stared at and searched the familiar, everything seemed changed. Again.

Three years ago Kate had flown back from Venice alone. Her parents had returned a few days earlier to bring Abbie back to Oregon. Kate had held out, hoping for some word. Those were the loneliest days of her life. She'd stayed near the airport, where it felt cold and impersonal but allowed her to blend in with the travelers, families, and lovers. Then she had gone home and left Jack somewhere behind.

Mason had met her at the airport while her family prepared for her arrival. She remembered the first glimpse of her cozy home and how instantly foreign it appeared. She didn't have a moment to really think about it for weeks. Then Kate began to be alone—family and friends had to move on with their lives and she insisted they go.

On her first trip home from the supermarket with her backseat loaded with groceries, she'd stopped right here with the engine running. The front tree had been smaller then and the lawn recently mowed by a helpful church member. The house had appeared the same as it had before she'd left with Jack—yet it wasn't. It was the first time she realized that the house she loved would survive and continue without Jack, without her. It wasn't hers to own. She was here for a season, and then the house would hold other lives. She'd still clung to hope and prayers, but a part of her had known that Jack's voice wouldn't be on the answering machine when she walked inside. Jack wouldn't eat the food inside the white plastic bags. Jack wouldn't be able to make this okay.

Kate saw that again now as she sat with the blue tile on the dashboard and the heater humming. Everything felt instantly empty and hopeless. Days before she'd been moving toward a new life, a future, a tomorrow not tethered by yesterday's sorrow. Now this tile, these people, this unreal story of Nazis and Allied resistance was crashing into her world and knocking it out of orbit—just as she'd thought it was back in control. Kate had to make a decision. This time the decision would be hers.

An hour later she was at Connie's. Kate's smiles and actions felt like drying clay that could easily crack under pressure or rapid movement. She found Abbie and Connie on the computer, working on the Connie and Tim O'Brien homepage. Connie updated her family news and photos weekly for relatives and friends. Kate gave Connie a brief summary with her asking, "What are you going to do?" But Abbie interrupted, excited about their trip the next morning. So Kate took Abbie home without any resolution.

Later Connie called several times to see if Kate was going to see her family, what she'd decided, whether she should search the Web for an international private investigator. Finally Kate quit answering the phone and didn't pick up when Mason called either.

Kate had to force her excitement about the trip. So much

hung over them to whisk away for four days. But Abbie fluttered around, getting her things in order. She filled Whiskers' food bowl and cleaned his water dish, then went to the neighbors to make sure they knew where his toys were located—she'd forgotten to tell them those things when she'd asked them to watch Whiskers.

"Mom, you have to read to me," Abbie called from the bedroom.

Kate relented beneath Abbie's "pleases." *The Voyage of the "Dawn Treader"* was perched on Abbie's covers. They had read little in the last week. The book had fallen behind Abbie's bed and was lost for several days. Kate began with chapter 2. The young king of the enchanted land of Narnia was explaining why he was sailing toward the world's end:

"'With Aslan's approval, I swore an oath that, if once I established peace in Narnia, I would sail east myself for a year and a day to find my father's friends or to learn of their deaths and avenge them if I could.'"

The words stopped her from reading, and Abbie curiously looked up from her pillow. Kate had read the Chronicles of Narnia as a young girl, but she'd forgotten that Caspian's journey into the unknown seas was for the purpose of finding people.

"Mom?" Abbie asked.

Kate started reading again as an unknown sea stretched before her and Abbie's lives. Did she dare sail where maps were not yet drawn? If only she could peek ahead to the last page and see that she and Abbie would be safe and better for taking the journey. But real life didn't always include happy endings.

In fact, it rarely did.

CHAPTER FOURTEEN

A mother and daughter in a silver SUV cruised down a winding road toward Crocker Valley. Kate didn't have the energy for this journey to pick up her elderly great-aunts and drive hours to her parents'. She didn't want to hear the aunties bickering, or be the responsible driver, or keep the secret of the last few days from her family members. There was much to decide and this felt like running away.

"Mom!"

Kate's heart jumped as she looked for something ahead in the road, then over at Abbie. "What is it?"

"Nothing," Abbie said, but her expression spoke, *You weren't listening to me again.* That expression was too common. Kate didn't know how often she'd blocked out a conversation or answered on autoresponse. During those moments Abbie could have asked, "Can I join the Charles Manson fan club?" and Kate would have answered, "Sure, honey."

"Do you think they'll notice how tall you've grown?" Kate asked lightly as an apology.

"Probably," Abbie mumbled. "Aunt Hannah will try to make me like fig jelly again."

"It finally worked on me," Kate said with a grimace.

"You like fig jelly?" Abbie groaned as Kate nodded. "That's why she's convinced I will get used to it. You gave in."

They laughed and were brought together, discussing the most awful Aunt Hannah creations, from liver-and-bell-pepper soup to lard butter. Soon Abbie decided they should sing. So Kate put in a bluegrass band CD that Jack had bought after hearing the group perform at an antique expo in Washington State. Abbie loved the CD and cranked the music. They sang loudly to the songs that reminded them of Jack while Kate tried to cast aside thoughts of broken blue tiles and life-changing decisions. For the past three years she'd acted out the role of a normal mother with her thoughts somewhere else. Now Kate determined to focus on the present, on this trip. It would take time to gain back what they'd lost. They needed laughter and smiles with Kate's thoughts and heart fully there. The decision sounded logical, but the battle had begun again.

"Let's listen to that one more time!" Abbie said, smiling as a song ended. She flipped the CD back and they sang even louder.

The miles clicked away. The farther from home Kate drove, the more distance she wanted from the blue tile, an elderly couple who wanted her decision, and even Jack Porter. This trip might provide the right perspective. She was pulled between two worlds. She couldn't survive there for long. Abbie grinned at her while singing a song. Kate knew one path would be chosen and the other forsaken.

Aunt Gerdie's baby blue luggage waited on the front porch. Aunt Hannah was in the garden, tending her plants with pink gardening gloves covering her hands and a wide straw hat covering her head like a mushroom cap. Upon their arrival, she immediately left the garden and hugged them both. Then she began to list all the reasons why travel did not go with old age.

"The last thing I want is hours in a cramped car so I can sleep in a bed that isn't mine. I never sleep well in strange places. And I don't like using the powder room at those rest stops, especially after we cross the California border—you know those California criminals are just waiting to catch someone unprepared. I'll have to bring my pepper spray. I've never understood why Kerby raised all of you in that state—it caused me many hours of worry and prayer."

"Hello, girls," Aunt Gerdie called from the porch, carrying a travel pillow. "Are you ready to hit the road?"

Aunt Hannah sighed long and heavy. "I better pack my liquid fiber."

After a short break in the house with Aunt Hannah trying to convince Abbie to try fig jelly on her scone and last-minute trips to the bathroom, they loaded in the car once again. Aunt Hannah insisted they each wear a straw hat to keep the road glare from their faces. "It's bad for your eyes, and skin cancer is always a worry." Kate knew all four of them looked ridiculous with their wide-brimmed hats. Abbie's kept falling over her eyes as they left Crocker Valley and turned back toward the highway. Aunt Hannah sat in the passenger seat with the large travel pillow tucked around her neck because she got carsick and had neck problems.

Aunt Gerdie, who was reading the *Crocker Valley Post,* leaned forward. "Aunt Hannah, did you know Henry Kronley died?" Kate remembered Jack had always chuckled at the way the sisters called one another "aunt."

"No, I certainly didn't," the older sister said, raising her head from the neck pillow in concern. "What could have happened?"

Aunt Gerdie held the paper in front of her, hitting Kate in the back of the head as she straightened the pages. "'Henry Kronley, age 86, died at his residence after a long illness.' Were you aware that he had a long illness?"

"He certainly looked fine the last time I saw him," Hannah said.

"I thought the same. I wonder what happened."

Kate glanced back at Abbie, who gave her a partial wink of humor. Kate didn't think the aunts had missed one morning of reading the obituaries. Even while out of town, when they wouldn't know the deceased, the aunts read the obits. Kate was sure it was the main reason for their daily newspaper subscription.

"We should send a card to the family." Aunt Gerdie plunked back in her seat. "I could hardly believe what my eyes were telling me. Isn't that such a shame, such a shame?"

"Aunt Gerdie, we're all dying fast at this age." Aunt Hannah tried to turn in her seat with the pillow stuck to her neck. "Abbie dear, your great-great-aunt is having a late-life crisis. You wouldn't know what that is, but it's a pain in the hind end, that's what it is. I've been quite content getting old and enjoying my garden. Now she suddenly wants to do all kinds of strange things."

"Like what?" Kate asked with a smile. She could just see her aunt getting the urge to skydive or something. The image of round Aunt Gerdie flying through the air with her short kinky hair flapping around her face brought a laugh to her lips.

"I'd like to go skydiving," Aunt Gerdie said.

"What?" Kate and Aunt Hannah asked in unison.

"I read about a woman in her seventies who did it and survived. I may be older than that, but why couldn't I?"

"So nice that she survived," Aunt Hannah said in disbelief.

"I've seen photos, and there is usually a handsome young

man strapped to you for safety. That was my favorite part of the idea."

Kate laughed, but Aunt Hannah's frown deepened.

"Or I thought about parasailing or a cruise—something to get me out of Crocker Valley before *I* end up in the obituaries."

"Aunt Gerdie, what is going on with you?" Kate asked as she left the small winding freeway and entered wide Interstate 5 South.

"She's going through a late-life crisis, I'm telling you." Aunt Hannah crossed her arms over her chest. "She wanted to buy a sports car last week and cruise the coastline with scarves around our heads and Jackie O. sunglasses. The woman is going to break a hip, I just know it. Some old people get Alzheimer's; some just go insane."

"We'll sing 'Born to Be Wild' and look for cute old men," Aunt Gerdie put in.

In the rearview mirror, Kate saw Abbie shaking her head like Aunt Hannah, but with a smile on her face.

"Getting old is for the birds, I tell you. You have to fight it with everything in you," Aunt Gerdie said determinedly.

"I'd rather enjoy my old age," Aunt Hannah said.

"Let me tell you something, young lady." Aunt Gerdie touched Kate's head. "Do all you can in this life. When you wonder what to do and you ask God to answer and he does, then you do it. Don't be some old woman and wish you'd crossed bridges or walked roads that looked scary at the time. Those are the ones with the best destinations. Are you hearing me say this?"

"Yes, Aunt Gerdie. I'm listening." Kate wondered what the words meant to her right now. Was it coincidence that her ancient great-aunt was giving this advice at this time?

"I hope you are listening. Life passes quickly, and we spend our time on a lot of insignificant things. We let fear keep us from some of God's greatest plans."

"Will you leave the poor dear alone?" Aunt Hannah tugged the brim of her hat down a little. "We want to enjoy ourselves, not get a course in life philosophy from an old woman. All us old folks have regrets and lost wishes—it comes with age."

Then they were quiet as they sped down the road with the other vehicles all moving toward their own destinations. Kate wondered if she'd someday be an old woman regretting great parts of her life.

CHAPTER FIFTEEN

By midafternoon Kate was the only one awake. Aunt Hannah expulsed small snorts from her passenger-side perch. Abbie's and Gerdie's faces pressed against pillows on windows in the back. Kate sped down I-5 South, crossing the Oregon-California border, where Aunt Hannah would begin carrying her pepper spray even if there was more wildlife than people in this part of California.

Kate enjoyed having the peace of the road to herself. A highway was a different experience when taking a road trip. The same soft whine sounded in her tires and mileage fell away at the usual pace, yet there was a whisper of excitement that could never be felt when driving on a usual errand or to a short destination. A journey was a blank canvas. Kate wished she and Abbie hadn't set a destination but had allowed the road to lead them. She'd done that once with two girlfriends the summer before their sophomore year of college. They'd packed maps, pillows, and junk food, then flipped a coin at major intersections and ended up in Austin, Texas.

Whenever she left for a trip, Kate would get that same tingle of excitement. She became aware of road noise—rumbling big rigs and the zip of cars. Suddenly she felt owed something— as if people should move aside because her car was spanning distances and claiming a chunk of America beneath its tires.

The enjoyment of the road wore off when her passengers awoke. Aunt Hannah needed the "powder room" every thirty miles from then on. Kate expected the drive from the aunts' house to northern California to take seven hours more or less. But with lunch, a snack, and powder-room stops, it took over ten hours before they descended from the mountains around Shasta Lake to dip into the top end of the Sacramento Valley.

Kate left the highway and drove familiar back roads. The towns of Anderson, Olinda, and Happy Valley were nuzzled in spring green. A line of hazy blue mountains surrounded them on three sides, watching with a lazy gaze toward the inhabitants below. Plateaus and open fields covered in green velvet would soon turn yellow beneath the scorching summer sun. Kate loved the month of May in her hometown, for grass colored the fields and the sky was crisp and clear after a rain. Oaks dotted the edges of fields, with gangly Digger pines clumped along seasonal streams. They followed roads Kate remembered like old friends. She saw the red metal roofs of Cottonwood High and remembered with a bittersweet feeling the graduation that tossed classmates from high school into the world.

"Abbie, that's my old high school."

Her daughter craned her neck to look out the window past Aunt Gerdie. "Is that where you played volleyball?"

"Yes," Kate said, as they passed the large gym.

The school looked new with its fresh paint and trimmed lawns, as if it were still the school she'd attended in the eighties, though improvements and new additions disturbed those memories. How many graduates had passed through those rooms since then? Where had all those people gone? The entire world had been spread before her as she'd sat on those concrete steps with friends, perusing college catalogs and dreaming of who they'd become. She'd felt able to do anything.

Memories flooded her: stubborn tears after breaking up with a guy she'd thought was "forever"; a failed trigonometry test; an argument with her best friend; cutting class and prom preparations; laughter in the hallways; a smashed bumper in her friend's classic Corvette. The years had been a tumult of good and bad as she had begun to shed the skin of youth and tried to imagine college and life as an adult. And here she was in that old play, trying to discover herself again.

"To be young again," Aunt Gerdie said from behind Kate. "I would do everything different."

"Are we near God's Point?" Abbie asked as Kate accelerated and left the school behind.

"How did you know about that?" Kate asked. "Did Grandpa tell you?"

"Yes. He said it's an important place where he once talked to God. He said pretty soon I'd be old enough to go."

"That's just like Grandpa. Look straight ahead at that line of ridge. We'll see it better from Grandma and Grandpa's, but that is where God's Point is located."

Within minutes they were turning down Old Oak Lane. Kate drove slowly up the gravel driveway. The trees in the yard and the small orchard seemed to have grown by feet since her last visit the week before Thanksgiving. Perhaps it was the leaves that gave them more height, or perhaps she hadn't really seen them in a long time.

"I think my hind end has fallen to sleep," Aunt Hannah said as they pulled to a stop.

The flowers bloomed in barrels by the porch and old Walton wagged his tail from his spot on the walkway. Kate had come home.

Kate's mom opened the front door, and her father came in from the corrals.

"Grandpa and Grandma Golden!" Abbie hopped from the car without closing her door.

They bundled into groups, dipping and turning to greet one another. Aunt Gerdie asked, "Were you surprised that we could get Kate to do this?" Aunt Hannah hurried inside to use the bathroom.

Her mother hugged her and said, "Kate, this is wonderful, and for Mother's Day weekend too. Cottonwood is ready with all the usual festivities."

"This will be Abbie's first Cottonwood Parade," Kate said.

"Well, it's about time." Her mother winked and turned to welcome Aunt Gerdie.

Kate felt a tap on her shoulder and turned to meet the face of her father. He put his hands on her shoulders and looked long into her eyes before hugging her. "Let's bring in your goods."

It took several trips before they dumped Kate's luggage into her old room and the aunts' into her brother's.

"Katie, this means a lot," her father said when they finished. She felt instantly guilty for it not being her idea. Now that she was here, it seemed so easy to come, except for Aunt Hannah.

Again her father gazed at her. "It's always good to have you," he said. But in those few words he'd really spoken much more: how much he missed her, how good it was for her to come, that he knew she had something on her mind, and he wanted her to tell him when she was ready.

Dinner and talk filled the evening. They sat on the back porch after dinner, and Kate realized where her love of outdoor evenings originated. Abbie explained all about the Narnian travels they were reading—of Lucy, Edmund, King Caspian, furry Reepicheep the warrior mouse, and the difficult boy named Eustace.

"They just landed at this island, and Eustace was complaining like usual. Do you want to know what happened, or are you going to read the book?"

"Go ahead and tell me," Kate's mother, Paula, said with interest.

"A pirate kidnapped them and put them on a slave ship."

"That's awful," Paula said.

"Mom, can we read some more?"

"The book is under one of the seats in the car. Why don't we read another story tonight?"

Abbie appeared disappointed for a moment, then smiled as if a lightbulb had lit an idea in her head. "Maybe Grandma could read one of her stories. I always like the one about the bread that rises out of the oven and all through the house, and the boy hides in the woods because he thinks he'll be in trouble for trying to make bread on his own."

"Give kisses and let's go find it," Kate's mother said.

Abbie made her rounds and followed Grandma inside the house.

"That girl is a storyteller," Kate's father, Kerby, said.

"She remembers much more than I realized." Then Kate worried—what if Abbie told Kate's mother about the blue tile in the package?

"Kerby?" Aunt Gerdie asked from the doorway with the paper in her hand. "Do you know a Walter Wundermeyer of Anderson? He died yesterday in a motorcycle accident."

"Still reading the obituaries, Gerdie?" he asked with a grin.

"Until I'm in one of them." She pointed a tired finger to the page.

"No, I don't know him."

"He was only sixty-seven. What a shame. At least he was enjoying life when it happened."

"Is she all right?" her father asked as Aunt Gerdie drifted back inside the house.

"Aunt Hannah says it's a late-life crisis."

"A few days away from Crocker Valley will help—it'll give her something new to share with the ladies at the library."

A chorus of crickets sounded from the thicket of flower beds and trees in the backyard. Somewhere a dog barked and a bug light zapped. Soft yellow faded to gray to black from the horizon to the top of the sky.

"It's beautiful this time of year. I could never fully enjoy spring because I knew the heat was coming soon to destroy the green hillsides," Kate said. "I wish it could stay this way."

Her father took a sip of coffee, thinking about her words. "Sometimes the best things don't last very long. If we had flowers and green every season, we wouldn't see their value."

Kate nodded. They were words well spoken, though she wished it wasn't so.

Night fell around them and they moved inside. Kate settled into her old spot on the couch with her feet on the coffee table and watched her father's favorite show on the History Network.

Only her childhood home could help her make her decision, Kate suddenly believed. Yet there was something more to gain. She didn't know what it was, but she was glad she'd come.

CHAPTER SIXTEEN

E xcept for the aunts, they all left early to park her dad's old truck along the parade route. Hannah was road weary, and Gerdie wanted to walk over and visit a "cute, old widower," as she called him, who lived down the street.

Kate, Abbie, and Kate's folks ate breakfast at the little restaurant on Front Street. The country-style eatery was crowded with costumed kids and adults. After omelets, hash browns, and Abbie's silver-dollar pancakes, they paid seventy-five cents at the Little League stand for steaming cocoa and carried the Styrofoam cups back to the truck.

The Cottonwood Parade brought the whole town to the streets. Abbie set up her lawn chair along the curb next to Grandma's and Grandpa's, while Kate sat on the tailgate. They waited for movement down the street—Abbie and Grandpa planning how she should ride his horse in the parade next year. An idea formed in Kate's mind as she watched them talk. *What would it be like to move back?*

In her childhood Kate had loved to roam the fields and wide, shallow waters of Cottonwood Creek. But as a teen she couldn't wait to leave small-town living behind. In college her visits had brought contempt for rural life and ways. But today she wanted it back. She wanted to bank, grocery shop, and grab an ice cream within a mile of each other. She wanted to take walks along the country roads of her youth and have Abbie attend her old schools. As if she had discovered a beloved childhood toy that had been stuffed away and forgotten, Kate knew she loved this place.

Looking around, Kate saw people she remembered along the parade route and at the different booths. Mother's Day weekend in Cottonwood was when families dusted off their cowboy hats, whether worn only once a year or daily. The Thursday kickoff barbecue started the four-day event with the Rodeo Queen being announced. Two days of rodeo and community activities brought together locals and tourists alike.

"There's something to be said for putting down roots," Kate whispered.

"Kate Bait!" Tayler, her brother, rounded her father's old Ford with two chairs in his hands. He tossed them in the back of the truck and grabbed her in a tight hug, kissing the top of her head. "It's about time you came for a visit."

"I had an old aunt practically drag me here," she said.

"Yeah, so I hear. That makes us feel good. I knew you should never have gone to Oregon for college—we could never get you back."

Kate punched him lightly on the arm. "Where's your wife?"

"Sarah's with Reece on the kindergarten float. Gotta keep those kids from falling off."

"That would be a good idea," she said with a laugh.

From down the street a marching band began to play. People young and old strained from the backs of trucks and along the streets for the first view of the Cottonwood Jr. High band that opened the parade every year.

"It takes you back, doesn't it?" Tayler said as they climbed in the back of their father's truck. He set up the rusty lawn chairs for them.

Kate noticed the soft lines that formed around his eyes as he squinted against the morning sun. Her brother had her father's looks—strong jaw and cheekbones, gray eyes, and sandy brown hair. His thirties had broadened his shoulders, finally making him look like a man and not the tall, thin kid he'd appeared for years.

The band came into view, and the flutes played a refrain before the rest joined in.

"There you were," Tayler said, pointing to the clarinet section. "Remember those shiny braces that would cut your lips?"

"Well, at least I didn't have to wear headgear at night like someone I know."

"At least I didn't—"

"Are you two being good up there?" Paula Golden was giving them "the look" from her perch below.

"Sorry, Mom," they said while elbowing each other. They were twelve and fourteen for a moment again.

"Did we have many dreams as kids?" she asked. A horse-drawn carriage carted a family of clowns past them.

"We didn't have great aspirations, but we sure had fun and great imaginations, if I do say so myself. With Mom reading so many classics and all that poetry to us, we didn't have much choice. Remember playing Moby Dick after lightning downed that oak in the front pasture?"

"I forgot about that," she said, laughing at the image of a young Tayler jabbing homemade spears into the tree trunk as if it were the whale. "Remember when we dug out that cave and used the dry creek bed for *Journey to the Center of the Earth*? We always had to play your favorite stories like *Captains Courageous* or *The Time Machine*."

"There was no way I'd let you hoist me up a tree as Peter Pan. I wasn't that stupid."

"Here come Reece and Sarah!" her mother called.

They both stood up and waved. Tayler and Sarah's son, Reece, wore a painted, cardboard pig snout and ears. He waved wildly at Abbie when he spotted her. Sarah was busy watching children and sent only a quick smile and wave when she heard their calls.

"Hey, pretty lady!" Tayler shouted, and Sarah blew him a kiss.

Kate smiled, happy his voice betrayed none of the strain of the last several years after Sarah's miscarriages and failed pregnancy attempts. Her brother did well on the small ranch he had always wanted, where he could watch things grow and the seasons change. But the difficulty of a marriage surrounded by grief and frustration had been his greatest challenge. Kate knew her brother struggled with not helping her more after Jack's disappearance. Tayler wanted to fix the world, but he couldn't mend his wife or his sister.

"Have I told you that I love you, big brother?" she said lightly, with her arm flung over his shoulder. Her lawn chair tipped and creaked beneath her.

Tayler's face was serious when he turned toward her. "Thank you, Sis. I love you too."

The afternoon brought Tayler, Sarah, and Reece to the Golden home for a family gathering. Kate's mother made stew and bread-machine sourdough while the other adults watched the kids on the swing set. With Kate's worries over Abbie's lack of friends, it was good to see Abbie run and play with Reece like any normal child. After a late lunch, Tayler pulled a box of old kites from the garage rafters. Everyone went to work rigging up a workable kite. The afternoon turned cool with slight breezes carrying high white clouds overhead. Soon colorful diamonds reached to touch the cottony sky.

Kate watched from outside the front pasture fence. Her

jacket sleeves covered the sharp barbs as she leaned against it. She'd felt detached from everyone for so long. Now she paused to watch her family. Life had continued on in spite of her three frozen years. Her nephew had grown taller and lived without memories of Uncle Jack. The seasons had passed over her hometown and the lives of the people in it. Her old dog had aged, and her father's horses now needed dental work.

While the world moved on, Kate had been stuck as if she'd fallen in some ancient bog with mud sucking her down. She wanted out, wanted to run, but always the questions, the hope that was dashed again and again, the faith that didn't conquer all—these things grabbed at her progress. A woman who'd spoken about losing a child had described it well: "You can't do anything. If I made a goal to do my dishes in a day and I actually did it, then I felt proud of myself. I was unable to pull myself out."

Kate watched bandaged kites flutter into the sky. Abbie ran with her hand clutching the string behind her, but her kite skidded and scraped the ground. All able hands were busy with their own clusters of bobbing kites.

She bent through the barbed-wire fence and jogged across the freshly cut field, feeling her hair bounce lightly onto her shoulders. Abbie was now tangled in the string. Kate's hands reached for Abbie just as Abbie's small shoulders slumped in defeat.

"Do you know how many times the Wright brothers tried to fly before they ever left the ground?"

"How many?"

"Oh, sure, ask for the exact facts." Kate cupped her daughter's chin. "I don't know, but they had to try a lot. And they needed each other to do it."

"Will you help me?" It was strange to hear her daughter ask such a basic question and seem unsure of the answer.

"Of course. I used to be a pretty good kite flyer in my day."

"Okay." Abbie's voice rose an octave. "Do you want string or tail? That's what Grandpa says."

"Whatever you don't want."

"I'll take the tail and run. You hold the string, okay?"

"I'm ready."

Abbie adjusted the red-and-white kite she'd covered with flower stickers and patched with silver duct tape. Then they ran.

The little kite fluttered and bobbed as Abbie let it go, climbing higher and higher. Kate let out the line, gauging the height and wind current. Abbie ran and jumped beneath the kite as if she could suddenly fly up and catch it. Above a field where they stepped over horse dung, the little kites, dipping and soaring, colored the sky. They worked hard to keep flying, to get higher into that sky.

Kate remembered that once she could fly. There had been a young girl not so long ago who carried a sheet onto the roof of her house on a very windy day. Tayler had mocked her idea, which only spurred her determination. Their mother was gone to town for an hour and the wind was right. A gust filled the sheet, then died away. From his perch in the mulberry tree, Tayler said she was crazy. She ignored him and concentrated. The trees began a soft swirl, then harder—the sheet billowed. She jumped. And hit the ground.

But she'd believe in flight again when the wind whipped hard against her face, bringing the hope of a time when she'd certainly soar. Little kites tied to the earth by a string but flying with all their might.

It's not over for me. I can still fly. In that moment she again believed in human flight.

Then the wind died down. *So much for wings,* Kate thought as the kites bobbed, struggled, and finally tumbled to the ground. It seemed that just as she'd made a breakthrough, God pushed her right back down.

"This is the best Mother's Day I've had since you and Tayler lived at home," Kate's mother said as they walked in from the field. "Remember this? 'Come to me, O ye children! And whisper in my ear, what the birds and the winds are singing in your sunny atmosphere. For what are all our contrivings, and the wisdom of our books, when compared with your caresses, and the gladness of your looks? Ye are better than all the ballads that ever were sung or said; for—'" she turned and put her arms out like a conductor and all the adults finished with her—"'for ye are living poems, and all the rest are dead.'"

"Longfellow," Tayler said. The children gazed in surprise. "Longfellow is Grandma's favorite poet, and that poem is the most recited one, as you can tell."

They began discussing different poets, but Kate felt the words of Longfellow's poem walk with her. She'd forgotten about that—how her mother would call her and Tayler "my living poems." Kate had called Abbie that as an infant. But she'd forgotten.

Kate worked daily among furniture and objects old and dead. Here was a life before her, not in need of restoration, but fresh and new and filled with the life only a child possessed. Kate watched her daughter run with Reece, their kites in hand. She realized in that moment how deeply she loved her child. The frozen places of her heart thawed, and she loved with a wonder she'd forgotten.

"Abbie!" she called. "Would you like to see my secret tree?"

"Can Reece come too?"

"Why don't we take Reece a little later and just you and I go?"

"All right."

The others went inside for hot cocoa. Kate touched the top of her daughter's honey hair that had turned stringy and smelled of wind. They walked hand in hand down the road along the side of the house, past the horse corrals and across a wild field.

"You have a secret tree?" Abbie asked.

"It's not such a secret anymore. I used to climb into the highest branches and watch Tayler come try to scare me. He couldn't find me until I started laughing. It's over there in that grove of oaks."

An overgrown path meandered through the green field toward a stand of wide, old oaks that had once been Kate's secret wonderland. The thicket of many-leafed branches kept the green grass from turning brown and was a place she could always find shade from the summer heat. There were at least twenty trees in the grove, with massive and moss-covered trunks decaying on the ground. Tayler and Kate had imagined the trees were felled by a tribe of Native Americans who surely had loved this place as much as they did. Silence was strong within the ring of trees, as if even the birds and insects knew this was a magical place. It smelled of moss and decaying wood and leaves.

"This looks like the Wood Between Worlds."

Kate smiled, realizing how much her daughter remembered from their readings of the Narnia Chronicles and also how true her observation was.

"I never thought of that. If there were pools of water beneath the trees, we could hop into them and try to reach another world."

"Don't you wish we could?" Abbie's eyes sparkled with imagination as she tipped her head toward the umbrella of branches and leaves overhead. "We could pop in and out of different worlds and maybe somewhere we'd find Daddy."

Somehow Kate had guessed Abbie was thinking of her father before she spoke his name. "Where do you think Daddy is?" Kate stopped at a downed log and sat down.

"I don't know." But Abbie said it in a way that made Kate wonder.

"Please tell me. I won't laugh at your thoughts."

The sun shone in soft patches through the overhead branches like light through stained glass.

Finally Abbie spoke. "In kindergarten, I told my friends Daddy was on a special mission that only very important people do. The kids believed me, and I believed it too. But now the kids at school don't believe it anymore. They say Daddy left us like Jeffrey's father. One boy said maybe you killed him and put him in a box in the ocean."

Kate tried not to react outwardly. "And what did you say?"

"I told him he watched too much TV."

They both smiled.

"I've thought of lots of reasons why he hasn't come back. What if he was shipwrecked on a deserted island like on *Swiss Family Robinson?* Or what if he discovered something really bad, and the bad guys aren't letting him go because of it. I wrote down thirty-one things that could have happened in my diary. When I grow up, I'm going to go look for him. And I don't think you should give up either."

Kate wondered what to say to that, though this time she wasn't worried. She knew they were making progress—Abbie's confession was proof. Maybe with their shared honesty they might find peace over the loss of Jack someday.

"Abbie, I'm glad you told me that. We'll stick close together from now on and tell each other what we feel. I know we're going to be all right."

When Abbie's hand reached for hers, Kate knew they'd made a promise. They stood and Kate wound through the grove, holding Abbie's hand and stepping over branches. Finally she stopped.

"This was my tree. I'd climb up there and feel bigger than

the world. Sometimes I'd bring my book; other times I'd sit there to think and escape my brother."

The wooden boards she'd nailed into the trunk were loose and some missing. Kate estimated the tree must be over forty feet tall, though it had seemed even taller as a young girl. The thick branches forked heavenward. She could see the remnant of one of her "rooms"—a scrap of plywood her father had given her when he built the saddle shed.

"Can we climb up?" Abbie asked excitedly.

"I'm not sure, but let's try."

Kate tested a board and it popped from the rough bark. Abbie laughed as it flung her backwards.

"Guess we'll try another way."

Kate tried boosting Abbie up, but then an old rope remnant unwound and broke. It looked impossible until Kate saw a fallen log with spiked branches poking out. Together they dragged and hoisted the log up against the bark. Kate scratched her legs and arms, climbing and helping Abbie until they made it. Once in the tree they climbed higher and settled in a branch intersection.

"We did it, Mom!"

They laughed together at the memory made and then gazed through the other branches toward Kate's old home, the fields, and fences. They spied old Walton, tail wagging, walking slowly toward the front porch and the horses eating new grass in the side field.

"From here you can see that ridge." Kate pointed to the long crest of a hillside that Cottonwood Creek had cut. "That's God's Point."

"Oh," she gasped. "Why did Grandpa first go there?"

"Well, his mother died in a car accident. She had prayed for him for many years, and he was feeling very sad about losing her. So he climbed up there and decided to wait until God talked to him."

"Did God talk to him?"

"Grandpa said God came in a soft, gentle breeze, and the words were spoken on his heart."

"What did God say?"

"He said, 'I am with you always, even to the end of the age.' "

"Wow. I want to go up there someday."

"When you're a little bigger."

"I can't wait to grow up."

Abbie's words surprised Kate, as they sat on different branches above her childhood grounds.

"Enjoy your childhood, Abbie. Don't spend too much time looking forward, because we adults spend quite a lot of time looking back. We need to enjoy the season we're in." She paused, considering her own words. "I think I'm beginning to learn that lesson after many lost years."

They sat in the tree, with Kate shifting now and then, realizing that branches weren't as comfortable for adults as for children. She told Abbie some of her old adventures in the grove and wondered why she'd never shared them before.

"Didn't you and Uncle Tayler have a secret treasure spot?"

"How do you know so much?"

"Grandma and Grandpa e-mail me."

Kate laughed at the idea. As a child in this tree, could she have ever imagined such a thing as e-mail and that her parents would be doing such a thing with her child?

"Yes, yes, we had a secret treasure spot. Instead of buried gold and jewels, we put our own treasures inside."

"Like what?"

"Let me remember—I had my favorite fake pearl beads, a feather I found that I was sure had come from a bald eagle, a postcard from Hawaii when the aunts went there, a silver dollar my grandfather gave me. What else?" Kate tried to envision the metal box they had painted gold and their ceremonial placing of treasures inside. "Tayler put a four-leaf clover that he pressed, a bunch of his favorite rocks which made the chest—as we called it—really heavy, and some other things like that. But after the first time we buried it, we'd dig it up all the time, put new things in, and take other stuff out. I needed those pearls for a slumber party."

"I can understand that," Abbie said in a grown-up voice that caused her to giggle at herself.

"We even made a map from a brown paper bag and burned the edges to give it that old look. Maybe we should do that for you at home."

"Is your treasure still there?"

"I don't think so. We'd move it around for a while until we found a hollow tree trunk to hide it in. But I seem to remember Tayler digging it up when he was home from college."

"Can we look? Please?"

Kate looked at the shadowed woods below and wondered if the treasure could really be down there somewhere.

"I guess we could—if we can get out of this tree." The climb down was harder than the climb up. When they finally reached the ground, the soft light from the overcast sky had fallen a shade darker. But it had been well worth the scratches and work to make the climb. Kate couldn't remember the last time she'd sat above the world in the arms of a tree. It should be mandatory for all adults—to remind them of the simplicity of childhood.

"We better hurry." Kate brushed bark from her hair. "My stomach is hungry, and night comes quickly within the grove."

"Where to?" Abbie asked like an adventurer on a quest.

"This way!"

Off they ran among trunks and fallen logs down a small slope to a giant tangle of roots that rose high above them with the giant tree stretched out in eternal slumber.

"We had a bad storm once when I was a little older than

you. This was the tallest tree in the grove then, its massive branches reaching above all the others. After the storm, Tayler noticed the branches weren't there. It was top-heavy and that storm had tumbled it right over, ripping the roots from the ground and leaving this pit at its base. We were sad about the tree; it was so beautiful. But it made a great place to play and hide treasure. I'm sure our treasure box is gone by now."

They hopped into the pit, now not as deep of a crevice because of years of leaves and decay. Kate couldn't see inside the tangle of roots. She reached her hand into the cavity with great care, afraid of what she'd feel. Her fingers touched something cold and metal.

"It's here," Kate said in surprise.

"It is?" Abbie's face shone with excitement.

Dirt and wood showered her arm as Kate pulled out the old metal box. They climbed out of the pit and set the box on a tree stump. The chest was rusted through on one corner, dirty from years in and out of the ground, with most of the gold paint worn off and the original silver metal showing through.

Kate was hesitant to open it. Once Tayler had hidden a pack of cigarettes in there when he was twelve. She didn't know what else was later hidden there during high school, since she had stopped coming to the grove by then. The lid creaked open and Kate tried to make a quick assessment, but Abbie was just as quick. Instead of old cigarettes, she found candy wrappers with tiny holes eaten through and some plastic toys.

"Look, a Tootsie Roll wrapper." Abbie held it up, but nothing was left inside.

"This is strange," Kate said as they carefully went through the contents that reminded her of the inside of a piñata instead of her old treasure box.

"Mom, this has my name on it," Abbie said, holding a yellowed envelope.

"Let me see that." Kate knew the handwriting even though the last letters in *Abigail Rose* were water damaged.

They were words from the past.

"Can I open it?"

Kate hesitated too long—Abbie was already lifting the tab with careful strokes.

"There's money and a note!" She showed Kate a ten-dollar bill and then handed Kate the note. "Mom, will you read it?"

Kate took the worn paper from her hand. She read it and read it again.

"Out loud, Mom."

> *"Surprise, Abbie. Here is some spending money while we are gone. Grandpa really likes Rocky Road ice cream so maybe you could treat him. Mommy and I will miss you while we're in Italy, but it won't be long until we return. I want you to always know how much your mom and I love you. We'll bring you back a surprise—it will be better than that huckleberry bubble bath I bought you in Montana. Oh, that smelled! We'll have to put some in Mom's bathwater because of that evil cold-water trick she pulled. I love you more than string cheese."*

Abbie and Kate stared at one another as if they had truly heard Jack's voice.

"I remember that, the 'I love you more than string cheese,'" Abbie said in a whisper. "Daddy told me to try string cheese when I was a little girl, and I didn't want to. He said that he loved string cheese, and I asked if he loved it more than me."

Kate nodded, staring again at the letter in her hand.

"Mom, God does answer," Abbie said softly. "Remember we prayed? Now we get a letter from Daddy."

"It just doesn't work that way," Kate said in shock, shaking her head. "This must be a mistake. We need to find Uncle Tayler."

CHAPTER SEVENTEEN

H e had found something. Lukas went through the papers again to confirm what he'd already read. The same facts remained on the page.

It was deep night—later than he wanted to know. He sat in Karl's study and stared at the packet of documents he'd discovered stuffed in the back of a file cabinet.

Lukas and Marta had left Portland right after their talk with Kate. And, though the call of home tugged heavily at him, he'd returned to Arizona for a few more days to help Marta. Again Lukas had gone through the files and papers in case he'd missed anything on Wolfram Meizer. It had taken Lukas a long time, for Karl's study was unorganized and filled with fishing, golfing, and community magazines that he'd saved for years—Lukas had located a stack from the eighties. Karl seemed to collect papers, canceled checks, payment receipts, comic strips, and e-mail funnies.

Then Lukas had found the white, oversized envelope.

Now he knew that Karl had had more information than he

originally revealed. Not only that, but Karl appeared to be involved in areas that cast the light of suspicion directly at him. Did Marta know about this? Lukas believed they'd shared everything. Perhaps she wasn't as trustworthy as he had assumed.

He rubbed his eyes and glanced at his watch, inwardly groaning at the time. He must be reading the documents wrong. The late hour caused his mind to work sluggishly, and stress fought against him. Yet there was the proof before him. Lukas glanced toward the open doorway. Down the hall, in the room she'd shared with Karl for years, Marta now slept. Did she know, or was this a secret kept from her also? He wanted to wake her and ask at that moment. But first, he must rest. He'd need sleep and strength before confronting her in the morning. If the words were correct, Karl seemed involved not only in Wolfram's work but also in the disappearance of Jack Porter.

Lukas would wait until morning.

⋄⇒◉⇐⋄

Tayler held the paper. His mouth twisted downward in what Kate knew was worry.

"I remember this." He nodded as the memory returned. "Jack helped me prepare the treasure box for a kind of cousins' fun night. We were going to do it while you and he were gone. Jack was worried about Abbie being left for that long. We put candy and toys in there, and Sarah and I were going to lead a scavenger hunt. I think you, Sarah, and Mom had gone to Chico that day—yeah, that was where you were because Sarah bought . . . that doesn't matter. But I remember now he put a note inside the box."

"How could you forget this?" Kate tried not to blame him, but her hands still shook from the shock of seeing Jack so alive on the page.

"It was one of many kid things we'd planned, like a three-legged race and stuff Mom was working on. You and Jack had made those envelopes for Abbie to read each morning of your trip. Remember?"

Kate remembered. They'd stayed up late the night before their drive to Cottonwood. They were delirious to the point of laughter after packing, and Kate had heard of this great idea of a daily letter. Jack had drawn a smiley face on each of her fingertips in the process of trying to write the notes. Their laughter and pranks made the process twice as long. But she remembered the letters:

> *Day One—We fly from California to Italy today. Draw us a picture and we'll bring you home some airplane wings.*

> *Day Two—When you wake up, it will be nighttime for us on our first day in Venice. We'll miss you.*

Kate knew this was as far as the notes had been opened. After Jack's disappearance, her parents had flown to Italy after getting emergency passports and were with her for a week. Abbie stayed behind with Tayler and Sarah. Kate wanted to be the one to tell Abbie what had happened, but she didn't want her expecting to see both her parents get off the airplane, only to be shocked by the news. So with Sarah's help Tayler had done his best to explain. But it wasn't until Kate arrived back in Corvalis alone that all of them felt the reality. The memory of Abbie's face, so pale and solemn when they first saw one another, was a stark contrast to the rosy-cheeked excitement she now wore as she talked in the other room with Grandma.

Kate took the note from Tayler and set it on the kitchen counter. The rest of the family discussed in hushed voices in the living room. She sought Jack's words again and again. They seemed the words of a man who loved his daughter and looked forward to returning. But what was certain anymore? If

he'd only given the slightest clue—something like, "Abbie, I
have to go away for a few years, but I promise to return. Don't
give up." Or "God's work is nearly done for me, but we will be
together someday." Even, "Abbie, I love you but I still must
leave. I'm very sorry, but I won't be back." The worst possibilities were better than silence.

"I need to get Abbie to sleep," Kate said. "She's sure this is
an answer to her prayers."

"Kate," Tayler said with his hand on her arm, "maybe it is."

"How can you say something like that?" Anger spread
through Kate.

Her sister-in-law glanced up.

"Let's go outside," Tayler said, taking Kate's arm. He opened
the sliding-glass door, and the cool of night touched her face.
"Mom will get Abbie to sleep and give good words of wisdom."

Kate hesitated, but her mother had heard Tayler and nodded
for her to follow him. Kate closed the door behind her and
waited for her eyes to adjust to the darkness.

"I once knew all these constellations," Tayler said as they
leaned against the porch railing. It was an expected move of
her brother's to divert them from the subject at hand.

"I don't fall for your tricks any longer, Brother. And besides,
you never knew any constellations besides the Big and Little
Dippers, except for the ones you made up."

"And I've forgotten all the ones I made up," he said. Then he
turned to her. "I don't know how to help you, Kate. I can't bail
you out. This is strange for me to say, since we never were
good at talking about spiritual stuff. But I know that God is
still with you and Abbie. I think you'll be able to see that
someday."

"One part of me believes that. I only wish I could see it
now."

"I'm not through with my questions for the Big Guy—questions like, why can't Sarah and I have more children? Or why

were *we* born in American luxury while another man lives his life in poverty? Things like that. I have just begun to see that God's love is greater than I can imagine and his ways are a mystery. I guess I should focus on God's and my relationship and not on all his dealings with the whole world. But enough of my musings. . . . To find this letter now, after so much time has passed . . . I don't know what to think. But maybe God is doing something in your life. . . . Oh, what does a rancher from Cottonwood know?"

"A lot, I would say."

"Really? Because I've wanted to ask you . . ." Tayler pulled up a metal love seat with vinyl cushions, the legs scraping across the wooden deck. He sat down and his face fell into the shadows. "Kate, did something happen?"

His question threw her off balance—from stars and God to this sudden directness. "What do you mean?"

"You tell me. I've noticed something different in you. I mean, of course you've been changed since Jack disappeared, but on this visit, there's something else. I asked Dad about it, and he said you'd tell us when you were ready." Tayler scooted over so Kate could join him. Both propped their feet upon the railing. "Or are my musings getting the best of me?"

Kate weighed what it meant to tell Tayler about the blue tile fragment and her meeting with Lukas and Marta. Telling required accountability. If she chose to get involved, her family would worry. If she chose to put the past behind, the fewer people who knew she'd passed up this opportunity, the better. She stared at the sky, but it gave no answer. It only sparkled with myriad stars in the night, unchanged by earth's problems.

Then she made a sudden decision. "Something happened. A few weeks ago I decided to put Jack behind Abbie and me and start a new life—or try to. Being here has made me consider coming home."

"Now I see why Jack's letter would upset you so much."

"That's not all of it. Less than a week ago I discovered new information that could change . . . well, I'll just say it. I found a blue tile—like the one I found in Venice."

Tayler's legs dropped from the railing and he sat up. "You found a blue tile—where?"

"In my house. It was mailed to me. And the people who mailed it contacted me right before I left for this trip."

"Kate, start at the beginning and tell me everything."

A pebble, even the smallest, dropped into a lake could not hide the ripples that spread and widened across the smooth surface. Tayler insisted that Kate tell the story to their parents and Sarah. Kate was at least relieved to have the aunties and Abbie already asleep. She told of finding the tile, of meeting Lukas and Marta, and then felt the impact of the story as if she'd been whisked away from a catastrophe. Seeing it now from a distance, she realized further the magnitude of what had happened by the reactions of the others. It seemed like a fantasy as they sat in her old living room and discussed a group of Resistance fighters who carried fragments of a broken antique tile.

"And you've kept this to yourself? Abbie too?" Her mother asked.

"I'm surprised she kept the secret—and a little concerned. Abbie thought she'd done something wrong by opening the package and putting the tile on my pillow. And I didn't want to tell anyone because it seemed futile to cause worry at this point."

"You need us more than you know," her father said, and Kate instantly recognized the truth.

They talked and strategized with coffee cups filled and refilled into the late hours. Her father led prayer several times for direction. Kate wanted answers, then and there, but there were none. No one told her what to do, though she knew they would support her decision.

"I see what this weekend at home is all about," her father said. "It's about coming home."

Kate turned to her father, expecting to see a smile and hear about her moving home so they could help more.

Her father's face was unwavering in its intensity as he spoke. "Sometimes a person needs to come home to face the world again. I don't mean Cottonwood. There's a place within us where we find who we really are and who made us. Once you've come home, then you can do what God put you here to do. We want our own path, and we tend to look over at the plans of others to make our list of wants. But God's path is the one to follow. It's going to be rocky and hard, Kate. But it's worth the destination."

Her father's words were many for him. And they were truth. Two roads stretched before her, and Kate stood at the fork—unsure, taking one step down, then back-stepping quickly.

"What is God telling you?" her father asked.

"I don't know. I can't hear him."

"He will answer if you really listen. And I know where you can find him."

CHAPTER EIGHTEEN

Lukas had not fallen asleep until the time he usually awoke. The smell of bacon and coffee had stirred him from slumber. He now leaned over the breakfast Marta had made—bacon, crepes, fruit—and wondered how to talk to her.

His fork scraped the plate loudly as he cut the crepe. The bacon was cooked exactly the way he liked it—a little crispy but not burned. Marta refilled his coffee cup and he thanked her.

"What is it?" she asked, sitting down across the table with her own breakfast.

This was his opportunity. "Nothing," he said.

"Did you sleep well?"

"Fine." He took a bite of bacon with his eyes on his plate.

"Are you feeling all right?"

"Yes." He gulped down his coffee.

"Then what is it? What's wrong?"

Lukas left the room and returned to drop the white packet on the table. "I found this."

Marta paused a second before taking another bite of food.

"Do you know what this is?"

"Yes," she said.

"Then you lied to me."

"No, I didn't—and neither did Karl. This was not relevant to our search."

"How can you say this is not relevant or that you did not lie? For one, you and Karl told me you had not been back to Austria."

"I said that *I* had not been back. Karl went and I stayed behind."

"Explain this to me now," his voice boomed.

"Calm down and I will," she said, her voice rising in a challenge.

Lukas held his tongue and settled back in his chair. They stared one another down with him losing. Her hands were shaking more than usual, and he felt sick at the thought that she'd known about the packet and hadn't told him. He wondered if it was truth she'd now speak.

"You know what is inside then," she said, tapping the envelope. "I will make it simple if that is possible. Karl believed he knew what Wolfram was seeking—an area where the Nazis had hidden something. He did not know the exact location since there were three possibilities. He also did not know what was hidden. I believe this began in 1994, but all the years blur together anymore.

"Karl never told me the exact details. But he found someone who knew Wolfram in South America—the wife of an exiled Nazi. Her husband was approached by Wolfram about a partnership. They had made other business ventures together. Then he died. She believed Wolfram poisoned him and collected the profits from their companies—she was shocked to discover she was not a beneficiary. But she was smart in one way—she made copies of all her husband's dealings without him knowing it. When Karl returned from Argentina, he came back with the information in that packet."

"Why would this woman give Karl the maps and German documents?"

Karl paid for this information. "It took a substantial portion of our savings and retirement. The woman wasn't married to an exiled Nazi for nothing—she knew how to get what she needed. After Karl obtained the map of the three locations, he contacted a diving specialist, an expert who had done underwater discoveries of ships and airplanes, things such as that. They were going over the three areas where we believed Wolfram was attempting to return."

"Was Karl trying to find Wolfram or this hidden stash?"

"He wanted both. I know what you are thinking—that we were in search of lost Nazi gold. You should know we were not interested in wealth. Other than gold, there is Nazi technology and records of companies that collaborated with them that have never been recovered. There are also hopes that documents will still be found giving families proof of their stolen artwork, bank accounts, and land holdings. You know the Nazis' attention to paperwork. They were almost fanatical about accurate information."

"Yes, I know."

She paused, apparently realizing her mistake. Of course Lukas knew, because once he himself had been a Nazi.

He spoke before she fully recovered. "Karl could have joined a Holocaust group to recover this lost information. Do you believe it is some of the lost Jewish treasure?"

"That is what we have assumed. But Karl could not join another group because of Wolfram. A major expedition could not be kept secret. Wolfram would disappear again. Karl's first goal was to find Wolfram. Karl believed that if we found Wolfram first, then we would hand over any information we found to the proper authorities."

"What happened after he met with this diver?"

"Karl came home for the winter. He kept in contact with the diver—his name was Rudy Blessing. Then in late winter, Karl could not reach him. He tried to e-mail again and again and phone him. Karl finally went to find him, but Rudy had disappeared months earlier. Karl found another piece of blue tile at Rudy's residence."

Lukas wanted to believe this and the pieces of tile fit together. "So that is how Jack Porter comes into this," he said in deep thought.

"What do you mean?"

"Rudy Blessing and Jack Porter worked together in 1989 in the Mediterranean. It is in these papers. Jack Porter worked on a dive to a ship that Blessing discovered."

"I did not know that." Marta paused, thinking. "But this explains why Karl sent Kate Porter the tile. After Rudy Blessing's disappearance, Karl shut down the search because he felt responsible for the man's death—we, of course, assumed that Rudy died as one of Wolfram's victims. Karl felt terrible and would rarely talk to me about it. He had really liked the man. It was the last straw for him. A few years later, everything changed. Karl wanted to start the search again. Now that I see the dates, that was the time when Jack Porter disappeared. And Karl must have wanted to help Kate because he felt responsible for her husband's death just as he did for Rudy."

"Supposed death. We do not know for certain."

"Well, yes, I guess that is correct. I have wondered about the Kate Porter factor and did not know the link. I believed Karl was helping someone linked to Wolfram, though I thought it strange—sometimes a wife from the old ways does not feel right asking everything. Now I understand. Karl was tortured over what happened. And that is why he called the reunion together. He had given up the search for Wolfram until Jack Porter. Then Karl said to me, 'How many lives will it take?'

Right after that we started searching for Wolfram again. He knew Wolfram had to be stopped."

"And he soon knew he needed us to help," Lukas said.

"Yes," she said softly.

"You should have told me earlier."

"It did not change the facts. You already had the map of the three locations, and you basically had the information, except—"

"You should have told me."

She nodded and placed her hand over his. "I am sorry. You know everything now."

Lukas turned his hand over and wrapped his fingers through hers. He was surprised by the great relief he felt at her touch and her words. Her face softened, though even in her anger he thought she was beautiful in a way only age and grace could be. Lukas didn't allow himself dependence on people, but he was getting very comfortable with Marta to the point of need. Enjoyment and fear were equal partners. But with the coming battle and after Karl's recent death, Lukas knew he was risking more than he should.

CHAPTER NINETEEN

Kate couldn't sleep. The clock read 4 A.M. She still had hours before they piled into the car and headed north, enduring the inevitable powder-room stops. She needed rest for the journey, but it would not come.

Kate rolled over carefully, not wanting to awaken Abbie on the other side of the double bed. In the night-light's glow, she could see the keys to her father's 1947 Willys jeep. He'd given them to her before bed. She knew what he was suggesting. Her family could give their opinions and advice, but only God could give a true direction. Her father knew where to meet him—God's Point.

Throughout the night Kate had wrestled with the thought of meeting God on the mountain. What if he wasn't to be found the way her father had found him there? Even more frightening, what if God actually *was* there, waiting?

Snatches of sleep carried dreams she couldn't remember and allowed little rest. Finally, she gave in and got dressed. There was a morning chill as the horizon grew light. She grabbed her father's jacket from the coat hook in the hallway and her mother's knit gloves, knowing it would be even colder on the ridge. The jeep took a few tries before it rumbled to life. She turned on the heater, knowing the old jeep would take half the drive to start warming up.

Kate turned down the driveway with the canvas top flapping in the wind. Kerby Golden now made the journey to the ridge an annual event. He'd make a day of it, sometimes bringing Kate's mom or anyone who wanted to go. When each of his children turned fourteen, he brought them there. They sat on an outcropping of rocks, gazing across the view of country and mountains all the way to portions of civilization. When Kate's turn had come, they'd gone in the evening. There her father had told her, in his few words, how much God meant to him and how man couldn't find true peace without a right relationship with the Creator. Kate had believed it then, though it was her only trip to God's Point. It seemed simple and clear up there above the world. Life wasn't so simple now.

She drove the paved road until it turned to gravel, then across a dirt road that cut through an alfalfa field.

Her father's annual pilgrimage had begun on the day after his mother's funeral. He was a young man then, newly married, with a baby on the way. He had been close to his mother. She had prayed for him for years. She'd spent a long time telling him about the peace only God could give and how life could not fulfill him without the love of Christ. As much as he had loved and respected her, he didn't need God. He didn't even know if he believed in one. His life was great as it was and much too busy to seek matters of philosophy. Days before she was hit by a car while walking along a country road, his mother had said the words that would haunt him. "Whatever it takes, I hope you find God. Life is meaningless without him." In his grief, he'd climbed the ridge of mountains and found the place he'd later call God's Point.

The road turned downward into the creek bed. An echo resounded up the canyon as tires clattered against creek rock. Kate sought the place where the river ran wide and shallow. She leaned over the steering wheel, making sure the winter rains had tapered off enough to cross. Dark cliffs rose above the opposite side of the creek, making a climb seem impossible. Kate knew the way toward the dry spring that transformed from a winter runoff into a trail up the mountain during the remaining months of the year.

The cool of the creek bed rose from the water and chilled her nose and cheeks. She turned up the collar of her jacket, thankful her hair hung long enough to warm her neck. Her feet had warmed beneath the slow heater. Kate drove between brush and trees until the trail grew too narrow. She parked and opened the canvas door. Kate felt uneasy about the woods still shadowed in the early morning light. It felt strange to be among the tall trees. Her father would say she'd lived too long in town. She headed up the trail. Twice she stopped and considered turning back, but in fifteen minutes she pressed up the last incline. Her air came in sharp, painful breaths.

Kate stood on the side of a small rocky clearing, not daring to step out any farther. Her father had cut a bench from a fallen trunk; it reminded her of a church pew. Yet, instead of resting beneath a cathedral's dome, the rough-hewn pew gazed up into the artwork of God. This was holy ground, she believed. It took several moments to feel brave enough to walk near the edge of the cliff and sit on the bench. The morning light grew in a soft, horizontal line as the sun spread its arms across the open, rolling country, miles to the east. Far below the creek, from which she heard gentle ripplings, lay unseen in the darkened canyon.

Feeling small, she wished for her father's presence beside her. This was his place. Her eyes closed for a moment as she took in the fresh morning scent. The world seemed to wait, but she didn't have the words to begin. It would be awkward speaking to God as if he were right beside her, all around her, or in the view before her. God was too large—it would be like conversing with a mountain as you stared upward from its base.

This was who she was. A girl from Cottonwood—against the vast world. She hadn't dreamt of being anyone great or exotic—she'd just wanted sunrises and sunsets with happiness in between. She wanted to give her best to whatever she did. She'd passionately loved both her husband and her child. She'd tried to love others and God most of all.

In this crazed world, why would God require more?

"Why?" she whispered.

Nothing.

No wind or sounds or words.

Then, *What do you want from me?*

A cold chill crept through her, and the bench seemed unnaturally hard. This was foolish. Everyone would be awake by the time she returned, and they'd have expectations. They'd know where she'd gone and wonder if God had met her there. She'd have nothing to tell them.

Kate rose to leave. He didn't stop her, this God whom people loved and devoted their lives to. He didn't stop her from leaving or chase after her with words of truth. She—who wanted to leave the mountain with a glow like Moses when he climbed down from Sinai with stone tablets in his arms— carried nothing.

This was not her place, not her God's Point. Perhaps there was nothing of the sort for people like her. She'd never received visions or heard God's voice. She didn't have dreams that set her course or miracles that changed her life.

Kate stumbled along the trail. It was much rougher going down. Ridicule followed and mocked her for coming all this way. Finally she could see the outline of the jeep against the cliff and the dry spring below the next turn. She took her eyes from the trail and missed seeing some loose rocks. Her feet slipped, and Kate reached for something to stop her fall. She landed hard, feeling the sting of rocks and hard dirt.

Her hands burned, and one knee pounded where a patch of blood oozed through her jeans. Limping the last steps to the jeep, she sat on its rough vinyl seat. She failed to pull her pant leg high enough to see her scrape. But then the pain eased, and she knew what it was—just a skinned knee like she'd had a hundred times as a child.

Below her the creek shone like a pathway of pure silver. And tears began to fall, gently and without direction. Kate wanted them to stop, angry at her weakness and at God's silence. Why couldn't he meet her on a mountaintop? How could the One who set the intrinsic balance of life and creation not be there to find her?

"A Christian isn't supposed to feel this way," she said aloud to herself. "A Christian is supposed to feel joy and peace, not turmoil and loneliness."

Then she thought of Jesus. Had he escaped turmoil, loneliness, rejection, and pain? What made her immune? Perhaps her faith was not that the sun would always shine, but that God would be with her when it didn't. Kate saw her old self before Jack had disappeared. They had been happy and safe. But when her bubble had been popped and her heart punctured, she'd been lost. She hadn't even known she'd built a fool's paradise around herself until it all fell apart. Then she hadn't known what to do.

Had God been with her? Kate remembered past times when he'd seemed as real as her own life. Had memory and those moments been only a fantastic illusion? She recalled those times—youth church camp, her wedding day, a long night when Abbie had a very high fever, and even the day Jack disappeared—when she had felt moments of God in her life.

She studied those memories for some falsehood. Then Kate

moved over the last few years of silence. And suddenly she realized he had not always been as silent as she'd thought. God had been speaking in his small, still voice through others, circumstances, and things she called "coincidence." The words had been spoken, but she hadn't listened.

Kate leaned against the steering wheel with its rough edges and closed her eyes in surrender. Words came to her: *You are not hidden from my eyes.*

She looked up. The canyon grew lighter as the sun neared the horizon.

"You aren't trying to knock me down, are you, God?" she pleaded. "I've been fighting you, when you only want to walk with me. You want us to do this together. Show me the way I should go. Show me how to be a mother to Abbie. And give me strength to walk the path you have ahead."

Kate returned to the house. Her father sat on the front porch waiting. Kate felt instantly sheepish at the question in his eyes as he approached her.

"I have an idea," he said, giving her his hand as if she stepped from a carriage.

"What kind of an idea?"

"I think you should start with that blue tile. Find its origin and age—you're in the right business for that."

Kate paused to examine his face. He wanted to ask her about her journey to the mountaintop but loved her enough not to. Yet, without asking, he knew what she had to do.

"Start with the blue tile. That's a good idea." Kate sighed. "Dad, I think I'll be going back—to Europe, I mean. I'm not sure how it will work with the shop and Abbie and everything. I never wanted to return there. It's been one of my fears."

"What is another fear?"

"Well, I'm a little afraid of finding out what happened to Jack."

"And what's your greatest?"

"Not ever knowing what happened."

"Then you must go to Europe. Even if nothing is found, you'll know you tried everything." He put his arm over her shoulder.

"I know."

They turned toward the front walkway.

"How did the jeep run?" he asked.

"It took me where I needed to go," Kate said. They smiled together and walked toward the house.

CHAPTER TWENTY

He leaned against the headrest and closed his eyes. The first rush of wheels as they lifted from the ground brought a sigh of relief. He was leaving the United States. Home awaited when the wheels touched earth again. The flight home had always brought relief despite the country he returned from—but this flight brought a longing stronger than he'd felt before.

People around him began to converse and order drinks. Lukas reached across to the seat beside him and found Marta's hand. She clutched his with a quick strength that made him look at her face. There were silent tears in the lines down her cheeks, and she did not look his way. While he found comfort on this flight at the thought of home, Marta was leaving everything familiar behind and returning to the place her plight had first begun. And Karl was not with her. Lukas tugged at a corner of his handkerchief until it pulled free from his pocket. She took it with her other hand.

Lukas turned toward the window as the plane passed

through the clouds. He thought of home and the journey ahead. This final chapter of his life would not be what he'd anticipated. Earlier that year he'd been approached to write a book and to lecture at the universities. He'd always planned his retirement to include many days at his mountain estate, enjoying a good pipe and readings in the Germanic literature he'd long wanted to study. Perhaps he'd get to know his grandchildren better, even his own daughters. And that would end his life, the last page closed.

Now this would not be his way. Life had rarely taken him where he wanted to go. Every vision of his future had been changed. The sins of his youth were never recompensed, no matter how hard he'd tried. And now he must find Wolfram—who once told him why he should join the Nazi Party, then ridiculed his struggle with the moral issues of the cause. Later he had become Lukas' enemy. They thought he had died, but now Wolfram was back to haunt him. Lukas had to remind himself that Wolfram Meizer was only flesh and blood, and a man who had taken much from him. Life had not brought justice to Wolfram. And so Lukas would bring it with swift revenge. He could now feel the hatred that would give him the strength. He would allow it to consume him enough to destroy the man who made Marta cry and who helped destroy his own life also.

The plan had begun to formulate. Marta was convinced Kate Porter would decide to join them in Europe. Lukas hoped not. But regardless, he would think every step through and move in ways Wolfram would not expect. It would begin with a letter, written by his hand. The words were already memorized. Somehow Lukas would find the right channels to contact, the letter would reach Wolfram, and there would be no turning back.

He wrote the words in his thoughts again:

> *Wolfram Meizer,*
> *Do you remember me? Do you remember I betrayed you*

*long ago? Has that kept you wondering what happened to
me—the one you could not reach?*

*I remember you. I remember Susanne in the snow. I
remember the muddy ditch where you left Jantes—did you
know his name? And I remember Karl. We are left—you
and I. Age burdens us and carries us near to the grave. Who
in the end will still be standing?*

Time will give the answer.

Until then,

Bruno Weiler

. . . Is he too as I am now? Does he still rise in the morning,
dejected, thinking who is lost to him? And at night, awakening,
think who is lost?

Does he see himself reflected in me? In these hours, does he see
the face of his hours reflected?

—Walt Whitman, *Leaves of Grass*

part *two*

"Our system is so terrible that no one in the world will believe it to be possible."

—THE KOMMANDANT OF AUSCHWITZ

CHAPTER TWENTY-ONE

Usually the man looked westward in this coldest hour of the night. He'd send a prayer in that direction, allowing the briefest moment of hope.

But this time, he paused at the doorway to stare at the mountains to the east—there was a thin line of light separating the ridge and the sky. The sight was mesmerizing, and he yearned to see all the colors of dawn. He could not recall when he'd last seen the dawn, and he didn't try to remember. The thought played through with the rising of the great sun, the sun he'd not see today or any day soon. With profound effort, he turned his face away.

The block building was dark and cold—colder, it seemed, than outside. Passing the red blink of the cameras mounted at every corner and the padlocked doors, his footsteps echoed in the stairway as he descended to the concrete floor of another hallway. Entering his room, he closed the heavy metal door without pulling the light chain above. His feet knew the steps to the edge of his simple cot, most likely an army-surplus item. Darkness surrounded him like a heavy fog, but it comforted more than imitation light. Fake light would be a mockery after staring toward the first inklings of dawn only moments before.

The way the pale blue in the east had reflected across the black waters would not leave his thoughts and that bothered him. He ached for daylight with almost a hunger, something he had not allowed for a long time. The routine he had established for survival was simply to function, making him a mechanical, subservient human, with few reminders of humanity. To confirm that he remained among the living, he retained a strange friendship, rare laughter, and his writings. The rest of what he had been was carefully placed in his inner locked storage, and someday he hoped to recover it.

He was nocturnal now. Perceiving in darkness came naturally to him like it did to other creatures of the night—a bat or raccoon, or perhaps a wise owl. At first he'd fought the change because it would be his surrender to them. During most of the day he'd stay awake with the knowledge that sunlight warmed the world somewhere above him, beyond his sight. But the change had come. To do the work required rest, so his body betrayed his will. He hated his weakness—especially when the light of this dawn revealed that he had succumbed to his captivity.

He walked the few steps to the tiny sink and touched the corners, already knowing his toothbrush had not been returned since the week it disappeared. They'd played their game with no rules again. It was always the smallest things to demean him, remind him who was in control. The toothbrush and eating utensils were their favorites. Sometimes only a butter knife came with his meal or a fork for his soup or nothing at all. He imagined them watching and laughing. Tonight there had been no meal waiting at his door.

Cold water felt good against his face, and he took long drinks bent over the sink. It didn't fill his hunger but helped.

His muscles ached after the full night. The coming summer months granted less hours of night and thus increased their workload. There seemed a greater urgency than before. He knew he would awaken to a decent meal—they needed him now and, though the game brought them pleasure, he must have energy to do their work. He found satisfaction in that.

Beneath his bed he found the lump of wood he'd been carving beside the ones he'd already completed and saved until he could give them as gifts. They were lined up, showing the progression of his time as the figures improved. The first one appeared to be a bumpy, misshapen horse, but the newest figures were smooth and detailed. A cat, an elephant, a flower with a stem, and a smiling girl—these were his gifts for the birthdays and Christmases he'd missed. Holding the wood in his hands, he considered flipping on the bulb. Instead he let memories carry him.

Somehow he must get out. They were smart and they knew his weaknesses. They'd found a way to keep him captive. It didn't require locks on his doors. It forced him to live in darkness and artificial light—either from fluorescent tubes or from the bulb dangling in the center of the room. But they hadn't destroyed him in the process. Somehow they still needed him. *That must be the way for this madness to end,* he thought. He must find their weakness.

Jack Porter had been trying for three years.

Jack awoke with a start. He could always hear footsteps before they reached the upper stairway. Though every muscle tensed, he didn't move from the bed. The sound proceeded down the stairway to the lower entrance, but he was unsure who it was until the weight and pace could be gauged along the concrete floor.

The locks to his door had already been turned. For the past week this had been the new routine after his return from the mountain. He wondered why they didn't trust their own mind games to keep him inside anymore.

The footsteps stopped, all four locks flipped one by one, and the door groaned open. He had to shield his face from the hallway light spilling inside.

"Your package is early this time." Ian set the envelope on the table.

"*Danke,*" Jack said. It brought a slight smile to Ian's face.

Jack waited until Ian left and turned all the locks before he rose from the bed. He wasn't sure he wanted to see what was inside. Again he wondered why the routine had been broken. Perhaps they knew he'd deciphered their method of bizarre deprivations—the missing toothbrush, a razor and soap one week and none the next. He'd thought he could predict an irrational pattern. But this was unexpected.

He would need the light, but they'd be watching. Jack tried to sleep instead, refusing to give them the satisfaction of seeing his eagerness to open the package. He couldn't do it for long. This was his one link to the outside, to his old life. These bi-annual arrivals had kept him from insanity, even the consideration of suicide. But the photographs crumbled away the protective armor he fought to wear, leaving him naked and unprotected. His ultimate weakness—they knew it as well as he did.

In one quick surge he jumped up and pulled the chain. The light flickered and burned into the room, chasing the shadows to the corners. As he turned over the manila envelope, he noted, as usual, that there was nothing to give him a clue. Then he pulled out the photos—all printed copies from a computer. Glancing toward the camera eye that stared at him from above, Jack arranged the three photos in a row.

No outside reaction, he told himself. His hands shook from

the effort as he held each photo to believe more fully what he'd
already seen.

If Jack had died three years ago, he'd have wanted his wife
to move on with her life. He would have said that and believed
it. But that was with the condition that death was as he'd envisioned. Jack had never gone for that white and cloudy vision
of heaven. If the Creator of this world was somewhere beyond
the wall of the universe preparing a place for his children, it
would not be colored fuzzy white. In his musings, Jack leaned
toward the vision of a vibrant heaven. Meadows, valleys, hillsides of dark greens—open spaces that rolled and stretched for
hundreds of years. Towering plateaus like he'd seen in New
Mexico and Utah with their red towers of rock stretching for
leagues and worlds. A thousand years could be spent exploring
the surface of steep ridges and peaks, deeply cut valleys,
islands covered with pines, and others with exotic flowers and
crystal seas. In the details of life he saw on earth—the
complexities, intricate design, and balance—how much more
eternity would be.

Jack's musings went long. He'd had plenty of time for them.

But what if he was wrong? he thought as he stared into the
face of his wife and then of his child. What if heaven or hell or
mortality was to be suspended between life and death? Wasn't
the lake of fire what he felt now—the pain of being banished
from life and love? Could hell be worse than this? It was hell
to look into the face of your wife and see that she could be
happy without you. Hell was watching your daughter mature
without your hand to touch her.

Kate was laughing. His old friend Mason leaned close beside
her, grinning. This was the first laugh, smile even, that he'd
seen on his wife's face in three years. Mason's hand was over
Kate's and their cheeks touched slightly. Jack had seen other
photos with Mason in the background or with his arms draped

around Abbie and Kate. Suddenly the meaning of the photos clicked together and Jack understood.

The photo of Abbie showed the complete loss of baby roundness in her cheeks. She was swinging on their porch swing with long, gangly legs hanging over—a Band-Aid on one knee. He didn't know about the scrape beneath her Band-Aid. He didn't know the many bumps and bruises the years had brought his daughter, when once he knew every detail. Her hair was a shade darker—from wheat to honey—and cut shoulder length in an older style. Did her hair still smell like the watermelon shampoo she liked so much? Abbie was only seven, soon to be eight—still a young girl—but it would not take long. The years they'd been apart, agonizing as they were, had actually swept by quickly, he realized as he looked into his daughter's face.

Jack moved to the third photo, of Kate alone in her garden. Sunlight shone around her hair. Though her face was shaded because of the glare from behind, he could see a gentle smile on her lips, as if she'd found peace among the dirt and flowers. Her hair had changed slightly, similar to Abbie's shoulder-length cut—one side tucked behind her ear with a section fallen against her cheek. He imagined they'd gone to get matching haircuts—a girls' day out. Kate watched him, looking deeply into his eyes, oblivious to how her gaze ripped into him. A part of Jack accused her for being happy, even envied that she could smell their daughter's watermelon hair and put Band-Aids on her scraped knees. It wasn't her fault, he reminded himself. She didn't know he was here, staring at her, yearning to pull them from two-dimensional. She didn't know she stared into his face. But mostly Kate didn't know he missed them so deeply it scared him.

Jack didn't understand the message in these photos. The others he'd received, now hidden beneath his cot, had warned him that they could reach his family whenever they wanted.

His thoughts of escape were destroyed by those images. Who did Kate and Abbie trust behind the camera lens? Who was that close that he could never reach them first?

That was the old message. But these photos spoke something new: "They don't need you anymore. Your family has moved on." He held the first one. Mason was turning toward Kate and making her laugh.

Kate and Abbie had moved on.

If Jack had died, he would have wanted it. But it was different to still be alive.

He must discover why he'd been given these photos and what worth there was in life without the hope of returning to Kate and Abbie.

CHAPTER TWENTY-TWO

Wolfram Meizer didn't need a mirror to know he was old. He felt it when his eyes opened and as he rose from bed in a body that groaned and creaked with every movement. Yet a glance in a mirror still startled him. Perhaps it was because he looked in one so rarely; inside he believed himself the man he once was. Age was the only thing he'd still to master. But he hadn't given up on that yet.

Papers were overrunning his office. On the television across the room CNN International reported a recent African uprising. The sound was turned low enough for him to ignore, but high enough in case anything of importance came on. It rarely did—unemployment in Russia, secret cloning operations, Britain's AIDS findings—nothing particularly relevant to him. Still he must always watch. Wolfram wished for a secretary in that moment, though he would never trust someone among his things. At least, never again.

He stretched in his chair, leaning far back while scanning the four televisions mounted inside a long open cabinet near the ceiling. Two screens showed complete darkness—one, the lit hallway; and another, Ian studying charts and smoking a cigarette. He must remind Ian to be sure to watch the screens of the dark rooms from time to time also—he'd become a bit lazy about that. With his mental memo in place, Wolfram returned to the screen of his laptop as he went through e-mails and made several phone calls.

Wolfram stood and raised his hands toward the ceiling; his back ached from the office work. He'd left the castle grounds for a few weeks only and returned to mounds of work—it never ceased to require his attention. He walked along the bookcase, and his eyes caught the book about Otto Skorzeny. It made him angry every time he saw it. So why did he keep it? As a reminder of what had been stolen from him and also to remember that men like Skorzeny were dead now. Skorzeny the officer, the German hero, the admired legend to neo-Nazis after the war. Yet all his stunts and books and freedom after the war didn't save him from death. With his death, his fame receded year by year. Perhaps such men didn't have to flee Europe after the war. They weren't hunted and didn't live in fear in those early years. But the youth of the world didn't remember the deeds of Scarface Skorzeny now—how he'd saved Mussolini from death by parachuting into the mountain villa where Mussolini was held. They didn't remember his postwar work with the American government or that his friends were the elite of the world. Few knew of such stories now.

Wolfram had outlasted most of them, and he had no intention of going anytime soon. There were many such things to comfort him, even if he was spending so much time hidden away in this secluded place. It would be worth it in the end.

With a flip of a remote, the cabinet above him closed, shutting away the tubular rooms. He thought again about what comforted him now. The work had grown old, but progress drew close to completion—he was sure of it. He'd push them a little more and finish it by autumn's foliage. Then he'd finally be justified, his work ensuring his name would be remembered. Soon he would have what he always deserved.

Wolfram Meizer enjoyed being *kommandant* of his world.

Wolfram pounded his fist against the table. A splash of steaming coffee spilled over, dampening one of the three newspapers he read every morning. The sunshine reflected from the drops on the patio table. Meizer's eyes stayed on the black words and images before him. He had heard the news, but seeing the printed version shocked him further. Not Otto Kauls—it seemed impossible. He read the words again.

> *Survivors and their families gathered outside the Latvian courthouse today after the indictment of Otto Kauls. Dr. Kauls is accused of war crimes and crimes against humanity after allegedly participating in the murder of several hundred Latvian Jews and other civilians during the summer of 1943. Lawyers for the 84-year-old doctor claimed that he was unfit to stand trial. The judge decided otherwise.*

Further down Wolfram read statements from the witnesses—a local civilian, the daughter of an alleged victim, and others. They had a tight case against him.

> *"I was in the woods and heard the shooting, many rounds, then a pause and more rounds. I crawled through the brush and watched Dr. Kauls walk among the bodies and shoot anyone still alive. One was an infant held in the dead mother's arms. There were bodies and blood all over the ground, old women and men, children and families. Those images never leave me."*
>
> *"My mother was used as a human guinea pig. Otto Kauls*

is no doctor; he is a monster. It is possible that my mother's brain and body parts are sealed in jars in that private collection he still possesses today."

Dr. Kauls lived in South America from 1945 to 1988 before he returned to Europe. He was found in the Lithuanian village where he had been living for the past ten years.

"Idiot!" Wolfram hit the table again.

The photograph captured a dejected and weak man, not the old friend he remembered as tan and strong, smiling across a table laden with Caribbean lobster, smoked salmon, and Banks beer.

Otto had not been a fool like some of the others. Nearly every month Wolfram found reports of Holocaust survivor settlements, another deported ex-Nazi, or a pro-Fascist group as the target of propaganda. It shouldn't surprise him. Decades and decades could pass and they'd still lord it over the world because they'd won. Groups with free thought who were aware of the underlying plots would forever receive constant attacks—even old men near their deaths could not find peace.

Footsteps sounded from the graveled garden path.

"Ian!" Wolfram stormed, rising from the chair.

The steps quickened and Ian emerged from the forest. "What is it?" he asked in a voice that betrayed his annoyance.

"Do you know about this?" He held the paper up as Ian approached.

Ian's eyes flickered slightly and Wolfram knew the answer. "I read it this morning."

"Do you remember him?"

Ian shook his head slowly, as if trying to conjure up the memory.

"When you had a terrible cough, this man took care of you. You were too small to remember." Wolfram paced the rock patio. He stopped when he noticed Ian watching him. He told his body to calm and control the stirring rage.

"Sit with me." The metal chairs screeched as they pulled them across the stone. Wolfram motioned for Ian to have some of the coffee in the carafe, but Ian refused. "What did you think of the report?"

"I think it is typical."

"Typical? That is all you can say? It is an injustice to rob an old man of his last days. Will they prosecute any Russians or Americans for wartime activities?"

"No," Ian said. "Only the Nazis or those who are against their beliefs."

"Yes."

"Our civilized nations try to say they do not believe in God, that evolution has been man's path, yet they are hypocrites." Ian—with his light, wavy hair and dark eyes that didn't move from Wolfram's—spoke so calmly and with so little expression that Wolfram nearly admired him.

"And why are they hypocrites?" Wolfram asked, taking the bait with pleasure. It interested him that Ian had come so far without his realizing it. This boy had initiative and thought for himself.

"They cling to moral laws and ethics when, without a God, there is no need for forced rights and wrongs. The strong will survive. The weak will not. When the governments realize this, our world will finally be free. Until then we will have these ridiculous trials."

"You do understand then."

"Yes."

"This—" Wolfram touched the page—"is from ignorance. This man was a doctor and scientist. Medical advancements are progressive because of men like Otto. Our world condemns how he obtained his knowledge, but his research is used in their modern science."

Wolfram leaned back in his chair and stared down the slop-
ing grounds. He saw images of twisted bodies and crying
German women. The Americans and British had murdered
thousands of civilians during the war. They dropped bombs on
Dresden and Hamburg—cities all over Germany. And what
had they done to the innocent people of Japan? It was justified
as "war necessity." The Nazis believed the same. If the Allies
had lost, perhaps they'd be up for war crimes. The ironies
never failed to anger him. If he were younger, if only he were
younger . . . Ian, silent across from him, was evidently thinking his own thoughts. That's when Wolfram caught the black
ink eyes of his old friend in the newspaper and knew just
how careful he must be. A part of him wanted to get out of
Europe—go to the Middle East or back to South America and
leave this work for Ian.

"I walked up for a reason," Ian said.

"Wait," Wolfram said, lifting his hand. "Let me drink my
coffee."

His cup was almost empty. He filled it again and stirred
some milk into the dark brew. Opening the paper, he began to
read through it slowly. Ian remained seated, seemingly unconcerned by Wolfram's demands.

Wolfram skimmed the business page, but his thoughts
bounced back to the idea of leaving. He knew he couldn't do
it; age and comforts kept him planted. And soon the castle
grounds would be finished. But even sooner, Wolfram hoped,
the original operation that had brought him back would at last
be complete. It was his final goal. As much as he'd tried for
years to stay away, he was drawn like some gravitational force
that wouldn't release him. It had pulled him during his
wandering years when he'd trekked the Andes, feeling at home
as he stopped in the small hotel of another exiled German.
He'd had women, alcohol, every pleasure he craved. Still, the
calling of something stolen from him, something that should

CINDY McCORMICK MARTINUSEN

have been his, worked and wore against him. It was the one thing he couldn't have.

When he'd done all he wanted and gained more than he'd imagined possible, he gave in to that call to discover what he would have had if the war had lasted another week, perhaps even a few more days. If he hadn't been forced to leave Europe. If he'd had a little more time. Wolfram would see it before he died, or this quest would kill him. He would not end his days like his old friend Otto Kauls.

Wolfram pried his eyes from the newspaper to the brightness of the morning, ignoring Ian's finger tapping the table. There was surprising comfort in the laws of nature; as Ian had said, only the strong would survive. Wolfram watched the silver threads of a spider's web that stretched wide across the tips of a green thicket. Suddenly a fly flew straight into the snare. It stuck and struggled. In a quick swoop, a black-and-gray spider flew across the silk and began a furious spin around its prey. Wolfram smiled and took a sip of nearly cold coffee.

"We must speak," Ian insisted.

Wolfram let the interruption pass this time. Ian had been up all night after all. "Then speak." Wolfram's eyes remained on the long legs of the spider as it twisted and turned its victim.

"I received a message about a man in the States. His name was Karl Olsen."

Wolfram turned toward Ian. He had gone to the city for one day only and had missed the call—this was business he had planned to keep from Ian. "Yes?"

"The message was that Karl Olsen is dead."

Wolfram savored the words like the first taste of fine wine. Unable to keep the smile from his lips, he stood.

"Then we are nearly finished."

CHAPTER TWENTY-THREE

Jack dreaded the instant shock of cold water creeping around the edges of his wet suit and sliding inside the worn cuffs. He'd soon warm; his body heat against the neoprene lining would raise the temperature and he'd lose the chill. At their depth the water would always be dark, even if it wasn't the middle of the night.

They'd spent an hour with their lights beaming against the particles and staring into the eyes of pike and whitefish that gazed with wonder before turning and sliding into the night. Jack knew this area along the steep wall of the lake well. There was only a slight slope from mountaintop to water's edge to lake floor. Jack could locate each deep gouge where under-water missiles had been tested during the Nazi era. He'd checked thoroughly to assure that the indentations had not formed cracks that would cause breakage or landslides above. Tonight he checked again. With their movement within the mountain—the months of drilling within the old salt mine—damage beneath them must be gauged regularly.

Jack turned to check Ian's location. Through the haze he could see Ian's light move against an area where the slope jutted outward. Jack knew there were other reasons for Ian's interest in the dive. He'd always come in the past when Rudy was well enough to dive too. Jack and Rudy both believed Ian had other reasons besides rock crackage for his dives. He was looking for something, and Jack had his theories. These lakes were full of mystery, but if Ian sought lost treasure, it would be found too deep for divers. It must be something else.

Jack moved away from Ian toward an area below the docks of the castle grounds. Jack had explored this area only once, checking for rock movement in a lower outcropping of rock. It took time to find it. Holding his light in front of him, he kicked smoothly through the water. This area had the greatest slope. He could follow the lake wall straight up to where it shallowed to the shore of the castle grounds. It was the only shoreline on this end of the lake with the sides surrounded by sheer mountains. Across the lake was a large shoreline where Jack had seen a distant village with lights that shone like beacons, reminding him of life outside the alpine prison.

On their most recent dive, Jack had found the long crack in the rock deep beneath the dock and upper grounds. If the crack grew and created an underwater avalanche, the estate could possibly be in jeopardy. It was a thought Jack had begun to consider.

He thought of it again as he reached the area and checked his gauges and waterproof watch for the time. Ian would expect him back in ten minutes or less. He had little geological experience and had wished for more on countless occasions, since they had been working him outside his field of expertise. The great "they" didn't seem to understand that he was an archaeologist, not a miner or geologist, when they brought him here. Yet Jack wouldn't give them reason to doubt it now—he needed them to need him. It ensured his safety as well as his family's.

He knew these people were serious. The first six months of confinement, with their taunting and photos, were proof enough. The following year and a half, he'd been moved around and then brought to Ian. Ian was who he saw now, their foreman or puppet—he wasn't sure. They'd worked at another site for some time before they'd settled here a year ago.

But two plans had begun to formulate in Jack's mind. If he could fake an accident, make Ian believe he had been pulled down by rocks and drowned, he might have a chance to escape. He'd put a reserve tank outside the boat and use it to cross the lake beneath the water. The danger should be removed from his family with his supposed death. Then he'd reach authorities and get help out to Rudy.

The other plan—the avalanche and possible destruction of the castle grounds—put his life in jeopardy. Since the most recent photographs had arrived, he'd considered this plan more than once. What did he have to return to? What did he have to look forward to?

Jack moved through the water, remembering the night he lost himself to a panicked need to escape. He'd had no plan, only pure desperation. Straight across the lake he swam, while Rudy and Ian worked along the wall. It took his logic only an eighth of the way across the lake to kick in and turn him back. The risk was too high. Someone very close took those pictures of his family. It would be nothing for them to reach Abbie and Kate.

In Jack's first months of captivity, they'd given him countless photos of victims—charred bodies, a headline of a family murdered while they slept, a black man hanging from a tree, a little girl shot with a doll in her hand. Those images turned him around. He wasn't here because of some amateurs—they had an essential reason for keeping him here. They'd worked too hard and long, taken too great a risk by kidnapping an American. There was something very important about these diggings.

Halfway back from his attempted escape, he had surfaced. Already Ian had lights skimming the water's surface. Jack waved his arms, feeling defeat spread over him at the loss of freedom so close yet too costly. When he boarded the boat, he made an excuse about going too far, though he knew Ian never really bought it.

The accident idea might work, he now thought as he recognized an outcropping of rock. He found the crack and noticed how it had widened by half an inch more and appeared to have cut deep. Jack turned downward to follow it, though he knew he couldn't go far. The pressure increased with the depth, and his equipment was too old to push far. He often feared a hose would break, so he kept careful watch. The crack in the rock widened as the light's beam followed its jagged line. Then Jack saw a large hole in the rock wall. He held the light with one hand and grasped the ledge with the other. A few rocks came loose and floated downward. He needed to be careful or the accident he wanted to fake could actually happen. The light beam sought the sides and then disappeared into the darkness of the gouge.

Jack swam downward and inside, just a bit. Then he realized that this was not the underside of an outcropping as he'd first believed. It was an underwater cave. The lipped ridge of rocks above the opening had kept the mouth of the cave from view on previous dives. Or perhaps some of their digging inside the cave had broken loose any blockage. The light gave no answer to its length. Jack backed out and examined the edges. The ridges in the rock indicated man-made qualities, as if the walls had been chiseled and widened. But he believed the cave was natural in origin. As he followed the wall down, he remembered to check his watch. It was time to get back.

Jack found Ian moving in his direction, no longer investigating the rock wall. When Ian caught him in his light, he gave him a thumbs-up. Jack checked his compass, and they swam until they saw the lights along the hull of the boat. Slowly they surfaced, following the line of bubbles from their masks.

Rudy waited beside the ladder, grabbing up the tanks, belts, and gear. Water streamed from their sleek bodies as they climbed from the weightless world of water into the boat. Jack peeled away the wet suit, and the chilly night air stung his skin.

Rudy tossed Jack a towel and then one to Ian. "It's not right for me to be left up here," Rudy said, rubbing his mitten-covered hands.

"Get well and you can come with us," Jack said.

"I'm trying; you know I'm trying." A cough burst from his lips as if to contradict his words.

"Get where it's warm, right now," Jack scolded.

Rudy nodded between coughs and descended the cabin stairway. Ian was putting away equipment. Jack knew he should help, but this time he sat in the stillness of the boat, breathing the cold mountain air. For a moment he stared across the water to the lights along the opposite shore. People had normal lives over there—eating in restaurants, watching television, laughing, singing, loving. He was separated by mountains and water, though much more than that.

"The locals wanted to know about our nighttime activities." Ian was watching him. "Remember the boats coming round a few months ago?"

"And what are we doing? Really?" Jack asked it like a challenge.

He knew the reason they'd brought him here—they believed he had knowledge that would help them. And they believed his archaeological skills were essential, though geological skills were more necessary. They couldn't hire another professional who could share their work with the world. Jack and Rudy had worked as a team in the past: Rudy was experienced in underwater archaeology, and Jack had worked at Native American caves in Montana. They were the perfect choice. What he didn't know was what exactly this group wanted him to find. Jack still didn't know after three years.

"We are remodeling the grounds of an old castle," Ian said with his usual serious expression. "Often at night we enjoy studying fish."

"If I knew what fish to look for, I might help find it." Jack said it casually as he pulled the towel over his head and rubbed the water droplets from his hair. He didn't want to see Ian's eyes probing his face or hear the lies in Ian's responses. In a twisted way, he liked Ian. Ian was part of the group who kept him here, though Jack had yet to sway the young man's allegiance or move him to some compassion. That had been one of his original plans. He'd worked little by little toward friendship but had fallen prey to his own game. The fact that Jack could actually like Ian—the person, the man—was proof of how warped this life in captivity had made him.

"Some knowledge can destroy you, Jack."

"How can my life be more destroyed?" Their eyes locked, and Jack noticed a slight flicker in Ian's expression before he turned away. He wondered if Ian ever imagined the life they had stolen. Ian knew about Abbie and Kate. But did he consider what it felt like? What had Ian's life been like before this assignment or project or whatever this was for him?

Tall and quiet, Ian ran his hand through his hair, sleeking it straight back. What thoughts moved through his head? He never revealed any beliefs or past or reason for his presence here. Ian only expressed what was expected in the moment.

He finished putting away equipment and turned back to Jack. "Let's go over the maps. You can show me what you found."

"What I found?" he asked, wondering if Ian already knew about the cave.

"I'm sure there are changes from our last dive. I found a few cracks that had deepened. Didn't you find anything?" Again his eyes did their probing.

"A few. I'll record the changes."

They descended the steps into the boat's tiny cabin. Ian flipped on a light over the table as they scooted around the booth seat. Rudy had made coffee and poured it into gray tin cups. Strange how much freedom Jack felt when on a dive or in the boat, as if this were a normal underwater expedition. Out here he was nearly an equal with Ian, and Jack enjoyed the luxury of real conversation with Rudy instead of their fragmented talks through the heating vents and their coded taps through the cement wall. These dives were rare now, something Jack actually looked forward to. Unlike his previous work in the soot and recycled air of the tunnel, these dives brought a dread of the night's end. The boat had a faint musty scent that Jack loved. It was the smell of mold and rope, closed-up cabins, and open waters.

Ian unrolled the map and set his cup, a compass, and a can of chili on three corners of the paper to hold it down. The renderings showed the lake from different angles. There were figures indicating depth levels around the lake, the widths at various points, previous dive locations, and sketches of the mountain ranges with marked areas of digs and blastings. One drawing depicted the joining of two mountains, where a spring began and flowed into a stream that cut to the slope of the old castle grounds that had been Jack's home for the past year.

Jack studied the map with Ian beside him.

Rudy sat in a chair and flipped through an Austrian newspaper that he'd found crunched under the table when he sat down. "Says here that Charles Schulz died. You know, the Peanuts cartoon guy."

"Snoopy was one of my favorites," Jack said.

"Everyone loved Charlie Brown. My favorite was when he gets that terrible little Christmas tree—"

"How old is that newspaper?" Ian asked.

Rudy looked and didn't respond. Jack could tell it must be old news.

"I found nothing changed here or here." Ian touched points they'd previously marked on the map. "It did not appear that the digging inside the mountain had protruded through the lake wall."

Rudy folded the paper and leaned toward the light. "Then the water we hit in Tunnel 8 could come from an underground lake or spring, though the solidity and depth of the rock makes that theory doubtful."

"What did you find, Jack?" Ian asked.

Jack studied the map. He could see where he had marked the crack he'd reinvestigated tonight, but there was nothing of the underwater cave. Ian again watched him.

"This area could perhaps have impact damage. There was approximately a three-quarter-inch widening in the crack and several inches' depth change. Something to watch in the future." Jack spoke casually as if it held little importance. He turned their focus to a structure area a hundred meters from the cave. "Ian, if you didn't find any damage to these areas and this is directly beneath the internal digging within the old salt mine, then I agree with Rudy—we did not reach the lake, but some other water source."

"Why can we never make progress here? Your calculations inside the mine must be wrong." Ian's voice had a harsh ring to it, enough for Rudy to put his coffee down.

"I've gone over them again and again," Jack explained. "Rudy has double-checked me. We aren't far enough to have reached the lake—tonight only confirms what I already believed. And if you blew out the wall of the lake from the inside, the water would fill the tunnel before anyone could get out. The water we cut into must be a spring."

"Unless we tapped into an underwater cavern," Rudy suggested. Jack wished he hadn't thought of it.

"Explain," Ian said.

"If there was already a cavern or a spring that ran into the lake beneath the rock, we may have broken through the top of it. The water didn't rush into the tunnel for one reason—we were digging downward. It also didn't have the pressure because there is some other outlet for it."

Ian nodded. "We must dive lower. Or we must go into the water from inside the tunnel."

Jack now suspected that Ian did know something about the cave. Or perhaps it was what they'd been seeking all along.

Rudy continued. "We don't have the equipment. I've read about teams cave diving. It can be very dangerous work. We'd need a diving bell, and if we go too far inside, then it won't be enough to have twenty to thirty minutes to decompress. Some deep cave dives require hours of decompression, so we'd need a chamber to transfer into after each dive. Beneath that kind of surface, every second is more valuable than in any other dive we've ever done. We'd need underwater scooters, lights, a wall mapper that fires sonar to find our way, along with a trailing cord to help us get back out. There's no room for error in this. This three-man team can't do it, especially with this equipment we're patching up after every dive."

"We'll get the equipment," Ian said.

Neither Rudy nor Jack spoke. They knew such equipment wouldn't be found on a black-market order form.

"There is little enthusiasm. Perhaps there are things you don't tell me, information you withhold, plans of sabotage? Do you want to leave this place? Until this is finished, you have no hope," said Ian.

Jack guessed that Ian was getting pressure. But it also

angered him that Ian again referred to their freedom, dangling it like a carrot before their faces. Jack knew it was a hope they'd never fulfill.

"*Will* we be freed, Ian?" Jack asked. "We've been here too long and know too much to be allowed to walk away. You know this group better than we do. What will they do when our work is done?"

Ian's face took on an expression of surprise. It brought fear to Jack and Rudy to see that Ian had believed the same lie that they had believed. But now Ian recognized the truth. Of course they would not be allowed to go home, even if their homes were still waiting—which for Jack it wasn't. The risk was too high for their captors to allow their freedom. In that second Ian knew it also.

Ian left the map and climbed the stairs from the boat's cabin.

Neither Jack nor Rudy spoke for a long time. Jack continued to stare at the map. "Why don't we blow this entire place up?" he said in a low whisper. It was an exhilarating thought. "We have access to the dynamite."

"You know why we don't. I have a nephew, and you have a family who are safe as long as we do what they say."

"If we could get enough sticks in the perfect places, there'd be no one to harm them."

"I know you aren't serious, Jack. But in case a part of you is, remember that these people are more than the few here. I've been with them longer."

"Who are they?"

"My guess is that they are linked with neo-Nazi organizations, perhaps even other fanatic groups," Rudy answered. "They must have connections in the States. Possibly the operation is smaller than we guess, but sometimes I feel it's larger than I imagine."

"We're getting close to what they want. Ian showed

emotions tonight—he's getting pressure and a lot of it. But we need to find what we can do."

"We wait."

"You've been here too long, Rudy. Don't lose your fight. They say inmates in prison reach a point when they don't want to leave anymore because those walls mean safety to them. That can't happen to us."

"It won't."

"Then what can we do?"

"We can pray," suggested Rudy.

Jack leaned back with his hands behind his head. He should have expected such a response, but hearing it now made him teeter between humor and anger. When Jack had known Rudy Blessing years earlier, their roles had been reversed. Rudy, a Catholic by family, not faith, had attended mass a few times a year and had his mother's rosary beads in the instrument drawer of the boat he lived on. Jack was honored to spend a summer doing underwater diving with the Blessing team in the Mediterranean. He'd been full of youth and spiritual faith back then, unafraid to share his beliefs with anyone interested, including an only slightly curious Rudy.

"Sometimes God wants action," Jack countered. "Prayer alone has taken us nowhere."

"Prayer has probably done much more than we know," Rudy said with a look that reminded Jack of the countless times God had helped him survive another day. Rudy's friendship alone had been an answer when Jack thought he'd go insane from his solitary confinement.

"Sometimes I think you like it here," Jack grumbled.

"No. I want freedom. It often amazes me, the strength of that desire—how God designed us to require it. But I can also see the great good in our time here."

"What great good?"

"I've come to truly understand. All pretense, obsession,

desires, possessions—it's all been taken from me. I had many dark moments before you came. My fight was with God even more than with them. It almost killed me. Finally I surrendered to God in sheer desperation. They kept me in this filthy basement for months—a place that would bring a man either to God or to insanity."

"I know that basement," Jack said, wishing to erase the memory of his six months there.

Wondering where Ian had gone, Jack looked up the stairway but saw no one. Another pot of coffee percolated on the stove, but he could still feel the stifling air of that basement. He remembered scratching his tallied days beneath the scrawls of other captives who had been there before. His marks would reach one hundred seventy-three, while one person had marked over four hundred. Had that been Rudy? They'd never talked about the means that had brought them together.

"I began to pray in that basement. I prayed for someone to talk to and, though it took almost a year, you came," said Rudy.

"So this is *your* fault?"

"I hope not," Rudy said with a laugh. "You had great faith when they brought us together. You came right when I was losing it again."

"I would not have survived without you." Jack took a quick drink of his coffee while his thoughts returned to a night he'd sunk so low that life hadn't seemed worth living anymore. It had been Rudy's words that saved him: "Think of this moment, then the next moment. You'll go insane if you wonder what your family is doing right now, what they are thinking. Get through tonight. Save a bit of food every meal in case the next one doesn't come. Hide something that will give you something they don't own. And do something for your family—write letters and poems or bring rocks from the diggings to someday give your daughter."

Jack had not told Rudy about the latest photos of his family—the evidence of their life without him. If he ever gave Abbie the wooden animals he'd learned to carve or Kate the letters he'd written, it would only be salt in their healing wounds. *What now, Rudy? What keeps me going?*

"Can you see the good that God does in the midst of bad?" Rudy put his elbows on the table and rested his chin on his folded hands. "When everything was taken, I could see what was important. I gained a greater view of life and death, even eternity. I know this is just a moment in eternity. This is my work right now. God doesn't want men to oppress men. But man's free choice affects even the innocent. One person sins and another pays the price. It's not fair—but a world that doesn't follow God will never be just or fair or happily ever after."

"And we're the ones paying for another's sins."

"God doesn't promise a 401(k), nice house, perfect family. He promises to never leave us or forsake us. *You* told me that a long time ago."

"That seems like a different man. I know I still believe, but sometimes it doesn't feel like enough."

"Have you ever been to a museum or an exhibit of a great artist, Jack?"

"Sure. I spent a week in Florence."

"Then you'll understand this. My favorite painter has always been Picasso—don't ask me why. There was this exhibit in Paris—I must have gone five or six times in a month. I liked to stand very, very close to a painting—as close as I could without making security too nervous. I'd stare at a small section. One painting included this awful pea green color within the outline of a woman's lips, and the strokes looked terrible from close up. But the farther I walked away, the more beautiful the painting became. The entire picture was revealed."

"So this is the awful pea green of our life painting?"

"Of our eternal painting, perhaps." Rudy stood and poured more coffee into Jack's cup. "Do you know what Oswald Chambers writes about prayer?"

"More Oswald?"

"I have his book in my room."

"How? I can hardly get paper and ink."

"I prayed and I asked. They must have ordered it from South America. The box said Amazon something."

"Amazon.com?"

"Yes, that's it. I still have the box."

"That's an online bookstore. A store on the Internet where you can order books with one push of a button."

"The Internet, yes. Interesting."

"No, unbelievable. They ordered you a book from Amazon."

"Ask and ye shall receive."

Jack shook his head in disbelief. "Just tell me what Oswald says about prayer."

"He says that prayer is absurd."

"I didn't expect that. But lately, I'd almost agree."

"Oswald writes that prayer is not practical but absurd. We should understand that prayer is stupid from the common-sense point of view. It feels like doing nothing. Haven't we heard a thousand times, 'All we can do now is pray,' as if that's the last resort or the worst-case scenario? Isn't the *prayer* word used in all kinds of absurd situations, like when we don't want to help someone or don't have anything else to say? 'I'll pray for you.' And yet prayer is the greatest mystery of all. It is faith. When we do truly pray, we are acting on the faith that the words we throw to the air are doing something. And prayer does. It breaks barriers and changes the nature of life."

"My mind would agree, but what I feel is different. I haven't seen barriers broken and life changed in a very long time. I don't even hear God as I once did."

"He has entrusted you with silence."

"Great—what a gift."

"Oswald writes: 'God is working for His highest ends until His purpose and man's purpose become one.' The best thing to remember is that we should live this life to fulfill God's purpose, not our own. For God's purpose will eventually be greater by far than our own, if we can only believe and allow him to move and change us."

"Trust in the Picasso?"

"It'll be even better than a Picasso in the end."

Both men were quiet, each lost in his own thoughts. Jack heard a slight creak overhead and then footsteps. Ian must be above them. Returning to the maps and sketches they'd charted again and again, Jack spotted the place where he'd found the cave and again decided not to mention its location, not even to Rudy. Until Jack knew more, he would let this be his own little secret.

CHAPTER TWENTY-FOUR

Wolfram closed the wooden blinds on the French doors and turned the lights low. The television in the corner was on mute but flashed from across the room.

He'd moved his favorite birds back into the office. Whenever he left the castle grounds, the cages were moved. No one entered his office while he was gone. The slight light calmed the birds, and they chirped softly. He hit the remote to open his surveillance cabinet. Wolfram switched a button that showed the security room with the lone guard watching monitors and reading a book. He listened for movement in the house—nothing. Rudy's room was dark, Jack had a light on and was carving wood at the table in his room, Ian had fallen asleep while leaning way back in his chair. The hallway to the barrack was empty.

The wheels of Wolfram's chair squeaked as he sat before the antique desk. With one hard pull and his other hand holding a latch, the front panel of his desk opened to reveal a red metal safe. He turned the dial and heard the click of the lock. Behind several stacks of currency—American and euro—he found a white handkerchief folded and held in place by a green rubber band. Wolfram withdrew the handkerchief and set it on the desk where the lamp shone a circle of light.

It annoyed him how his hands shook constantly. He noticed it when drinking his coffee and sipping soup and now as he pulled the rubber band away.

The two tile fragments in the handkerchief differed in size and did not fit together. Whoever cut them had not gone for form or precision. Three pieces were missing that would join his two, and soon he'd have one of those fragments. Wolfram wondered which one it would be. He knew what he hoped. Then only two pieces would be left, and he may not even need them, though he would want them eventually. This whole tile had almost been his once—before it had been broken into five pieces. The betrayal of a woman had stolen that from him.

Wolfram remembered that Susanne Olsen had been Karl's sister, bringing a chuckle to his lips. Karl Olsen was dead now too. He remembered the giant of a man he'd seen only once, through the scope of his rifle. Karl had been moving through the forest steadily and with great care. Wolfram's view was perfect, like watching a cat sneak up on a lion. He was the lion watching from above. His finger rested on the trigger when he heard something behind him. Climbing the back of the ridge was another of their Resistance comrades. This one was not so lucky as Karl Olsen. The following years would prove his mistake in not killing Olsen first. The man had caused him much trouble, keeping his name on watch lists around the world. Bounty hunters came after him, investment required partnerships, and he was forced to monitor every move he made—it grew tiring.

Wolfram moved the tile fragments, arranging them in differ-ent ways. He'd had one piece for over fifty years, since he found it wrapped in cording around that kid's neck. Wolfram had been stunned to see it there. The boy didn't talk easily, but it took little time for him to reveal that his team members each had a piece. Wolfram thought he'd have the pieces back within the week, that he'd get each one of the four remaining men. But he couldn't predict the war's end or his need to escape without the chance to get them all back. It took decades to get the second tile fragment.

He picked up the telephone, though it was the middle of the night in America. He wasn't even sure what time zone the western states were in and he didn't care. The voice that answered didn't sound groggy but alert. Perhaps they'd been awaiting this return call.

"You should speak to me only," Wolfram said without introduction. He knew he would be recognized.

"Of course. I gave little information to Ian, enough to receive your return call quickly."

"Next time only speak with me. Now I want details." Wolfram hated the man's accented German, but Wolfram's English was even worse.

"We had two men in Arizona for several months. I decided I should be there for the actual confrontation. We watched for a few days. Our subject brought two men to his home. I will send you the information we found on them. One will be of particular interest."

"Would these be older men, his age?"

"Yes."

Wolfram nearly smiled. The remaining two tile fragments. "And do you have photographs?"

"We will send the files at once."

"Good."

"The two men were not there when you met with Olsen? Olsen had a wife also."

"They were all gone when we met the old man."

"Did he know who you were?" Wolfram wished he could

have seen Karl's face and heard his words. Had he known those were his last moments alive?

"Yes. He mentioned your name."

"Good. How did it occur?"

"Without much assistance."

"I do not understand."

"He was old. We threatened him, pushed hard to get the item—it was too much, I suppose."

"And you left behind the object that I asked?"

"Yes."

"And the item—"

"I must first ask you. When will we have what you promised?"

"I am working on that." Wolfram leaned back in his chair. "Old secrets can be hard to find."

"You've been working on it for a while. There is a lot of pressure here, and it's difficult keeping the wayward ones in line. They have little patience."

"Precision is key. Impatience will destroy the cause."

"But we need something to keep them satisfied. Some proof, perhaps, that this is worth waiting for, as you have promised. Our men respect you greatly and do not doubt your word—I do not mean to imply that. But it would help the restlessness if there was something definite to show them."

Wolfram drummed his fingers on the desk as he listened. He nodded slowly, then a bit faster. "I understand. I will send a copy. It is a document from October 1944 that I stole from top secret Gestapo files. It describes plans for the greatest weapon that would make their work in atom splitting—"

"Do not tell too much on the line."

"And now, when will I have what you took from Karl?"

Wolfram looked at the missing spaces between the two tiles.

There was a long pause. "We did not get it."

Wolfram pulled the phone away; he could feel the anger rise

within him. "Franklin, you had better explain," he said through clenched teeth.

"You said we would not use names."

"You have other things to worry about right now."

"We believed Olsen had given the piece to us. But after our leave, I realized it was the exact piece I had left in his office— it was one of the copies. It's a delay—we'll get the original." Franklin spoke as if it would be simple.

"Yes, you will." Wolfram's hand slammed over the tile pieces. "If you knew how long I've waited for that." Wolfram regained his composure. "Keep searching. And there are two others. This is essential to what you request of me."

"We will get them," the voice said with confidence.

"Send those photographs of the men at Karl's."

"They will be there within the half hour."

Wolfram slammed the phone. His left hand remained over the fragments. He needed at least three pieces of the tile map to complete what he'd begun—without them he searched aimlessly. Fool Americans could not get the job done, as he'd always suspected. They could talk big, but the results proved their inefficiency.

Wolfram sat in the dull light of the room. The birds were now quiet. There was a new set of maps he should look through, but the warmth of the room and comfort of his chair kept him reclined. Wolfram glanced at the clear, plastic case on the corner of his desk. It had rested in that place for so long that he rarely saw it there. It looked like a paperweight with a small speck in the center. The speck was a tiny, glass capsule. That capsule had been his companion for almost ten years before he had confined it in the clear case. Many had used theirs, biting through the glass while in a cell awaiting trial or at the moment of capture. Instant death was their escape as cyanide exploded through their system. Wolfram had never needed it. Close at times, perhaps. But here it remained at his side, a testimony to his endurance and destiny.

He reminded himself of this as he mulled over the last thoughts of Karl Olsen. They were not as he had hoped. Instead of fear, Karl had felt contempt. He had given the fake tile fragment, believing he'd taken another jab at his opponent. Wolfram closed his eyes and breathed slowly. Karl was dead. Karl was in the grave. Karl would soon turn to rot. Wolfram thought of the many bodies he'd seen—twisted limbs, mouths gaping, eyes wide with surprise or more often with nothing-ness inside. That was Karl Olsen.

A ding sounded on his computer, breaking the stale air. Wolfram clicked a button and watched the file download. He printed the file and waited. It took only moments for the faces to come through. Wolfram set the papers beneath the lamp-light. The first showed three men meeting at an airport. Three old men who looked nothing like the soldiers they'd once been. And then he knew what Franklin had meant about being surprised. One man in the photo was tall and burly, smaller than Karl Olsen, but a large presence anyway. He carried a briefcase, and a carry-on bag was beside him. The expensive suit looked comfortable on him, even after his flight. This man was conditioned to traveling and dressing well.

And Wolfram knew that face.

"Former finance minister Lukas Johansen. Why do you greet Karl and Oskar as if you are old friends?" Wolfram leaned close to the faces. He pulled back with a sharp intake of breath as the knowledge hit him. "Bruno Weiler, you old, betraying fool. You have been here all along."

⊷⟞⊜⟝⊷

The gravel under his tires crunched louder than the high-pitched whine of his golf cart. Wolfram knew he looked ridiculous to his employees, motoring around in his buggy to investigate the progress around the grounds. They could laugh when he wheeled away, but they would never dare laugh to his face.

He stopped suddenly and backed up a foot away from a young boy. The engine idled, and he remained on the cushioned bench. The apprentice gardener glanced up with a potted plant in his hand.

"What kind of plant is that?" Wolfram asked in German. A blank expression etched his features. The boy didn't understand. Wolfram leaned over and smacked the boy in the face with his leather gloves. The boy didn't move, only stared with fear in his eyes.

Wolfram turned the wheel and drove toward the house. A better system was required for him to get the work from these men. Ian would calmly explain that Wolfram himself had requested workers who did not speak German. Wolfram wasn't even sure where these men had come from—Romania, Bosnia, Turkey perhaps. He hadn't cared at the time. All he wanted was men who would do the work for enough pay to mind their own business, not be able to talk to locals if they ever left the grounds, and could return without ever knowing the exact location of the castle. The money brought them and did its work. Wolfram knew he should be understanding—but if he wanted to know what kind of plant was stuck into his soil, he deserved an answer.

He drove around a wide stairway dressed with overflowing potted geraniums to the upper level and entrance of his house. Storming down the hallway, he intended to put some fear into his housekeepers. He loved the fear he saw in their eyes. They might complain and make threats about quitting behind his back, but they would do what he asked. Why? Because Wolfram had money. And money made people shut up and do what he asked.

As he passed the aviary built into one side of the hallway, Wolfram stopped to a gathering of chirping. The birds fluttered and hopped from the branches of the potted trees. Their water was full, but the food wasn't. He hadn't fed them yesterday.

"You need me, don't you?" he said in German. "I will feed you when I want."

He walked into his office. The room was warm and smelled of bird feces. The four cages in the corner sprung to life as he closed the door. These birds had water and food—he'd checked earlier that morning. Wolfram walked around his desk and sat in the overstuffed leather chair. He leaned his head back and rocked. As his mind sought possibilities for a better operation, he opened his eyes to stare at the birds.

Something about caged birds drew his fascination. He could watch the four cages, each of different height and volume, for hours. The largest cage held his newest recruit—one he'd watched and chosen from the larger aviary in the hall. The finches were in constant motion, chirping as they hopped and skipped from nest to perch to swing. He liked to see the progress of their movements from the small cage to the larger ones. Could birds be jealous? Did they watch the lone bird in the largest cage and want what it had? Did they peer at Wolfram with black, beady eyes and desire his freedom? He watched to discover—he'd been studying different species for years.

A psychoanalyst friend in Quito, Ecuador, found Wolfram's view on jealousy fascinating. Their discussions in smoky cafés were often long. But Wolfram believed the man was really more interested in the workings of Wolfram's mind than in the conversations about bird behavior. The friend once said, "Jealousy is never satisfied," as if to warn Wolfram. Wolfram agreed on the surface, but underneath he knew that nothing in life brought satisfaction, except in the pursuit of it. Jealousy fed his life; he'd admit it to anyone. But not his own jealousies.

Wolfram loved to pursue what others wanted. The birds wanted what he had; he knew by the way they watched him now.

He'd first discovered the power of jealousy long ago, and all because of Paris. Wolfram had never been to a city away from his own country other than Vienna. When he received the orders with Paris as his destination, he immediately wrote to his mother, telling her in words only she could understand. "Mother, you know the place you've dreamed of going—I will be there next week." It was a short assignment escorting a midlevel officer, but he'd be in Paris and at such a time. The grand city was no longer France's Paris, but Deutschland's. Germany's Paris. They had conquered their great rival.

Wolfram had had an afternoon to himself—the officer demanded privacy after meeting with a Frenchwoman of great beauty. Wolfram walked the Rue de Rivoli toward the narrow point of the Obelisk where he glimpsed the Eiffel Tower beyond. A surge of adrenaline pumped through him as he crossed the busy streets and then stood at the Place de la Concorde. The twenty-acre square with cars, cyclists, and German military driving round the outskirts was the heart of Paris. He turned a full circle—Eiffel Tower, Seine River with the Parliament rising over the bridge, gardens, and Musée de l'Orangerie containing Monet's treasures, the columns of La Madeleine. In the center island stood the shining gold-plated, 3,200-year-old Obelisk that had once adorned Luxor in Egypt before its gifting to France.

Wolfram breathed the autumn air that day in 1940. It amazed him to think that Napoleon had marched where his feet now walked. King Louis XVI had ordered the beheading of Austrian-born Marie Antoinette, along with a thousand others, at this place. Wolfram imagined the blood in the square stone grooves. This site was the pulse of France and her history. And Paris' heart, history, and future now belonged to the Nazis.

Wolfram peered down the long Champs-Elysées. It was not as busy as usual. People were afraid. At the far end of the long street was the boxy frame of the Arc de Triomphe. Parisian architects had designed the city well, with sweeping gardens that rose to meet monuments and framed entrances to palaces. Nazi banners waved everywhere. The French flag was nowhere in sight. Swastikas fluttered in the morning breeze to remind all Parisians that now they were German property.

Later he had explored the streets. He noticed an older woman wearing a scarf that reminded him of the one his mother wore when she went to market or to the theatre with his father. She claimed it was from Paris. She yearned for Paris and its fashion and must be quite envious of his journey here. Wolfram would buy her a new scarf and enjoy the questions she'd ask, trying to act like a doting mother rather than coveting every detail all to herself. She'd brag to her friends and display the scarf, but the jealous part of her would never forgive him for achieving her dream—something she'd never have.

Paris changed him. Wolfram knew that even as he explored the city. He saw what it meant to conquer and own what belonged to another and to have what someone else wanted. Never before had he possessed something in such a way. Germany possessed France. He was Germany. His mother's wish to see Paris—he possessed that too. It filled him with a strange yet great power. Later in the day, he had found his own Frenchwoman and had taken what he wanted from her.

Wolfram's return home did not give him the satisfaction he'd imagined. When he arrived with the scarf and postcards, his mother wasn't there. His father waited at the hospital, and the black-and-red scarf would soon be placed in her coffin. A mixture of alcohol with some medicines she was taking, they said. But Wolfram had discovered the truth. The Jewish doctor he'd forbidden his mother to see had killed her. The man must have given her the medicine before his deportation. He couldn't believe that someone as proud and strong as his mother could have made such a mistake. It was murder—it had to be. Wolfram was determined to find his mother's killer, even transferring his post to be a guard at Mauthausen, where he believed the doctor was sent. It had taken months to discover that the old man had died in the cattle car en route from Dachau to Mauthausen.

Wolfram inspected the precision neatness of his office— everything had a place now. The birds chattered, perhaps plotting a way to reach the larger cage or freedom itself.

Wolfram was meant to possess. That time in Paris had been the catalyst for what had lain dormant since his creation. Some were born to own, while others were born to be owned. It was part of the line of evolution. The strongest knocked the lowest from existence. It was how the human race had grown and survived. No cave dwellers remained—there was proof that the human animals must be destroyed. Hitler had seen it, though his greed had made him impatient for too much too soon, destroying what should have been the Germans. There would be new changes—very soon. Evolution was now in their hands—to choose what should be created or destroyed. The natural world had ordained it. Mankind would make it happen.

Wolfram looked outside. The gardens that swept in a straight line to the house must be completed.

And Lukas Johansen must be found.

CHAPTER TWENTY-FIVE

Jack walked the path his feet knew by heart. Every night he left his barrack home in darkness and returned in darkness. Tonight he slowly walked back with the dust of a mountain coating his clothes, skin, and throat, and clogging his ears.

Palov, the most outgoing member of the small manual-labor crew, shouted a good-bye. Jack had at first assumed he and the rest of the crew were locals, before he realized they spoke a Slavic language. He still didn't know if they'd been hired legally or if they'd been stolen from other salt mines. None of them spoke English or German, so Jack lifted his hand as their paths parted. Usually Palov made hand motions, asking Jack to drink beer with them as the shift ended. But Jack always had to smile and wave them on. It was clear they still didn't know he was captive here. Most likely they believed he was partners with Ian and free to quit the job and move on.

But tonight all the crew was tired. So Palov and the other three men plodded away toward their temporary housing in the crook of the mountain.

Jack was weary too. His back ached, and the holes in his boots kept filling with dirt and rocks. Jack imagined a hot shower, a sharp razor, and clean sheets to find rest in. It was maddening to think that he, Jack Porter, was actually being held prisoner. He worked and lived in a nighttime mountain paradise with the same constellations over his head that had been there all his life. When he remembered his prior world, it seemed impossible—surreal even—that this was happening to him. It was easier to surrender to the knowledge while inside his concrete room. Out here and during the hours of his workday, it was hard to comprehend that he could never go with Palov and the others, that he couldn't get on a boat and go home.

And yet it was so. The mountains and water became his jail cell, his family the lock that kept him inside.

Jack reached the barracks and entered the main hallway. Ian's door was open, and a light burned inside.

Ian met him as he passed. "Would you like a shower?"

Jack nodded, partially resenting that he must have permission, the other part thankful to not wait the four days until the weekly luxury. Ian unlocked the bathroom several rooms down and closed the door when Jack entered. The water was cold, the soap rough, and he couldn't stay under long. But he was clean.

Jack dried the hair that dripped down his back. The towel was thin and stuck to his body—it didn't smell fresh either. Several months had passed since Ian last granted a razor and scissors to him and Rudy. Jack dried his face and the short beard that was ever his annoyance and dressed in the same worn clothes he'd had beneath his work coveralls. A few raps at the locked door brought Ian back.

"We aren't making the necessary progress," Ian said when Jack emerged. A shiver ran down Jack's spine, and he longed for the wool blanket on his bed. He envied the thick red jacket Ian wore.

"We are doing everything we can," he said.

"It may not be enough." Ian disappeared into his room. Jack heard a television and had the strong urge to see it. Instead he turned toward the hall and basement stairs.

The light blared a one-hundred-watt glow over his head. Jack was cold all the way through and now regretted the shower. He wrapped himself in the blanket and sat at the small wooden table, hoping the bulb would add some heat to the room. He glanced at the vent in the bottom corner of the room and wondered how Rudy fared beyond the cement-block wall. Rudy's health was improving too slowly. Jack hoped summer would get rid of the plaguing cough and allow him to gain weight and strength before another winter.

"Now I'm making plans for my future here," he whispered in disgust. His voice sounded strange in the room, as if the walls muffled the words as soon as they were spoken.

From beneath his bed, Jack brought out a pen and paper. He stared at the paper. A week had passed since he'd last written—since the day the photographs had arrived. He had returned to those images each morning he awoke as a reminder of the reality he'd now entered. Tonight he would write again. The blank pages awaited his words.

The first page should be easy to write. It was the throwaway page that would be read while he worked. Jack had discovered the way to keep his supply of paper and pens from being taken. If his letters were amusing or if his readers thought he'd reveal something, they would allow him to write, providing ink pens and soft, onionskin paper. They believed he didn't know. Jack always left a single hair on the stack of fake letters. It was often gone upon his return. Jack had begun to play their game, even though their rules changed often.

He couldn't think of the words he would leave to be read. Instead he went straight to the ones he could only be rid of once they were there on the page. His pen touched the paper, paused, and then moved quickly.

> *I have lost count of the days, but I think it is toward the end of May. I will ask Rudy the date next time we speak; he never loses a day. I have not written you for a while. There is little left for me to say. My writings to you have given me strength and hope to continue. Now I know I am only a shadow of what I once was. Once I was a man with definitions and characteristics I could describe. This place has taken that away.*
>
> *Now I know that I wanted you to wait for me, even if I was only bones in the ground. I wanted to be the lone thought in your head. I wanted what we shared to be strong enough to bring us together again. This is the part of me so filled with self. It shames me to admit, but I want you to long for me as I long for you. I have labored over the possibilities and tried to turn time back. If only I would have gone with you that morning in Venice. I won't say those words again. Right now you are sleeping, somewhere around the world. You do not know that I am alive or that I write you as I once would explain my day after Abbie had fallen asleep. I wish I could hear of your days again. But now I write my last letter to you. My own desire for you must be released. I must love you enough.*
>
> *God perhaps will choose to use us as individuals now. We must believe in him instead of the love we once shared. Our love is only strong through him. And I will love you forever. But I must be free from you as you are free from me. Perhaps then I will find a way out. Good-bye, Kate.*

He leaned back in the chair and decided he would destroy this letter. The writing of it was necessary, but he would not want to see it again.

"Jack," came a whisper mixed with a round of muffled coughs.

He flipped off the light and crawled to the vent in the wall. "I'm here," he whispered.

"How did it go tonight?"

Jack laid the blanket on the floor and stretched over it with his ear close to the ridges of the vent. "Not great, according to Ian. We could use you."

"It's bad when I miss the tunnels. This room is driving me crazy. Any thoughts of another dive for you and Ian?"

"Possibly. Get better and we'll talk about it."

"I'm trying." Rudy paused. His voice sounded different when he spoke again. "I've been thinking that, in a sense, this is my fault. Jack, they chose you because of me. They found a recommendation I wrote about you, and they made contact."

"I can't believe you'd say that."

"But the correspondence was what convinced them that you were the one. We would work well together, and your family would keep you here."

"You've been in that room too long. It's my turn to encourage *you*, I see."

"I don't need encouragement. What I want to ask is that you'll forgive me."

"There's nothing to forgive."

"It would give me peace just to know."

"Then I forgive you." Jack leaned his head against the vent. "Now, good rest."

"Good rest."

Back on his cot, Jack considered Ian's words. The operation was a failure so far. But Jack suddenly knew what they sought. It *was* the underwater cave that he'd found. They believed it was inside the mountain—their molelike diggings were in hopes of finding it. The salt mine had produced little—Palov and his men worked in a field they did not know. It was all for show, while Ian, Jack, and sometimes Rudy worked in the tunnels forbidden to the other men. Jack spent his nights mapping and searching old tunnels for anything left behind by the previous occupants. Ian would study those maps and the few objects Jack had found. The greatest excitement had come when they found the underground spring.

He bolted upright. It wasn't an underground spring as he suspected. They had reached a section of the cave. Jack tossed off the blanket and began to pace. If this was true, then the cave went deeper than he'd imagined. He could hold the key to what these men wanted. It could be his chance out.

⋅⊱≡◦⊂≡⊰⋅

The sun sought to scorch the skin on his face and neck as he stood on the end of the dock, staring across the waters pocked with waves. Wolfram lowered his hat over his face to shade his eyes. Two boats secured to the dock knocked gently against the bumpers. Wolfram would enjoy a ride in the large cruiser back to civilization. He'd been secluded too long and missed the outside world of noise and constant activity. The quiet of mountains and lakes brought too many voices from the past sliding into his thoughts.

It won't be long, he promised himself. The castle grounds were nearly complete. The remodeling of buildings and the castle expansion were nearly finished. If the other work could be completed, he would be free from this place and his future secured.

"I want to own a mountain," his father had once said. A young Wolfram had watched from the slight crack in the cupboard, where he'd crept to escape his father's unpredictable rage. The boy watched in both fear and awe as his father settled himself into the chair—his legs spread wide and hands behind his head. Wolfram's mother had given him a cup of coffee on a silver tray with a silver milk server. She never lacked in detail. He watched his father pull at his mother's dress and wrap his hand around her thin leg.

"What would you do with a mountain?" his mother asked, slapping his hand.

"I would own something great," he said, and with one swoop he swept Wolfram's mother onto his lap, toppling the silver tray. She was angry and he laughed as she cleaned up the mess. But his father would never own a mountain or anything else for very long. He would end his life a pauper with every investment gone wrong.

A crisp wind blew from the water, and Wolfram walked from the wooden dock with steps slow and heavy. What made him remember that moment from his past? He had many memories from within that hideaway where he had found safety and could spy without being found. But only that one memory when his father put his claim on a mountain came to mind now. Wolfram had forgotten that. He usually kept those memories locked away. He was no longer that weak and timid child. He was no longer the son of a man whose anger destroyed his own life.

"Father, I *do* own a mountain," Wolfram whispered.

On the side of one mountain was the entrance to what had once been a salt mine. The one thing he'd never owned now waited somewhere in that mountain or in one of the surrounding ones. Though he was close, he knew patience was required. Yet it ground at his nerves that after so many years, he was this close but not close enough.

At least no one else knew the secret that only the highest-ranking Nazis had long ago ordained. Wolfram had made a careful examination of that fact in the last decades. Ernst, the one man Wolfram had tracked in Argentina, a Nazi in hiding as he was, had worked in the operations offices. He had the maps of three locations but was unsure which one had finally been chosen as the top secret location. Wolfram promised they would work together and build a Fourth Reich. But Ernst proved himself not as loyal as he claimed. In the end, Wolfram had the maps without the use of a trustworthy partner. At first he had thought he could find the location without the blue tile. He now knew this was the site, the other two locations distractions, but a year here had proven his need for the five pieces that made up the tile.

If not for that witch, he would have succeeded long ago. Wolfram had planned everything with precision. He'd bargained with one camp inmate at a time—food for information. They had eagerly told their stories, not only for survival but for a chance to betray the officers and guards who held them. His work paid off, and he found the inmate who would be used in the delivery of goods to the secret location in the Alps.

Wolfram could find pleasure in the memories of his work. His commanding officers had never suspected him of having intelligence beyond working as a guard. As the war ended, he saw the need to use extreme caution in everything he did. The time had come for such precision planning again.

He reached the white golf cart and paused to gaze above the gardens, beyond the castle and past the groves of pines and birches. Hidden behind the trees was the flat roof of the barrack. They were sleeping now—Rudy and Jack. He would work them harder. He'd find Lukas Johansen and Oskar Gogl.

This time he would succeed.

CHAPTER TWENTY-SIX

Jack's eyes could not adjust even though he stood in the shadows. They had grown stronger in the darkness, but full sunshine pierced even his squinted lids. Ian waited beside him as Jack rubbed his eyes and tried to think why he was leaving the bunker during the daytime hours and where he could be going.

The diggings had yielded little. Over the past year, he'd progressed through a cave, found objects both from the WWII era and others possibly of Roman and Celtic origin. Yet everything was quickly taken away, making an analysis impossible. Had he failed and was now to face the wrath of those who held him? Ian gave no warning, but he never did. Jack thought of ways to make himself and Rudy valuable—that was the key to survival.

Ian checked his watch and motioned for Jack to follow. Jack could barely open his eyes once he left the afternoon shadows. How ironic that the sunlight he'd longed for now killed his eyes. With every step along the wooded path, Jack's forebod-

ing grew. He recalled well his first six months of imprison-
ment. Would he meet those two men again—the only two men
he had depended upon for life? They had enjoyed their role as
gods, taunting him and promising every harm imaginable.
They knew about Kate and Abbie and liked to tell stories of
women and children they'd met and abused. Jack knew they
were mostly stories and that the photographs were probably
archives, but the words and images worked at him despite his
own logic.

Jack stopped along the stone pathway beneath the shade of a
birch tree. He waited for Ian to turn toward him. "What is this,
Ian?"

"Come."

"What should I expect?"

Ian said nothing, which concerned him even more. Perhaps
they knew about the underwater cave. Or could they have
done something to Kate or Abbie? Jack could feel his strength
drain and panic spring into the empty spaces.

"God, help me," he whispered to himself. With these words,
peace fell over him—an actual, true peace even in this moment. Jack realized this could be his walk to death, his last
moments in the sunshine. Fear tried to inject its sting, but
something stronger took it away. He was no longer afraid of
leaving this world.

The woods opened and the curved path joined a wide walkway flanked by gardens all the way to the water's edge on his
left. They moved upward, with the dock and shoreline behind
them, toward a large white mansion remodeled from the
framework of a castle. He'd seen only glimpses of the house
through the trees, its roofline from the mountain entrance
above, its dark outline during the midnight dives. Now he
could see where the original structure, a stone turret and
walls, joined the remodeled section. It was huge and grand,

forcing him to realize the monetary resources of those who kept him here. Money such as this meant power.

They ascended stone stairs, headed across a cobbled square and then up another set of stairs through the front double doors. Jack walked with his shoulders straight. They would not destroy his spirit today. The door creaked, long and loud, as it opened. Jack heard the birds before he saw them. The long hallway, with its tall ceiling and magnificent rooms opening through different doorways, seemed designed for the giant at the top of a beanstalk—he was definitely Jack. Everything was bigger than necessary, yet the rooms were silent.

As they passed a mirror, Jack caught the reflection of a stranger walking with Ian. A haunted man with circles beneath his eyes and chin and cheekbones narrowed from weight loss stared back. His hair had more gray, and he appeared nearly fifty when he'd yet to hit forty. This man was not the Jack Porter he once greeted in the morning mirror. The sight of himself stole some of his confidence. Waiting at the end of the hallway, Ian motioned for Jack, knocked lightly on the door, then opened it.

Jack's eyes had weathered the full brightness of day and then the dull light of the hall. Now he entered a study where sunshine streamed through the open French doors at the opposite end. As they walked through the room, Jack took in a few details until the television caught his eye. He recognized Larry King on CNN—the first news he'd seen besides scraps of outdated papers in three years. Jack smiled as he passed it, somehow believing that God had given him that glimpse as encouragement.

Through the open doors, they approached a man sitting at a white patio table. Even from the back, Jack could tell he was old and was surprised by his age. As they moved around, he studied the face that perused a newspaper. He must be over seventy, perhaps even eighty. But there was pride and strength about him in his straight posture and air of royalty about his large head. His hair, thick and brushed straight back, was dyed black, and he had large sideburns. A tailored suit fit well over his large frame, the tie smooth beneath a dinner jacket. They were at a secluded estate, yet this man dressed impeccably for his afternoon soup. Obviously his polished shoes had not walked in the dust or the gravel outside. As he leaned forward to sip his soup, he touched his tie.

Jack had expected a compound of terrorists, neo-Nazis, or anti-American forces. He'd spent hours trying to discover who these people were and what they were after. Yet he had seen no one along the paths outside or in the rooms within the house. Jack peered back into the room and around the private garden for the faces he expected. There was no two-way mirror or camera with an eye on him. Could he really have been kept here all this time, not by the great "them" he had imagined, but by this "him"?

Jack knew there had been at least three men who'd entered his hotel room in Venice. In seconds they were inside, and he was unconscious from some object to the head. There had been other men when he was transferred to different locations. Where were these men now? An old man sipping his soup brought an absurdity to his struggle.

Jack fought the instant shame. This man, this old and crumbling man, could not have destroyed his life, caused his family and himself immense pain, forced him to live in the night and work within the walls of a mountain. He could not be held captive by the desire of this lone man. Could he?

Without acknowledging Jack's presence, the man took a long drink. As he drank, his long earlobes moved. The man leaned back and stared for a long time. Another drink, another stare. How could older people stare as if seeing something behind their own eyes? Was that how great plots were discovered? Perhaps that was why they kept him at exhaustion level—so as not to drift into the places where the mind made most anything possible.

At last the old man spoke, but in German. The reason for Ian became clear. He was the interpreter. "Come forward," he said through Ian.

Jack moved in front of him. The dark eyes that studied him made him self-conscious. He realized this was part of the game. The loss of every small convenience cut into his human dignity. This crotchety old man enjoyed a sunny afternoon and used Jack as a pawn. Yet Jack felt no fear, none at all. He felt stronger than he had in a long time.

The man spoke and waited for the translation, then continued. "Your work here is almost done. You will want to go home then."

Jack tried to ignore the tinge of hope that stirred. There was no home to go to, he reminded himself. It had all changed. This man had done his work well. He'd fed Jack hope until the end came near; then reality was his destruction. His family had moved on, so there was nothing else for him but this. That was what this man wanted him to believe. Without Jack's faith beyond understanding or logic, this man would have succeeded.

God, give me strength. Tell me what to do and say. I need the will to fight and be strong for whatever future you have for me.

"My name is Wolfram Meizer," he said through Ian, then waited for a reaction. "I am your captor, your king, if you will." As he motioned for Jack to sit across from him, he smiled.

"Why did you bring me here, Wolfram Meizer?" Jack sat in the chair while Ian remained standing.

"You are here to be my hands. To do as I tell you and move where I want you to go."

"No, why am I here at this table right now?"

"I wanted to see you in person. I want to tell you how

important it is for your work to succeed—and soon. Your work must get finished, Jack Porter. I wonder if I can trust your work."

"What will happen to me after I finish your work? And to Rudy?"

"Rudy does not get better and cannot work. What good is he to me now?"

"Rudy is essential," Jack said, anxiety rising. He would need to protect Rudy. "I am unable to work without Rudy."

"If you neglect your work, Rudy may be neglected also."

"What if I find it?"

"It?"

"The secret I'm supposed to find without knowing what it is."

"You will have freedom."

"I do not believe you."

It took a moment for Wolfram to get the translation. It made him laugh. "You do not have to believe me," Wolfram said in English.

"I have no choice, you mean."

"*Ja, ja, das ist* it. No choice."

Yet Jack *did* have some power over this man who sat with such confidence. He now knew the discovery of the cave was the best thing that had happened to him in three years.

It became the new routine. Jack would work through the night in the salt mine, return to the bunker and sleep, to be later awakened and brought to the house. Wolfram would be in his office or his smoking room or on the patio with his afternoon meal. He always sipped his soup from the same white bowl and drank his coffee from the same white cup, with saucers under each. Every day he ignored Jack's presence for the first several minutes, then he would wave him forward at a given time. Jack would sit down and Wolfram would stare into other places. Jack had the feeling Wolfram precisely planned not just each and every moment of his own life, but of Jack's and Rudy's lives also.

On Jack's fourth visit, when Wolfram turned his attention his way, Jack said boldly, "I would like a Bible."

"In English, I suppose."

"Yes." Jack nodded.

Wolfram spoke to Ian, who left the patio for the office. He returned a few moments later with a thick, leather-bound Bible in English and handed it to Jack. Why would he have such an item? Jack wondered.

"Anything else?"

Jack paused, a bit taken back. "Oswald Chambers' book *My Utmost for His Highest* and a John Grisham novel—one of his most recent ones. And a razor." Jack then realized what he should be asking for. "Most of all, some antibiotics for Rudy, if not a doctor to see him."

Wolfram spoke and Ian responded, "He wants you to write it down. He says you are good at writing." Wolfram gave a sly smile. Jack relished the fact that Wolfram thought he had surprised him, as if Jack didn't already know about the letters.

The next day Jack brought the paper with his requests. He'd added pears and oranges to his list for both himself and Rudy. Rudy had once said how much he missed eating pears to the point that he prayed every night for some. Jack had smiled as he wrote *pears* on the list. God did have mysterious ways.

Fatigue was becoming a great enemy. Wolfram seemed to forget Jack needed rest, especially with the increased pressure to finish the project. Ian's weekly work schedule pushed the diggings beyond dangerous. They used explosives more often. Jack made plans to smuggle some into the barracks, but Ian inventoried them after every shift.

Despite the weariness he fought, Jack looked forward to his time with Wolfram. The old man seemed to find pleasure in talking to Jack. Sometimes he'd speak about nothing of importance: his annoyance about an area of his gardens where pansies had died from an unexpected frost, or the overload of advertisements on television. But mixed within these mostly one-sided conversations were bits and pieces of the Wolfram Meizer Jack was interested in deciphering.

As evening fell, Jack would return to the barrack and record Wolfram's words. Every day he tabulated the little phrases. He hid these pages inside a ripped part of the lining beneath the cot—something he could do against his captor. Through the bits of conversations, day after day, Jack discovered who held him and why. He scanned the record of their conversations and began to understand the mind of Wolfram Meizer.

> *May 31*
>
> *Wolfram talked and stared, and I wondered if he sometimes forgets I'm there. He'd comment on something on CNN, and I realized how he uses it to work on his English. Often he gets the news story completely wrong. It's strange having Ian speak his words for him. I often wonder why Wolfram repeats some things. Some of his words today: "Man must be of value or there is no value of him living."*
>
> *There was a CNN story on former Yugoslavia that sparked his interest. He said, "We almost won, you know. The tunnels were being dug, and we needed a little more time. Did you know the technology we were gaining?"*
>
> *June 1*
>
> *Nothing of importance today. We sat in his smoking room. The newly remodeled walls are already tinged with the scent of smoke. He puffed on his cigar and wanted to hear about my work in the States.*

June 2

Wolfram said, "In Gusen, a camp near the Danube River, we had planes built. And all underground."

June 3

There is more than I can remember from my conversation with Wolfram today. I'll write what I can recall. It was like getting a whole view inside his mind. I don't believe Ian had heard Wolfram speak about these things before. That in itself is a concern. Does Ian wonder why Wolfram gives me so much? I wonder.

We were in his office, and CNN showed a refugee camp in former Yugoslavia. The video made Wolfram lean forward in his chair.

After a lengthy stare, he spoke. "If we had one cold night, they died like rodents eating poison. They were animals, licking soup that dripped onto the filthy floor. They broke every rule and deserved punishment. It is their fault we lost the war. Did you know that?"

I asked who he spoke of.

"The Jews, Italians, Poles, criminals, and weaklings."

"Weren't they starving?"

"You should see what people do when they don't have food."

"I can understand a little."

He ignored my comment and continued. "We must look toward the larger picture. I once had a commanding officer with this great career who became obsessed with finding a family heirloom. It was some coins and a brooch that belonged to the Austrian Empress Sissi. He would not give up when he could have saved himself at the end of the war. Instead of making preparations to leave Europe, he kept searching. Ridiculous. Many people were killed because he couldn't get it."

"He never found this heirloom?" I asked.

"No. One part was found by the family not long ago, but the brooch is still missing. I saw one woman die at a camp over that brooch, and there were others also. Even the officer died in his pursuit."

There were other comments that I'll try to remember and add later.

June 5

It's strange how these years around Ian—though he usually speaks perfect English, and I think he speaks several languages fluently—and with Rudy's bits of German, now I can sometimes understand Wolfram before Ian translates. Ian did not come for me until it was time to work again. The rest was needed. But Wolfram said nothing of importance to record, except I did see the video screens of our rooms in a cabinet when we passed through the office. The door hadn't been closed all the way, but I pretended not to see.

June 6

Wolfram was full of thoughts today. "Hitler lost his genius to gluttony. He gobbled too much and it destroyed us. It will be different the next time."

I didn't respond, so he looked me in the eyes when he said, "The armies prepare around the world. You must know where to align. The hatred of men as well as their loves can be used to make them do nearly anything."

June 7

Today I asked if Wolfram had ever let any of his birds free. He stared at them in their bizarre, different-shaped cages—with one bird in the largest cage, and four in the smallest. He said, "Once I let a little bird go to see what it would do. But it didn't know how to fly anymore. I let the cat inside. It would have died anyway."

June 8

  For the first time I saw true fear in Wolfram's face. He was talking about the Jews, trying to convince me of the truth of an international plot. He said, "They are not human. They just look like it on the outside. Don't ever let them fool you."

  Suddenly he faced me as if he was looking at me for the first time. "You not Juden?"

  I wanted to say yes just to give him a scare, see him choke on his soup.

  Ian spoke before I could decide. "Nein, Papa."

  I did not know if I'd heard Ian correctly. I asked, "He is your father?"

  "Yes. He is my father."

  Now much more is clear about Ian.

  I'm writing what even seems of small significance. Perhaps this will be for a purpose I don't yet know. Tomorrow I'm to get a tour of the remodeled castle. Rudy confirms that this is good—it's giving us knowledge that will be useful. I keep wondering why. Why is this happening now? I think it is perhaps a bored Wolfram who likes to play with our minds. But I also think he is getting quite desperate to find what is in the mountain. I pray before I leave my room and hope these bizarre meetings will produce a way to escape.

CHAPTER TWENTY-SEVEN

Wolfram went through the plans one final time. The last phase of the grounds' development was days away from completion. His contacts in the States had located Oskar Gogl living comfortably in Maine. Lukas Johansen would not be difficult to track down.

He stretched and checked his watch again. There were several hours before Jack Porter would arrive. The hours with the man were amusing. Jack continually tried to understand him and seek a way to freedom. The young man could find no peace in his position. And Jack wasn't telling the entire truth about his explorations; Wolfram had that feeling the more they spoke. There was not enough fear in Jack Porter's eyes— that was the proof.

Wolfram walked to the kitchen to see what his housekeeper was preparing. He rarely saw the older woman. Hilde was paid well and needed little time away. She adhered to his stringent rules, and he'd never caught her in even the smallest infraction. She had been well trained long ago.

Hilde looked up, surprised to see him in the kitchen. His feet thundered over the stone floor.

"*Grüß Gott,*" she said softly as she kneaded some bread dough. Her arms were thin and her sleeves pulled up.

"*Grüß Gott,*" Wolfram replied. He noted that Ian had brought a white bag of medicines, pears, and oranges from his morning trip to town, which brought a smile to his face. That made him wonder about the mail, so he left the kitchen and walked to the sideboard by the front door. Wolfram went through the bills and catalogs. Then he saw a large envelope with a return address from an acquaintance in Vienna. Inside he found a note from the man and an unopened letter. The letter had been sent to Wolfram in care of this man, who had forwarded it on to his village mailbox.

Intrigued, he opened the letter and met the words of Bruno Weiler. His hands began to shake. The memories returned with the rising of his rage. In a mad swoop he cast the mail onto the floor and slammed his hand through the mirror on the wall. Blood gushed from the wound as he crumpled the page in his fist.

Bruno—or Lukas—his old betrayer wanted a fight. And Bruno Weiler would get his desire.

Never say you've come to the end of the way,
Though leaden skies blot out the light of the day.
The hour we all long for will surely appear—
Our steps will thunder with the words: We are here!

In blood this song was written, and not with pen or quill,
Not from a songbird freely flying as he will.
Sung by a people crushed by falling wall—
Sung with guns in hand, by those whom freedom calls!

From "Zog Nit Keyn Mol" ("Never Say")
Written by Hirsh Glick in the Vilno Ghetto of Poland (April 1943)

part *three*

Some call this island the World's End,
for though you can sail further,
this is the beginning of the end. . . .

—C. S. Lewis, *The Voyage of the "Dawn Treader"*

CHAPTER TWENTY-EIGHT

Rain streamed down the car windows like so many tears Kate had yet to cry. She'd held the tears inside, not shedding one in the weeks of May and June as she prepared to leave her world behind. Her cottage home was now behind her, awaiting the couple who would house-sit for the summer.

She was going to Europe. Suddenly, in a confusing flurry, the time had come. Abbie was quiet as they left Corvalis, Oregon, and headed for California, where Kate would leave her daughter with her parents and catch her flight. The idea of parting had caused them both much anxiety.

"Do you think Reece understands I'm not going to Australia?" Kate asked.

Abbie smiled bravely and even giggled. "I don't think so. A few days before school ended I had my last e-mail lab. There was a note from Reece. He wants you to get him a postcard of a koala bear and a kangaroo."

"I'll get an atlas out and show him where Austria is."

"I know—like the bologna between the bread of Germany and Italy—that's what Grandpa told me."

"Grandpa is very wise."

Kate guided her SUV from Highway 34 to join the flow of faster traffic on Interstate 5 South. Connie called Kate on the cell phone three times with questions about her trip. What she really was trying to say was finally said on the last call.

"Okay, it's just that I won't know what to do without you. I'm joining this summer Bible study and I wanted you to do it too. And summer swim club and everything. But then I'm also so proud of you and excited and—I mean, Europe for the summer! This is amazing! But, of course, I won't say a word to anyone. I love you, my friend."

Kate said the same and they hung up—again. For the thousandth time she wondered if this was a mistake. It helped to have her family's support and also Marta's, who called a few times a week with new thoughts about Kate's trip.

Kate's realization weeks ago in Cottonwood had started a domino effect that made this trip possible. Abbie was out of school by the beginning of June. Kate's most faithful customer, Mrs. Charles, bought several pieces Kate had previously refused to part with, providing the money for the summer in Europe. Kate's father would manage Restorations from afar, with Connie as his contact and bookkeeper after she decided to close her in-home day care—the smashed marshmallows under their pillows had been the last straw. Trudy had asked for more summer hours before Kate could even approach her. It all worked out—and this time Kate didn't write it off as coincidence.

Marta warned Kate to keep her destination a secret from all but her closest friends. Kate had anticipated that, yet many people's suspicions would mount unless she planned something. She could hear the rumors otherwise: "She's spending

the summer in Europe? I thought she struggled financially."
Or, "Always expected to see something suspicious from her."

Kate wanted to divert attention without lies. If the need
arose, Kate would say she needed to get away, and Abbie
wanted to spend time with her grandparents. She'd said it a
few times and then hurried away or changed the subject. Time
moved so quickly that few people had asked.

Then Mason had arrived at her doorstep a few days ago.
"You've been vague on the telephone when you actually do
return my calls. Every weekend you've been busy, and now I
hear from Jane that your mom is ill and you're moving there
for the summer, possibly for good, and Connie might take
over the shop. Kate, what's going on?"

She invited him inside, but he didn't move so she came out
on the porch.

"Is there any truth to this?"

"Not much. But I am leaving for a month or so. I meant to
tell you, but it just never seemed right. So I've avoided you."

"At least you're honest." He wore a grim expression she'd
rarely seen. "You're still searching for him."

"I have some things to get together in my life."

"What happened to us?"

The words they'd spoken at the restaurant seemed long
ago—before finding the blue tile, before meeting Lukas and
Marta, before going to California, where she'd found the
strength to seek Jack one more time. Kate hadn't forgotten that
she and Mason were supposed to be testing the waters to see if
a relationship was possible between them. She'd just avoided
it—and him. Now she knew how unfair that had been.

"I'm sorry. But it was too soon."

He looked at the ground. "So where are you going?"

She bit her thumbnail, and he waited for her answer.
"Europe," she said. "I met some people who are helping me
find out what happened."

Mason shook his head. "Kate, when will you understand? He wasn't the man you've turned him into."

"What do you mean? Tell me that you saw him with another woman or that he behaved differently behind my back. If you can say that, then perhaps I can believe you. Perhaps it will change my mind."

"I can't say those things. But you've made him into a saint by this memory you cling to. He wasn't a saint or some hero. He was a man, just like I am. Life is worth living, Kate. You can't live forever in the past."

"I need to know. I've prayed for answers, and now this opportunity has come."

"It tells me a lot that you didn't come to me."

"You aren't a part of this." He was hurt by her words, but Kate knew it was the truth. This was her path to be taken without him. She studied his face and the hand that rubbed his chin. Kate realized Mason didn't have the rough hands she often yearned to hold her; his were long and soft and beautiful hands, but they weren't the ones she longed for. She needed Jack.

"I'll be here when you return," he said gently.

"Don't wait for me any longer."

"There's nothing else I can do," he said, forcing the words through his teeth.

"That isn't true."

"Do you care for me?"

"Very much." She reached for him, then pulled her hand away. "I think . . . I mean, I believe we could have loved one another if our lives weren't these lives. Does that make sense?"

"No. It makes no sense at all."

"You don't want it to. I think you've known it all along."

He nodded after a few moments. "Good-bye, Kate. I'll be here when you return."

"Mason, don't wait for me. I can't say what tomorrow will bring, and you need to walk your own path."

Kate had watched him until his car disappeared down the street. He was behind her now, left with everything else she'd known for so long. She'd settled into a life sans Jack and was just getting familiar, even comfortable, with the prospect of a future. Now Kate had chosen to cast it aside for a great unknown. But she wasn't alone. God would be with her every step and mile and continent ahead.

⋯≡◉≡⋯

Kate had one full day before she left her family and child behind. She could tell that her mother worried, but both her parents supported her decision. Her brother wanted to come with her, but Kate wouldn't take him from his own family. She'd call if help was required, and Tayler had already applied for a passport just in case.

While everyone else in the house was tucked into their beds, Kate sat on the bed and opened her Bible beneath the round glow of the butterfly lamp that had been hers as a kid. She started turning to the book of Colossians, but her eye was caught by words in the Old Testament book of 2 Samuel. She read of King David and the death of his infant son. David had been heartbroken, but one of his statements echoed through Kate again and again: *"I will go to him one day, but he cannot return to me."* She realized that whatever had happened to Jack, he could not come to her. But she would go to him—be it on earth or in heaven.

Abbie rolled toward her and mumbled something in her sleep. She smacked her mouth softly, then was still again. Kate watched her daughter, with her hands folded beneath her cheek, and knew that she couldn't leave her behind.

It would be morning in Austria, Kate calculated, so she

grabbed the address book from her purse. Kate tramped to the darkened kitchen for the phone and punched in the long series of numbers before she could talk herself out of it.

A woman whose voice she didn't recognize answered the phone in a flurry of German. Kate asked for Marta and the woman grumbled something else, then set the phone down with a clatter. Moments passed before Marta came to the phone.

"I have to bring Abbie," Kate said quickly. "We'll rent a bungalow or whatever you have over there."

Marta chuckled. "It will be wonderful to have a little girl in this house. We could all use it."

"Lukas won't be so welcoming. He isn't happy with me, so how will he handle a child? If he isn't nice to her—"

"Don't worry, Kate. I will prepare Lukas. You make the arrangements. Does she have a passport?"

"Yes. We got her one after Jack—in case he was ever found and we needed to come over. I brought it to my parents' with me."

"You have known this for a while then?"

"No, though I guess I hoped. Could it be dangerous for her?"

"I do not believe it any more dangerous than leaving her there. We are safe in Lukas' home. We have made few plans and will make the rest when you arrive. But she will stay here with me if you need to go anywhere we have concerns. Or you will stay here. Or perhaps you fly her home if it is difficult. Anyway, bring the girl, and we will establish the details after your arrival."

"Thank you, Marta."

Hours passed without sleep. Kate read her Bible and then a new novel that she'd bought for the plane ride, though she should be reading more about WWII and the Nazis. She turned off the light, but her mind wouldn't relax. Doubts came with the darkness. Should she take Abbie? What would it be like to return to Europe? Kate considered calling Mason in the morning to say good-bye. She'd certainly call Connie. What should she bring for Abbie on the plane? Her daughter's birthday was coming—should they come home or celebrate it without family? What was Kate thinking? This entire trip was pure insanity. Her entire life was being disrupted, and for what? Possible answers?

Kate wrestled with her thoughts, something she'd done often but did even more so tonight. At last she gave up and remembered to pray. She prayed for herself and for tomorrow. Then she went through the list of her family and friends, trying hard to remember what each was experiencing. It made her realize how consumed she'd been with her own life. But she continued to pray for even the unknown in their lives. For Aunt Gerdie's late-life crisis and Mason's future and on through the rows of faces she saw in the darkness. And sleep finally came.

CHAPTER TWENTY-NINE

Lukas had settled into his old routine at home. Messages, appointments, and mail had awaited former minister Lukas Johansen. He worked through them, feeling needed and productive again. Marta spent hours on the computer, making arrangements to sell her Arizona house and get her mostly boxed-up possessions into storage. She also organized for Kate's arrival.

He could feel the tension in his daughter Anni at the idea of having a stranger with free decision-making power in the house. Anni had become quite comfortable in the house she'd never lived in as a child. It had been three years since he had allowed her to move in. Marta was sensitive to the young woman, but Anni had never been easy to manage, and Lukas had never been good at talking to any of his daughters, especially Anni. But in all, he was happy to be home. Home was like a nice slow pipe after a hectic day. And the weeks in the States had been more than hectic.

Back in his element, Lukas had decisions to make. He had

invitations to teach at several universities—Innsbruck was closest. The publisher for his book deal had left several messages. His retirement years were supposed to be this way. Years ago the political buzz had pointed toward his appointment as chancellor of Austria. After all, he had worked well under Chancellor Kreisky's administration from 1970 to the early 1980s. Austria had experienced years of growth despite the scandals that never fled political life. Jewish Chancellor Kreisky was criticized for appointing wartime Nazis into his cabinet, but no one in government knew Lukas could be counted among their ranks. Lukas understood Kreisky's desire to unify Austria and to put the past behind, though Lukas also found it intriguing that, decades earlier, Kreisky had been forced to flee Austria because of the men he appointed as cabinet members. Sometimes Lukas would gaze around at his colleagues and realize he was sitting in a room of former enemies. They would have killed Kreisky under orders of the Third Reich. At the beginning of the war, Lukas guarded men like Kreisky; and by the end of the war, he would have killed these ex-Nazis. Now they worked together for the good of a new Austria—whatever that meant to each of them.

The political climate shifted away from Lukas when the Social Democrats lost a majority and a coalition government formed. It didn't bother him because politics were his life now, but he wouldn't accept the position of chancellor, not with his past. Though his secrets were well covered, he'd seen skeletons escape closets that had seemed to be shut tight. Someone in that position would be very carefully scrutinized, especially after the President Waldheim scandal. Waldheim had claimed he had no knowledge of his unit's atrocities, but few believed him. Lukas quietly backed those who wanted him brought up on war crimes. The Waldheim case deserved to be looked at. Lukas knew colleagues who had an old Nazi Party badge— most everyone joined during the late 1930s when *Nazi* meant being the political favorite. Later a Party number was practically necessary for survival. But this wasn't simple politics or even service in the German army. Waldheim was an Austrian president who had been a Nazi SS in the Death's Head Division—and the members of Death's Head served their name well. Waldheim's and Austria's images were tarnished in the eyes of the world. For Austria, it wouldn't be the first time or the last.

But Lukas always stepped back when the scandals came. Sometimes he expected a bony finger to point at him. His benefactors who helped after his prison time had instructed him carefully, even paid for minor facial alterations. But Lukas would still feel fear rise when an unexpected camera appeared in his face. Why he was spared, he didn't know. His work in the Austrian Resistance perhaps helped, or maybe his skeletons were truly buried deep.

Lukas was out of the political arena now. He missed Vienna enough to still travel there often. Marta had been to Vienna only a few times as a teenager. They'd go for a week soon and he'd show her everything.

He made mental plans in front of the fire one evening. The Kunsthistorisches Museum, home to some of the world's finest art, would be high on the list and the Hofburg Palace, where once the imperial Habsburgs ruled the Austro-Hungarian Empire. Some summer festivals had started already, performing his favorite operas at the renowned Vienna Music Festival that drew the world's wealthiest and most influential guests. Soon enough he would show Marta everything.

Kate Porter was due to arrive in a few days. Lukas wished they'd already taken one trip to Vienna. Once the American woman came, it would be time to concentrate on what he'd been avoiding since his return.

A fire blazed in the living-room fireplace. Lukas sat in his wing-backed chair and sipped the coffee Marta brought him.

She sat in a chair beside him, staring into the flames. He wanted to ask how she was doing, but instead he tried to watch and gauge her progress. Her adaptation appeared to be going well. Marta hadn't known how much she'd missed the Alps, she said. Now Lukas found little jars of wildflowers around the house, though he'd yet to catch her in the act. One morning he'd found the flowers outside his door.

From the corner of his eye he saw that she was still deep in thought. In their short time together, he was amazed at how comfortable he felt talking to her, even if their discussions led to disagreements. There'd been no one in his life like that. Perhaps he trusted her because Karl had trusted her, or because she'd always been faithful through the years. He only lost courage in asking how she was doing. Did she still cry over Karl at night?

Marta sipped her tea delicately, her lips gently touching the cup. He wondered how she pulled her long hair into the soft curls around her head. She nodded to herself as if deciding something, then turned to face him. He was about to smile when he noticed her determined look.

"What?" he asked.

"I want you to welcome Kate and Abigail in a generous manner when they come."

"I am allowing them to stay at my own house. That seems like a generous manner, especially when there is a child involved." Lukas was irritated to no end about the child coming. There would be toys to avoid and no rest from the noise.

"We need children around us. This place may be beautiful, but it can be very cold. Your daughter does not like me here."

Lukas didn't like that Marta had felt an empty coldness to his house. He wanted her to feel welcome. "Anni does not like anyone."

"She reminds me of her father."

"You are not correct. I like you very much, Marta Olsen."
He hoped to get a smile from her, but she ignored him.

"Your heart is not in this search for Wolfram. You do not
wish to do this?"

"What I wish is not relevant. I wish to be a much younger
man. I wish for a little peace. There is little choice in this
matter."

"You are home in your mountain haven. Nothing can touch
you here."

"I do not fear for my life, Marta. I believed we were pursuing Wolfram for revenge."

"I am tired of revenge. Justice, not revenge, remember?
Nothing will make it all right. Nothing will bring back those
years we've lost or return Karl to me. Don't you yearn for
peace?"

Lukas shifted in his chair and felt her study his profile.
"Peace is something I have never known except for brief
moments. But I do long for it."

They watched the silent flames consume the oak logs with
only an occasional snap of surrender. Lukas thought back to
the beginning. When he'd first dreamt of belonging to something great. He'd believed the Nazi Party was that—it promised a future and development for a better tomorrow. The
controversial aspects had seemed minor compared to his
thoughts of a greater good, until these issues had become reality and he had been faced with the guilt of being swept up
without using his mind or his conscience.

He sighed. "I wish someone could have told me that the
decisions of youth haunt even your dying days. We talk of
justice and revenge—should I be exempt from them?"

"You went to prison for your crimes," she said. "Lukas,
what exactly happened in those years before you came to us?"

The images were never far from his mind's eye. Once he had
confessed those sins in this very house to a young American

woman named Darby Evans. It had been months since he'd
last checked on her, now living in Salzburg. She was the only
one to hear his words, the only one it made sense to tell. But
he wanted to tell it again. He kept waiting for someone to
condemn him, to call him the murderer he was and confirm
his own words.

"I killed a young woman."

Nothing changed in Marta's expression—not a twitch or
movement in the lines of her face.

"Tatianna Hoffman was her name. She died to save her best
friend." He folded his hands together and rested his elbows on
the arms of the leather chair. "I knew both Tatianna and her
friend during our childhood—we grew up in the same village.
It was my first firing squad." Lukas could see his victims as
clearly as the fire before him. Tatianna so thin and changed
from the carefree village girl he once knew.

"There were others in the line against the wall. But I killed
Tatianna. I could have chosen one of the men, or I think there
was a child there, but I suddenly cared for her. I aimed true so
she would not suffer. It was the first time I had cared in a very
long while."

Marta watched the fire, and he wondered if she had heard
him.

"Her best friend survived the war by fleeing to America and
had a child—a daughter who later had a daughter of her own.
I met that young woman this past year. She told me about
God's forgiveness. And I actually saved this woman's life."

"You saved the granddaughter's life—of the friend who
escaped the war? Recently?"

"Yes," he said in a whisper. "Was this God giving me
another chance to make right what happened with Tatianna?"

"Perhaps." She nodded. "*Ja,* perhaps."

"It brought me closest to peace, the closest I have been since childhood. Then I went to a reunion in America to see my old comrades."

Marta was wiping away a tear. Lukas hadn't seen her cry in weeks.

"Why this?" he asked, wanting to reach across the gulf of space between them to touch her cheek.

"I do not know."

"You do not cry for me?"

"Yes, I cry for you, Lukas. I cry for your heart and life and that we brought you into this when you were at last leaving the past behind. I cry for your unshed tears."

He wondered how she knew about the tears that never found him.

"You need not cry for me. Redemption may not be so easy as I hoped, but I do not deserve your tears. Cry for Karl or Jantes or Susanne. Even cry for Tatianna and now this woman Kate Porter, who has lost her husband. Look how God forever faces me with young women—and this Kate brings a girl child. I even have three daughters. Could God not give me sons? Women haunt me since Tatianna."

"I think that is part of your peace. Let them comfort you, not make you afraid. Do your daughters know this story?"

"No. Three daughters who know nothing of what their father has done, or even his birth-given name."

"Perhaps it is time to tell them."

Lukas turned quickly toward her. "How can you say such a thing? They must never know. Am I not already haunted enough without seeing my own children hate me? They think I am a leader who fights for his beliefs. How do I tell them that once I was the enemy I have fought so long against? Never say that again. There is one last danger, and that is Wolfram. We must focus on him. If I do not seek him, he will seek me."

"Wolfram will leave you alone. Karl was seeking him so he—" Marta stopped, and Lukas realized that perhaps she wished they'd stayed far from Wolfram. He had not told Marta of the letter he sent, sure it would eventually make it to Wolfram's hands. He could not hide now.

"He will not leave us alone," Lukas said. "I've been wondering about the tile pieces. We will look at Karl's piece when Kate Porter returns it. Wolfram may want more than just an old revenge."

"Then we have work to do before your death. I believe in the end, you will find your peace."

"I hope you are right." Lukas thought of Karl on the floor of his house. There had been no peace for his friend. He deserved it even less.

⋅⇥⟪⟫⇤⋅

All that was familiar had been pushed behind her.

Flights were on schedule. Kate and Abbie had a barely manageable amount of luggage. They had left Redding, California, before the sun rose and changed planes in San Francisco and again in Frankfurt, Germany, to their final destination of Innsbruck, Austria. Abbie loved flying and saved her packet of pretzels as a souvenir. She watched the Disney Channel on the trans-Atlantic Boeing 777 and followed the digital map on her monitor that showed their present position and point of destination. When they flew over England, Abbie enjoyed picturing the children from the Chronicles of Narnia and the queen of England below them.

Kate and Abbie both peered through the plane's small window on the last flight. The snow-covered Alps shone like panes of cut glass, reflecting light at differing angles. The peaks looked like a dozen ranges that had collided together, stretching in every direction along the horizon. Kate had never imagined the white-capped domes to be so imposing. Villages and winding strips of roadway could be distinguished within deep valleys as the plane descended toward the skiing village of Innsbruck.

Kate's airport instructions were simple—after baggage claim and customs, look for Lukas' daughter Anni, who would pick them up. She was there—a thin woman in her thirties with bleached blonde hair. There was no welcome in her eyes. She casually held a sign in one hand that said "Porter," while holding a cigarette in the other.

"I'm Kate Porter. And this is Abbie."

The woman nodded. A man rose from a bench and helped with their luggage.

"I am Anni Johansen," the woman said in a thick accent. Clearly she did not enjoy her assignment as chauffeur. "This is an employee of my father's."

The airport was small, so in minutes they were riding in a gray sedan, with the couple in front and Abbie and Kate in back. Neither the woman nor the man said much to them. The soft leather seats and gentle rumble of the vehicle rocked Abbie to sleep, her head against Kate's shoulder.

"How long until we reach Lukas and Marta?" Kate asked, leaning forward.

Anni glanced first at the man who was driving before answering. "In one hour we arrive at my father's estate," she said, with a half turn her way. "How many days do you and the child and Marta stay with us?"

Anni's tone indicated what she thought of company in her house.

"At least a few weeks," Kate said.

Anni said nothing else for the rest of the drive.

Kate watched the world outside the speeding vehicle. Pines grew from the mountain slopes to the rim of livestock-dotted fields. The colors shimmered with an energy all their own here. Just yesterday she'd left Cottonwood with its already heat-washed landscape, where the color was slowly being sucked from trees and fields, even the sky—like water drained from the thirsty land. But Austria's colors had awakened from the winter's nap with new greens, the bluest skies, and mountains that chose their own tints throughout the day—whether borrowed from the lakes below or the shades of sunset.

As the sun dipped behind the mass of mountains above the valley road, it dawned on Kate that she was really in Europe again. Though this was a much different Europe from the water-locked streets of Venice, she'd actually come to a place she'd never wanted to return to. And she wasn't afraid.

Iron gates opened wide for their arrival when the driver hit a digital switch on the car's console. Through tall pines the house shone in the shadows, illuminated by miniature lights along pathways and in the surrounding gardens. Unlike the quaint Austrian homes Kate had admired on the drive in, with decorative trimmings on the gables and wooden flower boxes bursting from every window, the Johansen residence was reminiscent of the old imperial Austro-Hungarian Empire with its air of sophistication and grandeur. She assessed the house at over a hundred years old, though it appeared spotless and new. The winding lawns were shaved short like a cut carpet, and a fountain bubbled in the center of the circular driveway.

"It looks like a place for a princess," Abbie said, rubbing her eyes as the car stopped. The man got out quickly and opened Kate's door.

Marta walked down the steps and embraced Kate at the car. Lukas stood in the entrance at the massive double doors.

"You must be Abigail," Marta said, bending to see her.

Abbie's sleepy smile brightened when she noticed the fountain. "The water looks pink."

"Yes, a special color for our special guest. You will see the dancing fairies in the morning. We need to get you out of the chill."

"Welcome," Lukas said without a smile. He reached to shake Kate's hand.

"Danke schön," Kate replied, which earned her an approving nod.

Marta had made dinner and done much to prepare for their arrival. She'd set up a playroom in an upstairs bedroom with a children's kitchen set and TV and VCR, where Abbie could also sleep if she chose. Abbie could hardly be pulled away from the room to come to dinner—dumplings and a beef dish with thick burgundy gravy. Neither Anni nor the man in the car joined their meal. Lukas spoke little while they ate, but he asked Abbie if she liked her room. Marta claimed it had been Lukas' idea, though he brushed it away as untrue. Kate knew Marta must be able to work miracles on him.

The tiring day and jet lag caused Kate's eyes to burn as Lukas and Marta drank another glass of red wine. Kate noticed Abbie's curiosity. Her daughter's past exposure to drinking had been a rare holiday toast or Jack's brother, who came to town every few years carting a twelve-pack of beer. Kate would have to explain to her that in Europe drinking wine was as common as drinking Pepsi was at home.

Marta noticed Kate's weariness and ushered them both upstairs. The room was neat, though a bit chilly. Two thick down comforters folded sideways on the bed would warm them. Kate couldn't wait to slide beneath the folds of the clean sheets and comforter. Yet when she lay in bed waiting for Abbie to return from the bathroom, sleep would not come. Nothing here was hers or had the scent of home. As Abbie came bounding in with her toothbrush in hand, Kate realized there was one thing that reminded her of home—her daughter. And if God had ever been near her, she prayed he'd be here with them now.

Chapter Thirty

Kate showered and dressed in their room, then left Abbie still asleep in bed. At nine-thirty the others would be awake. She heard someone in the breakfast nook.

"Good morning," Kate said, hoping to see someone other than Anni in the room.

"*Guten Morgen,*" Anni replied in a cool tone, returning her gaze to the newspaper in front of her.

"That's right, *Guten Morgen.*" Kate glanced around, feeling awkward.

"Do you want coffee or tea?" Anni didn't look up from the paper.

"Coffee would be nice. Where are the cups?"

Anni pushed her chair from the table with a loud scrape and retrieved Kate a cup of coffee. She motioned to the cream and sugar on the table. Before Kate could even thank her, she'd left the room.

"I see you met Anni once again," Marta said as she entered the nook.

"Yes."

"She is Lukas' middle daughter. The oldest lives in Germany with her husband and three children. His youngest is at university in Paris."

"I don't think Anni likes having company."

"She treats me the same. But you will not see her often." Marta motioned toward a small hallway leading to an area of the house Kate hadn't seen. "Lukas waits for us. Did you sleep well?"

"Yes, very well." Kate's stomach grumbled. But she was at the mercy of this family. Kate liked her independence and didn't know if she could stay in the house for long.

Lukas' study was a few doors down the hallway. Marta knocked on the closed door before entering, though she didn't wait for an answer. It could have been a study for someone like Ernest Hemingway, Kate thought. A great place to write novels in, with its oversized leather furniture, rock fireplace, and bookcases along the wall. A beautiful antique desk dominated one side of the room and was surrounded by boxes of files. Pinned to one wall were maps and photos that didn't match the neatly framed art on the other walls. Lukas sat behind the desk, also lined with stacks of files.

"Good. I want to get started. We will have breakfast soon. The girl has not awakened yet?"

"Abbie," Kate said, looking at him directly. "The girl's name is Abbie, or you may call her Abigail."

Lukas grimaced and stood up, moving toward the map on the wall behind him. Marta sat in a leather chair near the fireplace.

"Did you bring the tile?" Lukas asked.

"Yes."

"I will ask to see it a little later."

"I ask that you be honest with me," Kate put in. "If you don't feel I need to know every detail of this—" her hands swept the room—"I understand. But I want to trust everything that is said here."

"Yes, it is agreed," he returned thoughtfully. He glanced at Marta, who nodded for him to continue. "We seek a man named Wolfram Meizer. I told you about him in Portland."

"Yes. I did some research on him. He was a guard at several camps and part of the SS Death's Head Unit, the Topenkopf—is that how you say it?"

"Good enough. Where did you find this information?"

"In a book about the men in the camps. It detailed many of the guards with their marital status, religion, the camps they served, and other descriptions. But if I found the right person, the book said he died in 1945."

"Do you have this book with you?"

"Yes, along with other papers I found."

"Very good. We will use that to search for other guards from Meizer's unit who may still be alive. Until recently, we believed he died in 1945. Now we know he is alive, and we have three locations to search. At one of these places, we believe we will find Wolfram Meizer."

"If we find him, how will that help us know what happened to my husband? We can't walk up and ask."

"What do you say—we will cross the bridge when it comes?"

Lukas' words didn't encourage her.

"When we find Wolfram, there are many options to be decided upon," Marta said. "It is something we should discuss. We can contact a Holocaust group or the Austrian government to press criminal charges against him."

"Let us find him first. Come, Kate, see the locations we will be searching."

She moved around the desk and stood beside him. The map of Europe had red pins stuck in three locations.

"Wolfram took this map from a Nazi in Argentina. This

man's wife provided Marta's husband, Karl, with a copy. The three locations were possible hiding spots for Nazi loot."

Marta leaned against the desk behind them. "There are priceless artworks, gold bullion, documents, and other valuables that have never been found since the war's end. Austria had paintings and sketches from the famous painter Gustav Klimt inside one of the most famous museums in Vienna. These were either stolen from the museum or taken by forced sales from Austrian Jews. Many paintings around the world have been proven to be stolen works yet have not been returned to the families of survivors and Holocaust victims. But then there are the works and gold never recovered. Some were lost in unreachable Swiss banks, and others perhaps locked in caches around the world."

"You believe one of these sites is one such hiding place?"

"It is possible."

"Why would he wait so long?" Kate studied the three points on the map—two in Austria and one in Italy.

"My husband believed Wolfram could not return because Nazi hunters sought him. Wolfram was also rumored to have murdered an exiled Nazi in South America."

"Let us not cover too much information too soon," Lukas said. "Let us return to the map. The first location is Schloss Weiss, a castle in northern Italy."

Kate compared the red pin near the Austrian border and its relation to Venice, Italy. The distance wasn't far. She'd spent hours studying maps of this area and surmising the routes for a kidnapping. Within a few hours Jack could have been taken to Switzerland, Austria, Germany, or France. It would take even less time for a fast boat to cross the Adriatic Sea and reach Slovenia or Croatia, even Bosnia or Herzegovina, where terrorists could demand a ransom. But none ever came. Later she had studied the water currents and made inquiries at coastal villages for any John Doe, or whatever they called an unidentified body in Italy.

The map brought back those memories she'd tried to push away. Nights of hopeless tears when she agonized over where on earth her husband lived or his body rested. He was somewhere. Kate never thought it would take this long or that she'd be in an Austrian estate looking at a map again.

Lukas was watching her when Kate turned from the map. "The castle dates to the thirteenth century, during a time when there was a regional feudal war. Apparently many passageways were built. These were convenient during the close of WWII as one spot in the ratline," Lukas explained.

"What exactly is the ratline?"

Lukas glanced at Marta as if to say, "She doesn't know anything."

Marta spoke quickly. "It was the line of places that Nazis used to escape from the Third Reich nations down through Italy and on to South America. A group called ODESSA organized it, and such points as the Schloss Weiss would keep these men and women along the journey."

"I've heard of ODESSA. The group consisted of SS members who formed a network to escape Europe during the war. I just did not know the term *ratline*."

"Now you do. ODESSA and the ratline have been used in Hollywood movies and much fiction, but the group and the route did exist. We'll talk about this information later. Marta's husband found testimony from a man captured in 1947 and accused of wartime atrocities. He named Wolfram Meizer as one of others who stayed at Schloss Weiss in 1945 before Wolfram escaped to South America.

"Locations *zwei und drei*—two and three." Lukas pointed to another red pin close to the third in upper Austria, not far from the German border. "This is the Salzkammergut area of Austria—the lake district. Our last two points on the map are both in this region. The believed Austrian Redoubt would have occurred here. The Redoubt was—"

"An area in Upper Austria where the Allies believed Hitler would make his last stand at the end of the war. They thought he would hide within the Alps with his top officers and military and keep the war from ending."

"Good," Lukas said, raising his eyebrow. Marta smiled. "I was raised in the Salzkammergut region. The lakes are deep and mountains rugged, much like here. There are also many salt mines and tunnels within the mountains. The Nazis had underground armament factories built by concentration camp inmates, where they built airplanes and weapons beyond the eyes of the Allies."

"Sounds like a perfect place to hide something after the war. But then, so did those secret passageways inside the castle in Italy."

"Yes," said Marta, "but we have ruled out the pin up there labeled *drei*."

"That is correct," Lukas said, sitting on the edge of the desk. "Wolfram will not be found at Toplitzsee, or Lake Toplitz."

"How can you be so certain?" Kate asked. The lake was small, elongated, and near another larger lake.

"There is one building on the lake—a restaurant. It has become a tourist site, with tours from around the region taking visitors on a Nazi treasure hunt. This lake is famous for legends of Nazi gold. They are certainly true stories. Eyewitnesses tell of SS officers dropping wooden crates into the water. Many divers have tried to discover what is inside the crates, but the lake is deep and dangerous."

"Karl and I watched a program about the lake."

"Yes. An American television network was a part of funding an exploration with Simon Wiesenthal Foundation. It was popular news in Austria for some time. Scotland has its monster in the lake, and we have our missing Nazi treasures."

"Did they find anything?" Kate asked.

"Yes. They used special equipment—what are they called in English?"

"Minisubmarines," Marta helped.

"That is correct. The crates were broken, but they recovered counterfeit British notes." Lukas sighed and sat in the leather desk chair. "There is much to explain."

"We will do a little at a time," Marta said. She brought a fold-up chair from the corner for Kate to sit in. "I will take a turn. Kate, you know who Heinrich Himmler was?"

"One of Hitler's top men," Kate said. Her father's History Network collector's tapes saved the day.

"Himmler headed Operation Bernhard, which would flood the economy with counterfeit currency. First the British pound and then the American dollar. They used artists, bookbinders, engravers, and printers in concentration camps to do the work of making the templates. They planned to murder the workers when the project was complete."

Lukas leaned an elbow on the desk and looked at the map. "It is said the war would have had a different outcome if they had begun the project earlier. A survivor of the project said they perfected the American hundred-dollar bill and prepared to print a million dollars a day. But the war was ending too quickly, and the project relocated."

"Now it ties into our two locations in the Salzkammergut region," Marta said. She rounded the desk to stand before the map. "Some of the counterfeit money ended up in Lake Toplitz. The inmates were kept alive—perhaps Hitler or Himmler believed they had time enough for the operation to save the war. The inmates were moved from camp to camp until they came here." She pointed from the lake to a town north and over a range of mountains. The third red pin was stuck on the blue outline of a lake within the range of mountains. "This is Ebensee. On the outskirts of the village was a subcamp of the larger Mauthausen Concentration Camp. Inmates were used to dig tunnels into the mountain for underground armament factories. The Operation Bernhard inmates were secluded from the other prisoners. And Wolfram Meizer was a guard at KZ Ebensee during the last six months of the war."

"It does tie together." Kate nodded. It was fascinating, something her father would be greatly intrigued by. But this was also very real for the present. "Yet the counterfeit money would mean nothing now."

"Correct. But this region became a kind of draining pot for those fleeing the greater Reich. Goods were shipped from Berlin to be hidden, and inmates were moved into Bavaria and Austria. Hitler had a mountain fortress outside of Salzburg. We don't know exactly what Wolfram discovered, but we believe it happened while he was at KZ Ebensee."

"The second pin in the Salzkammergut region is between Ebensee and Lake Toplitz."

"It is Waldsee—*see* means "lake." And *wald* means "forest." Lukas and I do not have much information about it. We began to organize everything this last week."

There was a knock on the open door. Anni looked at them in front of the large map and then at the papers and boxes with a mixture of annoyance and curiosity. "The child is awake," she said to her father.

"Thank you," Kate said, quickly moving around Marta and to the door.

"She is in the kitchen," Anni said as Kate passed her.

Kate's feet echoed down the hallway as she turned the corner to where Abbie sat on a stool, sipping something in a teacup. Her hair was tousled and she still wore her nightgown.

"Good morning, Abbie."

"I called you," she said with a small pout.

"I'm sorry. I didn't hear you. I should have come and checked."

"It's all right. The lady who picked us up at the airport yesterday made me some tea. She gave me these yummy things to put in it instead of sugar. One popped into my mouth too." Abbie giggled and pointed to the pink dish with brown crystal squares inside. Kate picked one up and took a small test— brown sugar and molasses. With a wink to Abbie, she popped one in her mouth just as Marta entered the room. Kate acted as if she were caught red-handed, which brought a good laugh to Abbie.

"This is the room I want to be in," Marta said, glancing at Kate, who swallowed the candy quickly. She smiled at Abbie. "Do you remember me from last night?"

Abbie nodded.

"Would you like some breakfast? You and I can make it for everyone."

"I want to stay with my mom," she said shyly.

"We can all cook," Kate said with a wink that brought another smile to Abbie's face.

As they boiled eggs and Abbie arranged meat and cheese on a plate, Marta said quietly to Kate, "Lukas must still be talking to Anni. This either will make things worse or we could see improvement. I do not hold my breath."

⋄⇒◎⇐⋄

Jack had folded the blanket twice before stretching out in front of the vent on the floor. He was cold as always and wondered if he'd ever again be completely warm for more than a few hours. His time with Wolfram Meizer would thaw him to the bone, only to be returned to the basement and on to the tunnels. If he survived this, he'd go to the Hawaiian Islands for a year and never be cold.

Rudy was trying a new experiment through his side of the vent. Jack waited in the darkness with his fingers pressed on the metal grate.

"Well?" Rudy's whisper echoed through the vent.

"Nothing so far."

Jack enjoyed the nights when they weren't too exhausted to stretch near their vents. He imagined them as young boys who lived separated by an alley, so they'd send flashlight signals back and forth. It made him smile to think of Rudy stretched on the cold concrete on the other side, now trying to find a way to pass a note across the span of a few feet between vent covers. He wondered what kind of arm Rudy had invented to push paper through—a wire arm made from collected paper clips or a contraption made of eating utensils. Jack liked to tell Rudy he was MacGyver in disguise and that if they only had a stick of bubble gum they could be free and safe with their families in only minutes. Rudy had never seen the television show, so he couldn't appreciate Jack's humor.

Jack felt a light touch against his fingertip. "I feel it." He scooted up and tried to reach through. The paper disappeared, then was there again, but not close enough. It hit the ridge and crumpled.

"A little more. I got it." Jack had to remember to whisper. He could hear Rudy's hushed celebration mixed with the deep-lung coughs that stayed with him.

"Now we have a new way to communicate if necessary."

"It's even fun," Jack said with a chuckle.

"I have some news," Rudy said in a serious tone. "I borrowed some books from Ian."

"Ian would do anything for you, Rudy. Have you ever asked him if he'd help us escape?"

"Actually, I did. But he said no."

Jack laughed quietly, imagining Ian's deadpan expression. "So what news did you find?"

"One book was about this region. It's in German, but I'm getting pretty good at reading German now—all those old newspapers and such have helped. Well, if I'm reading correctly, then it seems that a dam was built on the village end of the lake over fifty years ago. Want to guess the exact date?"

Jack leaned close to the vent, thinking. "Maybe early 1945?"

"You just made the winning answer."

"What do I win?"

"A trip for two into a scenic underground tunnel system."

"Thanks. So the dam was complete just prior to the end of WWII. Anything else?"

"Not really, but I did find that a bit of a coincidence. Maybe what these people are seeking is really inside that dam."

Jack was in thought. "Did the lake level rise at all when they constructed the dam?"

"Ah, *that's* what it was saying. I couldn't figure out a few words. But I think it rose something like ten meters once spring melted the mountain snow and filled the lake. By then the war was already over. The village had to restructure, and homes were torn down during the dam construction to make way for the rise in the lake level—I'm sure that was unpopular, but citizens didn't argue with the Nazis by then. They knew what would happen. I thought you'd find that bit of our lake history interesting."

"Yes, I do," he said. Now Jack knew how the cave opening had the man-made markings. The lake had been low enough for divers to work there, so perhaps the cave hadn't even been under the water at all at one time. Ten meters was around thirty feet.

Jack wanted to tell Rudy about his discovery, but the vents couldn't be trusted with that knowledge. Perhaps their new note system? Rudy was saying good-night and Jack was glad he was off the floor. The cold quickly went through the wool blanket and into his skin.

He later looked at the paper Rudy sent through and laughed, knowing Rudy also thought of them as boys passing secret notes. It read "Will you tell Melissa that I like her?" There were three boxes marked: *yes, no,* and *maybe.*

But those were the same choices he gave himself when he thought of telling Rudy about the cave. He decided that somehow soon he must tell his friend. The new knowledge might give Rudy the energy to fight this illness he couldn't conquer. Jack decided they needed another night on the lake. He'd tell Ian he was concerned about more cracking.

The cave was waiting to reveal its secrets.

CHAPTER THIRTY-ONE

Lukas wanted to ignore what he saw happening before his eyes. He'd done it many times before, believing everything would work out. But Marta had asked him to talk to his daughter. Anni was the hardest of his children to speak with, perhaps because she was the most like him.

She had paused after Marta left the room, then turned to leave also.

"Anni, please come inside," he said. It was a relief to speak German again after talking with Kate and Marta in English.

"A game of chess?" she asked, nodding toward the chess stand in the corner with hand-carved marble pieces lined for battle. "I remember when you taught me long ago."

"You had come for the summer and were bored to death."

"This fortress can be dull for a fifteen-year-old."

"I suppose," Lukas said. He recalled how different his childhood had been with a father who enjoyed the tavern more than home. At fifteen he had run away several times, hiding at his friend's house until his aunt in Vienna volunteered to take

him in. Life was better for a time, until his wandering met the
idealism of the Nazi Youth. Immediately he'd been drawn in
with promises of position, honor, and duty. He'd once had a
friend who was half Jewish and that posed the greatest problem in his new beliefs. But the more propaganda he read—the
scientific facts about the degenerate traits of the Jews and the
reports of their plots to control the government—the more his
anger grew. At one rally, he found himself shouting and chant-
ing with all the others, and it scared him to hear his father's
voice from his own lips.

"You don't seem interested in chess with your daughter."

Lukas turned to Anni. She had always worn her anger on the
outside, in her body language and tone of voice. He recalled his
vow to be a different father to his children than the one he'd
been born with. Lukas' daughters had gone to the best schools,
had money and position, and he never once had yelled at them.
But all that hadn't brought his children closer to him.

"Is there something you want to say?" he asked Anni.

The challenge came swiftly. "Why did you bring these
women here?"

"Kate's husband is missing. We may be able to help." Lukas
rarely told Anni anything of his business besides what she
needed to do. He felt like her employer instead of her father.
There was little warmth between them, and he didn't know
how to break the wall that had grown so high.

"You are a home for refugees? Last month we gain the older
woman and now this one and her child. On every trip, Father,
you return with more women."

There was pain mixed in her sarcasm. Lukas was sure of it.
Anni rarely showed emotion other than anger. Anni's mother
was constantly frustrated by her middle child. Vera was the
quintessential Viennese woman—hospitable, charming, never
ruffled, full of pride in herself and family. If one of his affairs
had not been such a public embarrassment, Vera would never

have left him. Once her pride was tarnished in the eyes of society, she would never return to him. Lukas missed the sound of
his daughters in the house, but he didn't fight for them. It was
Vera's place to raise them.

Lukas recalled how Anni had called him late one night
several years back. He'd never heard her voice sound helpless
before. He had driven to Vienna to pick her up, and Lukas was
stunned to see her so sick and vulnerable. He took her straight
to the hospital, where she was treated for a drug overdose.
They later drove from the hospital to a rehab center, where she
stayed three months. Lukas visited once a week though they
rarely talked. Their way of growing close was through a game
of chess. He hated to lose. And he had started to lose regularly
the last weeks before she checked out. Lukas had offered her a
place to live and a job. This hadn't been her first trip to rehab—
only the first time she'd called him. He knew that without a
place away from her old life, she would be calling again. Anni
had accepted his offer.

"You have made it clear you don't like this," he said carefully. He wondered if Anni knew she was a special case, not
just one of many women he liked to help. Marta and Kate
weren't here for that reason. It just happened. Did Anni understand this and know how much he enjoyed her living at the
estate? "I would appreciate it if you were polite with my
guests. They are guests for a while and then they will leave."
Did Anni know she was more than a guest?

"If that kid gets into my stuff or is too noisy, I don't know
how much I can take."

"But you will try?" Lukas realized he was saying the same
words Marta had said to him.

"I suppose." As she rose to leave, she glanced at the map.

He should tell her everything. Anni had helped him before
in his business matters, which were sometimes bordering on
illegal, proving herself loyal countless times without questions

or the need for answers. But he wouldn't risk her being involved in this. The danger that lurked on the edges was too great. Lukas couldn't lose his daughter to the battle begun long ago. Wolfram Meizer had already taken enough.

⟡⟞⟝⟡

After a short nap for Kate and a quick tour of the estate grounds for all of them, Lukas deemed it time to work once again. Marta had established right away that they would talk about their mission only within the walls of Lukas' office, not when they were eating, on a walk, or in front of Abbie. Kate found it humorous that Marta called the search a "mission." Two senior citizens, Kate, and Abbie were members of a secret mission. Who would have thought?

Kate brought her tile to Lukas' office, where a fire crackled in the rock fireplace and the lamps were turned on. Marta had opened the shades to the one window in the room, though afternoon brought little light in.

Abbie was upstairs, playing in her new room after discovering a dollhouse that she might have claimed to be too old to play with at home. But she was arranging the rooms and dressing the small people when Kate returned downstairs.

They stared down at the four tile pieces: Karl's larger triangle, the copy made from Jantes' original that they'd found in Karl's office, the smaller piece Oskar had sent by courier, and Lukas' squared section. By now Kate had heard about Oskar Gogl, who hoped to join them soon. But with his wife's medical problems, he wasn't sure when. Only one portion of the square tile was missing.

"What do you think?" Marta asked Lukas.

"I don't see anything special about it."

"Do you know where the tile came from?" Kate said. "What is its origin?"

Lukas and Marta looked at one another before Marta spoke.

"Karl's sister was part of the Resistance group before Lukas joined us. She brought the tile to a drop point with instructions for Karl to divide it into five pieces—one for each team member—and to bring it to the next meeting." Kate caught the solemn way Marta's eyes flipped toward Lukas, then back to her. "Susanne was killed before the next meeting, so the full reason was never discovered. Everything was terrible in those last months of war, and we never thought the tile was the real key. But this is what Lukas has begun to question. We wanted to see the pieces together to decide."

The tile drew their attention again. The copied tile was slightly different from the others, with its darker color and grainy edges crumbling easily. The other three were a bright cobalt blue with a raised pattern; their broken edges exposed a white, grainy texture.

"I did some research on this," offered Kate.

"Really?" Lukas said, moving around to sit behind his desk. Kate noticed that he seemed tired tonight.

"I'm an antique dealer, remember? I may specialize in more early American pieces, but I have resources."

"And what did you learn?" Lukas asked.

"I think most important to know is that this is not an antique."

"How do you know?"

Kate picked up information she had brought from home and reviewed what she'd learned. "I won't read everything, but first of all I never realized the great history in tiles and the many varieties. Victorian encaustic tiles, Dutch and English tin-glazed tiles, European stove tiles, medieval floor tiles, Italian, and on and on. It was the thickness of the tile that gave me the first clue. Different centuries have different characteristics of thickness and hardness of their tiles, along with the actual process of making them. But twentieth-century tiles tend to be the thinnest of all. This tile fit that model."

She picked up a piece and turned it around in her fingers. "There are other characteristics to determine the time period of a tile. For example, eighteenth-century tiles usually were chamfered to slope inward so they would abut neatly with the others. Or some seventeenth- to early eighteenth-century Dutch and English tiles had two opposing nail holes in the corners.

"The blue color probably came from a metallic oxide from cobalt. The majolica painting technique used variations of color and tone—see how the blue had darker shades in areas. The raised edge was probably pressed into it, or the clay was poured into a mold."

"Would this have to be made in a factory?" Lukas picked up one of the fragments.

"Single potters were capable of doing such work."

"What are you thinking?" Marta asked.

"I am not sure," Lukas said. "If it is not valuable by age and it obviously has nothing buried within the clay—I often wondered if that was why Susanne told Karl to divide it. She may have thought there was something inside, an SS intelligence note perhaps? I am just giving ideas here. If we knew the answers behind the tile, we could better predict what Wolfram would do." He leaned far back in the chair, staring at the ceiling. "*Vas,* I mean, *what* is your conclusion on the age?"

"After I read everything, my guess would be no later than the early 1900s. I'll leave these descriptions for you both to go over, but that's my thought."

"This is good," Lukas said.

Kate enjoyed his rare approval while it lasted. She picked up a file with a list of questions stapled to the inside flap. "How could I forget?" she said, looking at the name on the page. "Rudy Blessing."

"The other missing victim," Lukas said, unconcerned. "Tell us about their connection. Let us get comfortable here."

"I will make some coffee and tea," Marta said. She left the room, and Kate was instantly intimidated by Lukas' presence. His dark eyes examined her beneath hooded lids. She plunged on as if her advocate, Marta, was still there.

"Before Jack and I were married and he was still in college, he went on a summer internship with Rudy Blessing's diving expedition. Jack spent the summer with Rudy's team on an underwater archaeological search."

"This is interesting," Lukas said. "We have a definite link. The two locations both have lakes, no oceans nearby. But with underwater archaeologists, lakes, wooden crates dumped into Lake Toplitz, and other lakes in the Salzkammergut region from which German armament and objects have been recovered, we have a pattern."

"The castle in Italy has a lake nearby also?"

"Yes."

Kate felt the question stirring, the one that had taunted and kept her from life for three years. She wanted to ask Marta, not Lukas. But she couldn't wait. "Lukas, please, I need to know one way or the other. Do you think Jack could be alive?"

His fingers were laced together as he rocked in his chair. He seemed in great consideration. "I will say this raises us one notch closer to that possibility."

⊷⇒◯⇐↜

It was past midnight, and it seemed they'd covered a hundred subjects. But Kate still had more on her list of questions. Dinner was long behind them, Abbie was sleeping, and they were all tired. They discussed the Blue Tile Crimes. There were a series of crimes in South America and one in Germany during the early to mid-1950s—a well-known doctor, several political figures, even a man named Ernst, a suspected Nazi in Argentina. All were murdered, and a blue tile fragment was left at the scene of each crime. Every piece was the same shape and pattern as the one Kate found on Jack's pillow.

It was Marta's idea to trace the raised design on the tile onto a piece of paper. Kate placed the paper on top of the tile and gently rubbed with a charcoal pencil until the pattern appeared. They examined it for a long time. The design that wrapped around the tile was neither congruent nor clear. If it had been art it leaned toward a cubist or perhaps a surrealist image depicted in a pattern of lines and shapes. Perhaps the shapes and design would have meant something to Wolfram Meizer, but it didn't reveal anything to them. Maybe the final piece would make the pattern clear.

"That tile belonged to Jantes," Marta said softly, picking up the copied piece.

"Jantes was the funny one in the group. He made us laugh until we cried. A handsome young man also—the village girls were at his mercy."

"Wolfram took Jantes' tile when he killed him and used it as a pattern for fake tiles he left behind at the crime scenes." No emotion showed in his face as Lukas rose to add another log to the fire.

"Why would Wolfram do these crimes?"

"Quite an intelligent twist if you think about it," Lukas said.

"I do not like to agree, but it is true." Marta folded her hands on her lap. "We believe Wolfram committed these crimes for his personal reasons—perhaps he was trying to get information or revenge. He would leave the tile piece to divert blame away from a single individual and make it appear to be the activity of a terrorist group—our group. I am sure you have heard of bombings or other crimes where a group then claims responsibility. Wolfram was doing that, but casting blame upon us. Perhaps we should have come forward, but we'd moved on in our lives. We did not want the suspicion, especially since we did not know who could be doing such crimes. Were there more tiles? Why did Susanne ask us to divide the tile? These and other questions kept us unwilling to come forward."

"But it also kept our group from reuniting and hunting Wolfram down. What is the best way to discredit something?" Lukas asked Kate.

"I'm not sure."

"You are a Protestant or Evangelical?"

"Something like that," she said. "I believe in the Bible."

"Good enough. Now when the Nazis murdered the Jews in the name of Christ or because they say Christ was murdered by the Jews, what does that do to your religion?"

"Besides making me angry, it makes Christianity look bad to those who don't understand it. Christ was a Jew himself, and the foundation of my beliefs stands against everything the Nazis did."

"Explain the foundation," Lukas continued.

"Jesus said to love God with all your heart, soul, and mind and to love your neighbor as yourself."

"But if no one tells these words to the victim who is hurt in Christ's name, what do they believe?"

"That Christ would ordain such a thing," answered Kate.

"Yes. This is not a great example, but you can understand how Wolfram used our group's name to do his evil, which in turn harms us very much. I think he thought if we were prosecuted or the press found the story, he could locate us quickly and get the missing tiles. Those tile pieces, and I am sure revenge, are very important to him. But we may never know for certain why he did this."

"Kate, do you feel like you've entered a spy movie?" Marta asked with a chuckle.

"That would make me a very old Bond, James Bond," Lukas

said, and Kate realized he'd made a joke. He even smiled slightly to himself.

"I was thinking *Mission Impossible,*" Marta said. "Will my instructions disintegrate in five seconds?"

"They might," Lukas said, stretching his arms. "We must rest, but this is what I believe we should do in the next few days. I will go to Schloss Weiss to see if I can pick up Wolfram's trail from there. Kate, I know about someone you can speak to. I cannot go with you. My former position in government makes it difficult to interview people about such matters. The news could raise a lot of suspicion—or get straight to Wolfram. There will be things you must do on your own."

"I understood that before I came," Kate said. The fire had died down, and a chill moved through the room.

"This man lives in Italy. He was in several camps and knew Wolfram Meizer. Karl had his name listed in the files. I found some information on him. His name is Francis Moore. He is a survivor of the camps, speaks excellent English, and has authored several books. He was at Ebensee at the end of the war."

"Where in Italy?"

"Venice, I believe."

"Venice?" Marta asked. She looked at Kate in shock.

"Yes," Lukas said, in a voice that questioned her reaction. "Kate has been there, so transportation will not be a problem."

"She shouldn't have to go there," Marta said.

Kate listened to them go back and forth, as if she were outside looking through the window. Her comfort in the idea of returning to Europe came from knowing she wouldn't be returning to Venice. Now she felt like God had tricked her in a way. Or had he only taken her a step at a time? How far was she willing to go from what made her feel comfortable to get the answers, to possibly get Jack himself?

"I don't know what to do about Abbie."

"Marta can stay with her here."

"I won't leave her."

"Then take her with you."

"No, I don't want to take her to that place," Kate said.

"You can do the trip in one day. It will be a long day."

"Lukas," Marta said, "she should not do this. Do you not understand this?"

"Do we want Wolfram? Does she want to know about her husband? This is not easy work, and we do not wait for perfect conditions. Wolfram does not sit and do nothing because his men might get afraid. I must go to Schloss Weiss and see what I find there. Kate does not know Italian or German—she would get nothing. Francis Moore speaks perfect English and has shared his story again and again. If you are too afraid of Venice, then I will go myself later or get someone, but it—"

"I will go," Kate said, "but only for one day."

"This is only the first step," Lukas said. "Do you know what we have begun? This will not be comfortable or nice all the time. This is a battle. This could be a battle for our lives."

CHAPTER THIRTY-TWO

Marta quickly became Abbie's adopted grandmother. Kate enjoyed time with her daughter and Marta outside the estate walls. The Alps were like Kate's tiny magical tree world in Cottonwood magnified a thousand times. They followed trails and collected handfuls of wildflowers. When Kate told Abbie she would be gone for a day, Abbie didn't seem to mind as long as Kate was back at bedtime for *The Voyage of the "Dawn Treader."*

"We still haven't finished it yet," Abbie said.

It eased Kate's mind to know Abbie would be happy for the day. The arrangements had been made by Anni, which made Kate a little nervous. She'd probably have train tickets to Siberia instead of Italy.

"I don't want to return to that city," she confided in Marta the day before she was to leave; they were walking from a mountain trail to the wide paths of the estate.

"I understand. We will wait until Lukas is feeling better and then I will go with him. Or I will go and speak with this Francis Moore instead of you."

"What's wrong with Lukas?"

"He is old, and he refuses to see a doctor."

"You can convince him of anything; don't you know that?"

"I lose my power when it comes to doctors," Marta said regretfully. "I did not think it wise for you to return to Venice."

"I didn't either. But I've prayed and thought about it. It will be good for me to go back and contribute to our group. You and Lukas can't do everything, even if sometimes I want to be a child like Abbie and have someone take care of me—for just a few moments."

"I know the feeling. We are strong women, you and I. We have to be. But even strong women need a shoulder sometimes. Let us care for each other until another shoulder comes along."

Kate nodded and patted Marta's back. She noticed gentle tears in the older woman's eyes.

⋅⊷══◯═══⊶⋅

Marta drove her to meet the midnight train. Kate was glad for a cheerful driver this time. She'd chosen that mode of trans-portation to avoid another Anni chauffeuring experience and to skip a day of frequent plane changes. Marta stayed long enough to give her a quick lesson in rail travel, then waved good-bye so she could get back before Abbie woke up. Kate was alone with a few other travelers at the tiny station along the railroad track. She could see her breath as she waited where she hoped the first-class nonsmoking car would arrive. As the chill creeped through her taupe panty hose, Kate wished she'd worn slacks instead of her straight black dress. Then the track began to hum and the flat-fronted red train zinged toward them, coming to a quick stop.

Kate picked up her bag, noticing how fast the other passen-gers hopped on. She had to take the nearest open door— second-class smoking. The doors slid closed immediately behind her and before Kate left the loading and unloading area, the train was whizzing along the track again. The cars had the stench of years of smoke layered like paint over the walls, seats, and any patrons who stayed for long. Kate kept walking through cars until she reached the empty nonsmoking section. Settling into a seat with a small table in front of it, she realized that this was it—her return to Venice.

Inside her black leather bag she'd packed her Bible. Kate turned straight to Psalms and read the verses she had underlined the night before. God was her strength, her refuge, her deliverer, her shield, her song—she kept reading those verses throughout the journey. The word *refuge,* in particular, stood out. Years earlier, Kate would have thought a refuge was a place of escape. But it wasn't so. Refuge was a place God kept her as the storm waged and as life continued. It wasn't a transported hiding place, but a peace in the midst of life. Only now could she understand that.

The day awoke gradually as she traveled and changed trains several times. The distance changed the landscape. White, flat-fronted buildings with brown window boxes and gabled roofs dotted the hillsides and villages in Austria. Across the Italian border, the scenery slowly gave way to red-tile roofs and sweeping vineyard hillsides the farther into northern Italy she rode. As the train left the mountains and rolling countryside behind to cross more cities, the colors seemed a shade less vibrant.

Francis Moore, the man she was going to see, had recently been admitted into long-term care in Venice. Lukas had contacted Moore's wife, who volunteered to meet Kate at the Santa Lucia Station at the west end of the Grand Canal. The smoky station was bustling with movement by the time Kate disembarked. Moving toward the main entrance where Marie Moore would be waiting, Kate paused. A wave of panic tried to overtake her. This was too real: the smoke, the voices surrounding her, and something slightly familiar she couldn't describe. Then she realized what it was—the scent of a city on water. And Kate knew that she should never have returned.

⤙═◉═⤚

Lukas rubbed his eyes as he leaned against the headrest in the back of the gray sedan. His usual driver and handyman, Rey, was at the wheel, but they had spoken little since their morning departure toward the south. Lukas' energy would not return, and a day in bed due to Marta's insistence had probably made it worse.

He hated being old. It made him grouchy.

Kate would be in Venice by now, he calculated. He wondered how she fared. Marta had given him a long lecture on his insensitivity in that situation. It had seemed a logical decision to him. Kate had been to Venice before so the city would be manageable. Francis Moore's English made him accessible to the young woman. Marta asked why he didn't give *her* the assignment. Lukas had tried to think fast and brush it aside as Kate needing to feel like an essential part of the group. This trip would be her contribution. Marta always had a comeback. She said Kate had assisted with her research on the tiles and her studies to know something about the war before she'd come. Lukas grew tired of the banter. He wasn't going to tell her why he hadn't asked Marta to go to Venice. He hadn't thought of it—that was all. She wouldn't have believed him.

But the deeper truth he'd keep to himself: he worried about Marta. She acted so strong on the outside, but he saw little signs of her grieving. And she had become attached too quickly to Kate and Abbie. He didn't want her hurt when they went their separate ways. Sometimes he worried that he had become too attached to Marta. When he imagined her gone from the house, he felt not sorrow but fear. Could he live without her? Could he live without wildflowers in little jars, without her kind rebukes, without her presence?

Lukas realized they'd crossed the open border into Italy. He needed to concentrate on this Schloss Weiss. But he'd keep Marta near the estate as much as he could. Until Wolfram Meizer was found.

⋆⟫━◯━⟪⋆

Marie Moore spoke only broken English, which didn't help Kate's anxieties about this trip. But at least they didn't travel to the area where Kate and Jack had stayed. When Marie and Kate arrived at Francis' long-term-care nursing home, Kate took in the Mediterranean-style gardens and arched breeze-ways. She had never seen such a comforting medical facility.

Marie accompanied Kate to the doorway of Francis' room. "A bad day for him today. This come sometime. He be old Francis tomorrow or next day. *Mi* man is strong." Marie smiled. "Come tomorrow?"

"No, I can't. I have to return to Austria," Kate tried to talk slowly so Marie could understand.

A frown replaced her smile. "Small time. Small time." Kate assumed that meant she had a short time with him.

The room had an overpowering smell of menthol and medicine. Francis Moore appeared tiny and frail against the white of his hospital bed. An IV ran to his bruised hand. Smiling, he motioned Kate to come inside.

When Marie spoke to him in rapid Italian, he answered simply, "*Si,*" and she left the room.

"Very good, she will leave us. My wife gets too concerned."

"It is the job of a wife."

"*Si, si.* And this husband will do as she asks. We will talk a short time. She is retrieving my book, an English version, from the hospital library for you to take. It is my memoir."

"Thank you," Kate said. Francis knew she had questions about his time at Ebensee. He wanted to talk while he could— that was what his wife had told Lukas. But now in his presence, Kate didn't know quite where to begin.

"You are Kate Porter, and I am Francis Moore." He pushed a button that raised the bed up straighter. His hair was pure white and his brown skin wrinkled, as if he'd spent all his days in the sun.

"I apologize for not introducing myself."

"It is fine. Now I am told this is about KZ Ebensee and Wolfram Meizer."

"That is correct. Would you mind sharing your story with me?"

"He is still alive, isn't he? Wolfram Meizer is alive?"

"We believe he is. We are trying to find exactly where."

"Why do you seek him?"

"He may know what happened to my husband."

Francis considered her words instead of asking for more details. He shook his head as he stared at her for a long time, examining words and memories in her eyes. "I do not need to know everything," he said. "But I want you to seek Wolfram for other reasons also."

Kate gazed into the man's eyes. A cold gray, they reminded her of an ancient star that fought hard to keep bearing light. Francis Moore had done a lot with his life since the war's end in 1945. He'd moved the world to remember and take a good look at itself and its future. But there was deep pain buried inside, pain Kate could recognize but never comprehend. Its vastness was too great.

"I understand," she whispered, because she did. He wanted her to seek Wolfram for him and for the others who could not.

"Have you been to Ebensee?"

"Not yet."

"There is a good museum by the Catholic church. The

Resistance Museum with good people who can help you. You should also see the camp location. It will help in your search to understand this man you seek." Francis closed his eyes in weariness.

"Is there anything you can tell me?"

"It is in my book. I put as much as words can say in those pages. It is a photograph, but only those who were there can truly understand." He closed those steel gray eyes. "I am too tired to tell it myself. You tell our stories when we are gone, all right?" With these words he opened his eyes and looked at her intently.

"I will try," she said, nervous about what this would mean to her. "I don't know how, but I will try."

"That is all we require."

Marie Moore returned Kate to the train station. She had come a long way for fifteen minutes with Francis Moore and his book. But somehow it was worth it. Outside the station, Kate ate lunch at a café beneath a red-and-white umbrella. She used the phone Lukas had loaned her to call the estate. Anni answered in a tone that told Kate she was interrupting. Quickly Anni informed her that Abbie and Marta had gone flower collecting or animal tracking or something like that; then she hung up.

Kate relaxed for a moment, watching a line of people who waited at a landing along the waters of the Grand Canal. Then with a sudden purpose, Kate paid her bill and went to the ticket booth. She watched the light wind ripple the waters as she carried the ticket to the now-loading group heading for the Piazza San Marco.

Plaster peeled from walls, flowers bloomed fully, and tourists and couples strolled the bordered walkways as the boat cruised the canal toward the wide mouth of the Grand Canal. Kate marveled at the ancient city once again.

With the jacket she'd needed in Austria tucked beneath her arm, Kate disembarked after passing beneath the stone-carved mass of the covered Rialto Bridge. The sunshine heated the pavement and warmed her fair arms and face. Within minutes, Kate reached her destination.

Venice was much more crowded than she remembered; tourists and voices in many languages swirled around her. But she was back. Her feet moved and stopped in the exact same places until she stood in front of the hotel where she and Jack had stayed.

It hadn't changed in the years since she'd carried the paper bag of warm pastry upstairs. Time hadn't worn on these walls like it did on the people who walked in and out of the arched, wooden door. Kate thought of who she'd been then. Nearly four years ago now. She'd stood here with excitement for the day ahead, not knowing that inside her room her husband was gone. She never could have expected what had transpired between that day and this one.

Kate stepped back to the edge of the canal until she looked up and found their window. The doors were pushed open, and white lace curtains fluttered in the soft breeze.

And Kate felt peace. Whatever happened next, she was going to be all right. This place had not stolen God's presence from her life, though it had taken her a long time to see that. God would repay what had been stolen—not necessarily Jack, but a life and a future. She never wanted to endure such pain again. But with the perspective of this sunny day in Venice, Kate could see that as an individual, she was better and stronger for all she'd endured. Pain and sorrow had brought a greater compassion into her life. The experience had wrenched her from the walled world she'd enclosed around herself.

With one last glance, Kate said good-bye to the place that had begun her new life. And she suddenly found that she wasn't afraid anymore.

CHAPTER THIRTY-THREE

M om, look what I made." Abbie plopped on the end of the bed with a straight line of a crocheted chain. Kate sat up and looked at the clock. It was past nine, and she could tell that Abbie had been up awhile. The soft, white comforter had kept her trapped in slumber after her long, tiring journey to and from Venice.

"You're doing a great job," Kate said encouragingly. "You told me on the phone you were learning to embroider."

"I started learning that yesterday."

"Mrs. Olsen has spoiled you."

"Mom, she's Frau Olsen."

"Yes, she is."

"Yesterday we had a tea party in the woods, and I helped make all the meals. Do you know how to embroider?"

"Not really," Kate said, a funny frown on her face.

"We'll learn from Frau Olsen together. I like doing things with my ole mom too."

"Your *ole* mom? Hey, little lady!" Kate grabbed her daughter and started tickling.

"Okay, okay, my young mom!"

"And don't you forget it," Kate said, touching the end of Abbie's button nose.

"Frau Olsen said she's going to make me an apron for my birthday."

"You told her your birthday is coming soon?" Kate stretched and sat up higher in bed.

"Yes. She said if we're still here, we can have a party."

"That sounds great, honey. But I think we'll be home by then." The thought of home made Kate realize that she hadn't called her parents or Connie since the first few days. Her best friend had probably found some movie script to match her life here and was dying to share it. Kate missed the way Connie made her laugh and how she seemed to barely hold her own life together, but then accomplished more than most people she knew. Kate hadn't even sent postcards yet.

"Come downstairs and I'll make you some tea, okay?" Abbie hopped from the bed and was gone from the room before Kate replied. She heard small footsteps pad down the hallway and stairs.

As Kate rolled over, Francis Moore's book fell to the floor with a clunk. She had read some on the train and planned to read more in bed, but the late hour and long journey brought sleep with only the introduction finished.

Kate now began to read. Within fifteen minutes she was hurrying down the stairs in her pajamas with the book in hand. She passed Marta and Abbie in the kitchen. "Where is he?" she asked.

"In the sunroom," Marta replied with a wondering look on her face.

"Abbie, I'll be back for tea in a few minutes, all right?" Kate was already out of the doorway when Abbie said okay.

Lukas appeared to be part of his chair with his back pressed in and his arms along the chair's arms. A plume of smoke rose gingerly from a pipe in his hand. The morning sunlight poured into the room. Kate had almost forgotten how his presence could intimidate her, and she suddenly remembered she was still in her pajamas and she'd not brushed her hair or put on any makeup.

"I found something," she said, hurrying toward him.

"I found some things also."

"Great. At the castle?" Her heart was pounding.

"Yes, but—"

"First, you must read this." She came closer.

He straightened and nodded to the chair beside his. "This must be Francis Moore's book. I have meant to read it for years."

"You will wish you had. Read this part here." Kate handed the open book to him and scooted the other chair close. She reread the words from beside him, so anxious that she could barely keep still.

> We had known something was suspicious with Theo. He worked on special assignments. The officers usually kept him separated from us. But Meizer also would take him for work details. Some believed he was spying on us to Meizer.
>
> You could see that Meizer was in a rage when the door first flew open. He stormed into the printing room and searched every face. Then he saw Theo.
>
> "Did you save the template?"
>
> "You told me to destroy it," Theo said. "What happened? I gave it to the girl. She said you wanted me to give it to her."
>
> "Do you know the coordinates in your mind?"
>
> "I can try. But I destroyed everything. You told me to." Theo was already begging.
>
> Wolfram turned into a crazed man as I had seen many times. He grabbed his gun and hit Theo in the face. Theo fell,

and Meizer went mad, hitting him with the butt of his pistol until it was covered in blood. Theo was dead.

Lukas was silent.

Kate took the book from his hands and turned the pages back. "Look what Theo did before the war."

Lukas read the words and nodded. "Theo Mochlmann was a tile maker."

"Now read this." Kate was excited. "It's Susanne."

A young woman had come to the camp. She had come twice before, I was sure, because we all moved to the fence to watch her. We did not care that this might anger Meizer. This girl was like seeing a stream in the desert. She was all we dared not hope for—her youth and innocence. She was afraid to enter; we could see that when she looked at us—a mixture of sympathy and disgust in her expression. We did not blame her, for we knew we must appear as filthy skeletons. One inmate claimed she had touched his hand gently and told him to hang on, that soon help would come. We wanted to believe in an angel at the time.

We talked about the girl and tried to find out more about her. Someone discovered she was Meizer's housekeeper and that she came to the camp to bring Meizer fresh bread and eggs for his morning breakfast. Of course we all speculated more. The houseboy relayed that she was not his mistress, though Meizer had that intention. Once when she came and he was drunk, he had proposed to her and tried to take her in his arms. She had blushed and pushed away. That is what the houseboy told us, but he knew we wanted to believe in our angel. So I never knew if what he said was true or not.

After Meizer murdered Theo before our eyes, he left the camp. The kommandant was angry because Meizer left without permission. We all believed he was going after our angel—that she was the girl Theo had talked about. We

*were afraid for her. I think even the atheist in our small
group began to pray. But we never knew what happened to
this girl because she never came to the camp again.*

*Hope was lost, but liberation was just around the corner. I
believe that some of us would not have survived if not for our
angel giving us hope.*

"Susanne," Lukas said, closing the book.

"Isn't it amazing? Karl's sister was their angel. She convinced
Theo to give her the tile that she brought to the drop point
Marta told me about. You were right about Wolfram wanting
the tile; he wanted the tile in 1945. He didn't find it—"
Kate paused as she realized it—"but Wolfram did find her."

"Please leave me now." His voice was strained, and it
surprised her to see his expression. He held the book against
his chest, crinkling his forehead as if in pain.

"Of course," Kate said solemnly, turning to go.

Then his voice stopped her. "Kate, get dressed."

"Why?" she asked.

"We are going to Ebensee."

"Mom, don't feel bad if you have to leave me." Abbie read her
thoughts as they sat drinking tea. Kate was drinking quickly,
and she noticed her knee bouncing up and down. She kept
listening for Lukas to come into the kitchen. She sighed deeply
and wondered again if she should have left Abbie in the States
with her parents. But they had enjoyed many moments
together since coming here—cherished moments, and now
guilty moments.

"I just have these things I need to do," Kate explained.

Abbie sat across from her with a too-large flowered apron
over her clothes. "I don't mind. I like Frau Olsen a lot. She
doesn't have a granddaughter—she doesn't have any children
at all."

"That's true," Kate agreed.

Abbie hopped from her chair and came toward her. Kate pulled her onto her lap. Her daughter's head was almost level with her own. Kate touched Abbie's braided hair.

"Mom, I need to talk." Abbie turned sideways to look at her.

"What would you like to talk to me about?"

"We talked before we came about why you were coming here. I was so happy when I got to come too. So I decided that you can't feel bad about going places. I know you are going places to find Daddy."

"You know it may not happen the way we want. Abbie, I must be truthful with you. We may never know what happened. We may not get him back."

"I know. But I keep praying and praying. If Daddy did die—" Abbie bit her lip—"then we will have to be strong and get through it."

Tears built in Kate's eyes as she hugged her daughter, whose words were bigger than she was.

The emotion continued to escalate as Lukas and Kate prepared to leave. Marta had confided in her about Lukas' love for the girl Susanne. Now she understood his strange mood when they'd read Francis Moore's book. And though Abbie's words gave her strength, Kate continued to feel guilty about leaving, even if it was only for the day—again. So it was with questions and sorrow that she departed for a concentration subcamp with Lukas.

Kate pivoted in her seat to wave at Marta, Abbie, and Lukas' usual driver, Rey, who seemed surprised that Lukas was taking the car without him. The massive gates opened as they approached, and Kate turned to watch them close her daughter safely inside.

Please, God, protect her when I'm there and when I'm gone. Protect us all and guide everything we do.

After a long silence, they began to talk.

"You didn't tell me what you found at Schloss Weiss," Kate said.

"That is correct. I nearly forgot. It is a hotel now. The owners were friendly and enjoyed visitors who like to talk. They tell me that a man of Wolfram's age rented the entire place for six months. The couple spent the winter in Greece with the money, and they suggested it was a sizeable amount. But then Wolfram abruptly broke the six-month lease and left. They seemed happy about it because they were concerned about closing the hotel during the summer."

"Do you think Wolfram was there to see if it was the location of the Nazi secret?"

"Exactly. I do not think Wolfram knew the location because he did not have the tile. While we are gone today, Marta is going to further examine the tile pieces for clues of why they're so important to Wolfram. Tonight we will do that together."

"Why would that inmate Theo help Wolfram by making the tile and showing him where the Nazi treasure was?"

"To survive, most likely. Wolfram probably promised freedom or food for the location of where the officers were hiding Nazi loot."

"What will Ebensee show us?" Kate asked, admiring the green meadows and tall mountain peaks surrounding them.

"I do not know if that place was the beginning, or the beginning of the end. But it will show us where this all began, and it will lead us to the end."

Chapter Thirty-Four

I t was all changed. Lukas recognized the landscape if he looked up at the way the towering mountains were shaped at this place in the narrow valley. But now the road was lined with houses. He remembered fewer trees and army vehicles that had dug deep ruts into parts of the road.

Neither he nor Kate had spoken since they left the main roadway to follow the KZ Ebensee signs. They were driving along a residential street when he saw the stone arch that had once been the gateway into the camp. He stopped in front of it. Instead of barracks and mud and U.S. Army personnel, there were homes and yards and children playing.

Lukas could not decide if that was good or bad. Who could live with such ground beneath them? with ashes and blood fertilizing their flower bushes? But then, why not have life grow from death and make laughter and love where blood and tears had fallen?

Kate wanted to read the gold-colored plaque on the stone arch. Lukas didn't get out of the car when she walked to it and snapped a photo. It had been his idea to bring the camera, to document everything in case something held a clue. Lukas wanted as much evidence as possible against Wolfram Meizer when the day came for the authorities to bring him before his victims. But Lukas also couldn't help feeling his own guilt. He knew that the ugliness that had burned within him had never been exorcised from his soul. It could never be.

"The plaque was placed there in 1995. A bit late, it seems," Kate said once she returned to the car.

"That was the fiftieth anniversary of the liberation. Some things take a long time to remember—and to admit."

"This is so strange," she said. "How could people live here?"

He had to follow the signs to find the cemetery parking lot that was shaded beneath trees. First he noticed the monuments behind the low stone fence—he'd seen photographs of the larger ones at Mauthausen. The monuments were erected by the countries of the world who had lost citizens to the Nazis. This smaller camp was obscure in comparison to the well-known camps like Dachau, Auschwitz, Belsen, and on and on. Yet this subcamp, which didn't even earn full camp status, had dozens of country monuments within the stone border.

Kate was already waiting outside the car, but Lukas' legs wouldn't move. Finally he got out, leaving the door open. He followed Kate to the iron gate, where they entered the place of the dead.

Now he remembered, though everything seemed put in its wrong place. Across the courtyard he saw the row of black ovens surrounded by bricks and plaques for the dead. He remembered the sign that hung over the crematorium. He'd memorized it after reading the words again and again. It was a dying man's last breath of dignity.

> Not ugly worms
> Must in the future be nourished by my body!
> The clean flame should eat me up.

I always loved the warmth and the light
Therefore burn my body and do not bury me.

"I've been here before," he whispered.

"Marta told me a little," she said softly, lacing her arm through his. It bothered him for an instant and he almost pulled away. He had only slowly come to like her, even respect her. But he knew she reached for him out of her own need also. And he suddenly needed her arm as he walked this ground again.

"I grew up just over a few ranges of mountains in Hallstatt. After Susanne died, we followed Wolfram's trail for months, not knowing he had returned here. We arrived at this place just after the camp had been liberated by your U.S. Army."

They walked toward a large white sign near one wall. It gave a short history of the camp with descriptions of where the barracks had been located. Lukas looked at it closely, getting the perspective of the camp right in his mind.

Kate read a section aloud. "'Ebensee was a subcamp of Mauthausen Concentration Camp. It was built on November 18, 1943, as a labor camp to construct a system of tunnels into the mountain for a rocket-research factory. Most of the prisoners arrived from Mauthausen or other satellite camps.'"

Lukas remembered. He remembered every detail of the day he had arrived. It was sunny and warm for early May. He'd forgotten how beautiful Salzkammergut was—when raised as a child in such magnificence one quickly forgot to really see. And the war had helped blind his vision to beauty. The Americans had arrived just a day earlier. Local Resistance groups had already been in contact with them, but Lukas, Karl, Edmund, and Oskar came quickly to find Wolfram and exact their revenge. Jantes' blood stained their clothing, and his agonizing death rang in their ears.

The corpses.

Lukas could see them now, and he abruptly yanked away

from Kate. He closed his eyes and opened them again. They disappeared for a minute, then returned. Pure white bodies, naked and disfigured, were stacked like firewood or just left beside a pathway. Living corpses reached for him. The stench of disease and death made them cover their noses. But many skeletal faces smiled—they smiled and cheered from stretchers—some half dressed, some not at all. Their feet were black from frostbite and wrapped with any bit of dirty cloth. Their teeth were missing and their eyes so sunken he wondered how they saw. And they smiled for him.

Lukas remembered meandering through the camp. Karl had given them the news they wouldn't believe at first: Inmates had killed the guard Wolfram the night before. They all wanted proof, but the body had already been burned. Karl argued with them, wanting more, when Lukas had walked away. He wandered without destination through the sickness and odor. Some of the German POWs were dragging bodies and piling them in heaps. Their shoulders were hunched and uniforms dirty, not the proud Nazis they'd once been—like *he* had been.

An American trooper was telling a liberation story to several other soldiers as Lukas passed. He heard the young man tell of an inmate looking through his kit bag and emptying a tube of toothpaste into his mouth, then kissing his hand and asking for an autograph.

"Most beautiful place in Europe," the blond-haired young man said. "If this area isn't paradise on earth, I don't know what is. But then we find this. We hear there are camps like this dotted all over the place—I never would have imagined one place so terrible on God's earth."

Lukas' time as SS *Unterscharführer* Bruno Weiler at Mauthausen flooded over him. It had been liberated also. If he had stayed with the Nazis, he would have been dragging bodies along a path. If Tatianna had not come and his eyes not been opened, he would have continued for five more years into the darkness of evil—an evil seeping upon stolen lives like fermenting wine. Five more years he would have partaken of that cup. Would he have become like those men—too drunk with the wine of darkness to truly see what they'd done?

The American soldiers were disgusted and angry. Battle tough, they were brought to tears at what they saw. The SS did not fear the Americans as much as they feared the prisoners. Revenge was allowed. Guards not protected by the troops were literally torn to pieces. Lukas remembered stopping in front of something twisted and strange on the ground. He'd stared at it for a while until he realized it was an arm, the arm of an SS officer—he could see a portion of the swastika armband in the dirt.

Then he had been recognized.

The inmate had been following him. Lukas saw the man walk boldly toward him with an American GI, when Lukas had paused in his dazed walking. Their eyes met, but Lukas didn't know the inmate.

He spoke a fragment of English. "He, he. He guard at Mauthausen." The man's finger shook as he pointed. Eyes from everywhere turned toward Lukas.

That's when Lukas had looked back, realizing he'd walked a long way. Karl and the others were nowhere in sight. And he knew it was his fate. He should be punished. Perhaps that would take away the disgust of this place, of his fellow Austrians, of himself. Not only the disgust but the guilt. Guilt so heavy and piercing, he didn't care if he lived or died.

"Come with me," the American said. "We'll ask you some questions at headquarters."

Lukas didn't resist. In that place, this place he stood once again, he didn't really care. The inmate had called him Bruno Weiler and, before they reached headquarters, Lukas had destroyed his papers stating his name as Lukas Johansen. Karl would eventually find him and try to free him, but Lukas didn't want it. He swore Karl to secrecy until he served what justice demanded.

But Lukas would never feel the relief and freedom, even when he walked from the prison years later. He'd admitted his guilt and gone to prison. There was no finger the size of a twig pointing and accusing him now. But the guilt would never leave him.

"Read more," he said to Kate, as if the sign were the prosecuting attorney.

"'In April alone, 4,547 died. There were too many for the crematorium. A thousand dead bodies were found when the Americans liberated the camp. The ovens could burn 8 bodies at once. They were kept working 24 hours a day and could not keep up.' Herr Johansen? Lukas?"

He looked her way. His eyes felt glassy until he blinked.

"You saved some of them. Marta told me. You saved some families and gave information that helped the Allies. You saved lives." Her voice was soft, but her words angered him. How dare she speak anything about that time when she knew nothing at all?

He said nothing, lest he regret what anger brought to his lips. He turned away from her and again saw the line of black ovens encased in brick, some with their doors open.

How many had he saved from the flames? Never enough.

◈═◈═◈

Kate watched Lukas sit on a concrete curb and lean into his hands. There were noises around—the cars on the distant highway, a saw cutting wood for a remodeling job within view of the graves. But the cemetery itself seemed to hold a silence all its own. Like the eye of a storm, it rested. Countries from around the world had brought their offerings of flowers— mostly silk and plastic arrangements—but some were fresh. This place had not been forgotten.

She walked around the manicured lawns surrounded by raised, bordered squares. A lone headstone rested in the center of the green grass. Kate realized the number etched into the stone was the number of bodies resting beneath. Who were they? It was easy to see just numbers and nearly pass by a smaller mass grave. Oh, only 208 in this grave compared with 1,377 in the last one. Or what about a large camp, where millions had died? But in this one grave were 208 lives. Each unique individual was born into the world with a cry and left the world the same way. Who had they been?

"Let us go," Lukas said, joining her, his steps slowing over the gravel. He followed her without speaking until they were inside the car and the engine running. He stared over the stone fence. "I thank you for your words. I know you mean well."

Kate nodded, wishing she could find something to say to help him. But silence seemed best.

"I cannot go to the museum today. This is enough. We will stop at the tunnels for a few moments, then return home."

Kate looked again toward the area where 208 people rested.

The sign was like a trailhead marker beside the road. Lukas stayed in the car while Kate hurried up the path to the entrance of the underground tunnels. A group of people were there, listening to a soft-spoken, handsome young man who described the background of the Ebensee subterranean "gallery." Kate blended in with the group and listened.

"One military agenda of the National Socialist Party toward the end of the war was to improve its missile industry. The Allies bombed many factories and so an underground facility was established. The A4, also known as the V-2 bomb, was under development here.

"Five hundred prisoners from Mauthausen were brought here in November 1943 to build the camp. It was extremely difficult work, digging into the mountain. If prisoners became ill or unable to work, most were returned to Mauthausen, where they died from exhaustion, illness, or murder. By the end of 1944, nine thousand prisoners were interned at Ebensee."

Instead of moving inside with the group, Kate stayed at the entrance. There was nothing else there but history now. Tours were given here every day during the summer months and on weekends during the off-season. Tours to remember and tell the story. But this wasn't where Wolfram Meizer was to be found.

Lukas was talking on the cellular phone when she returned to the car. She closed the door after getting into the leather seat, and then she noticed the look on Lukas' face. "What happened?" she asked, fearing the worst possibilities.

"I have been asked to the invitation-only opening of Garten Wald."

Kate was perplexed.

"It is our second location, a restored castle grounds located on Waldsee—Forest Lake, not far from here. The host is unnamed, except for being its honored proprietor."

"It's Wolfram Meizer. Why would he invite you to this?" Kate asked, stunned.

"He believes himself smarter than we are. Another surprise move on his part."

"But you can't go," she said.

He set his jaw. "Of course I will attend."

Kate was silent as the car rumbled to life. She tried to picture this Garten Wald—"Garden Woods" was its translation. It would rest on the lakeshore of Waldsee, similar to the alpine lakes she'd seen so many of, probably secluded but not uninhabited. It seemed completely impossible, but what if Jack was at Garten Wald?

"We found Wolfram," she whispered.

"No. He found us."

CHAPTER THIRTY-FIVE

Jack and Rudy had perfected their system of passing information through the vent between their rooms. Rudy passed through a "wire arm," as he called the contraption that carried their notes. Through that process, Jack was able to get Rudy's information about the building of the dam on Waldsee in the 1940s. Rudy was also good at drawing cartoons. He'd leave one for Jack when he returned from the tunnels. Jack gave reports of each night's expansion in a coded message, in case they were ever caught. Then he told Rudy about his discovery of the cave. Rudy confirmed Jack's suspicions—Wolfram was searching for a cave or tunnel the Nazis had used during the war to hide something of great importance. Rudy had figured that out from bits of conversation over the years.

"Why do you think he asks me to the castle every day?" Jack asked Rudy through the vent.

"When Wolfram gets bored of watching his birds in their outside aviaries, he brings a few inside. He likes to put some of his birds in bigger cages to see how they react and how the other birds react to their position. Then those birds are moved to the smallest cage of all."

Jack thought about Rudy's words. "So when were you his favored guest? And why were you demoted to the small cage?"

"It has been many years. We weren't on Waldsee then. And I believe Wolfram grew bored of me. I think he suspects that you know something you don't tell him. So he attempts to sneak information from you."

"You mean the way I attempt to sneak information from him?"

"He tells you exactly what he wants you to know. Though he must be getting old by now, and his brain isn't always as sharp."

"It's amazing that Ian is his son," Jack said, folding part of his blanket to make a flat pillow.

"I'm praying for that boy's soul. Let's not get into a debate over him again. Ian sees more than we know—we think we fool him all the time. He's probably saved our behinds from Wolfram a time or two."

"Maybe, but I think the *Mein Kampf* doctrine is tattooed into his brain tissue," Jack said.

"Some things only come about by prayer and fasting—that's what the Bible says."

"Fasting? If we fasted, we'd die."

"There are many ways to fast besides abstaining from food, my friend."

"Our entire lives are a fast—an involuntary one."

"That doesn't count. Quiet a moment," Rudy said in a firm voice. "Someone's coming."

Jack heard the footsteps also and crawled quickly to his bunk. He distinguished two sets of footsteps as they approached. They stopped at his door and the locks clicked open. Instead of Ian's tall, narrow frame, nearly all the hallway light was covered by the presence of Wolfram Meizer in his doorway.

When the chain was pulled, harsh light flooded the darkness. Wolfram walked inside and examined the room. Ian entered behind him and stood near the small table.

Wolfram spoke to Jack, but Ian did not translate. They both waited and looked at Ian. The old man was expectant, eager to receive a response. He turned to Ian and spoke what Jack understood as "Tell him."

"What is it, Ian?" Jack asked. It took another moment for Ian to take his eyes from Wolfram. But instead of translating, he spoke to Wolfram, who laughed heartily, saying, *"Nein, nein."*

"Ian, what is it?" Jack was trying to think of the small cage he was about to be placed inside.

"He said your wife is here."

"Who?" The word was his, but the voice sounded strange in his ears. He couldn't say her name in this place. Had Wolfram brought her to this prison? "She is here? The estate?"

"That is what I asked," Ian said. "But she is not here. She is in Austria. Your wife has been here for several weeks."

Wolfram seemed satisfied by Jack's stunned emotions. He picked up a wooden kitten, Jack's best carving yet, and scrutinized it closely. As Jack looked out the open door, his sudden urge was to race outside and lock Ian and Wolfram inside. But Wolfram was too quick. As if he had read Jack's mind, Wolfram headed for the door himself, the carved kitten in his hand.

Ian and Jack stared at one another for a minute; then Ian left him and locked the door as he went.

"She is here," Jack whispered to himself. "Kate is here."

⊷═◉═⊷

The days passed in rapid succession, moving them toward the date of the gala event at Garten Wald. Marta was angry that

Lukas was going to attend and wanted to go with him. He refused. Kate had kept her distance for a few days and let them work it out. It was time well spent with Abbie. Lunches in hand, they would follow pathways dotted with wildflowers and studied maps that showed routes to the Naturfreundehaus huts that extended all the way across the Alps. Kate's legs were sore every day for a week. They took photographs in fields of flowers and brought back specimens to press and frame when they got home.

At night Kate used the Internet to gain more information. Marta and Lukas reached a peace settlement and joined her again. They began tracking Wolfram Meizer's past activities. The same maps of Austria that Kate and Abbie used to plan their future cross-country trek were used to study Waldsee and the surrounding mountains.

Lukas made contact with departments in Vienna and the Salzkammergut and found descriptions of the property Wolfram had bought on the secluded end of the lake. It took time to track, since Wolfram had used false names and corporations to shield the true ownership, but using Lukas' contacts and some assumptions on their part—the activities of Wolfram Meizer began to unfold. One report told of the ruins of a castle and an abandoned salt mine that Wolfram had purchased in the late nineties at an enormous price. Mountains towered around the lake except where the village rested on the western edge. The rest of the lake sloped straight up, making it impossible to travel the circumference of the lake on foot. The restored Garten Wald resting in the flattened joint of two mountain ranges could only be reached by boat. Lukas also obtained an old diagram of the original tunnels of the salt mine before Wolfram had bought it.

Every day Kate fought the urge to rent a car and drive to Waldsee herself. But it couldn't be risked. She kept herself busy with Abbie. They called home and Cottonwood several times.

Connie was excited to hear from her and reported that Whiskers had a surprise for them when they came home—three new kittens. Kate, Abbie, and Marta shopped at the local village; Lukas insisted on going with them, though he sat on a bench in the small park and smoked his pipe. Kate and Abbie finally sent off a few postcards—to the only people who knew where they really were. Kate had debated about sending Mason one. In the end, she decided not to and told herself she'd call him tomorrow. She'd been saying that for weeks now.

The morning of the Garten Wald gala arrived. It had been decided that Kate would go along and stay at the village across the lake. If Lukas didn't return by the scheduled time, Kate would call the local police. Lukas wanted Anni, Marta, and Rey to remain at the estate. He hired extra security for the grounds, which relieved Kate's worry about Abbie's safety. Wolfram Meizer had a plan, and they had yet to discover what that plan was, besides drawing Lukas into his lair.

She would be away only one night, Kate thought as she loaded her suitcase into the car. She saw Anni peer from a window and then disappear inside. The young woman was consistently in a bad mood.

Once in the car, Lukas began to pull from the driveway. Kate turned in the seat for her usual backward wave to Abbie and Marta.

"Lukas, stop!" she said suddenly. Kate could see Abbie running down the road after the car. She got out quickly, before Lukas had completely stopped. "What's wrong?"

Tears streamed down Abbie's cheeks as she tumbled into Kate's arms.

"Abbie, are you hurt? What is it?" Panic streaked through Kate. She held Abbie back to look for blood.

"I didn't tell you. I almost forgot."

"What?"

"I love you, Mom."

"I love you too." Kate's face was level with Abbie's as she wiped away the tears. "You don't have to cry, honey."

"And, Mom, please, please come back."

Kate put her hand over her mouth. "I'll come back," she said quickly. Then she realized that it wasn't something she could promise. "I will always do everything in my power to come back to you."

Tears poured from Abbie's eyes. "Bring Daddy back too."

⤐═◉═⤙

Wolfram Meizer buttoned the jacket over his stomach and gazed into the mirror. The snow-white shirt and black tuxedo fit his shape to perfection. He strolled through the house, his castle, where every light in every room was turned on, except in his office, of course. Stopping before the floor-to-ceiling windows in the master parlor, he gazed outside.

The musicians were set up on the front terrace, the caterers had candles ready to light on the decorated tables, and food was prepared in his kitchen. Tiny lights lit the pathway along the wide entrance from the boat dock to the terrace and the castle doorway. Tonight the world would meet him. He had started well-placed rumors that the mystery host was a wealthy German businessman relocated from South America—the truth was often the best deceiver. Didn't everyone want to see the grand reconstruction of Garten Wald and meet the mad owner no one knew much about?

Wolfram had selected his guest list carefully: cabinet leaders, members of the Viennese upper class, old money moguls, Party leaders. The choices would seem random, thus making it suspicious in an intriguing way. The rumors of intrigue would bring the ones on the list hurrying to the village. Others would ask themselves, "Why was that one invited and not me?" "How can I get on that guest list?" the intentionally uninvited would ask. Yet others would think, *There is a plot of some kind brewing.*

Wolfram took a deep breath to prepare for the night ahead. It would prove to be one of the best of his life. And there was one guest on his list he had waited decades to meet again.

⟶≡◖≡⟵

Jack had tried to rest, tried to figure out a plan, tried to understand why he wasn't brought to Wolfram's office any longer, and why no one was allowed to do the nighttime work. Rudy had been no help. They talked for a short time through the vent, but then Rudy grew tired and needed rest. Jack could tell that Rudy didn't understand the desperation of the situation.

Jack had tried to discover Kate's location, when she had come, and what she was doing in Austria. He'd found out nothing. But tonight something was happening, and Jack was willing to do the impossible.

He went to the door and began pounding until he heard footsteps. Suddenly, the door opened, and Ian stood in the doorway.

"Ian, have I ever asked you for anything for myself?"

"No."

"I must ask tonight. Have I ever given you reason not to trust my word?"

"No."

"Then trust me."

Their eyes locked, each evaluating the many months they'd spent together and what it had meant. Had friendship developed over that time? Had the friendship fostered trust? Had trust grown strong enough for each man to risk his own life in the other's hands?

"What do you ask?"

"That you help me find my wife."

"I know already."

"Where is she?"

"At the village tonight."

Jack was stunned at the thought of Kate—his Kate—across the lake where the lights called to him. "I must see her. And I need your help."

CHAPTER THIRTY-SIX

Three boats had been chartered for the occasion. A string quartet played softly as Lukas walked to the boarding station. His invitation was carefully examined while a reporter talked in front of a camera, pointing to where the lights of Garten Wald shown across the water.

Lukas was welcomed aboard the wide, flat boat. Drinks and hors d'oeuvres were offered on the open bow by waiters in black-and-white uniforms. Other guests lounged along the railing and the glass-sided cabin, holding drinks and tiny plates. Flags crackled gently in the evening breeze—Austrian, European Union, and another gray-and-red flag with the letters *GW* within double diamonds. Lukas wondered if somewhere in the design the letters *SS* or *NAZI* or a swastika could be hidden from first glance.

Lukas stood along the railing, facing the water. In no mood for small talk, he had already tried to avoid several familiar faces and a member of the press he remembered from Parliament. But he couldn't enjoy solitude for long without seeming surly, so soon he was engaged in conversation with a small group of people he'd known in Vienna. They discussed a new proposal of speed limits, then debated the origin of the wine they drank.

Lukas remembered that a king once said of his wealth, "Meaningless, meaningless. It was all chasing after the wind." What did Lukas really have? His daughters did not know him. He owned properties, several businesses, a casino, and investments in a hospital. As time passed, his work in the government now seemed irrelevant. It was all really worthless.

But Wolfram was building more than an estate in the side of a mountain. There was too much at stake here, and he had too much help. It was a legacy for the future. A legacy Lukas would stand against; yet he was walking right into its headquarters.

The boat landed along a dock. As Lukas and the other guests disembarked, he noticed the woods growing down to the edge of bordered gardens. Flowers arranged in intricate designs lined the wide, cobblestone path and stairways leading up to the castle. Wolfram had prepared an elegant first impression. Lukas distanced himself from the other guests he recognized and assessed the grounds as they moved toward the main terrace, where he could hear a violin playing. The entrance to the salt mine was dark but visible in a cutout section above them. Lukas also glimpsed the flat roof of a structure beyond the wooded area behind the castle and farther up. Would Wolfram dare have Rudy Blessing and Jack Porter locked in one of those buildings? He would believe anything of Wolfram. His old enemy was an intelligent and devious man. And when suspicions arose, Wolfram welcomed his critics with open arms.

The remodeled castle had a white turret on one end with a GW flag waving from its cylindrical roof. Lukas saw three floors of lit windows, and he estimated the house to be twice the size of his own. The group climbed the steps to the castle, where earlier guests talked in circles. More guests were arriving at the docks below.

Lukas made his rounds of the groups he was familiar with along the terrace. Trays laden with an assortment of foods covered a table at one end opposite the orchestra stage. Candlelit tables drew groups while others wandered through the house. Most people were interested in meeting their mysterious host. One rumor said he'd returned from Africa after making a fortune in the sapphire industry, another that he had connections in Hollywood. Rumors always ran wild.

Lukas decided to go inside, when someone spoke from a microphone on the stage. "Welcome, my guests. I am greatly pleased to greet all of you."

Applause filled the terrace. Many stood in the presence of their host. If a hundred years had passed, Lukas would have known this man. His nose was larger and his jowls now hung like a bulldog's. He'd gained weight upon his once-trim physique. He still wore his jet black hair slicked straight back. Wolfram was the aged version of the man he'd long known.

Wolfram had been a reckless youth, but he now stood and spoke with an air of royalty. "I am Wolfram, though that is not the name given to me at birth."

Although his name would not be recognized, a stir of voices questioned one another in curiosity.

"I invited you here to enjoy an evening, explore the grounds, and discover the magic of Garten Wald. New friendships will be established here tonight as Garten Wald opens officially. I envision a place for you and other dignitaries to come and enjoy Austria, be it for business or for pleasure. At one time, rival peoples met here under the neutral invitation of the castle lord. Peace was found between the two peoples. May this again be the purpose of Garten Wald."

Light applause followed. Someone behind Lukas whispered,

"What does he believe—that peace accords will be formed on the grounds?"

Wolfram continued. "I have a humble token to show my sincerity for peace and unity among party members, peoples, and the nations. Please, if you will."

A large display covered with red velvet was rolled onto the terrace. The television crew's cameras pivoted immediately to cover the event.

"I invited you here for something more than a mere party. I also want to share my journey. It is not a past I am proud of. Perhaps some will understand it as their own; others will find it difficult to understand, but tonight it must be spoken at last."

Chairs had been moved and wineglasses set down as every face turned, captured by Wolfram's words.

"I spent my childhood days in a village not far from here. My home was not a happy place, and I grew to be a young man seeking something to believe in."

Lukas knew that now the lies had begun. Wolfram had been raised in Germany, not Austria.

"My story is not unlike many Austrian stories. We found the Nazi Party to give us hope for a new beginning. Yes, they spouted their anti-Semitic and racist views along with the message of a greater vision. But anti-Semitic views were already ingrained in much of our culture since the time of the great Crusades or even the Roman age. The fear and misunderstanding of different peoples have always bred hatred. It is not right, but it is fact. And so, as a young man seeking something to believe in, I found the Nazi Party."

Across the crowd and beneath the small white lights, Wolfram's gaze met Lukas'. They had not stared into each other's eyes in decades, and yet it was all there between them—the memories and hatred alike.

"I had a different name at that time."

A cold sensation, quick and consuming, passed through Lukas. With a sudden light of realization, Lukas knew Wolfram's words even before he spoke them.

"My name was Bruno Weiler."

No one reacted to the name or noticed the flash of a smirk Lukas perceived as Wolfram glanced his way again. Wolfram continued with Lukas' story of joining the Nazi youth and of the Anschluss, when Austria was joined with the German Third Reich, and Hitler marched across their border to the cheers of many, including himself. Lukas had moved back involuntarily toward the shadows, away from Wolfram's sight and the eye of the camera. Wolfram was telling Lukas' history and claiming it as his own. It was not a past Lukas liked to remember, but it was his nonetheless. That Wolfram would claim to be Bruno was a twist of mad genius that Lukas didn't fully understand. It brought more fear than anger.

"In 1941, I was assigned the position of guard at Mauthausen Konzentrationslager. Finally, I understood what Hitler and his party were about. But it was too late. No one dared disobey the orders, or he would soon wear the uniform of an inmate. I participated in a firing squad where a woman from my own village was killed."

How did he know about Tatianna? Lukas wondered. He'd never spoken of the girl whose death opened his eyes to what he was doing and who he'd become.

"I cannot say what changed me, but I knew I must help stop this madness. I began to keep records on weapon-making sites and military secrets that I eventually gave to the Allies. I also worked with the Austrian Resistance. At long last, the war ended. But the past came back when I was arrested for Nazi crimes. My comrades could have helped me, but I chose not to fight the charges since I continued to feel terrible guilt. I could have escaped judgment by revealing that I had worked with the Allies and the Austrian Resistance, but I felt the sins of my time at Mauthausen deserved more than a few years in prison.

"Some will say I betrayed Austria. Others that my sins can never be forgiven. I understand both lines of thought. I can only walk the path I believe is right."

No one spoke as Wolfram lowered his head, then raised it to study his audience.

"So now I offer another small token as proof of my repentance." Wolfram gestured toward the velvet-covered display. "I was in South America in 1992 and bought a small art collection. This past year I discovered the collection's original owner was a Jewish family. The paintings were stolen from them during the war. Tonight I proudly return the works to the family. The Neumann family was informed of my gift and sent the grandson of Holocaust victims as a representative. David Neumann, would you please step forward?"

Lukas watched a middle-aged man walk from the audience. Unsmiling, he joined Wolfram on the stage. Wolfram took the edge of the velvet covering and tugged it down. There were gasps and applause as the distinct form of a Klimt painting was revealed.

"I hope this is yet another link in the reparation of peoples in this nation. The rest of the collection is inside, available for you to see. This is a special event. No one has seen this collection in its entirety since the late 1930s. Thank you all for coming."

Loud applause and cheers continued as Wolfram and David Neumann shook hands. People around Lukas talked. One commented, "Political walls are hard to break down, but men like that can do it."

Groups began to move close while others already sauntered toward the house. Lukas waited on the outskirts, talking to people he'd seen at dinner parties in the past. He was composed as always on the outside, but his eyes kept glancing in Wolfram's direction. Wanting to leave, he tried to consider what Wolfram would expect from him. There was a handful of people still alive who knew Lukas' old identity. But none, least of all himself, would want to refute Wolfram's claim. It would be messy and jeopardize everything. Yet how could he allow this man to take his identity? Lukas felt like the door to a very small cage had just been closed around him. Worst of all, he didn't know what Wolfram fully intended to do.

Lukas stayed with the chatter of men and women he'd known for years, though really knew nothing about. They were diverse in backgrounds and politics but all intrigued by the man who had invited them here tonight. The crowd lessened as music and dessert were offered in the water gardens. He scanned the patio in quick darts of movement, but Wolfram was not to be found.

With feigned interest in the painting, he made his way forward. The work reminded him of another Klimt painting, with the woman's long drawn face, dark colors, and mosaic design in her flowing robe.

If Wolfram meant to assay the suspicion in his countrymen, the revelation of a piece of artwork like this would certainly give the answer. It would be widely disputed where he obtained the piece. The usual Nazi rumors were unneeded because Wolfram had actually admitted his past in public. Wolfram knew how to gamble. The gift of the art collection to a wealthy Jewish family could be considered generous retribution, as well as the fact he'd already gone to prison for his crimes. Disgust and anger pulsed through Lukas. He recalled the bodies of Susanne, Jantes, and the white corpses with open eyes and cold fingers at Ebensee.

"Former minister Lukas Johansen," a voice said behind him. Lukas had felt the man's presence before he spoke a word. He turned to face Wolfram Meizer.

"It has been many years," Wolfram said.

"Not enough." They stared coldly at each other, like a challenge. "Bruno Weiler, is it?"

Wolfram laughed. "I believed you would find that interesting."

"What makes you want to be Bruno Weiler?"

Wolfram's gaze did not waver. "Let us talk first."

"After so many years, now you return to Austria."

"The world cannot compare to Europe."

"Especially when you want something." Lukas spoke in a low, precise tone.

"Some desires grow with age."

"But what exactly did you lose so long ago that you seek again?" Lukas gazed toward the dark mountains, knowing Wolfram watched every movement.

"Only solitude and peace in my native country," Wolfram answered.

"You will be returning to Germany?"

"You remember everything, Bruno—I mean, Lukas. Germany may be my birthplace, but Austria is home."

"I find that interesting."

"I think my confession interested you, or angered you? I also remember a young woman who once interested you. I believe her name was Susanne Olsen?" Wolfram taunted.

This is where it is leading, Lukas thought. Wolfram would strive for his weakest point to drive home the dagger, but Lukas was prepared to deflect it.

Wolfram leaned close as a group passed; a few people glanced their way curiously. "I did not realize it until Karl. My contacts discovered that Lukas Johansen is meeting Oskar Gogl at Karl Olsen's home. I wondered why a former Austrian minister would do such a thing. Lukas Johansen could not be my old comrade Bruno Weiler. He could not be the betrayer of my confidence and *der Führer*. How could I have missed that all these years? Was it your facial changes or my stupidity?

Bruno Weiler would not simply disappear in the labyrinth of postwar chaos. I allowed my own situation to keep me from pursuing him fully."

"I am sure your exile to South America did not make it easy," Lukas said, seeking Wolfram's own weakest place. Once he had known this man to fail beneath the lure of drink and a beautiful woman, but the older version of that man would most likely find pride his greatest failing. "Why were you forced to flee Europe when many others stayed, even worked for government agencies? Did you not have aspirations in the Party—want to be *kommandant* of a subcamp, king of your own little world? Ah, I forgot. You were demoted down to camp guard. It is not wise for an officer to get drunk with one of his men and not realize secret military plans were stolen from beneath his nose. Did this not happen to you more than once, and you did not know until I was far away? You led me to the Party, and I walked out with your future as an officer."

Wolfram took a step closer, his face now a sneer. A young man walked toward them with a tray of wineglasses. "Not now!" Wolfram said loudly. He regained his composure, even smiled. "She called for you. Susanne."

Lukas did not say a word as Wolfram laughed.

"As she died, she called for a man named Lukas. I wondered who that could be but never knew until recently."

"And is it not ironic that because of my betrayal of you, I was brought into Susanne's life?" Lukas said in an even tone. "She cared for me, not you. She called for me."

Again Lukas took the smile from Wolfram's face. Yes, pride was his weakness now.

"Men do not take from me. Not even you. Susanne was a temporary fancy. I enjoyed her more seeing her die."

He would not hear it, Lukas told himself. He would not see the body in the snow or the way she turned his way as they walked together. *Keep her out, or you will not be strong enough.*

Lukas realized he had long since clenched his fists at his side. He wished for a weapon so he could destroy this man with pleasure. But first he needed to see all the cards Wolfram held.

Feeling sick and full of adrenaline, Lukas paused before speaking again. "What about Jack Porter?"

"I have no idea what you speak of." There was not even a glimmer of fear on that self-confident face.

"What of the pieces of broken tile?"

Wolfram's manner turned serious. "That interests me."

"I will trade the tiles for Jack Porter," Lukas said quickly. "You can find your treasure with the complete set, isn't that right?"

"Jack will not go without his comrade, I'm afraid."

"Then trade the tiles for both men."

"I need the men and the tiles, and I don't think you trust me with both." Wolfram reached around Lukas and slapped his back hard.

"You will be exposed, Wolfram."

"Did you not hear my grand confession? I am Bruno Weiler, who paid for my Nazi crimes after the war. I make the world right even further by returning Jewish heirlooms to prove my change of heart and alliance."

"There are others who know you are not Bruno Weiler."

"*Ja.* The other guards from Mauthausen who are still alive. Old men who will not refute me or reveal their own past. It is worth the risk. For what can be exposed—that I am not Bruno Weiler? Then who is the real Bruno Weiler? Former minister Johansen may have a very ugly skeleton in his closet. We have some members of the press here tonight. And I have a nice microphone. Is there anything you would like to say? You should hope and pray no one begins to search my background. Only your own will be in jeopardy."

Wolfram laughed heartily, bringing many eyes their way.

"You do not see it, do you? We are very much alike, you and I. Very few attributes separate us. We started out the same, our families, our beliefs—we were even friends. But you lost the vision of a greater world. You scratch away at idealisms that are completely meaningless. Ah, you do not like that word, do you? We are equal men, Lukas Johansen. But I am free from what burdens you. Will you ever be free from your guilt? Men like you never are. So you help me or you will have more guilt upon your soul—Jack Porter's life is in your hands. And do your daughters know who their father really is?"

⊷═◉═⊶

They moved quickly along the edge of the woods, watching for guests while passing the dinner party. Jack followed Ian closely, barely seeing the people through the thick brush they stayed behind. They reached the water, and Jack spotted the tiny dinghy pulled onto shore. There were a flashlight and an extra gas can in the boat.

"Remember the arrangement," Ian said. Jack nodded and shook Ian's hand. He would keep the promise no matter how hard it would be to return to the barrack. His word had been given, and Rudy's life depended on it.

"Jack," Ian said, "I will help you and Rudy survive this. When we make the find, you will be freed. I give you my word."

"As I have given mine," he said.

"You must look better than that," he said, pointing at Jack. Ian tossed him a bag he carried. Jack unzipped it to find a set of clothing and a pair of shoes. He had wondered what to do about his appearance once he arrived at the village in rags. It wasn't what he'd envisioned for meeting Kate, and he'd hoped to borrow someone's laundry hanging from a clothesline.

"Thank you, Ian. Thank you for everything."

Jack used the oars for the first fifteen minutes on the lake, then tugged the string to the outboard engine, guiding the rudder carefully along the rugged shore toward the village lights shining in the darkness. The night was still and the water smooth. Only the urgency pounding within him interrupted the late hour. The boat's motor echoed too loudly, and he couldn't stop looking back, half expecting to be trailed. Instead he saw the casual journey of a well-lit boat leaving Wolfram's dock.

He turned the motor down to a slow, trolling speed. It seemed like hours, but Jack's watch said it was only one when he approached the town along the water's edge. He could distinguish the lights now from their sources on doorposts, streetlamps, and walkways.

Civilization. There were people strolling along a cement walkway in the cool of a summer night. From the darkness beyond the realm of town lights, he sat and watched them. There was little time to waste, but the sight of these people— of lives so close and so far away—mesmerized him as if he were a boy seeing a candy shop for the first time.

The boat putt-putted quietly as Jack sought an inlet along the rocky shoreline. He turned the motor off and coasted toward the shore. When the aluminum hull grazed the shore, he stepped over the edge. Water pressed against the rubber of his high rain boots as he dragged the bow onto shore and tied it off to a tree. He washed his face and arms in the cold lake water, then crouched in the darkness for what felt a long while before grabbing the duffel bag and pushing through the dense undergrowth. If someone stole the boat—he couldn't think of that now.

After Jack had changed his clothing in the brush, he found a dirt trail up a rise and through the trees. The shoes were a little loose and the pants baggy, but there were no holes or stains. It seemed that eyes stared at his every move from the darkness. A twig broke beneath his foot and he stopped to listen. No one was following. No one knew he was here. Jack told himself this again, realizing the wide gulf between captivity and freedom.

The trail turned from dirt to stone and light shone ahead. Then Jack entered the light. It felt both magnificent and terrifying to walk like any other man in the world. He didn't have to stay on one pathway from the barrack to the tunnels to the castle to the barrack. He could run all over, even ride in a car somewhere. It was the oddest sensation to be free, even if that freedom was for a very short time. No one understood it. The woman he saw through a window, the couple strolling along the street. He saw people here and there as he came to the village square. They took little notice of him, though he nearly expected applause and cheers at his arrival. Jack loved the tiny village. It looked so quaint and cozy even at night. He would love to explore it with Kate on his arm. And now she was only minutes away.

Jack followed the directions in his mind, reciting what Ian had told him as he made each turn, until he stood before the sign that read *Zimmer frei*. Ian had explained this was similar to a bed-and-breakfast in the States but less expensive and very homey. Kate was in room 10. She was up there now; Ian had come that day and confirmed it. His wife didn't know he was coming. He didn't know what she'd say, though he'd spent hundreds of hours imagining this moment. He kept feeling fear instead of joy. It was too overpowering, so Jack sat on a bench outside the hotel.

The time had come. But could he really go inside?

⋖═◉═⋗

Kate had never seen Lukas like this. He paced her room and explained the details of his encounter with Wolfram Meizer. She was stunned to realize that Jack was truly alive. He was alive!

"Marta would want us to call the police."

"But we know it would be too dangerous for your husband right now."

"Will you give Wolfram the tiles?"

"I do not know. He told me under his breath that he will kill Jack unless we bring the tile pieces to him in three days. He wanted the pieces now, but I said Oskar's was in the United States. I must go to Vienna tonight. There is something I must decide and people to meet with about it. You will come with me. I will get you a room there."

"Why Vienna? Shouldn't we get back to the estate?"

"I need more help than Marta right now. But I must get Anni to meet me in Vienna. It is time for me to talk to my daughters."

Kate knew what he was saying and saw the turmoil in his face. "I will stay here and take the train in the morning."

"No." He shook his head.

Kate put her hand on his arm. "Lukas, I will be safe here— Wolfram is too busy tonight. Go do what you must. Tell your daughters and be free of it. I will meet you tomorrow at the estate."

He nodded and put his hand over hers. "Thank you."

⋄═○═⋄

Lukas had left only fifteen minutes earlier, but Kate already regretted not going with him. She stood at the window and looked down at the street where he had gone. Even at this late hour people walked in the square and sat on benches. She closed the curtains so that not even an inch of window showed through. The room was cramped with a twin bed, table, antique wardrobe, and bathroom.

The walls began to close around her. She was alone. Jack was alone, but he was alive. Lukas believed he was just across the water. Earlier, on their drive to the bed-and-breakfast, Lukas had pointed out the lights of that castle. Now Kate had the overwhelming desire to see those lights again—the lights of the place where she now knew Jack could be living. But Lukas had told her to stay in the hotel, for her own safety.

Kate undressed and put on the white cotton shorts and shirt pajamas she'd brought. All the while she dreamed of how she could get to Jack. Perhaps she could somehow get aboard or rent a boat and do her own investigating. If he couldn't come to her, she'd go to him. If not for Abbie, Kate would have taken the risk. But she kept seeing her daughter's tears and feeling those slim arms clinging to her.

Kate was looking for her toothbrush when someone knocked on the door.

The door creaked open and, instead of Lukas, a stranger stood before her. Kate tried to shut the door when he said her name.

"Kate."

She paused, trying to see his face. The light in the hall cast shadows over his unkempt hair and scruffy beard.

"Kate, it's me."

It was Jack's voice; she'd almost forgotten the sound. She knew the recorded voice of her husband from watching home videos over and over again. But this real voice was brought from memory to reality. She'd recognize it anywhere. He stood there, waiting for her. But Kate couldn't move. Her hands were shaking and her feet unable to take a step.

He was here. Jack. But he was more than a stranger; he was a ghost. Kate wanted to run or slam the door in his face. She'd longed for him just seconds before, but now Kate knew— worse than losing Jack was to have him suddenly back and not be the Jack she knew.

His expression read the fear in her eyes. He appeared hurt.

"Jack!" was all she could say.

He nodded, and the light from her room fell on his face as she released the doorjamb and it creaked an inch wider. His eyes were Jack's eyes. They were red and rimmed with tears.

"Jack," she heard herself say again, softly. But she couldn't move toward him.

"Katie, I have a million things I want to say to you." He took one step and then another. The distance closed between them. His arms reached for her. His embrace was awkward, and his touch felt foreign and cold against her skin. She tried to hug him back but couldn't.

"You're here. This is really you."

"Yes, frightening sight that I am," he said with a chuckle. He quickly closed the door and turned on a lamp. He glanced around as if someone might be there. This Jack looked older and beyond tired; he was haggard. The beard changed him completely—he'd only once grown out beyond stubble.

"Please, tell me about Abbie. Tell me everything." He grabbed her arm, reminding her of a starving man in desperate need of nourishment. It frightened her, but she considered how she would feel if she'd been the one taken from family and friends for so long. "Kate, I wish I had time to hear about every day. You can't imagine—"

"Abbie," she whispered, wondering what her daughter would think when she saw him. "Abbie will be so happy. How . . . how did you get here? Wait, we need to get out of here, back to Lukas'." Kate was stunned that at last she had Jack— the goal she'd worked for for more than three years. It was over. Jack was here.

"No, Kate. I can't. I only have a few hours."

"What are you talking about?"

"I promised I'd return. That was the only way for me to do this. I gave my word."

"Go back? To Wolfram?"

"Yes. There is a man there, my friend. If I don't return, they'll kill him."

"Rudy Blessing."

"Yes. Then you know about everything—why I've been here?"

"A little, yes."

"What did you believe? Did they leave you a note, or was there blood to make it look like I died?"

"I didn't know you were alive until tonight. All this time I knew nothing."

He grabbed her and embraced her for a long time. This time it didn't feel as awkward. Her hands clasped his back and his breath grazed her neck.

"I'm sorry, Kate. I tried to find a way to get back to you."

"You can't leave again," she said. Her emotions were tied up. "I know you had no choice before, but let's leave now. Abbie has to see you."

He sat on the edge of her bed, his face in his hands. Moments ticked by as Kate studied him—his shoulders were hunched, and his hands weren't the rugged ones she'd known. These were cut and callused, as if they'd worked a hundred years.

"We don't have much time," he mumbled, then stared at her. "I forgot how you looked. No, I didn't forget, but I didn't remember what it was like to be in a room with you. I have to stay focused—we must make a plan."

He wanted to plan, and she still had a hundred questions. How did he get here tonight? Why couldn't he have gotten word to them earlier? Why would he come only to leave again?

"Jack, what happened that day?" she asked.

"Can that wait? There is much I want to talk about. I must hear about Abbie. There are so many things."

"Start at the beginning and tell me everything."

"We don't have time. If I asked you the questions that have been killing me for days and weeks and years—like why are you here? Why are you in Austria?"

"I came to find you, to try one last time." She saw the great emotion in his expression. "Please, Jack, I need to know what happened."

"You mean that morning in Venice?"

"Yes," she whispered, feeling as if she were talking about two other people. That couple could not be her and this Jack. What put this great gulf between them?

"It was easy for them," he said. "They knocked on the door not long after you left. I thought you'd forgotten something. When I opened the door, they hit me. I remember little of the next few weeks and didn't know I'd lost weeks of time. The first six or so months were like that—a dark haze of solitude. I was moved around after that and finally began to do what they chose me for—to find the location of some Nazi loot. We were in Italy at a castle there for a while."

"Schloss Weiss," she said, trying to imagine him in these places while she had waited and sought him from home.

"It was all planned. Remember the grant I was awarded to attend the conference? It was Wolfram's doing, though he went through several organizations. He's a powerful man with links to neo-Nazi groups in the States and Europe. He pays them to do most of his work. He's a man who enjoys playing with others' lives. They chose me because I'd worked with Rudy that summer. They e-mailed me, pretending to be him, telling me about a grant to go to this conference. We e-mailed back and forth in the months before our trip."

She watched his hands. Those hands she'd once known well.

"I'm sorry, Kate. I can't imagine what you've gone through."

"And you," she whispered, looking at him again. This time he didn't seem so much a stranger. She could see more of the Jack she'd once known. They talked quickly, hearing the time tick away in their heads. Kate tried to think of ways to keep him from leaving. He kept asking about Abbie, their families, friends, what people thought had happened, and her life without him.

She hadn't noticed the worn brown bag he'd brought. Jack opened it and handed her something. "This is important. Who took them?"

"How did you get these?" she asked as she flipped through the stack of photographs.

"Wolfram."

"How did he get them?"

"Kate, who took these pictures?"

"Connie. But—"

"Connie, your best friend, movie buff Connie? Does she know you are here?"

"Yes."

"That's how Wolfram knows about you being here."

"You think Connie could be involved—with this?"

"I have been receiving these photographs since after my first six months. You're certain she took them?"

"I'm sure. I remember all of these. She has a digital video camera and tapes everything—not just us. But these photos, I remember. We had a barbecue last summer at her house." Kate realized how awful that sounded. They'd had a barbecue and he'd been imprisoned. Then she stopped at the one with Mason's arm around her and the next one with them laughing and another with Mason. She wondered what he'd felt when given those. The progression of Abbie's age was a surprise, reminding her how long he'd been gone.

They sat in the quiet, knowing the time wouldn't last long.

"What time is it?" he asked, then saw the clock. "I must get back soon, but I'm getting Rudy out with me. In one week."

"No, we don't have that much time. Wolfram wants the tile pieces—you may not know what those are—but the tiles probably show the location of the treasure Wolfram seeks. We believe that he'll use you to retrieve it once he knows where it is."

"I already know the location."

"Of the treasure?"

"I found a cave on our last dive. I'm sure it's what Wolfram had us looking for."

"Then the cave is underwater? If this is it—unbelievable. Did you know that Wolfram has been seeking this treasure since the war?"

"I've known very little, though they've sent me underwater, inside mountains, and exploring the remains of buildings, castle foundations—whatever they led me to. I was never told what I was actually looking for. How do you know all of this?" Jack asked.

"I'm working with two people who were part of the Austrian Resistance and sought Wolfram during World War II when he was a Nazi guard. They thought he was dead until recently. It's a long story, but this could change everything." Kate was beginning to find hope in the idea of Jack going back. "If we could retrieve this treasure—"

"No, you couldn't do it without someone seeing you—and in such a short amount of time." Jack thought for a moment. "Tomorrow night. Let's do this fast and get it done. I'll insist on Rudy going on the dive. I think I can manage that much. Do you think you can get a boat and wait alongshore, let's say, two hundred yards away?"

Kate nodded at his determined look. They discussed the impossible—a simple plan to end their three years of separation. Kate realized as they talked that if the plan didn't work, if this was the only moment granted them by God, the moment she'd begged for, they'd lost much of that time discussing tomorrow night's plan. But it had to be done.

"Tell me more about Abbie," Jack said, as if also realizing

the passing of their precious time together. "Is sparkly pink still her favorite color?"

Kate smiled, remembering how Abbie's eyes had grown large at anything that sparkled, especially pink. "She likes purple now, but she collects sparkly stickers."

"Do her eyelids still have those soft blue veins when she sleeps?"

"Not really. But she still does that turn toward the wall right before she finally falls asleep, and remember how she used to smile and laugh in the middle of the night? She did that again last week for the first time since—well, you know."

He nodded. "What's her favorite ice cream?"

As Jack went through his list of questions, Kate felt as if he'd come home from a very long trip, hungry for all the news.

"Abbie has never stopped believing we'd find you, Jack. She's the only one who still believed." Kate wanted to admit her own guilt and say how sorry she was for giving up.

He put his hand over hers. "I didn't believe either. If you knew how many times I prayed for a night like tonight. And now it's gone and I never said all I wanted to say. Kate, I understand that you had to move on. Tomorrow could be the beginning of another struggle, learning where we all fit into each other's lives again." He was looking at their hands, touching her fingertips one at a time. "I don't expect you to feel the way you once did. I'm not the man you married. I know that."

"Jack, come back to us tomorrow. We can work that out later. Just come back to us."

Kate walked to the dock with him. They stood in the shadows. The air was cold now, as night was turning toward dawn.

It was time for him to leave.

Would she see him again? Would this be the good-bye she'd once thought she wanted? Perhaps the pain of a good-bye was greater than not having the chance to say it.

He took her hand as they stood there. Everything would

move fast now. It would be over by the next dawn, for better or worse.

"I'm going to walk away and tell you that we'll see each other tomorrow. I can't stand good-byes."

"I remember."

Jack looked up at the sky. Kate knew he was searching for a sign of dawn on the horizon. It would come soon enough. Then his eyes turned toward the moon, high in the sky. "It's a blue night," he said. "Do you remember that?"

"Yes." She noticed the way the night seemed washed in a blue haze. "The first night of our honeymoon."

Jack smiled broadly, and she glimpsed the husband she once knew. She suddenly wanted to rest within his arms, close her eyes, and never move from the warmth she knew she'd find there.

Instead she simply said, "Abbie says a blue night means her daddy is coming back."

"I believe she's right. God gave us tonight."

"Jack, I don't want you to go." She stared at the ground and his worn shoes. "I understand why you must, but I don't want you to go. This isn't enough time."

He reached for her hand and pressed it to his lips. He kissed each finger and she felt tears on her skin. "If you knew how good you feel to me. If you only knew. God must give me the strength. God, give me enough strength to leave you."

"Jack. Jack, look at me." Kate turned his chin to face her. "This hasn't been enough. I'm not ready to let you go. I've missed you so . . . but I know you must do this."

He kissed the palm of her hand and took several steps away. "I left some things in my bag in your room. Something for Abbie also. If anything goes wrong, give it to her. But I plan to do so myself."

"You must give it to her." Kate said, already hating the

distance between them—the distance that would continue to grow until he was gone once again.

Jack took several steps backwards, then turned and walked into the shadows of the trees.

"Wait," she called, hurrying into the dark to find him. He waited and then pulled her tenderly against him. His hands touched her hair and shoulders and grasped her hands.

"I still love you, Jack."

"I will always love you," he whispered fiercely, then met her lips with his own. The kiss was fierce, and passion ignited within her.

But before Kate could take a breath, he was gone.

CHAPTER THIRTY-SEVEN

In two hours Lukas entered Vienna. He'd been on the phone all the way there. He'd talked to several advisors and friends about his options. Though they grumbled about the hour of his call, they knew Lukas well enough to set up the meetings for the next day. Lukas found his usual hotel on the Ringstraße, with its view of the Stadt Park. Anni would be here in a few hours. He settled into his suite and felt a great weariness pour over him. It was impossible for him to pull all-nighters anymore. Once he could go days without sleep.

Those nights of meetings that lasted until sunrise, the flights from city to city—everything he had given his life for since the war's end was for nothing now. His reputation was about to be destroyed. He would be labeled, and that would follow him and his family forever. He would see it in the faces of old colleagues and friends. That he loved his country, his children, and the freedom of men everywhere would not matter. Because he had been a Nazi, he would be considered "anti-Semitic, guilty, a murderer and a torturer." All the good he'd done would be lost beneath this name of what he'd fought against.

In addition, he would have to prove he was Bruno Weiler, which could be tricky but not impossible, and the inevitable scandal. In telling the truth, Lukas knew he risked losing everything. Wolfram knew it also and counted on his cowardice to keep his silence.

Yet Lukas felt a sense of peace, even with the coming storm of a shambled life and career and with others' lives hanging by a thread. Wasn't it a tinge of peace because at last he'd be free of his horrible past? There was comfort even in the worst circumstances when a man stood up for what was true and good and right. That's what he'd seen in Tatianna's eyes before he'd pulled the trigger and ended her life. That was the peace he'd heard in Susanne's laugh and observed in Abbie as she played.

Lukas thought of an idea. What if he traded his life for Jack and Rudy? Wolfram wanted him dead and wanted to see his face as he died. Lukas knew Wolfram. He remembered how Wolfram thrived off the suffering of others. It was adrenaline and power and nearly joy to him. To have free will at killing Lukas might give Wolfram more satisfaction than finding the treasure. Perhaps Lukas could do one final thing to redeem the past.

God, are you a God who could forgive what I've done? Would you forgive a man like me?

Lukas awoke in a chair to the sound of knocking. He quickly tucked in his shirt and buttoned the top button. In the next few hours he had three daughters to face. He'd chosen the toughest one first.

Anni came inside and stared at him with concern. Then she glanced around the room to see if anyone else was there. "Your entourage of women is missing," she said wryly. "I am not used to seeing you without them."

"Anni, come sit down. There are things I must tell you. I have wanted to tell you for a very long time."

"This should be interesting. I had to drive almost till dawn—is this some dark family secret? I'm not really your daughter—something like that?" Her expression challenged him. This child of his was so like him. Lukas didn't know how to figure out his own thoughts—how could he ever perceive hers?

She followed him into a breakfast nook area of the suite. They sat in chairs opposite each other, and Lukas struggled to think how to begin.

"So what is it? Some borderline illegal activities?" Her tone was sarcastically comical. She had been part of some of his shady dealings, and he knew she'd wondered when he'd suddenly cut off business associates in the last year. She said he'd found his conscience.

"What do you know about my time during the war?"

"The war? I know nothing. You don't talk to *me* of such things."

He knew she alluded to long conversations with Marta and now with Kate Porter. He realized that she was deeply angry and jealous.

"You do seem to have an affinity for women," she threw in. "Except for me."

"Anni, let me speak. You are my daughter. I have not been the father I could have been, and I know that now. But you are my daughter. There is nothing in the world like your flesh and blood in human form. When I first saw you and your sisters— so unique and delicate." Lukas stopped. When speaking to his daughters, he always lost his words. Why were the walls so much higher when it came to the ones he loved? He knew with great certainty how deep his love for Anni was, even as she sat across from him popping a cigarette from her case and lighting up as if she cared for nothing and no one. He feared the love he felt for her, seeing her suddenly as the fragile-hearted girl she'd once been. His love for her and her sisters was the only thing that could completely destroy him.

"I must tell you about my past."

"Does it really matter, Father?"

"Do you already know?" He hoped she did.

"I know very little about who you are today, let alone who you were before I was born. Mother never spoke to us about anything besides etiquette and how we should behave in public. Any serious questions were rerouted." Anni took a long drag from her cigarette.

"August 11, 1941, I was part of a firing squad. I killed one of them. A young woman named Tatianna."

Anni slumped in her chair.

"After that day, though it was not instantaneous, my allegiance changed."

"Your allegiance to whom?"

"I was an SS guard at Mauthausen Concentration Camp."

"So we have a President Waldheim scandal in the works? That is what this is about? Well, you are no longer in office so that will help. It will be bad for Austria, but it's not like the country hasn't survived other scandals."

"My main concern is not the scandal. It is for my children. You are not surprised? You do not hate who I am? Tomorrow it will be in the news, and this will not be an easy time. I have much to explain. Though I am a former minister, there will be a lot of controversy, tabloids, rumors, hate mail, support mail that I will not want. You will not leave me?"

"Father, I cannot judge you. Perhaps I would have worked for you then, as I work for you now."

A heaviness descended upon Lukas. What had happened to his daughter? Where had he gone so incredibly wrong that she could not perceive the difference between light and darkness? He had chosen the name *Anni*. It sounded innocent and pure—full of imagination and adventure. Yet she was none of those things. He had destroyed her somewhere between the day of her birth and this moment when she sat in her chair smoking.

"You are not ashamed?"

"I don't care what you did decades ago."

She wasn't bothered that the word *Nazi* would be forever remembered with her family name.

"Anni, you should. You must care!"

"But, Father, I don't."

⋯═◦═⋯

Kate didn't think she had slept at all, but how could those hours have gone without a few snatches of rest? And now the cell phone was ringing. Kate jumped from bed and dug into her jacket lying over a chair for the phone. It was Marta.

"First, where is Abbie?" Kate couldn't wait to tell Marta what had happened. Even now it didn't seem real. She had seen Jack. Jack really was alive. A carved horse and a pile of papers rolled inside a rubber band lay on the table as proof. Kate had opened Jack's letters but couldn't read them. It was too much, too soon. And it wasn't time to tell her daughter. Not until she could bring Abbie's father home.

"She is making tea for us and wants to read the end of a book you two have been reading."

"A book? Yes, *The Voyage of the 'Dawn Treader'*. I forgot about it."

"Would you like me to finish it with her?"

"No, it's something I want to finish as much as Abbie."

"And you received some mail."

"From who?"

"A woman named Connie—Abbie said she is your friend."

Kate sat on the edge of the bed. "This is important. Open the letter and tell me what it says."

"Just a moment."

Kate got up, put her jacket around her, and turned the dial up on the radiator in the corner. She opened the curtains and morning light flooded the room.

"You want me to read the whole thing?"

"Yes," she said.

"It says, 'Dear Kate and Abbie. I finally found the movie that fits your journey to Austria—it's *Clear and Present Danger,* except that it's Jack who is missing instead of Harrison Ford's wife; they were in Paris, while you were in Venice and now you're in Austria; and it's terrorists who have the wife in the movie, but that could be true with Jack, you never know. Wait, maybe that was *Patriot Games,* not *Clear and Present Danger.* And I think the wife was kidnapped in London, not Paris. Well, I don't know, but this is a quick note as I rush out the door. I actually had a stamp and an envelope and your address handy, so what a miracle—I sent a letter! I'm really writing to remind you to call me or e-mail me or even a letter will do! I put some new photos on the Web site, too, if you have a computer over there to check them out. You should see what Trudy did to Restorations—you'll like it, I promise. Well, I hope. Ta-ta for now! CALL!'"

The letter sounded strange in Marta's accented English as she struggled with Connie's expressions. But as the letter ended, Kate suddenly understood. It was impossible to believe that Connie could be involved with Wolfram. And she wasn't. At the bottom of Connie's stationery and business cards were the words, "Check out our fabulous Web site with family and friend photos, movie reviews, and a lot of interesting stuff about us!"

"That's it!" Kate said. Connie's second love was her Web site. She'd put the entire disk from her digital camera right on the site for anyone to click through and see. All the photos given to Jack had to have come from there.

"What is wrong?" Marta asked as a beep sounded through the line. "Wait one moment. I must get the other call, and I always have trouble seeing the buttons . . . ," she muttered until the line switched over. In a couple of seconds she was back. "Lukas said to hang up. He will connect us to a three-person call."

Kate hung up, nearly laughing and crying at the same time. Connie's obsession with photos, movies, and the Internet had given Wolfram or his connected group ample opportunities to threaten her husband. There was no photographer hiding in the woods, or spy who had worked herself into their lives, or best friend who brought mochas while plotting espionage tactics. It was so simple it was preposterous. Wolfram must have discovered her presence in Austria by other means—not Connie.

"This is Lukas, and Marta is on the line from the estate."

"Great, I have so much to tell you both."

"Listen for a moment. Kate, I do not want you to go back to the estate. I already met with two of my daughters and the third is flying in any minute. I have appointments in the next couple hours for an exclusive interview. I will tell this journalist about my past from being a young guard at Mauthausen to the Resistance and Ebensee. It will air on the news at noon."

"What?" Kate said in horror. "You can't do this! Not now!"

"Tell us why you do this," Marta said calmly.

"Wolfram gave us an ultimatum. Three days to deliver the tiles. The press will be at the estate after this, so you and Abbie will be even safer there. And this is a move Wolfram will not expect. It is social and political suicide on my part; he would never expect me to do that. I have worried about the effects on our country. The world will label us again—"

"Lukas, you don't understand." Kate stood, glancing at the

stack of letters and the carved wooden horse that Jack had left behind. "I saw Jack last night."

"Last night? Where is he now?" Lukas demanded. Kate could hear the surprise in his voice. Kate quickly explained their meeting and why he had to return.

"What is your plan of escape?"

"Jack found an underwater cavern—it's what Wolfram has been looking for. Jack is going back to reveal the location to Wolfram's son. Jack trusts Ian—he's the one who helped Jack come to see me. I didn't like this idea at all. But Jack says it's the only way."

"It will not work," Lukas said quietly. "If Wolfram finds out, it is finished. He needs the men and the tiles to retrieve his treasure. Now he will not need the tiles. Once he has what he wants—I know this man—he will not let them go free. He cannot."

Everyone was silent.

"Did you find out why he needs the tile?" Marta asked, her voice shaking more than usual.

"I am certain that once together, the pieces reveal the location of this treasure Wolfram seeks," answered Lukas.

"It is time to get help," Marta said and flew into a stream of German directed toward Lukas.

"*Nein!* Marta, *nein!*" Lukas kept saying.

"English, please!" Kate said. "Marta, we don't have time. If I go to the police, it will take too long for them to believe me, especially since I am a suspect in Jack's disappearance. How long until a search warrant—do you even have search warrants? It doesn't matter. We have no concrete evidence! We have nothing that will bring immediate action."

"My hands are tied now. I will be followed and watched because of this scandal and many old friends will disappear," Lukas said.

Kate stood before the open window now, trying to think of a way. The line crackled when she moved.

"I know," Lukas said finally. "I am going to tell Wolfram's true story to the media. They will barrage him, and not even the castle will be secluded enough. It will distract him and give us more time if we need it. If this Ian can be trusted, they might succeed without Wolfram knowing. Marta, if this doesn't work in a day or two, we will go to the authorities."

"But what will stop Wolfram from getting nervous and . . . and destroying the evidence?" Kate asked.

"Kate, I assure you, Wolfram wants that treasure—he has waited nearly sixty years. And he wants me. He is not going to destroy his chances too soon."

"I hope you are right." She bit her lip and sat on the edge of the bed.

"Lukas, are you sure about all of this?" Marta said. "Your reputation, all these years of your work—it will all be ruined. You know that?"

"Yes. There is no other way. And it is time to tell it."

"We are here for you. I am always here for you," Marta said it softly, and Kate felt like she was intruding between them.

Kate cleared her throat. "I'm bringing a boat and waiting by the shore tonight as Jack and I planned. I'll do it alone if I have to. After their dive, I'll pick Jack up."

"I will send someone to help and delay my interview a day. But this now depends on Jack. And I hope this son of Wolfram Meizer can be trusted."

CHAPTER THIRTY-EIGHT

Jack returned before daylight. He hated to change back into the coveralls and rubber boots. He wanted to turn around and return to Kate. There was too much to mend between Kate and him in just a few hours. And how he longed to see Abbie! But he was determined to carry out his plan to save Rudy. Soon enough they'd all be together.

Ian wasn't by the shore when Jack returned. So he left the boat as he'd found it and crept back to the barrack. He peered toward the house as he passed, seeing the remnants of the party in garbage bags lined up at the edge of the terrace. A few lights were still on.

He didn't find Ian when he reached the barrack, and Rudy's door was closed as he passed to enter his own room. He shut the door. The darkness no longer comforted him. The room smelled and was dirtier than he remembered. It was cold and empty, and again he questioned why he'd returned. He knew the answer—he could never live knowing he'd deserted his friend. But what if that cost him everything—even his own life?

Jack bent down to listen into the vent. Perhaps Rudy had heard him arrive. There was no noise, but he felt a crumpled paper sticking just inside the ridges of the vent. He pulled his end of the wire arm and took the note. The only catch in their letter exchange was that they had to read them in the light. Jack found his stack of blank paper and put Rudy's note under the second page, then turned on the light. He sat on the bed, leaning against the wall. Then Jack realized his mistake. He'd entered the barrack as he always did on the nights he worked the tunnels. But last night he was supposed to be in his room all night.

Jack glanced up at the camera, its red eye always watching. He hoped Ian had thought of it. Jack didn't know the working of the security or how much Wolfram really watched, but that too was in Ian's hands. And where was Ian? Jack needed to talk to him. They had much to plan while the daylight hours gave them time. Tonight they needed to dive.

He looked down at the blank paper and flipped it over to Rudy's note.

I always laughed when people claimed to have prophetic dreams. But I hope the one I had last night was just that. It was the strangest dream. I was in the darkness and you were with me. I heard a voice calling my name, but it wasn't you, and you couldn't hear it. It kept calling, and I felt this great anxiety and asked, "Why can't you hear it?" You said maybe it was only for me. So I shouted, "What do you want?" The voice stopped calling my name but then said, "It is time for you to come home." Then I woke up.

This could be my own subconscious at work. But the strangest part is that when I woke up, I didn't feel cold, at least not for a while. I think I'm getting well at last. I don't

like to say God spoke to me, but let us hope he did. Maybe
we're going home.
　　I'll talk to you soon.
　　Always,
　　Rudy (aka MacGyver)

Jack smiled at the letter, especially the MacGyver part. He'd
have to watch reruns of the show with Rudy when they got
home. As he began composing a letter to Rudy, he heard the
sound of footsteps.

It was Ian.

-»≡◐⊂≡«-

Wolfram stretched in his bed. It was a massive four-poster that
rested in the very center of the large room with tall ceilings
and oversized, hand-carved furniture. Light poured through
the curtains in long dusty streams. He recalled last night and
his successful dinner party. It would be in the papers today—
front page in Austria, perhaps an inside article in the international papers.

The phone rang.

"Yes," he said. Already they reached him.

"You better watch the news this afternoon. It will interest
you greatly."

Wolfram recognized his ally from Vienna—a government
insider who kept him informed.

"Is it good?" He wondered if the lights had made him look
younger last night.

"You must get prepared. The rumor is that Lukas Johansen
is about to share some secrets."

Kicking the covers away, he stood with a thud against the
rock floor. "He wouldn't dare. It will destroy him."

"I think he knows that. But destroying you may be more
important to him."

◦→⟫═◉═⟪←◦

Ian had pulled all the equipment they had, so they checked hoses and batteries in the equipment shed. They should go through every piece—test it, review safety precautions and function. Technology had changed equipment dramatically in the fifteen years since Jack had interned with Rudy's team. Jack had done dives after that time, but this was an expedition, not a simple dive. They would have to be thorough with the time they had.

Jack mapped the cavern entrance and made sketches to where it reached the opening in Tunnel 8. He didn't know if the cavern went straight into the mountain—they knew nothing. This would be dangerous work, perhaps the most dangerous work he'd ever done. Both his and Rudy's life could depend upon tonight—that is, if Jack made it out of the cave alive. If they went too far, they'd try for the tunnel, though Jack didn't like this idea. Kate would be waiting on the lake. She'd be worried if it took too long.

Jack stopped for a minute to recall that he'd really seen her. After so many days of agony and times begging God for just one more moment with her, he'd actually been with her, touched her skin, and heard her voice. If they could just get through one more day apart.

Ian had agreed to most of the plan. He'd been stunned to learn that the cavern they'd sought inside the mountain had been right below them all along. Their dives had missed the mouth of the cave disguised beneath the outcropping of rocks.

Jack and Ian went over the plan. They'd make the dive, retrieve whatever they could, then Jack and Rudy would be free. Unless there was too much to recover. Unless they didn't find it tonight. There were many factors working against them.

And then Jack heard the worst news of all. Rudy would not be diving with them. He wouldn't be in the boat either. Jack's

quick plan constructed with Kate in her room was falling apart
before it began.

"Where is Rudy?" Jack asked.

"He's sick again," Ian said.

Jack almost said he knew Rudy wasn't sick. Rudy was
getting better; he'd said so in his letter. But now his trust in
Ian was crumbling. "I want to see Rudy."

"We can see him after the dive," Ian said. He stood up and
walked outside the shed, leaving the door open. Jack could see
the dock through the trees. One of the boats was missing—
Wolfram's cruiser. He wondered why.

They waited until the evening shadows were long over the
water. Jack knew Kate wouldn't be waiting along the shore yet.
But within hours, they might be together. Then there'd be no
more good-byes.

The water seemed forever unchanging. Jack loved the world
beneath the surface, where swimming was like flying; it was a
place of wonder for him. He couldn't move too quickly, voices
couldn't shout, and everything seemed slow and defined. At
times he'd felt guilty enjoying the dives—it was such a
contrast to the dirty work in the tunnels.

Jack and Ian carried everything to the dock. Jack passed
Wolfram's boat, realizing that he had returned sometime
during the day. Ian seemed unconcerned as he climbed aboard
the older fishing boat. He flipped on the lights beneath the
hull, and they beamed into the water just like on any other
dive. There would be no need to take the boat out since the
cave's mouth was right below them. There was no need for
Rudy to be in the boat.

Jack stopped. No need for Rudy . . . "Where is he?" Jack
grabbed Ian's arm and swung him around. "I'm not doing this
if you don't let me see him."

"He is fine. This time, trust me," Ian said. His gaze was

unwavering, and Jack had little choice. Jack believed that Ian really thought Wolfram would let him and Rudy free after this. But Jack knew otherwise. He'd compiled enough Wolfram quotes to understand that the man had no intention of letting them go. The only birds he'd released were killed by the cat—that said it all to Jack.

They dived into the water and for a second Jack's worries disappeared. He couldn't deny that this fascinated him. If this had been a legitimate expedition, he would have volunteered for such a dive in a heartbeat. They were diving where no man had gone in nearly sixty years. They were seeking what Wolfram had spent his life trying to discover. The Nazis had gone to a lot of work to hide this place.

Ian followed Jack; both wore backpacks and waist bags of supplies—they barely needed weight belts. The only sound was the whirl of their two pieced-together scooters that resembled handlebars with a small engine and had a light to lead the way. Rudy had built them before Jack's involuntary recruitment. They moved along the lake floor for twenty feet until it plunged downward. He'd guessed it was about thirty feet from the surface to the cave's mouth. Jack's light found the widening crack in the rock face. Then they reached it.

The whirl of engines stopped. They examined the entrance. Jack pointed out areas he'd earlier described to Ian as to why he believed the cave was natural but had been widened by man-made means. Ian nodded slowly, then pointed inside. Jack took a steel stake and hammer from a belt bag and, with Ian's help for leverage, drove the stake into the rock wall. Rock crumbled and fell away, but the stake was secured. Ian clipped the latch end of the cable he carried to the stake. Jack took the other end and hooked it to his belt. The lead line might prove their only way out again. They checked their watches. Jack didn't like the time—they were attempting too much for one dive.

Jack went first. The darkness was different inside the cave—

not wide and expansive beyond the beam of light, but black and cold and eerily silent. He moved with the scooter in front of him for light, but with the engine still off. The rock was smoothly cut at the opening, shored up by concrete reinforcement arches. Their lights searched the cavern floor for any evidence of the cavern's secrets. Soon they reached the rough, natural walls that narrowed rapidly as they went. When Jack felt a tug on the cable, he turned to see Ian unraveling a kink in the line. Jack began to realize they'd never make it.

Almost immediately, Jack noticed that the bubbles from his tank no longer streamed behind him as he swam but rose straight upward. Checking his watch for the time and direction on the compass, Jack motioned to Ian. There was a steel ladder attached to the rock. They swam upward, sometimes with a hand on the ladder rungs to move them along.

Above him, the light appeared strange, as if the beam narrowed. Jack was about to check the bulb when his head broke through the surface into air. Ian popped up beside him, looking surprised. Streams of water ran over their masks. Ian tested the air and pulled out his breathing apparatus. They removed their tanks, masks, and flippers and turned off the valves on their oxygen tanks. Water dripped softly, echoing through the cavern. Jack unhooked the latch of the cable and attached it to a rung of the ladder, then climbed the last few feet to a flat area of the cavern floor. The air was cold and musty.

"This is amazing," Jack said with a long whistle. "We're in the attic room of a cave."

"One intentionally designed," Ian said as he stepped over the water from the ladder to stand beside him. "Unless there is some kind of air vent, we'll use up the oxygen and have to go to our tanks."

Jack picked up his light, shining it on an object a few yards ahead. Crates stacked against the rock wall bore the faded red emblem of the swastika. "This is it," he said.

They walked carefully over the rough floor in their rubbery wet-suit stockings. Their lights illuminated the small room. They examined overhead to check for weakness or breakage and down a narrow corridor. The ink-thick darkness dissolved the rays, making it difficult to see anything ahead.

"Let's see what's in the crates first," Ian said, his voice betraying his excitement. Jack fought his own—this could be the most significant find of his life. Yet what he was about to discover would soon be in the hands of an insane old man.

"What are we looking for? Can you tell me now?" Jack asked.

"My father saw top secret documents in 1944." Ian paused, looking over the first crates. His hand touched the top as if it were sacred. "He was never supposed to see this information— it was only for the highest-ranking officers and ordained by Himmler himself."

"What did the documents say?" Jack moved to the other side and tugged at the wood, holding a flashlight on the box. Even after so many years, the nails held strong.

"They described a tunnel system built to hold as much trea- sure from the incarcerates as possible. That is the best English translation I can give."

"Treasure looted from Jewish victims." Jack stared at the crate again.

With his large pocketknife open, Ian worked at the edges. "Exactly. The cavern was supposed to also hold the plans of the worst weapon to be used against the Nazis. It was a weapon that could annihilate the Third Reich."

"Something that would destroy them? Why wouldn't they use it against the world?"

"My father believes their discovery of this weapon came too late in the war for them to build it, but that if the plans were ever revealed, it would end the future of another rise in the Nazi Party. They would wait until Germany could rebuild and then recover the plans for this weapon. But the few men and inmates working on it all died or were killed long ago."

"And this was all in these papers?"

"Nazi Party leaders were fanatical over precise paperwork. Their obsession to detail incriminated them after the war with what they'd done. They believed words like *final solution* instead of *mass genocide of the Jewish population* or *resettlement* instead of *shipping to the gas chambers* would be adequate—"

The sound of wood breaking stopped them both. Jack held the light as Ian pried up the corner. The wood cracked and snapped until the lid pulled away. They both peered inside.

There was an inner cover and then two metal boxes side by side. They each took a handle on the ends of one box and lifted. It was heavy and awkward and thudded to the floor, sending an echo through the chamber. Ian lifted the lid with a creak of the hinge.

Their lights didn't reflect gold bars or jewels, but yellowed crinkled paper. Ian took out a handful of moisture-damaged pages. He read them over as Jack picked up his own stack. The papers were in German. There were names and numbers in the columns and rows with stamped words at the top and bottom.

"What is this?" Jack asked.

"Some of that Nazi obsession to paperwork I was speaking about. These papers are records of the people sent to the camps." Ian looked at Jack's set and pointed out the columns. "You have names, dates, country and city origins, family members. And look, here is what was taken from them. Two fur coats, one gold tooth, a ring—that was one woman. When the camps closed, these documents were supposed to be destroyed. I didn't know they kept this much detail. Many camps succeeded in destroying the evidence, while other camps were caught off guard when the Allies moved in faster than expected."

Ian thumbed through the papers quickly. Then, working together, they lifted out the second metal box.

"It's all the same." Ian stood, staring at Jack in awe. "What if they made copies of everything? What if this is the complete record of all the victims? Let's open these other crates."

Quickly they opened every crate. They all contained metal boxes full of documents. After the last crate had been opened, Ian leaned back against the rock wall. Jack watched him. It amazed him that here they were deep inside the mountain with a treasury of information before them. This was not what Wolfram had wanted to find.

Then Ian began to laugh. He laughed harder and deeper until tears beaded at the corners of his eyes. He said something in German and laughed again. Jack had rarely seen emotion of any kind in Ian—this was stunning.

"*Treasury of the incarcerates* was referring to their information. Don't you see? We have made the most significant discovery since the war, what Jewish and Holocaust organizations have been searching for. This will help survivors and their families—they'll know the fate of family members and what was stolen from each individual. Look at this! An account number for a bank account with the monetary amount!"

"Swiss banks opened."

"And not only Swiss, but all over Eastern Europe."

"And no secret weapon?" Jack said it quietly, not knowing what reaction he'd get from Ian. He glanced at his watch and realized they'd been inside far too long.

"No secret weapon. The greatest one of all!" Ian said. "These papers are the weapon. These people are witness to the world—their final act of justice. It's proof and testimony of the Nazi deeds and the Holocaust."

Jack suddenly understood it all. More valuable than treasure, these documents were the complete record of what man was capable of doing to man. What did Ian intend to do with these records? Immediately Jack knew he needed to protect these documents. He must protect them with his life, if necessary.

"I thought the typical neo-Nazi didn't believe the Holocaust ever happened."

"Not all believe that, and there is none who is typical. And I don't recall telling you I was a neo-Nazi."

Jack didn't know what to say. Did he really know anything about this man he'd spent several years with?

"My father will not be happy," Ian said. "We won't get them out tonight. These crates will break apart if we try to use the boat winch to extract them through the tunnel."

Jack was facing Ian, but Ian was moving toward the back of the cavern. "What do you intend to do with the papers once you get them out?"

"There's another turn here," Ian said. "What is this?"

A moment later Jack heard Ian cry out and then the sound of sliding and a splash of water. He raced to the back with his flashlight. Though he couldn't see Ian anywhere, there was a gaping hole under a ledge of rock. Jack lay on his stomach and slid to the edge, using his legs as wedges against the rock. He shone his light straight down. He saw what looked like a rock slide down to the water. The water wasn't calm and stationary. It moved from one side of the hole and disappeared under the other. An underground river.

It was the perfect garbage can. Anything dropped down the rocky tube would eventually be buried within the mountain or emptied into the lake. Jack knew Ian could never hold his breath long enough and there would be no oxygen all the way through. Then Jack saw two hands grabbing the rock edge and Ian struggling to hold on.

"There's a current!" Ian shouted. "I can't hang on—!"

Jack slid over the edge a little farther. If he could get a rope to Ian . . . then a thought quickly flashed through his mind: *If he didn't reach Ian, he could escape, save the documents, be with his family, get Rudy away.*

But Jack couldn't do it.

He leaned over just an inch farther . . . and then Jack began to slide too. Reaching desperately for the sides, he tried to turn. His wet suit on the slippery rock didn't hold, and Jack plummeted into the water. He slammed into Ian, who barely kept his grip.

"It's a river!" Ian shouted. "We aren't going to make it!"

"Yes, we are!" Jack shouted back. He flailed his arm, trying to find a better grip. The rock cut his hands, and Jack knew they wouldn't last long. He wished for the oxygen tanks left above them in the cavern attic. Then he remembered the tunnel. It must have tapped into this stream; it was right in this area or perhaps above them. But were they already past it? There was no way to tell.

"Hold your breath and swim!" Jack yelled, then turned around. "Ian!" he shouted, not seeing him. Jack's fingers were sliding, and he couldn't hold. Taking one last breath, he dived beneath the rock and into the churning river.

CHAPTER THIRTY-NINE

The boat had a small cabin and an outside
deck—hardly room for the three people it held. The couple
had met Kate at the lake at dusk. She had expected Anni or
Rey to be the "help" Lukas had promised. Instead this man
and woman introduced themselves as Brant Collins and Darby
Evans. He had rented a boat from the village, and together
they boarded it, dressed as if they were out for an evening
cruise. Kate was afraid to trust these people she didn't know,
but she had little choice. They were Americans, she learned—
or Brant was half—and they lived in Salzburg right now. They
talked little past the introductions.

Once night fell, they changed into black clothing in the
cabin and turned out the lights on the boat. Brant drove at a
snail's pace, moving closer to the castle grounds, where they
could see Wolfram's boats tied to the dock. Lukas must have
filled them in on the story, which was a relief for her. Kate
could barely speak without emotion. Inside her bag she'd

packed the letters Jack had given her. If this didn't work out, they were all she'd have left of him.

Kate looked through the night-vision binoculars. She could make out equipment on the stern of the fishing boat and the lights, so Jack, Rudy, and Ian were already in the water. Kate checked her watch, but they were on time. She didn't know how long they could stay under. Was it twenty minutes? two hours? Brant and Darby didn't know either. She searched the water for Jack and Rudy to surface. That had been the plan—she'd have a boat and Jack and Rudy would simply swim the two hundred yards to meet her. Jack had several optional plans for himself in case Rudy wasn't able to dive, but her only instructions were to wait near the shore until dawn, if necessary.

Darby sat beside Kate. Her presence was comforting. "How long have you been married?" Darby asked softly.

"Almost twelve years." Kate's eyes stayed on the water, searching for movement. They may not get much time to reach Jack and Rudy when they did surface. Kate wondered if the plan was still as they'd established it. Jack had a lot to do in a very short time. She'd stay here until dawn and return every night until she knew one way or the other.

Brant brought a thermos from the cabin and sat beside them. He poured cups of coffee, then rested his arm around Darby's shoulders. They weren't married, Kate knew, but a glance at Darby's hand showed a ring. Engaged. They could understand a little how she felt.

"You must owe Lukas a big favor to be out here like this," Kate whispered. It seemed they should whisper.

Brant and Darby looked at one another.

"We do," Darby said. "But we want to be here too. Lukas should have called earlier."

Their eyes met, and Kate's stomach trembled with fear. *Should have* were words she didn't want them to say in recalling this night.

Kate stared across the rippling water. No one had appeared. It was taking too long.

Darby descended the stairs into the cabin while Brant sat near the bow and watched the water, checking through the binoculars from time to time. "Let's take turns for a while. I'll watch first. Kate, I'm sure you don't want to sleep, but it might be good to try."

She thought of the little sleep she'd had and knew it was good advice, but it seemed impossible. Yet there was one thing she wanted to do. Kate opened her bag for the pack of letters.

Beneath the outline of the mountain and a million stars in the sky, she began to read by the glow of a tiny flashlight. She flipped through the letters, reading snatches of the days they'd spent apart—the moments of Jack's despair, the simple times he'd recorded as if to remind himself that he still lived and breathed, the days when hope shone through. And within the words, Kate met her husband again.

> *They've moved me again, and I've kept track of the days by cutting marks in my shoes. I must know the exact days that I'm away from you. Today is 107. Can I make it to another?*
>
> *What do they want from me? What could this be for? They won't tell me and I say it's a mistake. I say that till my voice is hoarse. They don't want me. Not me. This isn't for me!*
>
> *Today I believe I will die in this place. My body will be crushed beneath the earth in a landslide, lost beneath tons of granite and stone. Or my will to live might fail in just one moment as I walk that trail from the mines—my body giving up, my spirit escaping this prison. I've sought insanity and death at times, wishing it was simply a decision.*
>
> *Five hundred days I have spent away from you. Five hundred days I have not touched you or spoken where you could hear me or I could hear you. It does not seem possible.*

*I wanted to write every day. I am surprised to see the pile
of letters that has grown over these days and years. But I
wanted to share my every day just as I long to know your
every moment. But there are too many now. You will never
remember them all. And I must save my paper; I do not
know when more will be granted. Maybe if I do a trick
they'll reward me—roll over, sit up, fetch a treasure within
the earth. And I think, why should I write to say the same
words again and again? I can't shout the words that I'm
shouting right now. "I'm here. I'm alive. Hear my voice and
don't forget me!"*

*Are these words to you or to God? I know nothing. The
anger has me tonight. And I don't care to fight it.*

*I want to smell your hair and touch your skin for just a
moment, though a moment would never be enough. I feel
desperate to get back to you. I believe I could kill a man to
do it. With my own hands, I could do it.*

*Kate, I'm a weak man. I can't breathe without you. I can't
do this any longer. Seven hundred and thirty-two days.*

Kate became anxious to know all his words, but at the same
time, they were more than she could take. Jack had been with
her for the briefest time. Now she knew what it meant to him;
now she knew who he was. But he was out of reach once
again.

She continued to read, moving in and out of Jack's world.
The tower of mountains above her became familiar as Jack
described them as the prison walls he loved to watch. The
crisp mountain air was breathed into her lungs, the same air
Jack wrote that he loved and resented at the same time. Light
caught on the ripples of the lake, and the lap of tiny waves
against the hull of the boat only brought Kate further to this
world where Jack had lived apart from her. This land and

water had become a part of him—they brought him peace in his later writings as he found peace with God.

> *Kate, I can't fully explain this. Call it my change on the mountain. But at last, I see God—even here, even now. It's what I should have seen a long time ago. Perhaps I knew it in my head, but not within me as it is now. I not only understand my need for God more than life, even more than I need you and Abbie. I believe it, feel it, and it fills me with the knowledge and peace of understanding. God is here with me. I can't deny that my anger continues to rise at times, but it's no longer out of control. I find myself marveling at the intricate design of it all. If this mountain can be so alive and balanced to bring summer flowers and winter's cleansing snows, then the One who made it can keep my life, even if I never leave this place alive.*
>
> *I think of Paul in prison, in chains. He wrote that to live is Christ, but to die is gain. I'm not ready to give up on life; I continue to want you and Abbie. But I know that God holds the design beyond what we can see.*
>
> *Almost three years—1,094 days. Even in this place today, my freedom stolen, my love for you and Abbie denied, I have found peace. I even find laughter and thankfulness. Was I ever this thankful for the love we shared? I had more than most people have in a lifetime. For that, I am grateful.*

Kate realized she was crying and had been crying for some time. She read one last portion of Jack's letters before folding them away.

> *Abbie, if ever you can read this, I love you more than string cheese, more than life itself. I'll see you again in every starry sky and every blue night.*

⇥▬◗═⇤

Jack was blind under the black water; he'd lost the light when he first fell into the underground river. As he pushed through the rough water-filled cavern, his hands stung from cold and open wounds. The river moved quickly, and he tried to move even faster while seeking the roof for an opening. He found pockets of air he couldn't breathe, knowing they would be toxic with no oxygen content. His lungs ached now and he still hadn't found Ian.

And then he knew—he wasn't going to make it. Jack knew that. And it was all right. He had been close—so close. He'd seen Kate. He'd had what he'd asked of God, another chance to see her. She had his letters. Abbie would have her gift. It was more than he'd had days ago. He could die knowing that.

Jack closed his eyes; there was no need to try and see. A few deep breaths and the water would fill his lungs. It would take only moments. He'd be truly free, and the cavern would keep its secrets.

His lips parted when suddenly he saw Rudy in the darkness. Jack opened his eyes. Yes, he saw Rudy's face staring down at him. He saw Rudy's hand reaching. Jack reached, and a firm grasp pulled at him. His body twisted and was dragged in the current. He kicked with his legs and sought another handhold. His face burst from the water and air filled his lungs. But it was Ian's face straining and Ian's hands holding his arm. Finally, Jack was free and pulled onto the platform inside Tunnel 8.

They lay on the ground, trying to breathe, rejoicing in breath.

"Where's Rudy?" Jack gasped.

Ian rolled from his back to his stomach. "What—what are you talking about?"

Jack shook his head and couldn't speak. It didn't matter. He'd see Rudy soon enough.

⊷⥱⊙⥬⊶

The sun would be up soon. It would rise through the window-panes and above the trees of his yard. Lukas sat in the cold room of his home with the telephone beside him and a lone lamp lit in the corner. Kate should be calling. She should call and say it was over.

But no one had called.

He wanted to help, but soon a television van would be parked outside the estate gates for his afternoon interview. And tonight he'd surely see old friends and ex-wives on the news giving their stories. "I always suspected," they'd say. There would be more in the coming days, especially after he revealed he was Bruno Weiler. Then Wolfram's castle would be mauled by media and paparazzi seeking answers, especially since Wolfram had claimed to be Bruno Weiler. But they must have Jack Porter and his friend free from harm first. It was a delicate matter, giving bits of information without too much and trying to discern the mind of his enemy.

At least his daughters would forgive him. Magda was the angriest, but she was also the youngest. Regina, the wise, oldest sister, seemed relieved to know the cause of his aloof-ness all her life. She cried as he told her the story and hugged him before leaving. Despite their different responses, they both promised to come to the estate the next weekend after the first full announcement settled. Anni had returned with him from Vienna. She drove and he slept. She continued to not care.

Lukas packed his old pipe and lit it, taking a long puff. It didn't relax him as he hoped.

"I thought smoking was not allowed inside the house." It was Anni, standing in the shadows behind him in the doorway to the sunroom.

"Why are you awake?"

"I couldn't sleep."

"Come in, then," he said. Her feet moved softly along the floor. She wore fuzzy, blue slippers and a robe. He had not seen her like this since childhood. Anni was always perfectly dressed, with makeup and hair in order whenever he saw her.

"Have you been drinking, Father?"

"I considered it."

"You are concerned about Kate Porter."

"Yes." He watched her sit in the chair beside him. She seemed much younger in this light. "I have other things on my mind also. I have you on my mind."

"Why is that?"

"I fear for you. You are who I once was. You seek something that is not visible but is easily found."

Anni did not speak, only stared at him as if finally realizing he truly could see her. How long had she thought she was invisible to him?

"My daughter, I fear what it will take for your eyes to open. Do you know what it took me? Oh, if you knew what I saw. Anni, if you could see my nightmares that come not from imagination but from memory."

He bent his head over his hands and began to sob. He didn't know where it all came from, but the tears, so deep and agonizing, tore through him and released their hold as they left. He couldn't stop it and didn't want to. At last what felt like a thousand years of agony and sorrow made their departure from Lukas Johansen.

Then Anni was on her knees in front of him, touching his head and hands. "Father, I will listen to your story this time. Tell me again. Tell me until I understand."

⋅→⇒◉⇐←⋅

"It's always coldest before dawn," Darby said. She put a blanket around Kate's shoulders, and Kate realized she was shivering. Gray had grown against the black horizon. Kate had never known a dawn to approach this fast.

"It's been too long," she whispered. "I know it's been too long."

"What do you want us to do?" Darby asked.

"I don't know."

They waited and Kate knew it was her call. "He's been down there too long. We'll go to the police at the village. Then my daughter will need me." Kate heard her voice as if it played on a tape recorder in another room. It wasn't her voice saying these words, not after all of this. Was being this close to Jack, having one last night with him, a gift or a torment?

"Let's wait a short time longer," Brant said from the stairs of the cabin. "It's the eleventh hour. Sometimes we think it's the thirteenth or fourteenth, but it's only the eleventh. We'll wait until all hope is gone."

CHAPTER FORTY

I t felt strange to walk. Moments before they had been clinging to life. Now Jack and Ian walked through the tunnel, injured and wet, but alive.

They both shivered—their wet suits left behind and their bodies bruised and fighting the cold in their wet swimsuits. Though they knew the route to the entrance well, they followed the small emergency lights on the rocky floor. They both had to push on the door, hitting it with their shoulders. It opened to the gray, early morning light.

"We must hurry," Ian said.

Despite the pain, they ran down the path, watching for rocks on the ground and movement around them.

When they reached the barrack, Ian went through the doorway. "Get dressed and ready. I'll be back very soon." But Jack couldn't go inside. What if they returned him to the life he'd lived so long?

Jack needed clothes, and he needed Rudy. Ian had saved his life minutes ago, so he must be trusted now. He pushed past

Ian and ran by the cameras in the hallway, down the stairs to the basement and to Rudy's door. It was unlocked.

"Rudy!" he called as he opened the door. The light from the hall revealed the room, but Rudy wasn't there.

Jack went to his room. No one was there either. No note in the vent. Jack found the clothes Ian had loaned him the day before—had that only been yesterday?

Kate, he thought. She probably thought he was dead. But they'd take one of Wolfram's boats. He'd find her again. As he dressed quickly, he let his eyes sweep across the room. This would be his home no longer.

Jack searched Rudy's room for any evidence of where he'd gone. He walked slowly around the room where Rudy had been working on inventions and drawn huge diagrams and figures on the walls. The bedcovers were a mess, some kicked to the ground. Rudy's room contained clothes, pinecones, a bird's nest, pieces of wood and wire, nuts and bolts. Jack couldn't believe he'd been allowed such things. And there, stacked neatly beneath his bed were a well-used Bible and his favorite Oswald Chambers book, *My Utmost for His Highest.*

Jack had never been in here before. It was Rudy, every last mismatched set of tools and objects in the room. But Rudy was missing.

Jack raced back up to the entrance. No one stopped him. The cameras couldn't touch him now. He turned toward the woods, where he'd wait until he could search all the buildings.

"Jack, stop!"

He turned, afraid of what he'd see. They didn't need him now. But Ian wasn't holding the loaded gun Jack had expected. Ian stood there in his red coat with his hands pushed into his jeans pockets in the relaxed pose Jack had seen a hundred times before. But it was Ian's expression that put icy fear inside him. Ian was breathing hard. He'd just come from the castle. On his face were sadness, deep and troubled—and anger?

"Where is he?"

"I took him to the castle two nights ago—when you left to see your wife. Rudy was cold and covered in sweat, so I moved him to the house, where the housekeeper could care for him. Wolfram did not know. The doctor is in the village, but there was no boat because you used it. Wolfram would notice one of his boats missing."

"What are you trying to tell me?"

"I could not go for a doctor in the daylight, so I planned to go tonight, but then all of this. I told Wolfram. I told him Rudy was sick and must get help. He refused. I told him that I'd tell him where the treasure was if he helped Rudy."

"What happened?" Jack demanded.

He realized Ian was crying. "Rudy died last night."

"I don't believe you." Jack shook his head. This couldn't be true—fatigue was destroying his mind.

"Wolfram promised. My father promised he would take Rudy to a doctor. Before we left last night, his boat was gone so I believed him. But he didn't take Rudy. The housekeeper stayed with him, but she didn't know anything."

Tears ran down Jack's face. He remembered Rudy's letter. It *had* been God's voice calling Rudy home. And in the dream, Rudy had said Jack couldn't hear the call. Only Rudy heard his name.

"There was a look on his face. It was peace," Ian continued.

"I saw him in the water tonight. It is Wolfram I want to see. Now."

Surprise flashed across Ian's face. Then he nodded. "Yes. We will go see Wolfram."

They found Wolfram sleeping beneath a thick comforter in a massive bed that dominated the entire room. The door creaked on its ancient hinges and brought Wolfram rising upward like Dracula from his casket. He didn't jump from the bed, only pulled the chain of the lamp and adjusted his eyes to see who had entered.

"Ian, *wer ist das?*" he boomed.

Ian's steps thudded across the floor. He stopped at the foot of the bed while Jack stayed in the doorway.

Wolfram was trying to see him. *"Ist das* Jack?"

"You let him die," Ian accused.

Wolfram yawned, stretching his arms above his head. His words were casual and surprised sounding.

Ian translated. "He says that he did not know Rudy would die. He is sorry. I will tell him what we found in the cavern."

Ian spoke slowly, holding Wolfram's interest. The old man rose from the bed to wrap a robe around his large waist. Jack had never seen Ian this way, so intriguing and explanatory. He moved his hands as if in a play, describing every detail. And then Jack could see the moment Ian dealt the blow. Wolfram's face turned white; he grabbed his hair and began to shake.

"You did not need the tiles that took many lives. Jack found the cave without the tile. And the treasure you sought is what condemns you." Ian laughed with tears falling from his cheeks. Jack knew he was speaking more to himself than to Wolfram. Ian took a few steps toward his father.

"Nein. Nicht mein sohn. You not take my son," Wolfram yelled to Jack as Jack turned to leave.

"He is not taking me. I am leaving you." Ian followed Jack out the bedroom door.

Wolfram's angered voice carried after them all the way down the hall.

"I loved him, you know," Ian said as they went toward the sound of morning birds singing in their cages.

"I understand. He is your father."

"I have tried to love my father. My life has been to do his

will, to make him happy, to say what he wanted. I did not know the difference until I met Rudy. That is what I meant. I loved Rudy. I wanted you to know."

CHAPTER FORTY-ONE

I t was beyond the "eleventh hour" as Brant had called it. Past the time for Jack to surface. But neither Brant nor Darby said a word to Kate. They stayed below in the cabin, often bringing her more coffee.

The light of dawn rose across the waters, and the birds began to sing. Kate's nose and cheeks felt like ice as she watched a mist drift and play upon the water. She'd never seen a more peaceful morning. It would be perfect if not for her great sense of loss. But this time was different. There was no panic, only a terrible grief that filled her until she was unable to move. Yet, below the sorrow, and as new as this day, came peace. It came from deep within, growing and moving through her.

She stood and dropped the blanket from her shoulders. Brant and Darby came up from the cabin and peered at Kate, their sleepy eyes showing their worry.

"It's time to go," she said, and the weight of grief nearly crumbled her strength. It wouldn't take long to break her to pieces, but for this moment she stayed strong.

Brant rose from the cushioned bench and stood beside her on deck. Jack's diving equipment remained on the dock like abandoned possessions awaiting a return. Kate now wished she'd called for help hours ago. Had Jack drowned below this boat while she sat back and read his letters? The horror of that thought gripped her.

"Let's go now," she said in a voice that moved Brant toward the captain's chair.

Kate glanced once more toward the water. Brant saw it at the same time. He pointed and Kate hurried to the edge. There was movement, not on the water but on shore.

Then she saw him. "Hurry!" she shouted.

The engine roared to life, the wind flew against her face. At any second she expected to see men chasing after them or for something else to go wrong. Jack was now on the dock with another man beside him. Brant pulled alongside them, and Jack reached for the rope as their wake bumped the boat against the dock. Jack immediately hopped over the railing and into the boat, with the other man following.

Brant didn't hesitate—he turned the boat away from the dock as soon as they were aboard. The wind whipped hard as Kate's eyes sought the castle grounds for movement or light.

Then Jack moved along the deck toward her. He reached for her and the gulf between them closed at last.

Wolfram Meizer sat in his office, dressed in his gray suit with the jacket buttoned at the front. His hair was combed back and he'd found a flower for his lapel. The TV was turned off, the video screens hidden behind the cabinet.

His birds were all gone, the cage doors propped open, and the French doors let cold air rush inside the room. The aviary was empty too. All his little birds gone loose into a world that would destroy them. Jack had taken Ian, and Ian had taken his birds.

He sat and sat. Suddenly he could hear them coming back. Their wings flapped with such a beating that Wolfram believed every bird he owned was now returning to him. He remained seated, waiting for them to peck their beaks furiously against the windows and find the open door. They had eyes like searchlights, bobbing and seeking the windows in his estate. Soon his grounds would be covered, the lawns trampled, and flowers smashed. The perfect design disrupted. They could not see what progress required. They were afraid to see it and tried so desperately to stop what nature needed. Birds had no intelligence; they couldn't even know envy as men could.

Then the flaps of wings turned mechanical and the cries turned human. Wolfram sipped cold coffee and sighed, long and heavy. With great care, he rose from the chair and walked to the plastic case on his desk. He opened the lid and held the capsule between two fingers.

They would destroy so great a future.

And so it came to this.

⊸═◎═⊷

Three months later

Many lives had crossed the pathway of Lukas' years. They were lives that would never leave him, and Lukas no longer wanted them gone. The faces didn't haunt him now; they were reflections of himself. Their blood no longer stained his hands but had blended with his own. They were part of him. And as such, he could share the stories of Jantes, Karl, the girl at Mauthausen—Tatianna—the others, and always, Susanne.

Autumn winds moved through the mountains, sweeping leaves from the long arms of trees to scurry end over end along the trail. Lukas walked his favorite path that morning, partly because the house was too silent, partly to feel the cold wind on his face, but mostly to return to the place he rarely went and now longed to be. He moved with purpose through the thick grove of tall pines so dark and damp, then stopped at the edging where the thicket paused into a hillside clearing. There Lukas stood in the shadows of trees. The view opened to a velvet green hillside with a crossroad trail worn through it. The sky brought filtered light through the black, rolling clouds.

He stepped from the trees and paused at the crossroad. The

descending trail led to the village below, the opposite path moved upward to span the alpine range, while the one ahead led across the clearing, past a tree stump, and disappeared over the ridge. He took that one.

As the wind gusted, Lukas slid his hands into the pockets of his wool jacket. Winter was coming quickly. He had much to do in the months ahead before the Porters returned to Austria. Lukas had given his help and checkbook to the small museum in Ebensee. Soon a new exhibit would open, telling a story that had taken decades to conclude. There, all five pieces of the blue tile would find their final rest among photographs and possessions from their group. How strange to see their things beneath museum glass. How strange, yet how essential was the need he felt to tell their stories and his own—even what he had done for both good and evil. It could change another life.

Another gust tugged his wool hat. Lukas pulled it down and closed the top button of his coat around his neck. The pathway felt familiar beneath his feet, though the time was great between the young man who used to race over these trails and the old man with slow steps that he now was. The old oak had given out years earlier when a storm pressed too hard against its roots. It had been enough to bring the tree to the ground. Lukas' groundskeeper had cut the tree for firewood, though the wood had never been burned.

The stump of the tree remained. He sat there with the wind around him and memories persistent in his thoughts. His eyes followed the path where it disappeared over the ridge. The trail would lead to Susanne's grandmother's house, where another family now lived.

It now felt right that Susanne was gone. He could not see her as an old woman, only as the girl she once was—brave and full of a love that would bring him sorrow. But it wasn't his fault. His sins had not caused her death, and she would be waiting for him—he could believe that now. Lukas remembered that last day when he waited at this tree to see her instant smile and the late-afternoon sunshine in her hair. He'd been waiting for her long after the year of her death. He sat a long while, knowing he would wait no longer after this.

The cold finally reached his bones though the contentment of the hike did him good. He turned back toward the trees and trail where he had restored the grounds of this old estate. A warm fire and a good pipe were in his thoughts as he journeyed back. Anni waited at the front walkway. He nodded a greeting and she nodded one back. His daughter looked young in her stocking hat, with a black scarf tight beneath her chin. Her cheeks and nose were pink with cold.

He thought of young Abbie and wondered how much she'd changed since he had last seen her. It would be late night on the West Coast of America; the girl he'd tried hard to dislike at first because of her youth and innocence would be sleeping, with her mother and father in the next room. Abbie had been granted a new life with her father. And the indomitable Kate, who had lived through so much these past few years, at last had her husband back and the mystery solved. Smiling to himself, Lukas thought that maybe some things did turn out all right after all. That's what Marta reminded him every day.

"We could get snow," Anni said, concern in her eyes as she watched his approach.

"*Ja*, the air feels right," Lukas said. They had spoken little since their world had changed. The media hounds, death threats, book deals, and the recovery of the lost documents beneath Garten Wald had all kept them from a serious talk. He offered his elbow and Anni accepted by sliding her arm through his.

"A game of chess by the fire perhaps?"

She smiled in her slight way and nodded. It brought a smile

to his lips also. Perhaps they'd all been granted new life, Lukas thought. These were the words he would tell his daughter. They were too long unspoken.

> . . . No one . . . doubted that they were seeing beyond the end of the world. . . .
>
> —C. S. Lewis, *The Voyage of the "Dawn Treader"*

I wish I could remember the moment I was first drawn toward the World War II era and the details of the Holocaust. What caused my deep need to read and reread these stories, to attempt to make sense of what can never be understood or explained? It began before high school, and certainly stories like Anne Frank's *The Diary of a Young Girl* and Corrie ten Boom's *The Hiding Place* were part of those earlier years.

But for me, writing on such a subject has been a difficult journey. Often I've felt unworthy to write about events and times that do not belong to my heritage. These people's stories do not belong to me. Writers are often told, "Write what you know." I've found that, instead, we must write about what moves us, what won't leave us alone, what keeps us up at night, and what we can't make sense of. That's why my first novels are about this spot in history that will never leave our world alone—and should never.

In October 2000, I returned to Europe for the third time. The first week was a whirlwind that took two friends and myself from Amsterdam to Vienna through six countries. It was a road trip with Anne de Graaf at the wheel and Tricia Goyer with her CD selections and ready camera. Trish and I would brave the Metro in Paris for the first time, two young women who were once nervous to meet real authors at our first writers conference. Anne drove from Paris to Prague in a day, and the three of us walked St. Charles Bridge that magical night of gentle rain. In quite another adventure, we sought the one last open crossing on the Czech/Austrian border (this involved protestors with farm tractors blocking the roadway, a very small ferry, and some shoddy directions). The trip held multitudes of laughter and moments we knew to be designed by the One who designed everything.

Yet not everything was picturesque. We passed several clusters of women along a Czech country road who, with the freedom of democracy, have become bound to the prostitution trade. We met Jewish siblings, young and friendly, but with the latest Israeli conflict heavy on their minds as the eighteen-year-old girl would begin her required service for the Israeli army. We also faced two days visiting three sites of Nazi atrocities—Lidice, Czech Republic, and Mauthausen and Gusen Camps in Austria.

Tricia had flown home when Anne and I came to the Salzkammergut lakes region of Austria. Near a quaint village, Anne and I walked among the monuments, ovens, and mass graves of KZ Ebensee Memorial. Through research, I met the dead in the ghetto song of a poet, in photographs of a woman and her infant who appear to be sleeping as I have slept with each of my children. I found them again at Ebensee as I stood above a mass grave and read the plaques surrounding the ovens. I wondered who these people beneath the earth were. Who were the individuals not granted their own resting place? What were their childhoods like, and what did they envision for the future?

Then I realized this site was not memory. It is our future. Ebensee Memorial will remain for generations. But at the same time, new monuments, mass graves, and memorials will be found in the lands of our world, including African countries, former Yugoslavia, and many more. This is not past us.

Cottonwood is my place of familiar roads, streams, mountain views, and people I've known since childhood. I talk to Tricia on the phone with the miles separating us and send

e-mails to Anne across the pond to Holland. My husband and I
set goals, go to the movies, or talk late into the night. My kids
and I study Eastern Europe, them for home school and me for
my next novel. And always, I daydream about Europe.

How does such a journey and a place like Ebensee change
life for me in Cottonwood, California? Sometimes I feel too
comfortable, too happy, too unaffected. But I also have been
deeply changed—in the way I view people all over the world,
what I want my children to understand, and this need to share
stories I often feel unworthy to write.

So this is my prayer for you—that your vision expand and
that God would take you on a life-changing journey as you
seek him first, because the vision is greater than yourself. My
first two trips to Europe were dreams. This last one brought a
greater vision. I'm not sure what God will do with it. I'm not
sure when or if I'll return to those lands I often daydream
about, but I know God works through all of our lives when we
allow him to be mapmaker and guide.

May your vision be clear and your journey sweet.

ACKNOWLEDGMENTS

My name appears on the cover, but this book is certainly a collaborative work. Janet Kobobel Grant, you are my agent, friend, and advice-giver in all areas of life. I thank Tyndale House Publishers for seeing my vision, for your amazing support, and for lending me the time and energies of Ramona Cramer Tucker and Lorie Popp—extraordinary editors who put much more than just a polish to this book.

In Austria:
Professor Reinhold and Elisabeth Wagnleitner—again, invaluable for me to glimpse life in Austria. Your assistance and friendship bring great gratitude.

Martha Gammer—abundant thanks for a personal visit to Gusen Memorial, the museum, a meal in your home, and finding us a place to sleep. You were a true gift.

Ebensee Museum—Dr. Wolfgang Quatember, Gabriela Eidinger, and Andreas Schmoller, for allowing me time and freedom in your archives, answering questions, and even bringing me coffee. My greatest memory was seeing Austrian schoolchildren learn about the Holocaust through the Anne Frank exhibit. You are doing a great work.

Research and Development:
Tricia Goyer—research assistance, manuscript reviewing, and just being you.

Katie Martinusen—manuscript review and the prayers that carried me.

Christy Harrington—manuscript review and honesty tempered with friendship.

Jeff and Becky Davis—information on decorative tiles.

Shelley Chittim—research on decorative tiles (and friendship).

Shawn Chittim, Shelley Chittim, Mike Chittim, and Joe Gazzigli—again, the Mount Shasta house was a perfect place to write. Thank you.

Dan Elliott—archaeology research.

Melissa Karlen—research about women in the Holocaust.

Neal Schiff of the FBI—suggestions and information on FBI and police procedure.

Todd Budde—information on insurance claims.

In addition to and including the above mentioned, both personal and professional help came from family and friends in a multitude of ways—from consistent prayer to deep friendships. I cannot name you all, so I hope you already know.

Cody, Madelyn, and Weston—my children who grant me such love and joy in all your unique and amazing ways. I am so thankful for you.

Richard McCormick—I'm proud to use the McCormick name, all because of you. You're a wonderful father. Gail McCormick—mother, friend, example. I agree we could use your maiden name too, but Guillemin McCormick Martinusen just gets a bit too long.

My sister, Jennifer Harman, gives support, encouragement, and love in a multitude of ways. Eleanor Martinusen, Teresa Price, Laurie Williams, and Lisa Peasha took great care of my children those afternoons so I could work. And, Lisa, your encouraging cards have meant a lot. Kim Shaw, we appreciated our substitute home school teacher while I went to Europe,

among other things you've done. Jenna Benton, Michelle
Ower, Robin Gunn, Marlo Schalesky, One Heart Sisters,
Tammy Martinusen—friendship and much needed prayer. A
huge appreciation to Anne de Graaf and Tricia Goyer—for that
amazing European journey (and thanks to Erik de Graaf, John
Goyer, David Martinusen, the husbands who stayed behind).
Maxine Cambra and the NorCal Writer's Group (keep writing
everyone!). Norita Brinton—for a dear gift when I needed it.
Teresa Martin—dinner for my family when we all needed it
and your kind notes. The Elegant Bean in Cottonwood—
Janelle Pierson, Piney Adams, and Linda Finken for those
MANY single shot, grande mochas with nonfat milk (sometimes), whipped cream (always), and light chocolate—but
then you knew that, didn't you? You know I'll always be back.

Another appreciation (I have a lot to be thankful for!) goes
to the communities of Cottonwood, Anderson, and Redding,
and to the readers who've shared their own lives with me. The
release of my first book, *Winter Passing,* has brought such
amazing support from friends, acquaintances, libraries, local
churches (my own especially), and local bookstores (Redding
Christian Supply and Barnes & Noble). I cannot express my
gratitude enough.

This book could not have been done without my husband,
David, allowing me silence, especially as the deadline arrived;
making dinners; tucking in children; and being my supporter
and encourager every day of my life—thank you.

As Paul wrote to the Philippian church, "I thank my God
every time I remember you" (Phil. 1:3, NIV). That goes to all of
you. I echo King David's words in the psalms: "I will give
thanks to the Lord"; "My soul finds rest in God alone" (Pss.
7:17; 62:1, NIV).

For more information on Ebensee Concentration Camp Memorial and the Museum of Contemporary History, or if you, a family member, or a friend is a survivor of KZ Ebensee, please contact the following address:

Concentration Camp Memorial Ebensee
Museum of Contemporary History
Kirchengasse 5
A-4802 Ebensee
Austria

SUGGESTIONS FOR FURTHER READING

The Voyage of the "Dawn Treader" by C. S. Lewis

My Utmost for His Highest by Oswald Chambers

From World War to Waldheim: Culture and Politics in Austria and the United States (Austrian History, Culture, & Society, Vol. 2) edited by David F. Good and Ruth Wodak

Here, There, and Everywhere: The Foreign Politics of American Popular Culture by Reinhold Wagnleitner

Coca-Colonization and the Cold War: The Cultural Mission of the United States in Austria After the Second World War by Reinhold Wagnleitner

The Camp Men: The SS Officers Who Ran the Nazi Concentration Camp System by French L. MacLean

Concentration Camp Ebensee, Subcamp of Mauthausen by Florian Freund

A History of Decorative Tiles by Noel Riley

An Illustrated History of the Gestapo by Rupert Butler

Hitler's Silent Partners by Isabel Vincent

Piercing the Reich: The Penetration of Nazi Germany by American Secret Agents During World War II by Joseph E. Persico

Yes, We Sang!: Songs of the Ghettos and Concentration Camps by Shoshana Kalisch with Barbara Meister

The Holocaust Chronicle: A History in Words and Pictures— Publications International, Ltd.

WEB SITES

Toplitz Lake—read about the recovery of artifacts from the Nazi era—*http://www.toplitzsee.at*

The Forgotten Camps—
http://www.jewishgen.org/ForgottenCamps/

Simon Wiesenthal Center—
http://motlc.wiesenthal.com/index.html

Austrian Press and Information, Washington, D.C.—
http://www.austria.org

Mauthausen/Gusen Information Pages—
http://linz.orf.at/orf/gusen

Mauthausen Memorial (English version)—
http://www.mauthausen-memorial.gv.at/engl/index.html

Holocaust/Shoah Research Resources—
http://www.igc.org/ddickerson/holocaust.html

United States Holocaust Museum—*http://www.ushmm.org*

Austria Tourism—*http://austria-tourism.at/*

City of Salzburg (English version)—
http://www.salzburg.com/engl/

Cindy McCormick Martinusen lives in her hometown of Cottonwood, California, with her husband, David, and their three children. They enjoy travel, camping, art and music, snow skiing, air-hockey competitions, and books. (The Chronicles of Narnia are their favorites.) The family is also currently home schooling.

Cindy is an avid reader; loves the mountains and the sea; and enjoys a variety of sports, especially skiing and playing softball on a team with longtime friends, her sister, and a coach she's known since third grade.

Her writing background includes the publication of articles, short stories, and a play. However, fiction is her great writing love. *Blue Night* is the sequel to her first novel, *Winter Passing*.

Cindy welcomes letters written to her in care of Tyndale House Author Relations, P.O. Box 80, Wheaton, IL 60189-0080.